Peccadillo at the Palace

Praise for *Girl with a Gun: An Annie Oakley Mystery*

"Bovée's debut novel brings readers solidly into the heyday of the Wild West shows, providing wonderful details about the elaborate costumes and the characters' remarkable marksmanship . . . There are enough entertaining elements to keep readers guessing, including romance, rivalries, jealousy, and at least one evil character from Annie's past. The prose has a charming simplicity, which keeps the attention focused on the action and the well-developed protagonist. A quick, fun read with engaging rodeo scenes."

—*Kirkus Reviews*

"A fast-paced plot keeps the pages turning. Readers interested in strong American women will welcome this new series. . ."

—*Publishers Weekly*

"Absorbing, heartfelt, and thrilling, *Girl with a Gun* shows off young Annie Oakley's skills as a sharpshooter and as a loyal detective. From the period details to the Wild West setting, I was completely immersed in the story and in the larger-than-life characters. It's a fun as a rodeo, and nearly as dangerous. Like Annie herself, Bovée's prose sparkles with precision and skill."

—Martha Conway, author of *Underground River*, *New York Times* Book Review Editor's Choice

"Kari Bovée paints a captivating portrait of the young sharpshooter, Annie Oakley, in *Girl with a Gun*. A diverting plot filled with unexpected twists and turns enthralls and satisfies the reader as Annie is transformed from a naïve Quaker girl to an independent young woman. This lively mix of historical fiction, romance, and mystery hits the target!"

—Susan McDuffie, author of the award-winning Muirteach MacPhee Mysteries

Peccadillo at the Palace

An Annie Oakley Mystery

Kari Bovée

Published by SparkPress, a BookSparks imprint,
A division of SparkPoint Studio, LLC
Phoenix, Arizona, USA, 85281
www.gosparkpress.com

Published 2019
Printed in the United States of America
ISBN: 978-1-943006-90-8 (pbk)
ISBN: 978-1-943006-91-5 (e-bk)
Library of Congress Control Number: 2018965478

For Kevin,

who never lets me give up on my dreams.

For Jessica and Michael,

who inspire me every day.

A Note From the Author about the Annie Oakley Series

Like most of us, I'd heard the name Annie Oakley before, but she didn't interest me until several years ago when my father encouraged me to watch a PBS American Experience biographical special featuring Annie Oakley and her rise to fame. I watched the show and became enchanted with this pint-sized wonder woman who was incredibly empowered at a time in history when most women weren't allowed to be empowered. She had talent, spunk, determination, modesty, and the courage to be herself—an expert markswoman and sharpshooter. She bested most men in the sport, including her husband, Frank Butler, and her boss, Buffalo Bill Cody—two of her most ardent supporters.

As a fan of historical fiction and historical mysteries, I thought it would be entertaining to put this feisty young woman in the role of an amateur detective. Based on everything I'd read about her, she certainly had the smarts, the compassion, and the desire to see justice served and order reign in the world. I've tried to maintain historical accuracy for the most part, but in this series I've played with some of the facts: I've altered time-lines, added fictional characters, embellished historical characters, and put Annie into situations she never faced in real life—and I've had so much fun doing it.

The prequel novella, *Shoot like a Girl*, is the story of Annie before she joins the Wild West Show. Although she doesn't play the role of amateur detective in this book, we learn what drives her to seek order and justice for herself and others though her relationship with Buck, a horse who becomes her lifeline during a difficult period in her life. From this experience, Annie becomes impassioned to seek justice for those who cannot seek it for themselves, and we see her spring into action in the first book of the series *Girl with a Gun*. This sets her on a course to make order out of chaos, and try to set things right in a world that can go oh so wrong.

I have delighted in imagining what was in the heart, mind, and soul, of this young woman who faced many obstacles in her life, only to become one of the most famous women of all time. It's been gratifying to put her in difficult situations and see her come out of a shroud of mystery, shooting her way to the truth. I hope you, too, enjoy these and future adventures I've created for this amazing woman of history—Little Miss Sure Shot, Annie Oakley.

August 1857

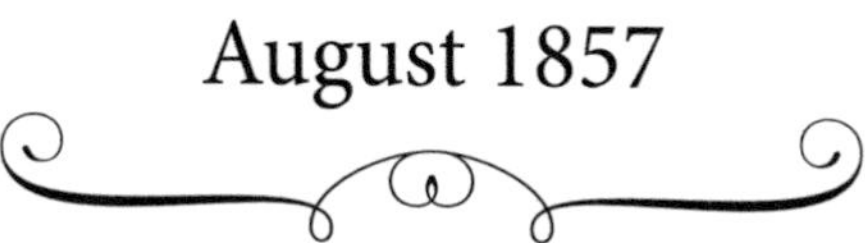

They must pay for their sins. I've made it my life's mission to make sure they pay. All of them: the imperialists who have caused the oppression of women and children, the poor, and the meek; and the rebels who use the innocent like me (whose only guilt is my birthright) to retaliate against the Crown. I will no longer be a pawn in their war. I will fight for those who have no voice.

They came in droves to our village in Cawnpore, in the middle of the night, with their tattered clothes, bare feet, and rotting teeth, like the dead arisen again for their revenge; ghosts stalking the living. They came shouting into the Bibighar where we had been told we would have safe haven. They came in swinging their axes, butchering the women and children like cattle.

Mother clung to me, holding three-year-old Alistair in her arms, her fingers sinking into my flesh. In the chaos, she pulled us to the ground and then told me to help her pull the maimed bodies over us to hide us from the soldiers. In my frantic effort to help, I grasped an arm and yanked too hard. The limb separated from the butchered body and

I froze in terror holding it above my head. One of the sepoy rebels saw me and stalked toward us, blood smearing his ragged shirt.

"You'll not have my children." Mother's voice echoed loud and determined.

The man laughed, his face in shadow.

"Very well, then, you shall not be separated from your children, but suffer the same fate as they."

He hauled Mother to her feet, Alistair still in her arms. She grabbed me to her side. The rebel wrapped a rope around Mother and me, tying it tight. Alistair shrieked in terror, and Mother clenched her jaw, her face stricken with rage. I stayed quiet, for I have been mute since Father left us. I told him I would not speak until he returned to us in the hopes that he would come back from the war sooner. But I fear he is dead, so my voice died with him.

The man dragged us, our feet tangled in one another's, our arms aching with the pressure of the rope squeezing the breath from our lungs. He pulled us out of the doorway of the Bibighar and down the steps. Mother leaned back against the pull, fighting every step of the way, holding tight onto little Alistair, tears of anger streaming down her cheeks, her jaw set against the urge to cry out.

The man led us toward the fort's well, long dried up in the summer drought. The screams of other women and children, dragged by their feet, their arms, their hair, skittered across my skin like fire and rang in my ears with the razor-sharp keening of a specter's wail. In the torchlight, we could not see the men's faces, only their white and rotten teeth, like fireflies in the night.

One by one, the men forced the women and children down the well. Some had to be thrown, others shoved, still others hacked with axes as they clung to the walls of the well like beetles fighting against the force of a waterfall. The men beat their fingers, their arms, shoulders, and heads, stuffing them down, one after the other, their screams boiling out the top of the well like burning lava.

When it was our turn, the man motioned to one of his comrades.

"This lot are fighters; make sure they don't escape." He then yowled as my mother sank her teeth into the flesh of his arm. He struck her on the forehead with the butt of his stick. Her eyes crossed and rolled back in her head. Her knees buckled, and she sank to the ground, pulling us down with her. Alistair fell free from the ropes. I wanted to shout to him to run, but the man swooped him up and threw him into the well. I heard his screams as he fell to the bottom, on top of the others, thirty feet down.

The man picked me up but I struggled against him, and like Mother, I bit his arm. He pulled my mouth off him and slapped me hard. Weighing more than Alistair, I was not as easily thrown in. I stuck my feet out, locking my knees against the wall and refused to bend them. The man took his fist and rammed it into my stomach, knocking all the air out of my lungs, and then I fell. Down, down, down I went, the moaning and screaming of the others below me rising like a cloud of doom as I fell into the pit.

I don't remember how long I remained in the well among the suffering. I don't know how I got out. When I woke in the hospital bed, the nurse told me I must be a miracle from heaven, or damned to hell, because I had been the only survivor. She nursed me, she fed me, she clothed me, and then she turned me out into the world to make my own way. Turned me out into a world that is unkind, unfair, and inhumane.

They will pay. All of them.

Chapter One

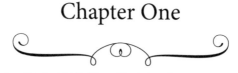

April 12, 1887, New York Harbor, Evening

Annie held onto Buck's lead line as the 180 horses, fifteen buffalo, and seven mules boarded the *State of Nebraska* steamship. The elk and deer had already been secured below decks. They loaded the animals two by two, as if Noah himself had come back to life, preparing for the flood. But no destruction of the world had been planned here, just a monumental excursion across the pond to pay a visit to the queen.

The Honorable Colonel Buffalo Bill Cody and his Wild West Show had been invited by the longest-ruling monarch to date, Her Royal Majesty, Queen Victoria, to celebrate her Golden Jubilee, and to attend the American Exhibition in London. The new manager of the show, Nate Salisbury, had arranged to charter the ship from the British for the journey.

Annie had received the news as she and her then fiancé, Frank Butler, were planning their wedding almost two years earlier. Both of them had left the show, Annie, to take care of her emotionally distraught mother, and Frank because of issues with his eyesight. Annie couldn't contain her excitement when the colonel told her the queen expressly wanted to meet her, and would she come back with Frank as her manager.

Her excitement, however, turned to nervous anticipation when she saw the big steamer. It didn't help that Buck was dancing with anxiety at the end of his lead line as she led him down the dock alongside the colonel and his two mounts.

"How's old Buck holding up?" the colonel asked Annie, his voice raised over the sound of his cowboy band playing "Tenting on the Old Camp Ground," a popular Civil War song. Ever dapper in his ornately decorated tan suede duster and embroidered thigh-high leather boots, he approached Annie through a throng of awestruck spectators, leading his white Arabian stallion, Isham, and another of his favorites, the dark war horse, Charlie.

"He's nervous." Annie reached up and stroked her horse's neck. "You know how he hates confined spaces." He hadn't settled from getting off the train from Ohio yesterday. Annie knew he hadn't slept, and his fatigue only increased his anxiety.

The swell of the crowd and the noise of people shouting their names fueled the horse's agitation. He pawed at the wooden planks of the dock. Annie swallowed the urge to throw up. She'd felt queasy the past few days, and the idea of sailing across the ocean for the next two weeks didn't help.

Annie's gaze traveled west where gray clouds were gathering on the horizon line below the setting sun. Buck sniffed at the breeze. Annie noted the metallic smell of the air, the heavy oppression of a coming storm. Would they truly set sail? Perhaps the storm would veer away from them, she thought, trying to calm herself. Buck snorted, reminding her that she had more pressing things to worry about at the moment.

"I've let the crew know that Buck is to be stalled next to Isham and old Charlie here for the voyage." The colonel raised his voice to be heard over another of Buck's frantic whinnies. "They'll have the largest stalls, covered, amidships, where the motion of the sea is minimized. Mr. Post will also wrap his legs once we've got him settled."

"Excellent." Annie tugged at the waist of the rose-colored moiré taffeta-and-lace dress that Hulda, her sister, had made for her. Hulda had pulled the corset strings too tight that afternoon as they dressed at the hotel for the bon voyage celebration that would take place as they left the harbor.

"Hulda, you are squeezing me too tight," Annie had said. "Let up a little. I can barely breathe!"

"You must be growing fat," said Hulda. "How long has it been since you've worn a corset, Annie?"

"Not long enough. I hate the things."

"Stop complaining. People will want to see you in all your splendor as we leave the docks."

Hulda had grown so like their mother in the last year—bossy, temperamental, yet sweet in her own way. Though not a national shooting sensation like Annie, Hulda, at nearly fourteen years old, was the beauty of the family, with soft, blond, wavy hair and bright blue eyes. She also had a gift for garment design and sewing. It hadn't taken the colonel and his new manager, Nate Salisbury, long to decide to hire Hulda as a costume seamstress after Annie presented the colonel with a beautiful buckskin duster with elaborate embroidery and beadwork, made by her baby sister.

Their mother had worried about Hulda traveling abroad. Annie, now eighteen years old, had been forced to grow up fast as a youngster, due to the family's impoverishment after her father's death. Soon afterwards, her mother's generosity to a suitor named Joshua had nearly bankrupted them, and it had fallen on Annie to keep the family fed and a roof over their heads. But Hulda still retained the innocence of a girl who'd never had such demands made on her, nor had she encountered the variety of people and experiences Annie had since her time in the Wild West Show.

Buck's shrill whinny pierced the air, and Annie covered her ears. She couldn't wait until she could get Buck on board, settled and comfortable, and herself back into her cotton and linen day dress.

The ship's loud steam horn rose sharply above the din of the crowd. Buck danced, nearly knocking Annie over.

"Best we get him settled on board before this crowd becomes a crush," said the colonel. "You know Buck's popularity. People can't seem to keep their hands off him, and he doesn't look in a state to be petted and fawned over."

"He's not." Annie let the line slip in her hand so Buck could move his feet more freely. He pranced and pawed, on the verge of a tantrum.

"You want Mr. Post or Bobby to lead him aboard?" the colonel asked. "I'd hate for you to ruin that pretty dress."

"I'll do it." Annie wished people would stop fussing about the dress.

"We'll do it together, then." The colonel gave her a warm smile. "In these stressful situations I like to handle my mounts myself, too."

The colonel, Isham, and Charlie took the lead as they walked down the dock to the livestock gangway at the rear of the ship. The crowd grew, and as far as Annie could see, a rainbow of colorfully dressed women with large-brimmed, floral-trimmed hats, and gentlemen with beaver-skin top hats and smart wool suits lined the docks. Their children, dressed with equal panache, stood quietly next to their parents, but their faces beamed as the colonel and Annie passed by.

A woman standing on the passengers' gangway pointed at Annie and mouthed something Annie couldn't hear. Her oversized red wool coat—tattered at the cuffs and bearing holes that needed mending—dwarfed her slight stature, but the intensity of her gaze worried Annie.

It wasn't often people didn't like her, but some didn't, just on principle, jealous of her success. The last time she'd been singled out in such a negative way, she found out she'd been accused of something horrific, and it had made the papers. Almost three years earlier, with Annie's rise to fame, a story had circulated that she'd tried to kill Vernon McCrimmon, Buck's previous owner and her own abuser, while under his employ. She had defended herself against the story, but the repercussions had taken a toll. Her reputation meant everything to her, and the idea that someone would slander her publicly left her feeling beaten and powerless.

What the general public didn't know was that Annie *had* killed Vernon McCrimmon—but later, in self-defense. He'd come after her with a knife, and after a hair-raising squabble, she was able to turn the knife on him. While she didn't regret her actions, she still had to live with the memory that she had taken the life of another, something that went against her own moral code as well as that of her Quaker religion.

The woman staring at her now brought up those uneasy feelings, and Annie tried hard to shove them to the back of her mind. She had to remain calm for Buck. The woman's sharp blue gaze shifted to Buck and settled on his prancing frame, a hint of a smile crossing her lips.

Buck gave a loud whinny, his head raised, neck taut, and eyes bulging, completely unaware of the woman. Annie turned to Buck to stroke his neck and when she turned around again, the woman had vanished into the line of people making their way up the boarding ramp of the ship.

With the possibility of a coming storm, Buck's nervous state, and the threat in the eyes of the strange woman, Annie suddenly doubted her decision to embark on the two-week voyage to the other end of the world. She hoped it did not prove to be a mistake.

Chapter Two

Once on board, Annie and the colonel walked their horses to the twelve-by-twelve-foot wooden pens that served as stalls, situated in front of the other horse pens, which were, indeed, smaller. Annie led Buck inside and slipped the halter off his head. She jumped out of the way as the horse started to pace, and scooted out the stall door held open for her by Bobby Brady, one of the show's players and Annie's dear friend.

Bobby had joined the Wild West Show a year before Annie. When Annie came on, she and Bobby had immediately formed a friendship, despite the fact that in the show's shootouts and competitions, Annie beat him every time.

Bobby also held a special place in the colonel's heart. The colonel had lost his only son at age six, and years later Bobby had stepped into the role. In addition to performing with Annie, Bobby often worked with the horses as a farrier, shoeing them and trimming their feet. He loved horses, especially Buck. Annie could see the concern on Bobby's face as Buck stamped and snorted, kicked and reared in his stall. How would they ever make the long voyage to England?

"I ain't never seen Buck so upset," Bobby said, closing the stall door. "Not since you first boarded him on the train to St. Louis."

"I know. He has a hard time in new environments."

"I feel right sorry for the fella. I know how he feels."

"Are you nervous, Bobby?" Annie used Buck's halter to secure the gate latch, to prevent him from busting through it.

"I'm downright scared, Annie. What if the ship goes down in the middle of the ocean? I ain't never learned to swim." Bobby's lips pressed together in a thin line, and Annie thought she saw his chin quiver.

She smiled at him. "Well, I know how to swim, and so does Frank. If the ship goes down, I promise we'll seek you out."

Just as Annie mentioned his name, Frank appeared, coming around the corner. Hulda trailed after him with a scowl on her face, her eyes trained on Annie's dress. Annie looked down at the front of the garment, which was wet from Buck's frothing mouth.

"They're waiting for you to go to the railing for the sendoff celebration." Frank came up behind her and set his warm hands on her shoulders.

"I'll be there in a minute. I just want to see that Buck is settling. Even the big stalls are small compared to the pen he stayed in during the show in St. Louis." Annie couldn't keep the concern out of her voice. She swallowed another wave of nausea and rubbed a hand across her belly as she noted the billowing clouds flatten, turning a deeper shade of ash.

"The crew will take the horses out for walks around the deck daily," Frank said, squeezing her shoulders. "You can't take care of everyone and everything, my darling." He smoothed his blond mustache, looking at her with the quiet compassion she'd loved from the moment she met him.

"I know, it's just—"

"You mustn't worry so, Annie," Hulda said, scrunching her brow in adolescent disgust. "If you want to worry about something, worry about what people will think of the state of your dress."

Annie ignored her sister's scolding. "I suppose we must make an appearance." Annie sighed. "C'mon, Bobby."

Bobby stood frozen to the spot, his mouth hanging open like a barn door on a sagging hinge as he stared unabashedly at Hulda. Annie stifled a snort.

"Oh, forgive my manners. Bobby, this is my sister, Hulda."

Hulda opened her blue eyes wide at Bobby. After twisting his hat completely out of shape, he took her hand.

"Delighted to meet you," Hulda said sweetly. Annie knew Hulda had seen the awestruck expression on Bobby's face and also knew she'd use his infatuation to her amusement. Poor Bobby. Annie hoped she wouldn't have to intervene when Hulda broke his heart.

Frank wrapped his arm around Annie's waist and pulled her away from the stall. Together the four of them headed to the upper deck to greet the thousands of fans waiting on the docks below.

From the ship's railing, Annie, Frank, Hulda, the colonel, and the other players who had already come aboard watched as the American Indian players, their wives, and their children pushed up the gangway to board the ship. Someone touched her elbow. She turned around to see two white-turbaned East Indian men in crisp ivory suits. The man in front bowed low at the waist.

"Miss Annie Oakley, I am Amal Bhakta, loyal servant of Her Majesty Queen Victoria. She has sent me as a personal escort to your troop. She is particularly excited to meet you, memsahib." His eyes never met Annie's, but he bowed again and gestured to the man behind him. "This is my valet, Benoy Patel."

"Oh, my." Annie turned to the colonel. "A personal escort . . . well, I never."

"Do you ever get tired of upstaging me?" the colonel said to her, his mustache twitching as his lips curved to a crooked smile.

She didn't want to admit it to herself, but Mr. Bhakta's words flattered her. Queen Victoria was the most powerful woman in the world, but Annie had been raised to view everyone as an equal, despite their talent or position. She also didn't want to admit that she struggled on a daily basis with the notion, due to her newfound competitive nature and ambition. She loved being the best at her game, and she felt a responsibility—or was it self-imposed pressure?—to continue to be the best.

"And you must be the great Buffalo Bill, King of the Wild West," Mr. Bhakta said, nodding his head to the colonel.

"Well, sir, I don't know about 'great' and certainly not a king, but I am flattered by your exceedingly good manners. Pleasure to meet you." The colonel stuck out his hand in greeting, but Mr. Bhakta only nodded once more.

"You always seem to cause a stir, Annie." Emma Wilson, Annie's friend and reporter for the *Chicago Herald*, sauntered up to the group, her hips swaying, drawing the eye to her wide-legged silk trousers. "May I get a few comments for the paper?"

"Hello, Emma," said Annie. "It's a long trip; can we catch up later?" The crowd on deck was becoming more animated and more excited as the people below bellowed and cheered. Annie could barely hear herself think. The cowboys, popping confetti-filled balloons and throwing streamers down to the crowd below, jostled the colonel on one side of her and Frank on the other.

"Of course, dear, but I promised my editor I'd wire your departing comments," Emma yelled above the din. "So tell me, what is it that you want to accomplish during your two years abroad?" With one delicately gloved hand, Emma raised her small pad of paper in the air and with the other she poised the tip of her pencil against her red lips. The steamer horn blew again, making the deck quake with its ferocity.

"I'm surprised you have to ask, Emma. You know what I want to accomplish. I want to represent my country. I want to support the show, support the colonel."

Emma raised an eyebrow. "Oh come now, that's all? You're the best sharpshooter in the Americas, Annie. There's a world to conquer out there."

She *did* want to excel, to prove her merit in another country. She just didn't feel comfortable talking about it. To stall for time, Annie nodded at Mr. Bhakta, who finally made eye contact with her and smiled with glowing white teeth.

"How will this trip make the difference for you?" Emma pressed.

Annie sighed. "Well, if I'm the best in the Americas, then I want to show England what Americans are made of—grit and determination." Annie hoped Emma would be satisfied with her answer. She knew Emma had a job to do, and she owed Emma a great deal for not reporting the story of McCrimmon's death, but she didn't appreciate the questions right now. The noise and the commotion made her want to go check on Buck. He must be out of his mind with terror.

"And your rivalry with Miss Smith; are you concerned she might outshine you? She is right on your heels, is she not?" Emma continued. "She's so brash, so brave, and her skills have improved."

Now Emma was hitting a bit too close to the belt, giving rise to the nausea that had plagued Annie of late. "Really, Emma. Are you trying to provoke me?"

"A little competition is good for the soul, good for ticket sales, isn't it?" Emma said, the corner of her mouth raised in mischief.

Although one of Annie's dearest friends, when Emma got into journalist mode, she could come off as ruthless. Annie knew she couldn't get away with soft answers. Emma wanted to needle her for the sake of a good story, and Annie had to admit that Emma's words got under her skin. Emma knew mentioning the rivalry between her and Lillie would do the trick.

"Lillie wants fame. I want to make a difference in the world." Annie couldn't deny that Lillie's skills had improved. And, if she were truly honest, she had to credit Lillie with getting her and Frank back together after a misunderstanding with Frank's former lover, Twila Midnight—who happened to be Lillie's adopted sister. But their rivalry in the show ring had grown stronger than ever.

Lillie had wanted to outshine Annie from the moment she was hired on. Annie knew this rivalry stemmed from Lillie's own insecurities due to a deeply unhappy childhood, but it still rankled. Their relationship was complicated, but they had both been there for one another when the chips were down. Annie sometimes thought of Lillie as an annoying sibling whom she would never understand. Sometimes they got along, but mostly they didn't. For the most part, they agreed to disagree.

"I want to empower women, Emma. I want to prove women are just as capable as men. After all, England is ruled by a woman." Annie's face flushed with the prideful declaration Emma had successfully dragged out of her.

"The queen rules Great Britain, but she was born into the role. She's a traditionalist. She's no suffragist," Emma said, her voice flat.

"Well, perhaps I can change her mind," Annie shot back.

Shouts interrupted their conversation. Down below, street children ran wildly throughout the crowd, clamoring to see the animals, props, and equipment still coming aboard. Several of the crew had trouble keeping the children off the Deadwood Stagecoach, a staple of the show, as workers prepared to load it on the ship.

"Thank you, Annie. Our readers will love this!" Emma stuffed her pad of paper and pencil into her pocket trousers. "I know these interviews make you cringe, but you are a sensation. You need to embrace it." She strolled away, the fabric of her pants swinging against the curves of her long legs.

Not long after the boisterous farewell—with the steamer's horns happily filling the air with bursts of noise, and confetti and streamers raining down on the onlookers—the *State of Nebraska* pulled away from the docks and slowly headed out of the harbor to the sea beyond. The sun had set amid dark clouds, and the summer breeze turned to a whipping wind so forceful that Annie, Frank, Hulda, and the others had to take refuge below decks.

After a steward showed Annie and Frank to their stateroom and

Hulda to hers, situated right next door, the trio set about unpacking their trunks and settling in for the long voyage.

The stateroom assigned to Annie and Frank was of good size with a double bed, bureau, wardrobe, and a small desk. The wooden floor was covered with an elegant red, blue, and gold Persian rug, which helped keep out the chill of the sea air. Two porthole windows were covered with blue curtains, and gas-lit sconces illuminated the corners of the room, casting a warm glow.

While the wind howled outside, Annie and Frank unpacked their trunks, as instructed by the steward, so they could be stashed below decks as soon as possible.

After relieving herself of her dress and the dreaded corset, Annie pulled one of the wooden, shoulder-shaped hangers from the wardrobe.

"Hulda will never forgive me if the stain doesn't come out of this dress," she said, draping it on the hanger. She then placed it on the wooden rung in the wardrobe, tucking in the skirt.

"I'm sure she will forgive you, dear. Although impertinent, your sister has a kind heart." Frank sat down on the bed to take off his boots.

Annie reached for a day dress from the trunk and stepped into it.

"What are you doing?" Frank asked, pulling off one of his boots.

"I'm going to go check on Buck, again. He was in such a state, earlier." After the farewell, Annie had gone to find him pacing in his stall, which didn't surprise her. He seemed to calm with her presence, and stopped only long enough to grab a bite of hay here and there. Satisfied he was eating, Annie then joined the others for an evening meal in the dining room. "I should have checked him after supper, but the steward wanted us to get unpacked."

"You're not going out there in this weather," Frank said.

Annie stepped into her dress and pulled it up to her chest, sticking an arm into one of the sleeves. "Oh yes, I am."

"Annie, please. You look exhausted. Let me do it," Frank pulled his boot back on. He crossed the room and took her in his arms. "Rest. I will see to your horse." He kissed the top of her head. She didn't realize she looked so tired, although she felt it. The past two weeks getting ready for the tour had been taxing on her both mentally and physically.

Annie relaxed in Frank's embrace. Somehow, he always made everything right with the world for her, although it hadn't always been that way. When she had first come to the show, she was hired on as a rival to Frank—the most famous sharpshooter in the world. The arrangement worked well, and they inspired one another to shoot their best, until Frank accidentally shot Annie in the hand while performing his famous card trick. Coming hard on the heels of the misunderstanding with Twila, Annie had told him they were through.

"Will you stand with him for a while if he's upset?" she asked. Annie knew Frank would deny her nothing, especially when it came to Buck. When Buck had gone missing before Annie left the show two years earlier, it was Frank, with the help of Lillie, who had found him, and then brought him clear across the country to North Star, Annie's home. Frank had proved his love beyond measure, and Annie had taken him back, immediately and without reservation.

"I will. You finish here and get into bed. You've been so tired lately." He pushed a lock of hair behind her ear. "I worry about you—always trying to make everything right for everybody else."

"I'm fine, Frank. Really," she said, laying her head against his chest. She loved hearing his heartbeat, steady and sure. "I have a fine Irishman looking out for me." She pulled away from him. "How does it feel, sailing across the sea again? Do you wish we were going to Ireland instead, to your home?"

"Perhaps someday. I would have liked to attend Uncle Sean's funeral a few years ago. He was so kind to me."

"He was the last of your family still in Ireland, was he not?"

"Yes. I received letters from him often until the day he died. He refused to come with us when we left Ireland. Uncle Sean was so passionate and so public about his political causes he had to be right in the thick of things."

"I'd love to see Ireland," Annie said. "I'd love to see it with you."

"I was so young when we left; I doubt I'd recognize anything. My parents built a better life for themselves—and for me—in America, and I'm eternally grateful."

"Well, I'm glad they brought you to America, too," Annie said. "If not, we would never have met."

Frank kissed her temple. "I'd better go see to your horse." He put on his coat and secured his hat squarely on his head.

As much as Annie wanted to accompany Frank, she couldn't deny the bone-aching weariness she felt in her limbs. For the past couple of weeks, she'd passed the exhaustion off as anxiety due to the upcoming trip, and hoped it wasn't a symptom of something worse.

Annie woke to Frank's snoring and opened her eyes to see daylight peeking through the porthole curtains. Something pulled at her waist, and she sat up to find she was still wearing her dressing gown, which was twisted around her body. A blanket had been placed on top of her. She hadn't even heard Frank come in.

She wondered how Buck was faring. She knew it was silly, but if she could have had Buck in the stateroom with her and Frank, she'd feel so much better. Having suffered together at the hands of the McCrimmons, the two had found refuge in each other and formed a bond that Annie had never experienced with another living being—not even Frank. She and Buck had breathed life back into one another—and since then, they had felt each other's pain and reveled in each other's happiness.

Frank alone understood this about them, and he would have woken her if Buck had been in a bad state. He must have settled down.

Annie got out of bed and went to the desk where Frank had laid his pocket watch. She picked it up, and her mouth fell open to see she had slept till noon! She looked over at Frank, who had turned over and quit snoring. His breathing was rhythmic and deep, and she wondered how long he had stayed up.

A knock at the door startled her. Running her hands through her hair, she walked to the door and straightened her dressing gown. She opened it to find Mr. Bhakta standing there.

"Oh, excuse me, memsahib. Are you not well?" he asked, concern creasing his brow.

"I'm fine, Mr. Bhakta. Just overslept. How may I help you?"

"Did your husband not tell you? I have planned a luncheon for your party."

"Oh, no! He didn't wake me when he came in last night, and he's still sleeping. Are you waiting for us?"

Mr. Bhakta shrugged, giving her a faint smile.

"I'm so sorry! We'll get dressed right away. We won't be twenty minutes."

"That will be fine." Mr. Bhakta bowed his head to her. "Please, do not worry yourself. I just wanted to see if you were well."

Annie bid him goodbye and woke Frank. When she knocked on Hulda's door, she found her sister had been up for hours, working on one of the costumes for the show. Annie told her about the luncheon and said she and Frank would be up to the dining room in minutes. Hulda put her things down and told Annie she would go there directly.

Annie and Frank dressed as fast as they could and headed toward the main dining room.

Mr. Bhakta had arranged a private table in a corner near the window. Potted palms screened them from the other passengers who were lucky enough to travel with the 120 performers and crew of the Wild West Show.

Positioned in the middle of the ship, one floor down from the upper deck, the dining room had been decorated with stately Victorian furniture, glass candle chandeliers, and Persian rugs of the finest quality. Quite like their customized Wild West Show tents, but without the chandeliers, of course. The teak-paneled walls and crystal sconces gave the room the ambiance of a grand hotel. Large flower arrangements graced each table set with silver candlesticks and crystal champagne goblets.

Seated at their table, Mr. Bhakta's guests also included the Sioux Chief Red Shirt, Lillie Smith, and the show's manager, Nate Salisbury.

"What do you think of the ship?" Annie asked Hulda, who sat with her mouth agape.

"It's the most beautiful and grand thing I have ever seen."

"Yes, but it will be nothing compared with the queen's palaces. I hope to see Buckingham or Windsor." Annie's excitement at the prospect momentarily squelched her queasiness.

"This is like a dream, Annie."

The floor rose up and forward and then down and back with a giant swell. Annie gripped the arms of her chair, and the items on the table shifted.

"Have we stopped?" Frank asked. "It feels like we aren't moving forward." He stood up to look out of one of the porthole windows next to the table. "Boy, is it dark out there. Looks like a heck of a storm brewing."

Just then, Mr. Bhakta entered the dining room and took his seat next to Frank.

"The captain has stopped the ship for the time being," he said. "Apparently, there is something wrong with one of the engines, and it is imperative they rectify the situation before the clouds open up."

"Is it serious, Mr. Bhakta?" The colonel paled, laying a hand over his belly.

"All is in hand, sahib." Mr. Bhakta smiled, putting his hands up in reassurance. "The captain says they will be finished within the hour. Nothing to worry about."

The floor rose up again, and Annie closed her eyes, the nausea returning.

"Are you feeling queasy?" she asked Hulda.

"Not at all." Hulda grinned. "It's almost like the carousel at the fair."

Annie wished she could share the sentiment.

Lillie Smith, who sat next to Hulda, frowned and waved a Chinese fan vigorously in front of her face. "My stateroom is so small I can barely turn around. And hot."

Annie wanted to chide her for being so rude, but she held her tongue, deciding that a row with Lillie would be inevitable at some point during the voyage, so better to wait for an argument worth her energy.

"I suppose you and the colonel have the largest rooms on the ship." Lillie shifted in her chair, her face pinched as she tugged at the tight waist of her dress that appeared two sizes too small for her ample frame.

"Nate and I are bunking together," the colonel piped up, annoyance in his voice. "So I don't want to hear any complaints from you, Miss Smith. If you'd like a larger room, I can take the difference out of your salary."

Lillie smirked at him and turned her head away, feigning interest in something else. The colonel's gaze caught Annie's, and his lips twitched in a half-smile.

Nate Salisbury, an elegant man with a perfectly trimmed beard and kind eyes, had just been hired on by the colonel for the tour. Annie had heartily approved of the decision.

"I feel quite humbled. Our room is very gracious," Annie said in an attempt to diffuse Lillie's negativity.

"And it's right next door to mine," Hulda added.

"Just as I figured." Lillie rolled her eyes.

"You may have my room, Miss Smith," said the chief. Tall and imposing with a handsome, stoic face, long nose, and a jaw that looked like it had been chiseled out of granite, Chief Red Shirt also had an attractiveness that came from within. Annie had connected with him the moment her dear friend, Chief Sitting Bull, had introduced them. Since Chief Sitting Bull had left the show, Red Shirt had replaced him as Annie's protector and friend. "I must stay with my people in the cabins below decks. They are uneasy on the water."

"Chief, you don't have to do that." The colonel, his face draining of color, pushed his plate away.

"My people have much fear crossing the ocean," Red Shirt told the group. "Many are feeling ill with the coming storm."

"Well, they aren't alone, Chief. I'm feeling a bit bilious myself." The colonel rubbed a hand across his belly.

"My people believe that if a man attempts to cross the ocean, he will be seized by a malady that will first prostrate him and then slowly consume his flesh, day after day, until at length the very skin itself will drop from his bones, leaving nothing but the skeleton. And if he dies at sea, he cannot be properly returned to the earth."

"Well, thank you for the cheerful tale. I know I feel much better," Lillie said, clutching her silk fan. She waved it in front of her face so violently she set the fringe on the colonel's coat to swinging. "But I'll take the room."

"Are *you* afraid, Chief?" Hulda asked. "How did you get your people to come aboard?"

"They trust my wisdom, and the colonel pays us well. We have seen plenty of death. We should not fear it." The chief reached for his wine glass and held it up to the group. "A safe voyage."

"To a safe voyage," they all sang in unison, raising their glasses.

Annie tried to engage in the conversation but could not stop thinking about Buck on the deck above her, possibly pacing and sweating in his pen with the sea growing rougher and the storm approaching. She hoped he hadn't got worked up again. Sitting through lunch would prove an agony until she could check on him.

She wanted to talk to Frank about it—he so often allayed her worries—but he and Mr. Patel were engaged in what looked like an intense conversation. It would be rude to interrupt simply because she was fretting over her horse.

"Mr. Bhakta." Annie decided to take her troubles into her own hands. She leaned toward him. "Is there a veterinarian on board?"

"Yes, memsahib. He is one of America's finest, I'm told. We want all of the Wild West Show's animals to arrive in London in fine form."

"Excellent. I'd like to talk with him about Buck."

"I shall arrange it." Mr. Bhakta bowed his head. "I'm sure he is with the animals now, with the approaching storm."

"No need. I'm headed up there myself, soon. I'm sure I can find him." Annie picked up a hunk of bread, hoping it would settle her stomach. She tore off a piece and put it into her mouth. It was sweet and soft, and to her surprise, it appealed to her. She finished it and then drained half a glass of water. Her nausea must be due to hunger.

"Miss Smith, are you feeling all right?" Nate asked Lillie, whose pudgy face was growing more insipid by the moment.

"Feeling a little green around the gills," Lillie said, waving the fan. Her face blanched and she stifled a burp. "Mr. Bhakta, is the voyage going to be like this for the entire two weeks?"

"No, Miss Smith. Perhaps intermittently. Shall I order you some ginger tea? It helps the stomach."

"No thanks. The way I feel, only whiskey will do the trick."

The chief raised his glass to her. "I agree, Miss Smith."

The luncheon meal seemed to go on forever, the ship pitching and rolling with the growing storm. Finally, Mr. Bhakta suggested they all retire to their cabins for comfort and safety until the ship was on its way again.

"Let's go see Buck," Annie said to Frank and Hulda. "I hope he's not out of his mind by now."

Annie's concerns couldn't have been more well-founded. Buck had worked himself into a lather. He paced frantically back and forth in his stall, his hooves digging into the pine shavings, spreading them to the corners. Soon he'd be pacing on the deck wood below, possibly damaging his legs.

"I have to get him out of there." Annie grabbed Buck's halter which was slung over one of the posts, while Frank opened the stall door for her.

"He seemed fine when I left him last night," Frank said. "He was pacing, but not agitated like this. Must be the swells."

Once Annie stepped inside, Buck stopped pacing. He stood stock still, but his whole body trembled, and he bumped his nose against Annie's stomach, desperate for some kind of comfort. The dusky smell of his foamy, sweat-stained coat permeated the air around them.

"There, there, boy. You're going to be okay. Let's get you out of here for a walk, eh?"

The horse lowered his head for Annie to tie the rope halter around it. She attached the lead line and led him out of the stall.

Buck surged ahead of Annie, his hooves clattering on the deck. Annie shook the lead up and down signaling Buck to back up. He threw his head in agitation, but obeyed. She tried to get Buck to move forward again, but he planted his feet, his eyes wide, his mind now catatonic, paralyzed with fear.

"Can we get the vet over here?" Annie asked Frank.

"I think he's with the buffalo below."

"Hulda, would you go fetch him?" Annie jumped out of the way as Buck, suddenly snapping out of his frozen state, tried to barrel past her. She shook the line again. "I don't think I'll be enough to calm him this time." Annie tried to keep her own anxiety at Buck's discomfort at bay. She knew they fed off of each another's emotions, and if she could stay calm, it would help him.

With a flip of her skirt, Hulda dashed away. Buck screamed a loud, frantic whinny, calling to the other horses. Some returned the alarm, and all swayed and pawed in their pens. Even Charlie and Isham began to weave back and forth in their stalls.

Large drops of rain fell onto the deck of the ship and made a *tick-ticking* sound as they hit the canvas cover over the stalls. Buck's ears perked up, and he lifted his head, as if preparing to flee.

The veterinarian came rushing toward them, Hulda on his heels. A compact young man with a brownish scuff of a beard and hair the color of sand, he carried a leather satchel.

"Looks like someone needs a little help," he said, nodding at Annie. Annie glowered at him, while wrestling with the 1200-pound mass of terrified horseflesh at her side. She glanced at Hulda, whose eyes had gone soft and dewy when the dashing young man had flashed her a grin. "Casey Everett. I'm quite a fan of yours, Miss Oakley."

"Right, yes." He pulled out a glass bottle and syringe from his satchel. "This is a sedative. A few drops of this, and your boy will be calm for hours."

"No disrespect, Mr. Everett, but could you tell me what sedative you plan to use?"

"It's heroin."

"But we will be at sea for two weeks." Annie struggled to push Buck away from her feet. "Will we have to keep sedating him? I've heard heroin is a strong drug."

"It's been my experience with the transporting of race horses, that once the horse is calm, he will see that no harm will come to him. He'll also realize his herd is here, and they are all in the same boat." Mr. Everett laughed at his own pun. He held the syringe in the air. "Here, let's see if we can get this boy—"

"Buck," Annie gasped, out of breath from her struggles.

"Buck, to stand still. Mr. Butler—" he nodded toward Frank. "Could you hold up one of Buck's feet?"

Frank moved past Annie and laid his hands on Buck's neck, stroking it, then ran his hands down Buck's leg. Trembling with fear, Buck froze, his feet planted to the ship's deck. Frank pinched the chestnut above Buck's left front knee, and Buck flung his hoof up into Frank's hand.

The horse struggled, probably worried at having one of his limbs immobilized, but Frank held on. Annie stroked Buck's withers as the vet prepared the needle for injection.

"I'm going to put the needle in as fast as I can. Miss Oakley, I'm going to need you to step aside."

Annie moved back and the vet stepped forward, jabbing the needle into Buck's neck, making him jump. Frank struggled to hang on in the skirmish. The vet plunged the drug through the needle, and stepped away. "You can let go now, sir," he said to Frank.

Frank let go of Buck's leg and quickly skipped backward to get out of the way as Buck strained against the line, becoming stronger in his terror-stricken need to escape. He reared up, nearly striking Annie in the face with one of his hooves. She jumped back and in doing so, lost hold of the lead line. Sensing his freedom, Buck spun on his back feet and headed straight for the deck railing.

In four large bounds, like a giant Pegasus, he soared over the rails and into the water, several yards below.

Chapter Three

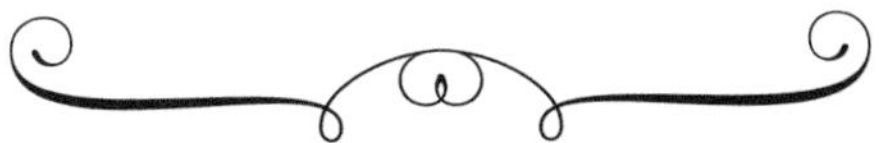

"Buck!" Annie bolted for the railing and hung over it, panicked to see her beloved horse flailing in the swells, his high-pitched screams echoing on the wind. She hiked her leg up over the railing preparing to jump when she felt strong hands pull her back.

"No, Annie," Frank cautioned, wrapping his arms around her. The rain came harder, and Annie shivered against the whipping wind.

"He's going to drown!" Annie struggled out of Frank's grasp.

"What's happened?" Mr. Bhakta and the vet came up beside her. Both looked over the railing at Buck paddling frantically in the water.

"Horses can swim, but not for very long," Mr. Everett said, taking off his coat, as if he were prepared to jump in after him. "The real worry here is that when the sedative kicks in, it will render him helpless. Then he will drown."

"Somebody do something!" Annie turned around, yelling at the crewmen on deck.

She turned back to see Frank and Mr. Bhakta topple overboard, falling fifteen feet into the water below. They landed with a heavy splash and both disappeared. Within seconds, Frank's head pushed through the surface, and he shook his hair out of his eyes.

"Frank!" Stunned, Annie gripped the railing, her heart thudding in her chest. The water around him took on a faint red or pink hue. "Are you bleeding? Why is the water red?" She called out to him, her voice high pitched with panic.

"I'm all right." His voice trailed on the wind. "I'm going to go after Buck."

"Where's Bhakta?" Mr. Everett shouted down to him.

Frank swirled in the water, searching wildly for the queen's man. Frank then ducked under, disappearing from view. Moments later he resurfaced, his arms wrapped around an unconscious Mr. Bhakta.

"Why does the water look red? Is Buck bleeding? Is Mr. Bhakta bleeding?" Annie searched Mr. Everett's face.

"I don't see what you are seeing," Mr. Everett said. His hair fell forward over his eyes as the rain, falling harder, pelted them. "The water is a bit murky, but I don't see any red."

"Somebody!" Annie yelled. Frank treaded water with one hand, and held onto Mr. Bhakta with the other. Buck flailed several yards away from them.

Annie, Mr. Everett, and Hulda sprang into action, yelling "man overboard," and directing the crew to lower one of the lifeboats. Several crewmen ran over and pulled at the rigging. They slowly lowered one of the small crafts into the sea. It plopped into the water several feet away from Frank. Holding onto Mr. Bhakta, Frank swam toward the lifeboat.

Annie braced against the rail with her hands, her fingers white from the pressure. She reached up, pushing her soggy hair out of her eyes, her hand shaking from the cold and the adrenaline surging through her.

Frank reached the lifeboat. Struggling to tip it, he got Mr. Bhakta's upper body onto the ledge. *Hold on, Frank.* Annie strained to see through the rain and the wind whipping her wet hair into her eyes. Buck was still floundering about a hundred feet from Frank. She pressed her fist to her mouth. *God, please don't take my husband—or my horse.*

With a mighty heave, Frank pushed Mr. Bhakta's legs into the boat.

"Take it up!" Frank yelled as steadied the small craft. The crew cranked the pulley and the lifeboat rose in the air.

Annie's heart pounded as she saw her horse, flailing in the water, all alone in an abyss of gray-blue sea. As fast as it seemed to come, the redness dissipated—or had it been her imagination? Buck's thrashing seemed to slow as the drug began to take effect.

"Better think of something quick for the horse!" Frank shouted as he swam toward Buck. Annie's stomach plummeted as Buck struggled to keep his head above water, and the rain came down in sheets.

"Swim, Frank!" she called out to him.

"Buck's weakening." Annie turned around, frantic, addressing the men who seemed to be doing nothing, staring at her as if she'd grown another head.

"Somebody do something, dammit!"

"Annie!" Hulda held her hand over her mouth. Her blond ringlets had loosened with the rain, and stuck to her face and neck. "You swore."

"If someone doesn't do something fast, I'll do more than swear." Annie hollered to be heard above the noise of the rain pelting the deck.

One of the ship's crewmen stepped forward, water streaming from his cap. "I believe we could use that to get the horse back on board." He pointed to the crane used to haul large loads onto the docks.

"Yes! We can make a sling and use the crane to get Buck out," Annie said.

"Brilliant idea." Mr. Everett nodded to the crewman. "Let's see how we can rig this thing up. Miss Oakley, don't you worry. We'll get them out safe. Now, you might want to go down below where it's warm. We'll take it from here," Mr. Everett shouted to her.

Annie looked at him aghast. "I am going nowhere until my horse and my husband are out of that water!"

Mr. Everett started to protest, but stopped when he met Annie's eyes. He then called to the other crewmen to help set the hoist.

Annie grasped the railing, peering down at Frank and Buck.

Frank's pale face glowed against the deep blue of the water. He was gasping for air against the rain and the swells, and his soaked hair streamed into his eyes as he struggled to hold Buck's head above the water. Immobilized by the drug, the horse had stopped flailing.

Unable to bear the sight of her beloved horse and her husband fighting for breath, Annie ripped off her jacket and her boots, climbed up onto the railing, and jumped overboard.

Annie hit the surface hard, plunging deep into the icy water, all the air pushing out of her lungs. Her dress and petticoats billowing over her head, she had to fight against the fabric to get to the surface. She popped up, and pushing the hair out of her face, swam over to Frank and Buck.

"My God, Annie, you could have killed yourself. What are you doing?" Frank shouted above the noise of the rain and crashing whitecaps.

"Everything I hold dearest in my heart is in this water. I want to be with you both." Annie yelled into the wind, the waves cresting around the three of them. "They are going to use the crane and a net to haul Buck on board. Are you all right, Frank? You aren't cut or bleeding?"

"No. I'm fine. Help me with his head." Frank's face strained against the water slapping against his chin. Buck's eyes took on a vacant stare, his body still, rising and falling with the waves.

Annie swam over to Buck's other side, scanning the water for blood, but there was none. The freezing waves lifted them up several feet and then sank so fast that Annie's stomach lurched. She shivered, the cold sinking into her bones. The sedative and Annie's presence had calmed Buck's thrashing, making it safer for them to be so close, but he was struggling to keep afloat.

The sky around them continued to darken, the charcoal clouds rolling over the massive swells. Rain pelted them, and with the water coming down from the sky and the waves heaving up, breathing proved an effort.

A net dropped from above, landing on the water with a loud thud. It oozed out upon the surface like oily paint, held fast by large knotted ropes and two timbers.

"We need to secure the net under his belly so the poles are at his sides." Frank motioned with his arms, the sleeves of his white linen shirt both clinging to his skin and billowing out in the water. The weight of Annie's corset and skirts grew heavier by the minute, and she struggled to get in front of Buck to keep his head afloat.

"Stay with me, fella. We've got to get you out of here."

A streak of lightning lit up the sky, and the rain fell harder, moving across the water like a shimmering sheet of glass.

"I can't hold him up, Frank. I'm too small." Annie yelled. "I'll secure the net under him."

Feeling the weight of her skirts dragging her down, Annie sank under the water, the waves tossing her back and forth. Reaching behind her, she fumbled with the buttons of her skirt, the buttonholes made tight with the swelling of the wool fabric. With a mighty yank, she ripped the buttons from the holes, her body sinking lower into the sea. She wriggled out of her skirt, her lungs clamping down. Her skirt rose above her head, floating toward the surface and she fought to swim upward, past it, desperate for oxygen. She surfaced and gulped air.

"Where'd you go?" Frank's voice echoed across the water.

"I'm okay." Annie swam to the nearest pole and disconnected it from the net, her body rising and falling with the swells.

"You hold onto these poles," she said to Frank." I'll swim under Buck with the net, and then we can secure the net to the other pole, and they can hoist him up."

A wave crashed over their heads. When Annie resurfaced, her husband and Buck had sunk beneath the water.

Quickly, net in hand, Annie dove under and could see Buck's lifeless body sinking. Frank momentarily resurfaced for air and then came back down to help her.

Working fast, they secured the net under Buck's belly and got it attached to the poles on either side of the lifeless horse. Frank gave Annie a thumbs up, and she quickly resurfaced.

"Pull him up, now!" Frank shouted to the men on deck.

Within seconds, Buck's body was drifting upward and breaking through the surface of the massive waves.

Annie's breath caught in her throat to see her horse, wet and lifeless, his legs dangling at awkward angles, being lifted into the sky. She prayed he hadn't taken on too much water. Her limbs grew weak, and she leaned her head back to float so she wouldn't go under. She felt Frank's arms go around her.

"You are a mighty force, Annie Oakley, and I love you. Hang onto me. They'll be sending down another lifeboat any moment."

The two clung together, tossed around in the waves, coughing and sputtering against the rain. As Buck's body disappeared over the railing of the deck, a lifeboat appeared and then descended into the water.

When it touched the surface, Frank tipped it sideways, allowing Annie to clamber in. Then pulling with all her might, Annie helped Frank drag himself in. The little boat pitched and rolled with Annie and Frank lying on the floor, exhausted, gasping for breath. Soon they could feel the boat rise.

Annie, still breathless, scooted closer to Frank and nestled into the curve of his arm.

"Thank you for jumping in to save my horse. I'll have to thank Mr. Bhakta, too. That was quite a valiant effort from both of you. I hope Buck is all right." Annie pushed the hair out of Frank's eyes.

"Well, darlin', I had every intention of jumping in, that's for sure, but somebody helped me."

"I don't understand."

"As I was trying to get my coat off, I noticed Mr. Bhakta standing behind me. He reached out to help me and suddenly, something came from behind us. Next thing I knew, we were both flying over the railing."

"You mean you were pushed."

"Yes, my dear, that's exactly what I mean."

~

The lifeboat cleared the railing and then thumped onto the deck. Annie scrambled out, thinking only of Buck.

The horse lay in a puddle of seawater, not moving, unconscious. Mr. Everett and Bobby knelt over Buck's head, checking his eyes and mouth. Mr. Everett held a wooden object, like a candlestick, in his hand and, after checking Buck's mouth, pressed the large end of the object against the lower side of the horse's heart girth.

"How is he? Is he cut? Bleeding?" Annie approached slowly, the wind sending a chill down her back, afraid to hear bad news. She held her hand out to Mr. Post, Buck's caretaker, and he grasped it with bony, shaking fingers. Rain dripped from his long handlebar mustache and rugged beard. His aged, watery eyes sought hers.

"I don't see any contusions. He's going to be fine, Annie." Mr. Everett said, his voice straining against the wind as he looked up at them. His eyes lingered on Annie's wet blouse stuck to her corset, and her petticoats clinging to her legs. She'd forgotten she'd ripped off her skirts and coat, but really, at a time like this, what did it matter?

"Mr. Everett?"

"Oh. Yes. The horse's lungs sound like they're clear, and he seems to be breathing normally. Once the drug starts to wear off, he'll come to, and we can get him back to his stall."

"Thank goodness." Annie's head swam with relief, and she sank down onto her knees, the pitching and rolling of the ship making it difficult to stand. Icy rain pelted her back, and the dampness of her petticoats and corset chilled her to the bone.

"He's going to be fine, Annie." Bobby patted the horse's neck, a grin splitting his face.

Mr. Post swiped at his eyes. "I don't know what I'd do if I couldn't take care of that yella' fellow anymore. I've grown right fond of him." Small, skinny, and aging more rapidly than Annie cared to admit, Mr. Post, she knew, took great pride in caring for Isham and Buck, two of the most famous horses of the era.

"You must get out of your wet clothes, Little Miss Sure Shot, and take shelter from the storm." Chief Red Shirt had appeared.

"Always so concerned about me." Annie stood up and reached for the lanky Indian chief. She pressed herself against his elaborate bone vest and the decorated braids that hung to his waist. "We saved Buck." Annie swallowed the hitch in her throat, relieved and grateful her horse and her husband were alive and well. But Frank's mentioning he had been pushed overboard created a whole new anxiety. Her initial uneasiness about the voyage when they'd boarded the ship returned, but for entirely different reasons. Was her husband in danger? And if so, from whom and why?

The chief patted her cheek. "It gives me great pleasure that your wonder horse will survive. He has a great spirit."

"The horse will be fine." Mr. Everett stood up, never taking his eyes from Buck. "But I am afraid Mr. Bhakta did not fare as well."

As fast as the rain and wind had come, the storm began to abate. Some of the ship's crew, Mr. Patel, and the colonel stood over the deceased Mr. Bhakta. Someone had placed a coat over his body, now soaked with rain and seawater. Annie, Frank, and Bobby joined them at Mr. Bhakta's feet.

"He's dead?" Bobby's voice cracked.

Mr. Everett knelt next to the body. He removed the coat and studied Mr. Bhakta from head to toe.

"Does he have any signs of injury? Any bleeding?" Annie asked. "I could have sworn I saw red in the water."

"It doesn't appear so." Mr. Everett moved Mr. Bhakta's limbs, looking for lacerations. "Let's get him—and us—inside, out of the storm. I'd like to take a closer look at him."

Frank and Annie exchanged glances.

"We'll come with you." Annie knelt down next to one of Mr. Bhakta's legs. Mr. Everett and Bobby lifted the man's chest and shoulders off the deck and Annie and Frank took his legs.

Once downstairs in the grand foyer, the Indian players and other passengers began to gather. Gasps and screams could be heard from some of the Indian women and children. The captain of the ship entered, pulling down the hem of his uniform. His captain's hat pressed down on his forehead, making it difficult to see his eyes, but from the stern set of his mouth and his subtle, if not invisible, mannerisms, Annie could tell this man aimed for perfection in everything—his dress, his crew, and his ship. He eyed her odd state of dress.

Now that she'd come to her senses, the stares of the other passengers and the captain alerted her to the fact she was barely clothed and what she was wearing clung to her skin. Bobby removed his coat and handed it to her. With a nod of thanks, she wrapped it around her shoulders.

"You realize, Miss Oakley, it is dangerous to jump overboard. Your life is worth far more than the horse's," the captain said sternly, hands behind his back. "I hope we won't have any more incidents of this nature."

Annie blinked, surprised at the condescension in the captain's tone. Didn't he realize Buck's worth—not only financially, but to her personally? Her heart pounded with indignation. As if sensing her rising temper, Frank squeezed her upper arm. Annie took in a deep breath, trying to calm herself.

"Sir, my horse and my husband were fighting for their lives in that water. I'm sorry if they inconvenienced you. Perhaps you should take up your complaints with the colonel, but we have a much more delicate situation here. Mr. Bhakta—"

"Ah, yes, I am aware." The captain raised his chin, and his gaze traveled over Annie's head and sought Frank and Mr. Everett's. "Please take Mr. Bhakta to my stateroom. I'll have the ship's Dr. Adams meet you there. I must get back to the helm. The engine has been repaired, and we are ready to get underway. I'll check back with you later." The captain clicked his heels together and turned from the group.

"But, Captain—" Annie reached out to grab his arm, but Frank steadied her.

"Simmer down, Annie."

"But he's so—and what about Mr. Bhakta—and you and Buck?" Annie sputtered, looking up into Frank's blue-gray eyes.

"I know, Annie. But he is in charge. You're upset, and with good reason, but please calm down. We've all had a great shock."

"You said you and Mr. Bhakta were pushed. I'm trying to remember who was standing at the railing with us, but I was so consumed with worry about Buck that I took no notice. Do you remember?"

Frank shook his head. "Everett was there with us, but I think he was ready to go after Buck himself. I don't see why he would have done it."

Annie sighed, resting her forehead against Frank's chest, the smell of wet wool filling her nostrils. "I don't like this, Frank. I don't like it at all."

Chapter Four

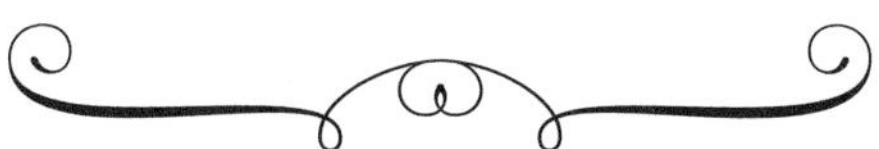

Frank held Annie close, his cold, wet shirt and waistcoat pressed against her equally frigid shift, making her shiver.

Moments later, a striking man in a gray suit with leather satchel in hand arrived. He motioned for Mr. Everett, Frank, and Bobby to pick up the body and follow him. Her teeth chattering from the cold, Annie put her small arms though the large sleeves of Bobby's coat as she followed the men to the captain's stateroom. She hadn't realized how much Bobby had grown in the past couple of years. She felt like a child wearing her father's clothes, but was grateful for the warmth.

"Please, step aside, people." Dr. Adams took one of Bhakta's legs and held an arm out to protect them from the crowd. "Go back to your rooms."

Once they had placed Mr. Bhakta's body on the captain's bed, Dr. Adams and Mr. Everett began to undress him.

"Miss Oakley, it might not be appropriate for you to be here." Dr. Adams gave her an indulgent smile while he let Mr. Everett finish removing Bhakta's shoes. He placed his arms behind his back in an authoritative manner.

Annie tried to temper her irritation at his insinuation that she was simply a weak-minded woman who could not bear the sight of a dead man. If he only knew.

"It might not be, but we are guests of the queen, and Mr. Bhakta was our escort. I'd like to know what happened. First hand."

Dr. Adams turned to Mr. Everett, a look of reluctance and resignation in his face. "Tell me what happened."

"I tried to resuscitate him when we got him back on board," Mr. Everett tugged at one of Bhakta's sleeves to remove it from his already rigid, lifeless body. "But it was far too late by then. I briefly examined him." Mr. Everett hesitated when he removed Bhakta's sleeve to reveal dark purple blooms of bruising on the dead man's arm. Annie's breath caught in her throat.

Dr. Adams leaned over the body, pushing Mr. Everett out of the way.

Mr. Everett stepped back, his hand to his mouth, his eyes wide. "I—I assumed he died of drowning."

"That is possible." Dr. Adams lifted Mr. Bhakta's chest and removed the rest of his shirt. Both arms showed the bright, purple mottling of bruising. "But my guess is that this man died of internal bleeding."

Annie shifted her gaze to Mr. Bhakta's face. Blood seeped out of his nostrils and from the corners of his closed eyes. She stifled a gag. The image was horrifying, but she didn't want to appear weak before these men who already seemed to judge her as faint-hearted.

"What could have caused it?" she asked, trying to sound unaffected.

The doctor straightened, his eyes never leaving the body.

"A number of things. Could be a hemorrhagic fever of some kind, in which case, we have to use extreme caution in handling the body so the disease doesn't spread." The doctor again leaned over the body. He reached a hand out to the face and gently opened the eyelids. Watery blood streamed out and down Mr. Bhakta's temples. The whites of his eyes were crimson. The doctor pried open Mr. Bhakta's lips, revealing bloodstained teeth and pomegranate colored gums.

Annie's stomach clenched, her nausea returning. Not usually the squeamish sort, she was baffled by her physical and emotional response.

"Excuse me," the doctor said as he pushed Mr. Everett, Annie, Frank, and Bobby aside. He quickly glanced at Annie and seemed about to say something, but he refrained and continued to undress Mr. Bhakta, down to his drawers.

Annie turned her back to the body, feeling the flush of heat come to her cheeks. She could no longer feign complete detachment. The only other man she'd seen in his drawers was Frank. She heard the shuffling of Mr. Bhakta's undergarment being removed, and then the bed creaked. She assumed Dr. Adams had manipulated the body in a manner to see his backside. The scuffling stopped, and Annie turned her head to see if Bhakta had been covered again. To her relief, the doctor had laid a sheet over Bhakta's private parts.

"No punctures or wounds," the doctor stated, crossing his arms over his chest.

"What could have caused the internal bleeding?" Frank asked.

"Certain drugs or chemicals could cause a bleed. Or, perhaps the fall displaced one or more of his organs. Also, some diseases can cause internal bleeding. I'm not absolutely certain he bled internally. Poison also presents like this. We should assume nothing." The doctor moved toward Mr. Bhakta's head again. "I can't say for sure, but the reddening of the eyes and gums are consistent with blood poisoning of some kind. But there is no evidence Mr. Bhakta has suffered any type of injury that would leave an open wound and cause the blood to become infected. Do we know if Mr. Bhakta showed signs of a fever or illness when he boarded the ship?"

"He seemed right chipper," Bobby piped in, his voice cracking.

"He certainly didn't seem ill to me. What about you, Frank?" Annie looked into her husband's face, the lines at his eyes deeper with worry.

"Not at all."

"Then we can probably rule out illness." Dr. Adams rubbed at his closely trimmed beard. He leaned over Mr. Bhakta's body and again pried open his mouth, this time more aggressively.

"What are you doing?" Annie asked.

"I'm looking for lesions in the mouth or down the throat. Blisters. Ulcers. Something of that nature."

"But why?"

"What time did Mr. Bhakta have his last meal, do you know?" Dr. Adams addressed Annie, ignoring her question.

"Well, he ate with us. I'd say at around twelve fifteen. I know for sure because I was worried about Buck and wanted to get back up on deck to check him within the hour."

The doctor took his pocket watch from his vest. "One thirty. And shortly after that, he dove overboard with Mr. Butler to rescue your horse."

"Frank?" Annie turned to her husband, hoping he would share with them what he had shared with her.

Frank ran a hand through his wet, blond hair. "Mr. Bhakta didn't dive overboard."

"I don't understand." The doctor shook his head.

"Neither did I. I had every intention to, of course—dive overboard to go after the horse—but before I could get my coat off, I was pushed—Mr. Bhakta was directly behind me, so either he pushed me, or he was pushed, too."

"This doesn't sound good to me," Mr. Everett said.

"That leaves me to conclude that Mr. Bhakta was well on his way to death before he was pushed overboard," said Dr. Adams.

"What do you mean?" A skittering of prickles ran down Annie's back.

Dr. Adams turned to address her. "We can't rule out the possibility that Mr. Bhakta was murdered."

"Buck is out there alone," Annie said to Mr. Everett as he pulled a blanket up over Mr. Bhakta's body to cover his head.

"Yes, we should go back on deck."

"I've got things in hand here, for the moment," Dr. Adams addressed Mr. Everett. "You've got your patient, I've got mine."

Mr. Everett straightened up slowly. "I'll take some blankets up there for Buck and make sure he is kept warm until he comes out of his drug-induced state. You two go get into some dry clothes," he said to Annie and Frank.

"We're coming with you," Annie said through chattering teeth.

"Annie, you're freezing." Frank grasped her around the shoulders.

"I'll be fine. Where do we find those blankets?"

Mr. Everett exchanged glances with Frank, who raised his hands in surrender.

On deck, Annie, Frank and Mr. Everett stood watching the prone horse that still hadn't moved. Annie's fingertips were numb, and her body began to tire from the endless shaking and teeth chattering. Frank rubbed her arms and shoulders, but her slim figure and tiny frame provided no insulation against the wet and cold of the storm. Frank tried to coax her indoors, again, but Annie wouldn't take her eyes from Buck, still lying on deck.

Pelted by rain and doused with the occasional wave breaking over the railing, Buck slept on as if he lay in a sunny field of wildflowers. Mr. Everett had covered him with wool blankets, but Annie wondered how much warmth those blankets could possibly provide, given the amount of cold water sloshing around him.

"Excuse me," Mr. Everett said, his shoulders hunched from the cold. "I'm going to check on the other animals. Give a holler if Buck wakes."

Annie and Frank nodded, and Frank took another blanket and wrapped himself and Annie in it. It was horribly itchy but provided protection from the wind.

"Poor Bhakta," Frank said.

"Yes, it's incredible. Who would want to kill him?" Annie asked. "Or you?"

"We aren't positive he was killed. Or that anyone is out to kill me."

"We can't be too sure," Annie said. "We can't rule out murder. If he was killed, it could have been anyone. A passenger? Someone in the crew?"

"Let's not jump to conclusions just yet." Frank held her closer.

"But Frank, you said someone *pushed* Mr. Bhakta overboard. It seems someone wanted to make sure Bhakta died. I wonder if the captain aims to investigate."

"Annie—" Frank's voice echoed a familiar warning.

"Don't look at me that way, Frank. You could have been killed too. We need to find out who this person is before they try again. Who knows who might be their next target?"

"I don't think you should get involved, Annie. Leave it to the authorities."

"Right now, I'm so cold I can't even think straight." Annie snuggled closer to Frank. "Maybe Mr. Bhakta wasn't a target. Maybe it was a random killing."

"Annie. Stop. You really have become somewhat of a worrier, dear." But Frank's voice betrayed his own worry. She couldn't help but love him a bit more for wanting to calm her fears, despite his own. He was her steady rock in every situation, but no matter what reassurances he gave, she wouldn't let this go.

He stroked her hair. "All will be taken care of. Look."

Buck was stirring and his eyes fluttered open. With great effort, he lifted his neck off the deck, curled his legs under him, and heaved a great sigh.

"Mr. Everett!" Annie called out to the vet and then rushed to her horse. She sat down next to him and flung her arms around his neck. Buck nickered softly and turned his head into her body.

Mr. Everett poked his head out from one of the other stalls and then rushed over to them, Bobby trailing behind him.

"Ah! Excellent. Once he stands, we will get him into his stall, rub him down and put a dry blanket on him. Poor chap must be freezing."

"Will he catch cold?" Annie asked, relieved, yet still worried.

"We'll get dry blankets on him and feed him some warm, sweet mash. That's the best we can do." Mr. Everett eyed Annie and Frank up and down. "I may not be a doctor for humans anymore, but I know you two could definitely fall ill unless you get out of those wet clothes and go indoors immediately."

"I've been trying to get this stubborn woman out of the cold for the past hour." Frank pulled Annie to her feet. "She won't leave her horse."

"Not until he's safely settled in his stall," Annie chattered. "What made you want to become a veterinarian?" she asked Mr. Everett, curious about his earlier statement.

"I've always wanted to work with animals. My father had different ideas for my education, so I became a physician. I never lost the desire to become a veterinarian, and decided to pursue my dream."

"Did that upset your father?"

"At first. After I saved one of his prized race horses from colic, he changed his tune."

With a tremendous groan, Buck set his front legs out in front of him and pushed up, getting to a sitting position where he rested a moment, as if gathering the strength to lift the rest of his body. Then he surged forward, uncurled his hind legs, and pushed up to standing.

The last time Annie had seen her beloved Buck so unsteady was when his legs had buckled from fatigue from overwork by McCrimmon. The man had beaten him nearly senseless when he couldn't pull a load. But this time was even worse, thanks to the sedative and ocean dive. Images of Buck leaping over the side of the ship raced through her mind, and she shook her head to clear them. As if reading her thoughts, Buck gave a low nicker.

"Looks like Buck thinks you should get indoors as well," Frank admonished.

Annie wrapped her arms around Buck's head. "Thank goodness you are safe, my friend. I hope you've learned your lesson. Panicking when you're afraid will land you nowhere but in trouble."

Buck let out a loud snort, shaking his head. He then shook the wet blankets off his body.

"Come on, now. Let's get him into his stall." Mr. Everett took Buck's lead line and led him inside. "Bobby could you run and get some cotton cloths and a couple sets of dry horse blankets."

Buck snorted again, releasing his previous stress and anxiety, and rubbed his head against the veterinarian, the cold water probably making it itch.

When Bobby returned with the cloths, Annie grabbed one and began rubbing it over Buck's neck and back.

"Oh, no you don't." Frank grabbed her by the arm. He took the cloth from her and flung it at Bobby. "Buck will be fine now. You *must* go inside, my dear. We can't have you ill."

Annie looked up at Frank with pursed lips and downturned brows.

"Now."

"I'll take care of Buck, Annie." Bobby was rubbing the horse's neck and chest vigorously.

"Very well," Annie said with a sigh. "Mr. Everett, you will give me a report once Buck is completely settled?"

"Of course. I think he's going to be fine."

Finally satisfied, Annie let Frank lead her downstairs and into the side door of the large lobby. The heated air hit Annie's face, making it tingle as it began to warm.

"Let's get you into bed." Frank hustled her to the hallway nearest their stateroom.

"Bed? It's only afternoon, Frank. I'll warm up once I get into some dry clothes. But what about Mr. Bhakta? We must find out what's happening, what Dr. Adams has determined."

"Annie."

"Very well. I'll change my clothes, but I won't get into bed. Not until I know what happened to Mr. Bhakta. You should probably get out of those wet clothes yourself. I can't have my hero getting sick." Annie knew she could soften his sternness. She always could, and tried to use it to her advantage as much as possible.

"I don't suppose there is another human being on earth who loves me as much as you do." Annie wrapped her arms around Frank's neck.

"You *are* a handful, Miss Oakley." Frank pulled her closer, rubbing her back.

"Nonsense!" Annie slapped his shoulder.

"Let's get dressed."

"Yes, sir." Annie turned to walk down the hall. She paused. "And Frank?"

"What is it now?"

"I love you, too. More than anyone else."

Frank raised an eyebrow. "Really? Are you sure?"

Annie nodded. "After Buck, yes!"

Chapter Five

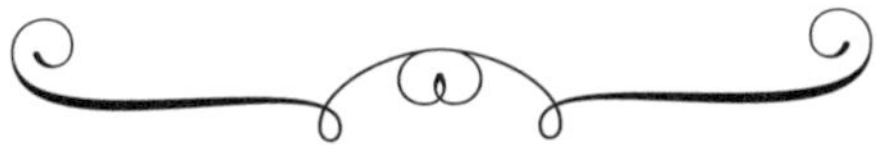

Annie, Frank, Dr. Adams, and the captain stood silently staring at the body of Mr. Bhakta, once again clothed and lying on the mattress of the built-in bed frame in the captain's stateroom. Annie hadn't had the chance to notice the masculine stateliness of the room before. Her gaze traveled over the heavy, leather-bound furniture and framed maps. The smell of pipe tobacco was so dense it seemed to ooze from the walls. A large Persian rug lined the wooden floor and held an oversized table with maps, compasses, and other navigating tools strewn across the top.

Annie, now in a dry, cotton dress and wool sweater, a woolen blanket wrapped around her shoulders, sank into one of the leather chairs next to Frank, who stood with the other men. She didn't want to admit it, but her arms and legs ached from numbness as her body continued to warm itself. Her stomach felt as if she'd been punched, and her head ached. She hoped she hadn't caught her death—to perish before she had a chance to be received by the queen. But she wouldn't have done anything different. She had to see Buck safe.

Annie still couldn't quite wrap her head around the fact that the esteemed friend to Queen Victoria had just died. Possibly been killed. The mere idea fueled the chill racing through her limbs, despite the heavy wool blanket she used as a shawl. Had he been more than a friend? Someone connected to the government? She didn't recall him introducing himself with a title, but he'd obviously been a royal appointee. She wondered how his death might impact those in the queen's circle, or the queen herself. Had someone aimed to kill Frank? Had he been pushed overboard because of his proximity to Mr. Bhakta? Or was something deeper going on?

"I think it best we do not tell the passengers that Mr. Bhakta's death is suspicious, but only that he drowned in an attempt to save the horse," the captain announced to the small group, which now included the late Mr. Bhakta's valet, Mr. Patel.

"But what shall we do with the body?" Dr. Adams asked, his waxed and twirled mustache bouncing up and down with each syllable. "We need it for evidence."

The group continued to stare at the soggy body of Amal Bhakta, as if he were a freak-show act.

"Seems a bit morbid to keep him—er—it." The captain frowned. "We'd usually give the deceased a burial at sea. Are you absolutely sure he was murdered, Doctor?"

"Not absolutely, but we must be certain. We have to keep the body."

"I see. Well, then. I suppose we can keep him in the refrigeration hold. Plenty of ice down there."

Annie winced. "Can we dress him in some dry clothes? It seems so. . . ."

They all turned to look at Annie with puzzled faces.

"Doesn't seem like it matters much, now, does it?" Frank said.

"I hate to be so indelicate, Miss Oakley." Dr. Adams placed a white sheet over the body. "But the fact that his clothes are wet will help with the . . . er . . . preservation of the body. We've got a way to go before we get to England."

"Mr. Patel, did Mr. Bhakta suffer from apoplexy?" Dr. Adams asked the bespectacled valet. "Do you know?"

Mr. Patel blinked up at the doctor through his wire-rimmed spectacles. "No. He was perfectly healthy to my knowledge."

"Right," said the doctor, fidgeting with his mustache. "It might be he ingested something harmful, either on purpose or accidentally. I will look through the books I have on board to gather more information on internal bleeding and blood poisoning. We'll also have to see the manifest. Question every single person on this ship. Captain? What say you?"

The captain pursed his lips in thought. "Yes. I suppose you are right. Until we can inform the proper authorities."

"Who has jurisdiction on the ship?" Annie asked.

"The captain acts as the law enforcement officer here," Frank said.

"Indeed, Mr. Butler." The captain rocked back and forth on the balls of his feet. "I will address the matter. Now, if you will please go to your stateroom, Mr. and Mrs.—er, that is—"

"But sir." Annie stood up. "Will you have time to run the ship and investigate a murder?"

"She has a point," Dr. Adams said. "If you'd like, I could start questioning the passengers."

"And the crew." Annie wrapped her hand around Frank's arm.

The captain's cheeks turned a pale shade of red. Annie knew she'd pushed too hard. She offered him a smile, but his eyes drifted toward Dr. Adams.

"I appoint you chief deputy in this investigation, Doctor. Please keep me apprised of all important details. I am sure we will be able to ferret out who would want to dispose of Mr. Bhakta."

"Or Mr. Butler," Mr. Patel spoke up, his voice as high-pitched as a child's. His small stature, concave chest, and large blinking eyes added to the impression that he had not yet reached the age of twenty, but at closer inspection, one could see the wisdom that etched his face, giving him a much older appearance.

"Why Frank?" asked Annie.

"His association with the anti-English Fenian Brotherhood."

Frank's arm tensed under Annie's hand. "I have no affiliation with the Fenian Brotherhood," he said. "I have never associated myself with any nationalist movement. I am an American through and through."

A gasp from the doorway caught everyone's attention. They turned to see a pretty young woman with dark auburn hair standing there, eyes wide and staring at the body.

The captain hurried to the door. "Miss Brady, how may I help you?"

The woman leaned around the captain to see inside the room. "I was looking for my mo—for Miss Parsons. Have you seen her?" The girl's eyes glittered with excitement, her gaze bouncing back and forth between the captain and the interior of the room. Annie thought she looked altered in some way, excited, distressed. Her cheeks blushed bright crimson, and she seemed out of breath.

"Are you quite all right, Miss Brady? Shall I escort you to your room?" The captain eased his way into the doorway, blocking her attempt to come further into the room. She stepped away, out of view. The captain said a few more words Annie could not hear and then came back into the room, shutting the door.

"She shouldn't have seen this," he said. "I don't want the passengers upset. The door should have been closed." The captain glared at Mr. Patel, whose gaze dropped immediately to the floor.

"Excuse my ignorance," Annie interrupted, wanting to take the heat off Patel. "What exactly is the Fenian Brotherhood?"

"It's a group of activists advocating for an independent Ireland, Ireland's complete separation from Great Britain. They believe that the government in London, namely the queen and the Conservatives, did as little as possible to aid the Irish people after the Great Famine," Frank said.

"The Fenians feel it is a form of genocide," Mr. Patel added.

"Frank, you've never been vocal about this cause," Annie said.

"I haven't. I've never been passionate about it. I don't know why I'd be associated with such a group."

"But your uncle—" Annie began until Frank's eyes darted to meet hers.

"He passed away some time ago," he said, giving her a cue not to continue. Annie would have to ask more about his uncle later. In private.

"Obviously, Mr. Patel received his information somewhere," said the captain. "It seems there is a notion, either misconstrued or somewhat confused, that you are active in Irish politics. We can't discount that information."

"Frank active in Irish politics? That's absurd," Annie said, her temper threatening to rise.

"We must find out who is perpetrating this rumor, and also find out if Mr. Bhakta was indeed murdered," said the captain. "Dr. Adams, are you up to the task, sir?"

"I'll try my best," Dr. Adams said.

"I'll leave you to it, then." The captain bowed slightly. "I must return to the bridge and to my duties." With his hands behind his back, he exited his quarters, his stiff, leather-soled boots creaking against the floorboards.

"Well, I have my work cut out for me then, don't I?" Dr. Adams approached Annie and Frank. "I do believe you, sir," he said to Frank; then he added to both of them, "I must admit, I know nothing about investigating a crime."

"We could—" Annie started to say something, but she suddenly lost her train of thought. Her head pounded and the room spun. She blinked her eyes to chase away the black spots that covered the room.

"Miss Oakley?" Dr. Adams reached for her arm. "Are you unwell?"

Annie shook her head, trying to clear it. "Yes, I was saying—I was saying—" Her vision blurred and then she saw nothing.

"Annie? Annie, can you hear me?" Annie heard Frank's voice in the distance.

"Mr. Butler, please step aside." Another male voice penetrated the *whirr* in her ears. "Miss Oakley." Annie felt a tapping on her cheek. She struggled to open her eyes, and saw Dr. Adams leaning over her and Frank next to him, his face etched with worry.

"What happened?" she asked, trying to sit up.

"Don't get up just yet," the doctor said. "You fainted."

"Fainted?" She couldn't believe what she'd just heard. She'd never fainted in her life. Her vision came in and out of focus, and she saw the black spots again. She closed her eyes, willing the spots away.

"Let's get her to bed," she heard Dr. Adams say. "I can examine her there."

She felt someone lift her, and could tell by the aroma of cigar smoke and leather that it was Frank who was carrying her. She let herself sink into the softness of his buckskin coat and fell again into unconsciousness.

When she opened her eyes again, she was lying in a bed. The doctor loomed above her, watching her face.

"You're back," he said.

"Where am I? Frank?"

"I'm right here, darling. We're in our stateroom." Frank approached the other side of the bed and took her hand. "You fainted again."

"What's wrong with me?" she asked Dr. Adams.

"I don't think it's anything serious. You've had quite a day," he said, pulling the covers up to her neck.

It all came flooding back. Buck and Frank going overboard. Mr. Bhakta.

"Yes, I suppose I have, but what about—?"

"No more talking or questions. You need to get some rest," Dr. Adams told her. He turned to Frank. "See that she stays put tonight. She should be fine in the morning, but if not, send for me."

"Will do, Doc." Frank said. Annie watched the doctor leave the room.

"But I—what about Buck?" Annie asked. "Where's Hulda?"

Frank ran the back of his hand down her cheek. "Mr. Everett is keeping his eye on Buck. Hulda is next door in her room. She, like the rest of us, is exhausted from the events of the day."

Annie relaxed into the pillow. Her head was still pounding, her stomach churned, and she felt exhausted.

"I'll see that Hulda has some supper and gets safely back to her room. But you sleep. I'll return in a while."

As much as she wanted to further protest and insist that she felt fine and could accompany them to supper, she couldn't seem to keep her eyes open. She closed them and then heard the doorknob click as Frank left the room.

But the truth of the matter remained. Someone may have killed the queen's friend, and that someone might be looking to kill her husband. *That* she could not let happen.

So tonight she would obey the doctor's orders and rest. Tomorrow, she would find out what happened to Mr. Bhakta and why.

The following morning, Annie woke early, grateful for a good night's sleep, but concerned that she still felt woozy. Thinking the sensation would pass, she got out of bed quietly to avoid disturbing Frank, who was snoring in blissful slumber. After quickly dressing, Annie headed upstairs to the main deck to see Buck.

The storm had given way to gleaming sunshine, and the blue water sparkled so bright that Annie had to shade her eyes with her hand. Even the brim of her straw hat could not keep the glare at bay. The wood of the deck, still damp with rain and warmed by the sun, infused the air with the woodsy smell of teak. It helped to diffuse the horrible, spoiled-milk odor coming from the ocean.

Annie pushed her straw hat further down on her head, the pressure making a squishing sound within the fibers. She walked toward the corrals to find her beloved Buck eating from a stack of hay in the corner of his pen. Someone had wrapped his legs—Mr. Post, probably. It looked like Mr. Post had also spent some time brushing Buck's coat and getting the tangles out of his black mane and tail. His body gleamed like the sun. And as Mr. Everett had predicted, Buck seemed no longer frightened, if not almost completely at ease on board the ship.

Annie entered his stall and laid a hand on his back, his coat soft as silk, watching him eat. She loved the way his eyes partially closed as he chewed the hay.

"He's a fine looking horse."

Annie turned to see the woman with the oversized coat who'd glowered at her when they'd boarded the ship. She was standing at the stall door. Her hardened face contrasted with the warmth in her eyes when she looked at the horse. When they shifted to Annie, the glow dissipated.

"Thank you," Annie said.

"I'm glad he's doing well this morning."

"Oh, yes. You must have heard."

"I saw the whole thing."

"I see." Annie furrowed her brow. "Why were you on deck during that horrendous storm?"

The woman pulled her coat tighter around her middle. "I'm sleeping in one of the cabins below. No fancy room for me. Third-class passenger. Only time I can stand being down there is if I'm asleep. Can't breathe. I need to be in the air."

Annie could certainly understand that. She was an outdoor girl herself. She left Buck and walked over to the stall door. "I'm Annie Oakley." She held out her hand.

"Yes, I know." As the woman took Annie's hand, her calloused palm indicated hard work and toil. "Gail Tessen."

"Pleased to meet you. You must like horses."

"Used to have them as a girl. A stable full."

"My. How fortunate." Annie eyed the shabby coat and the fraying hat. Obviously, the woman had fallen upon hard times. From the look of the weariness on her face, the hard times had outweighed and outlived the good ones.

"It was a different time, then." The woman's eyes slid over to Buck and a faint smile crossed her lips.

"What takes you to London?" Annie asked.

The woman's eyes darted away from Buck and away from Annie. "Family business."

Annie let silence fill the air. She wanted to observe Miss Tessen more intimately. Now that Annie had come closer, the woman avoided meeting her eyes.

"You say you were on the deck yesterday afternoon, during the storm?" Annie asked again. She didn't want to spook the woman so tried to proceed as gently as possible.

"Yes."

"Did you notice anything unusual? Anything that might stick out in your mind?"

Miss Tessen's lip curled. "You mean other than a horse soaring overboard? No."

"Whom did you see on deck?"

"What is this? Why all the questions?" Miss Tessen frowned, a look of insult skittering across her features. "I merely came by to look at your fine horse and see that he hadn't come to any harm." The woman's blue eyes finally met Annie's, cutting through her like a knife.

"I'm sorry," Annie said, taken aback at the woman's venom.

"Ta." Miss Tessen waved her hand. Her expression softened. "It's I who should apologize. I've a bit of a temper. And I didn't sleep well last night. That tomb down there will take some getting used to. All those savages with their crying babes. I'm sorry; of course you'd want to know what upset your horse. All I saw yesterday afternoon was the poor creature, scared out of his mind, you and your husband, the vet, and the Punjabi fellows rushing to the rail. I was sitting over there—" she indicated the wooden crates stacked against the ship's railing—"for cover, and waited till they hauled your horse back on deck. I took a chill and went down to the tomb to warm my bones."

Annie looked over again at the crates, and realized from that angle, Miss Tessen wouldn't have seen them bring Mr. Bhakta aboard.

"Thank you, Miss Tessen."

"That horse is special."

"Yes, I know. I'm so happy he's alive and well. I just wish Mr. Bhakta had survived the incident."

"What do you mean?" Miss Tessen flinched at Annie's words.

"Well, Mr. Bhakta went overboard, but he didn't survive the fall. He drowned." Annie paid special attention to Miss Tessen's expression. Her face went blank.

"Pity. Who was he?"

"Our escort to England. A friend of Queen Victoria's."

"Someone important." Miss Tessen nodded, her eyebrows raised.

"Yes."

A flurry of chocolate and tan striped taffeta skirts pulled Annie's attention away from Miss Tessen.

"Annie, dear." Emma Wilson was cruising toward them, wearing a large, floral-brimmed hat dipped below one eye.

"Emma, just the person I want to see."

"Glorious day, is it not?" Emma grabbed the brim of her hat on both sides and turned her face to the sun.

Annie turned to introduce Emma to Miss Tessen, but the woman had gone. Just as well, Annie thought. She had important matters to discuss with Emma.

"I saw Frank in passing," Emma said. "He said you fainted."

"When did he tell you this?" Annie asked.

"At breakfast in the dining room just now. Are you all right, dear?"

"Yes, I am quite restored. It was nothing. Just exhaustion." She didn't want to mention her queasiness. "Did he say anything else?"

"Nothing." Emma shrugged.

Annie pulled Emma away from Buck's stall and led her to the ship's railing where she could see anyone who might pass by.

"Did anyone say anything to you about what happened yesterday afternoon?" Annie asked.

"No. Terrible storm. I stayed in my stateroom writing. Why, what happened?"

Annie told her of Buck's mad escape and Mr. Bhakta's death. She also mentioned the Fenians, and the possibility that Frank might be in danger—a possible target.

"But is he affiliated with the Fenians?"

"He says no, although he had an uncle who was involved in political causes," Annie said, wringing her hands. The mere idea of Frank in danger made her blood run cold.

"And you doubt him?"

"I intend to discuss it with him further," Annie said, feeling the little crease between her eyes deepen.

"Don't look so downhearted, darling. You let me question Frank," said Emma. "I'll be discreet. It might be less harsh coming from me. And, as you know, I'm naturally nosy."

"Some would say curious." Annie smiled at her flamboyant friend.

"No. Nosy. An absolute busybody. That's why I make such a good reporter."

"Which brings me to another, similar matter." Annie batted her eyes at Emma.

"I see an assignment coming on."

"The captain has asked the doctor to conduct an investigation of sorts in regards to the incident yesterday, but . . . someone could be after Frank. I want to conduct a little investigation of my own. We need to question everyone."

"Everyone?" Emma's eyes widened.

"Yes. Most everyone is with the Wild West Show. I've only seen a handful of people who aren't. I'm not sure I want to interrogate my coworkers."

"I can see how that would be uncomfortable for you. Not to mention exhausting. Are you suggesting that we team up? Holmes and Watson?"

Annie laughed. "Yes, I suppose."

"Then I'd be delighted. When do we start?"

Chapter Six

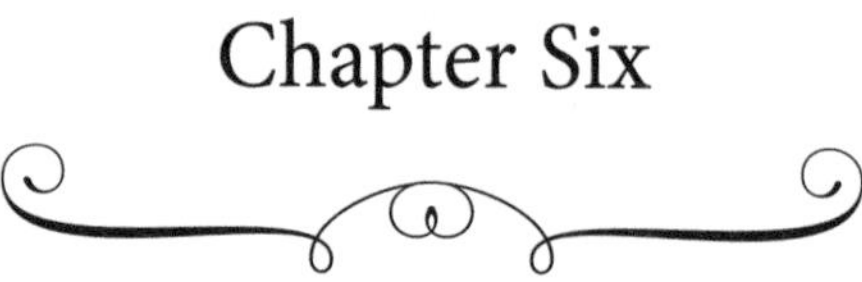

In the dining room, early that afternoon, Annie and Frank sat at the elegant table laid for luncheon, their baked mutton cutlets and roasted sweet potatoes growing cold as they waited for Hulda to arrive.

Annie tapped her fingers on the white lace tablecloth with one hand and clenched the linen napkin in her lap in the other. In addition to her irritation at her sister's tardiness, the conversation she'd had with Emma about investigating Mr. Bhakta's murder and the possible threat to Frank's life had made her twitchy. Initial inquiry had been easy with Gail Tessen. The woman had walked up to her to see her horse. Could she engage the other passengers in casual conversation as well, or should she approach them in a more direct manner?

The smell of rosemary wafting upward from her plate distracted her from her worries. She wished she could have someone remove her lunch. The smell made her want to retch—and reminded her of Hulda's delay. She sipped at the ginger tea she'd ordered.

"Really. As I live and breathe. That girl must think all day long of ways to vex me."

Frank, his face buried in a newspaper, didn't say a word.

Annie knew her tiffs with her sister annoyed him, and he tried to steer clear of them as much as possible, but still, it made her even more anxious when he seemed oblivious to her irritation, or her unease with the fact that someone may have tried to kill him. Why wasn't he more concerned?

She studied his posture: relaxed, at ease, intent on the paper. They'd been married for almost two years, and she thought she knew him well, but he'd lived more of a life than she had because of his age, and she knew there were things about him she didn't know. Up to now, there'd been no reason to ask.

"The chef has gone out of his way to provide such a lovely luncheon for us." Annie slapped her hand down on the table. "Can't she see she is being rude?" Annie cast a glance at Frank who nodded his head and murmured an agreement under his breath, never taking his eyes off the newspaper.

Annie's attention was drawn to the ornate wooden arch, flanked with large potted palms, at the entrance to the dining room. Hulda breezed through it wearing a bright crimson frock trimmed with white lace. She stood out among the others—a blood-red poppy in a field of white roses.

As she boldly approached the table, a white-gloved waiter instantly appeared at her side, pulling her chair out for her.

"Why, thank you, kind sir." Hulda flashed a bright smile and batted her eyelashes at the waiter. Annie refrained from rolling her eyes, embarrassed at her sister's boldness.

"What's for lunch?" Hulda asked, holding up the silver filigree spoon to inspect her hair in its reflection.

"For heaven's sake, Hulda, show some decorum," Annie gasped in exasperation.

Hulda put the spoon down with a scowl on her face. "I thought I had a hair out of place. Besides, is it really wrong to make sure one looks presentable?"

Annie took a moment to observe her sister's attire. She'd been so preoccupied with the glowing color of the dress she hadn't paid attention to the way its square collar plunged deep at the corners, showing off her sister's prematurely developed, ample bosom. She wore a thin silver chain around her neck, culminating in a tiny silver heart, nestled strategically between her breasts.

"That dress, Hulda. Where did you get it? I know I've never seen it before. And the necklace."

"I made the dress. Lillie told me I was beautiful and I should . . . enhance my beauty. She gave me the necklace." Hulda self-consciously pulled up the neckline of the dress.

"I should have known." Annie bit down her annoyance. "Lillie dresses . . . inappropriately." She wanted to say "like a harlot" but didn't want to seem unkind or lose her temper again. Annie always thought Lillie's boldness with her dress and sexuality was a ploy to hide her lack of accuracy with the rifle. Sometimes it worked. Lillie had a knack for riling Annie, but enlisting her younger sister to do her dirty work made it more of a personal affront.

"You know we don't present ourselves—that way. And you shouldn't accept gifts."

"Says the famous Annie Oakley, who just received a very expensive Winchester from the colonel."

"That's different. It's part of my job."

Hulda smiled, but not in a way that Annie appreciated. "It's my job to make pretty costumes and clothes," she said. "It might be nice if you weren't always so drab. You *are* in show business. Don't you want to feel pretty?"

Annie looked down at her tan woolen jacket, brown leather belt, and equally lackluster skirt. She could have worn something a little fancier for the luncheon, but the thought of the confinement of a starched blouse and tight silk skirts made her throat close. She wouldn't have been able to speak at all.

"Feeling pretty is beside the point, Hulda. 'When one is truly trying to seek first the Kingdom of God, he will not be a slave to fashion.'"

"Really Annie, you sound like Friend Percival from home." Hulda curled her lip.

Annie bit back a retort, embarrassed at her own hypocrisy. Had she not enjoyed all that came with being famous? She'd received a number of gifts, dresses included, from fans and admirers. When she first joined the show, Frank had bought her a set of Colt .45 pearl-handled pistols that Annie had thought the most beautiful piece of fashion and weaponry ever, not to mention the beautiful costumes Kimi used to make for her. She'd like to think she used that fame toward bettering her fellow man, but sometimes she did struggle with her own competitiveness and ego.

"Well, if you must know, little sister, I'm not just known for my superior shooting skills; I'm also known for my frank opinions and modesty."

Hulda shot her a look. "By modesty, you mean your buttoned-up attire?"

Annie took in a deep breath at her sister's insolence. "Enough, Hulda. Our mother raised proper Quaker girls. In the future, try to be a bit more modest. Don't embarrass yourself—or me—and eat your lunch." Annie realized her voice had risen an octave and looked around to see if anyone had witnessed her outburst. She noticed for the first time the ornate wood paneling, the beautiful inlaid parquet floors, and the opulent crystal-and-china table settings. Perhaps her sister was right. The environment might call for more elegant attire, but she'd never admit it to Hulda.

Annie sensed Hulda squirming in her chair and looked around the room to see what might be causing her distress. Bobby, seated a few tables over, was staring open-mouthed at Hulda in her peacock's attire, but Hulda didn't seem to notice him. Something or someone else held her attention. To her left, Annie spotted Mr. Everett taking leave from his table and walking toward them. Hulda visibly beamed as he sauntered over, his chocolate brown eyes trained on her. A connection had sparked between the two, and Annie felt her protective instincts kick in.

"Mr. Everett, please, come sit by me." Annie patted the chair next to hers. "Tell me how you think Buck is doing. I thought he looked quite well."

"Yes. The boy has rallied." He pulled out a chair and sat down.

"Did you have to inject the heroin again?" Annie asked.

"Not so far. Looks like it will be smooth sailing. Until the next storm."

"Let's hope that doesn't happen." Hulda said. "Mr. Everett, have you had lunch yet?"

Annie noticed her sister's cheeks flushing a shade of crimson, almost the color of the dress, and her indigo eyes darkened. A niggle of worry buried itself into her stomach. Her nervous horse and the recent murder seemed enough to contend with without having to play mother to her younger sister.

"Yes. Just. I say, Miss. . . ."

"Mosey," Hulda said, her voice a bit too eager. "Hulda Mosey."

"If you're not hungry, would you care to take a stroll on the deck with me?"

"Oh, well, yes, I'd love to." Hulda scooted her chair away from the table.

Annie laid a hand on Hulda's arm. "Really, Hulda. You must eat, and didn't you promise Bobby you would help him with the animals?"

"I did no such thing. Where did you get that idea? And as for lunch, I'm not hungry," her sister said through clenched teeth.

Annie knew the fib about her sister promising to help Bobby was wrong, but she wanted to keep the growing attraction between Hulda and Mr. Everett at bay. Mr. Everett was far too much a man of the world for Hulda, and years her senior. Frank was thirteen years older than Annie, but that had been different. Their relationship had grown out of rivalry, then friendship, and finally love.

Still, Annie knew it wasn't a winning argument, and if she said anything, her sister would just resent her even more than she apparently already did.

"Let her go," Frank said, lowering his paper. "The fresh air will do her good. Seems we're all feeling a bit peaked today."

"I feel perfectly fine!" Annie said, giving him a look.

Hulda lifted her shoulders with glee, smiled prettily at Frank, and then scowled at Annie as she took Mr. Everett's arm. As they left the room, Annie's gaze traveled over to the colonel's table where Bobby was watching Hulda leave with the veterinarian, his face crumpled in disappointment.

Annie released a sigh, resigned to the unpleasant idea that her sister had come to an age where flirting and courting were a natural hazard. She'd certainly been sneaking kisses with Mick Easton by that age. If only Annie could figure a way to turn Hulda's interests in Bobby's direction. Annie knew she could trust Bobby, and that he would never hurt Hulda. They'd only met Mr. Everett a few days ago.

"Aren't you worried about her, Frank?" Annie asked.

Frank lowered his paper to his lap and his spectacles from his nose.

"Would worrying help?" he asked. "She's a sensible young girl, and she's probably bored out of her mind with the rest of the cast, who are all much older than she is. Mr. Everett is closer to her age than the rest of us, other than you."

"Hulda is only thirteen. I met you at nearly sixteen. Mr. Everett must be in his early twenties at least—older than me! Bobby is much more suitable for her." Annie said, astonished at Frank's calm.

Frank turned to her, his brows raised. "Mr. Everett may be older than her, but you are a fine one to talk."

A jolt of pain stabbed at Annie's heart, and that pain made her anger rise. Her life with Frank had been so easy, so natural; he must have forgotten about all the hardships she'd told him she'd endured before they met.

"I didn't have time to be a child, Frank. I had to grow up in a hurry. It pains me that you forget. Hulda has not experienced life as I have. I worked myself nearly to death so she wouldn't have to do the same. She may not look it, but she is younger than her thirteen years in many ways. I was older than my fifteen years."

Frank finally lowered his paper and reached out to grasp Annie's hand.

"I'm sorry to have upset you. I've never seen you as anyone other than an accomplished woman. I understand what you're saying, and your argument is sound. She's not ready for a serious relationship with an older man. I will speak with Mr. Everett."

"And Bobby?"

Frank laughed. "The boy is so tongue-tied around her, I don't think there's much to worry about. He would make a good friend for her. He's a fine fellow."

"He is indeed." Annie agreed. "But he hardly has the captivating good looks of Mr. Everett."

"True. It's probably just a passing phase for Hulda. An older, accomplished gentleman is taking an interest in her. She's got a good head on her shoulders. Much like you, my dear."

"But you will speak with him?"

"I promise." Frank squeezed Annie's hand and raised his paper again. Annie relaxed in her chair. Frank's logic often settled her worries, but this time, she found only partial comfort in his promise. She didn't care for the idol-worship in Hulda's eyes when she looked at the dashing veterinarian. Thirteen years old, or thirty years old, the sentiment was unseemly. No one individual should be idolized over another. People were equals in her mind. She just wished the rest of the world would catch on.

She thought of the way she'd been treated by Vernon McCrimmon. She had been younger than Hulda at the time. After their father died, Annie had been responsible for putting food on the table by shooting game in the area. During a drought, when the animals and birds had fled in search of water, Annie's mother had farmed her out to the Darke County Infirmary, the poorhouse, and they had placed Annie with the McCrimmon family in Preble County.

She had finally escaped, taking the beaten and abused Buck with her. The fact that she had let the abuse go on so long shamed her. She tried to justify it by telling herself she had to help her family—but the shame still clung, like the dirty sackcloth dress she used to wear.

Now, as if she didn't have enough to worry about on this voyage, her sister's virtue had been added to her list.

Chapter Seven

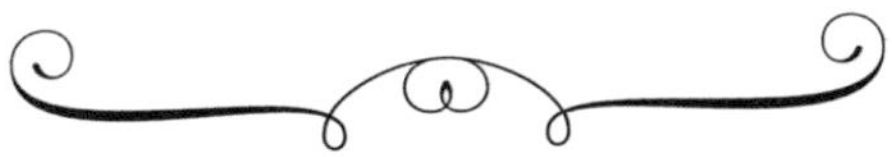

Refusing to feel sorry for herself any longer, Annie scanned the grand dining room, trying to decide how to proceed with her questioning.

Her eyes settled on two women, one of mature age and the other probably seventeen, not much younger than Annie, seated with their backs to the room. A tall, willow-thin man seated with them faced the room. Like the younger woman, he looked to be in his late teens or early twenties—Annie couldn't tell—but he did not carry himself as elegantly as his lunch companions. He seemed uncomfortable in the refined setting, like a giraffe at high tea.

The tables had been strategically set to encourage conversation, and it looked as if the trio had rearranged the place settings to deter any attempt at socializing.

"Frank, do you see those three people there?"

"What's that?" He lowered his paper.

"Those people. The man with the two women. Why are they seated like that?"

As if the younger woman could hear them, she turned around,

making eye contact with Annie. She was the same girl who had come down to the captain's stateroom when Dr. Adams was examining the dead Mr. Bhakta. Had she heard Frank and Annie talking about her? It couldn't be. The trio was clear across the dining hall. The woman turned back around to face the wall.

"It seems they don't want to be social," Frank said. "Perhaps their stomachs have made their complexions green, and they are embarrassed at the state of their faces. I know I'm not feeling well today—not sure I can look at luncheon, much less eat it."

"You are unwell?" Annie reached out to smooth Frank's hair.

"My stomach. Feeling a bit cold as well. Must have caught a chill from being in the water. How are you feeling after yesterday's adventure? You look positively radiant, aside from the crease of worry on your delicate brow." He smiled in a teasing way, and Annie punched his arm.

"Stop making fun of me. I do feel quite fine." The nausea came and went, and had momentarily subsided, though eating was the last thing she wanted to do. "But I can't help thinking about poor Mr. Bhakta. We could be sitting in the very same room as his killer."

"Those three hardly look like killers."

Annie threw her napkin on the table. "I can't believe you are being so casual about this, Frank. Someone pushed you overboard. Aren't you the least bit troubled? Aren't you concerned?"

Frank put the paper down, looking at her in earnest for the first time all morning.

"No, I'm not concerned, and I don't want you to worry. I can't imagine why anyone would want to harm me. It just seems unfathomable. More than likely the culprit was after Mr. Bhakta, and I happened to be standing there, too. I may not have even been the intended target."

She scowled at his response. Annie remembered that she'd said she'd let Emma question Frank, but the moment had seemed ripe for her own inquiry.

"What about your association with your uncle and his political causes?"

Frank's eyes flickered up toward someone walking by. "Like I said earlier, I hadn't heard from him for years before he died."

"Did he discuss his causes with you? Was he one of these Fenians?"

"He sympathized with the Fenians; that much is true. But there was nothing in his correspondence that attempted to involve me in his cause. He simply reported his opinions."

Annie studied his face, looking for any signs of unease, discomfort, or offense. His eyes slid back to his paper.

"Do you think you have any disgruntled rivals from your shooting days? Any disgruntled lovers?"

"Annie!" Frank lowered the paper.

"I'm sorry, dear. I'm just trying to understand why someone would be after you."

"According to Mr. Patel," he reminded her. "Idle gossip, in my opinion."

"But why would Mr. Patel make that up?"

"I'm not sure. The fact is, someone pushed Mr. Bhakta overboard. I just happened to be in the way."

"Maybe, but still, Frank, we can't discount what Mr. Patel said."

"Annie, you—of all people—know how things get out of hand with the press. I'm a known Irishman. Now, I am traveling to England with you and the show to see the queen. People fabricate stories. There's been much unrest between the Crown, Mr. Gladstone, and the Irish."

"Gladstone? Who is he?"

"The former Prime Minister of England."

"Oh yes," Annie said. "I've read about him in the papers. I thought he was a liberal and sympathetic to the Irish plight."

"He is, but he won't condone the violent crimes of some of the radical Irish independence groups."

"Like the Fenians?" Annie guessed.

"Yes. He brought on the Coercion Act for Ireland—a way of suspending habeas corpus."

"I don't follow."

"It was also called the Protection of Persons and Property Act. It allowed for the jailing and internment of agitators involved in the Irish Land War, without giving them any sort of a trial. Caused quite the commotion over there."

"So the Fenians were being imprisoned without trials?" Annie asked.

"Exactly."

"That must have angered them."

"I imagine so." Frank folded his paper. "And Gladstone still hadn't recovered from the negative publicity from what was called the Phoenix Park Murders of 1882 in Dublin."

"That sounds dreadful. What happened?"

"Two British diplomats were murdered while taking an evening walk in Phoenix Park. It was speculated the killers were Fenians. Gladstone had been trying to compromise with the Irish Nationalist leaders. He stuck his neck out for the Irish, and then the Irish gangs made him look foolish by killing the chief secretary of Ireland and his undersecretary."

Annie tapped her fingers on the tabletop, thinking about Frank's words, trying to see the connection to Mr. Bhakta's death.

“That still doesn’t explain why someone would kill Mr. Bhakta,” she said.

“No it doesn’t,” said Frank.

But Annie intended to find out.

The lunch party had started to disband when Dr. Adams stepped between the large potted palms flanking the entrance to the dining room. He weaved his way through the dispersing passengers who’d finished their lunch and made his way over to Annie and Frank, a large leather book in his hands.

“Hello, Dr. Adams, care to sit down?” Frank asked.

“No, I don’t really have time for lunch.”

“That looks like some ambitious reading,” said Annie pointing to the book.

“Ah, yes. Ship’s manifest. I was just returning it to the captain’s stateroom. I like to study it, to familiarize myself with all of the passenger’s names, in case of illness or—well—anyway, I stopped by to see how you were feeling, Miss Oakley. Any more lightheadedness?”

“No, I feel fine, Dr. Adams. Thank you for your concern,” she said, distracted by the leather book he had tucked under her arm. She’d love to get a hold of that somehow—she wanted to study it, too.

“Very well, I’m glad to hear it. Now, I must attend to the Indians below decks. Never seen such a scared and sick lot.”

Miss Brady, still at the table with her companions across the dining hall, turned to look at Annie again. Annie had grown used to people staring, but it still unnerved her. She tried her best to blend in, but somehow she couldn't. Perhaps Hulda was right about her state of dress. Her drabness made her stand out even more than she realized. When the girl turned away again, Annie whispered to the doctor, "Do you know who those people are? The two women with their backs to the room? And the gentleman?"

The doctor turned to look at them.

"I believe that is Anne Parsons and her companion, Becky Brady. I'm not sure about the man."

Before Annie could ask for more information about the women, Frank uttered a strangled noise and gripped at his stomach. "Oh my," he groaned.

"Feeling all right, old chap?" Dr. Adams asked.

"Just a bit of seasickness, I think," Frank said.

Annie noticed perspiration dotting his forehead. "Should you go lie down, darling?" she asked.

"It will pass." Frank gave her a reassuring smile.

She studied him a few seconds longer but decided not to press. He was a proud man and wouldn't take to her clucking over him in front of the other men, nor did he relish admitting to any kind of weakness.

"I'll leave you, then," Dr. Adams said. He moved to another table with several couples dressed in velvet and wool finery, greeting them quickly before leaving the room.

Annie's gaze travelled back to the trio seated across the room. The young woman occasionally fidgeted in her chair, and looked over her shoulder as if nervous about something. Her behavior was odd, to say the least, piquing Annie's interest.

"That woman over there is acting strangely, Frank. She almost looks frightened of something."

"Perhaps she is afraid of sea travel, like the Indians." Frank wiped his mouth with his napkin and set it on the table. "I think I'll go for a stroll on deck. Come with me?"

"No," Annie said, her eyes still on the young woman. "You go ahead. I think I'll wait for Emma. Frank, while you're on deck, will you look for Hulda? See that she's not making a fool of herself with Mr. Everett."

Frank pushed his spectacles up his nose, giving her an incredulous stare. She knew her request seemed ridiculous, but his checking on Hulda would ease her worries. Without waiting for his answer, she smiled sweetly at him.

"Of course, dear. Anything for you," Frank said. Annie noticed his face had gone sallow.

"Are you sure you are all right?"

"Yes, yes. Fine. Nothing to worry about. I'll go find Hulda for you."

"Thank you. I don't know what I'd do without you, Frank."

He gave her a peck on the cheek and strolled away from the table. Annie watched him leave, admiring the square set of his shoulders and the casual way he walked, graceful as a lion.

The two women and their companion stood up as if to leave. Annie rose from the table and, smoothing her skirts, walked toward the entrance to the dining hall, measuring the distance between her and the threesome so they would exit together. She wondered what she could possibly say to them without seeming obvious. The older woman wore a beautiful plaid scarf. What better way to start a conversation than with a compliment?

Annie weaved her way in and out of the tables and, as she had planned, ended up right next to the older woman.

"I've been admiring your scarf. Wherever did you get it?"

The older woman's hazel eyes settled on Annie's. "Well, thank you. My companion made it." The woman held her arm out to the girl. "This is Becky Brady, and I'm Anne Parsons." She indicated the man. "This is Mr. John O'Brien. It's a pleasure to meet you, Miss Oakley. Imagine our luck to be traveling with the Wild West Show." The woman's voice carried the hint of an Irish brogue.

Becky Brady, a pretty girl with russet ringlets and auburn eyes, gazed at Annie with a hard stare, making Annie's insides twinge with apprehension. Not everyone admired her, she knew, but outright rudeness always startled her. Like when she had first seen Miss Tessen. The woman's gaze had seemed to cut through her like a knife, but after speaking with her, Annie realized she was harmless, just unhappy. Still, Annie always made an effort to be kind, and it unsettled her when others didn't.

"Nice to meet you, Miss Brady, Mr. O'Brien."

Mr. O'Brien bowed a greeting but remained silent. Annie turned her attention back to the older woman.

"Have you been to one of our performances?" she asked.

'No," the woman said with an indulgent smile. "I've been in Ireland for the past few years. I just moved to America about six months ago."

"I see. What takes you to England?"

"My companion, Miss Brady, has an ill friend. We are going to look after him for a while."

"Oh, I am terribly sorry. I hope he is restored to health soon." Annie directed her attention to Miss Brady, hoping to make a more positive connection, but the girl's eyes seemed to look right through Annie, as if she weren't there at all.

"Becky? Miss Oakley is speaking to you." Miss Parsons bumped the girl with her elbow and at that moment, Annie noticed that Miss Brady's thick, wavy hair matched the hue of Miss Parsons's identically. Suddenly Miss Brady snapped to alertness.

"What have they done with the Indian man?" she asked. "He was a subject of the queen, is that correct?"

"Becky, don't be so impertinent. Why would Miss Oakley be privy to this information?" Miss Parsons's brow creased in embarrassment.

"Yes, he—was," Annie said, surprised at Miss Brady's cheek, but relieved they seemed to have no idea of her motives for engaging them in conversation. "Mr. Bhakta was the queen's servant, sent to escort the Wild West Show to England."

"Do you know where the body is?" Becky asked.

"Becky!" Anne Parsons's face grew red.

"We are traveling with a dead man, Mo—Miss Parsons," Miss Brady addressed the older woman. "It makes me uneasy. Do you really know how he died, Miss Oakley? Does anyone? He could have been killed for all we know." Miss Brady's voice shook as if she were about to cry.

"My companion has delicate nerves, Miss Oakley." Miss Parsons's cheeks flushed pink. "Please excuse her abruptness."

"Of course. I think we are all uneasy about the death of Mr. Bhakta. I'm not sure where the body is," Annie lied. She needed to distance herself from Buck's overboard event so as not to draw suspicion for her questions. "I'm sure the captain has everything in hand. I'll leave you to your afternoon. It was a pleasure meeting you."

"What do you say, Becky?" Miss Parsons again jabbed Becky Brady with her bony elbow.

"I thought you'd be full of yourself," said Becky. "It was quite nice of you to speak with us."

Annie smiled through her shock at the girl's continued brashness. "I'm a regular woman, Miss Brady. No better or worse than you."

"Oh, well, that's where you are wrong, Miss Oakley—your talent with a gun surpasses us all."

It was an unusual statement for the young woman to make, but before Annie could ask her to expound upon it, the trio left Annie standing in the doorway of the dining room, completely baffled. She shrugged off the girl's words and refocused her attention on something much more pressing—getting a look at the ship's manifest.

Chapter Eight

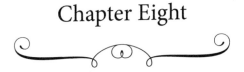

Annie grasped at the locket watch hanging from the delicate gold chain around her neck and looked at the time. She had a few more minutes before meeting with Emma. She headed out of the dining room at a fast clip just as Emma breezed through the dining room entrance in emerald- green taffeta trousers. A chocolate-brown waistcoat with jewel-toned, intricate embroidered designs cinched her small waist, and her ivory, puffy-sleeved blouse buttoned high up on her neck made her look as regal as a swan. No hat graced her head, but she wore a headpiece of pheasant feathers that streamed down her back, and a sage-green, silk shawl wrapped around her shoulders.

"There you are, dear. I hope I haven't kept you waiting," Emma said, out of breath.

"No, I was just going to . . . run an errand."

Emma pursed her lips. "Sounds mysterious. Do tell."

Annie hooked her arm through Emma's and led her out of the dining room into the expansive, chandelier-laden foyer. Rich, walnut-paneled walls lining the area shone with a candlelit glow, even during the day. Had the clock not just struck two, Annie would never have known the time of day due to the lack of natural light in the glowing foyer.

"Have you spoken with anyone?" Annie asked.

"Indeed. Several from your troop of merry players."

"And?"

"Nothing. Although, I can't imagine there would be. Most of the Indians haven't moved from their berths below decks. They are convinced that the colonel is leading them to their deaths. The news of Mr. Bhakta's demise has made their situation worse. The chief is keeping them well in their cups. Liquid courage."

"What about the cowboys?"

"I've only spoken with Bobby. Sweet boy. Wouldn't hurt a flea."

"Of course not," Annie said. "He's devoted to the colonel and would do nothing to cause any trouble." The two of them stopped in front of a large painting of a sea captain. Annie wondered if he was the ship's previous master.

"I can't imagine anyone in the show who would want to cause harm," Annie continued. "I know most of the cowboys fairly well. Even the animal caretakers, prop people, cooks, and general laborers. It doesn't make sense that any of them would kill Mr. Bhakta."

"No. It has to be one of the other passengers on the ship," Emma agreed.

"Which brings me to my errand," Annie whispered. "I want to go to the captain's stateroom. Apparently that's where he keeps the ship's manifest. I'd like to look at it, to get the names of the passengers who aren't associated with the show."

Emma looked over one shoulder and then the other, making sure no one could hear them. "I think that's a splendid idea. Do you know where his stateroom is?"

"Yes. One floor below. It's where we first took Mr. Bhakta's body."

"Lead on, Sherlock."

Arm in arm, Annie and Emma headed toward the stairs and then descended a flight. Once on the next floor, Annie led Emma toward the stern. Her breath caught in her throat as one of the cowboys passed by in the hallway.

"Afternoon, Annie," he said, tipping his hat.

"Donald," she said, and let out her breath as he passed. She pulled Emma to walk faster until they reached the captain's stateroom door.

Annie knocked. They waited in silence and when they heard nothing from behind the door, Emma grasped the handle.

"As I thought," Emma said. "Locked."

"Oh, dear. We won't be able to see the manifest."

Emma reached up to her elaborate fascinator and pulled out a hatpin. "We might be able to yet. Good thing I used two of these this morning. Watch to see if anyone is coming." She knelt down and put her eye to the keyhole. "I think I can make this work." Emma stuck the hat pin into the keyhole and wiggled it around. After a few agonizing moments, a click sounded from the door.

"Yes," Emma whispered.

"Wherever did you learn to do that?"

"My gentleman suitor in the police force. Remember? The one to whom I was engaged in defiance of my mother's insistence I marry money? He told me of a burglary case where the thief used a hatpin to pick locks."

"Amazing," Annie said in awe.

Slowly Emma opened the door. "Hello?" she said in a raspy whisper. When there was no answer, she urged Annie forward. "You go inside; I'll stay here and watch the hallway."

Annie slipped into the room, her heart beating like a rabbit's in a trap. She made a quick scan of the room and spied the manifest sitting on the ornately carved walnut desk that faced the door. She walked around the desk and just as she put her hands on it to open it up, she heard Emma loudly clear her throat and the door click shut. She heard Emma talking to someone. Was it the captain? Holding her breath, Annie waited.

In seconds, Emma peeked her head through the doorway. "Just grab it and let's go!"

"I don't want to take it. That's stealing."

"We've broken into the man's room and you didn't have a problem with that," Emma said, unable to hide the exasperation in her voice. "We'll only be borrowing it."

"Just give me a minute," Annie said. She took the pen from the inkwell and a blank piece of paper from a stack at the corner of the desk and, scanning the names, jotted down the ones not familiar to her, her hands shaking. She made a horrible mess of the paper as she hurriedly dipped the pen in and out of the inkwell. At least she hadn't made a mess of the desk—yet. Her hand froze in mid-air as she heard the door click shut again, and Emma's muffled voice just beyond it.

"Why, Captain!" Emma said, loudly enough for her to hear.

Annie felt the blood drain from her head. How would she explain herself to the captain? Why hadn't she listened to Emma and just taken the manifest? The sound of her heartbeat thudding in her ears, she closed the book as quietly as she could, put the pen back in the inkwell and was preparing to hide under the desk when she thought she detected the voices moving away from the door. She stood, frozen to the spot, waiting.

Yes, the voices were definitely growing fainter. She tiptoed to the door, laid her ear against it, and could hear Emma's tinkling laugh far down the hallway. Somehow, she had successfully diverted the captain from entering his stateroom. Annie scurried back to the desk, opened the manifest, and continued to write down the unfamiliar names. She counted fifteen.

She grabbed the blotter next to the inkwell and rolled it across the paper so as not to smear the names into illegibility, or ruin her dress with large inkblots. She blew on the paper for good measure, then folded it into a neat square and placed it in her pocket.

Setting the manifest back where she had found it and the pen back in the inkwell, she checked to make sure the desk was as tidy as it had been before. Then she hurried to the door and laid her ear against it again, checking for voices or sounds of movement. Nothing. Carefully, she opened the door and peeked her head out to find the hallway blissfully empty.

Giddy with relief, Annie nearly skipped down the hallway, feeling as if she'd just gotten away with murder.

Annie found Emma where they had met before, in the foyer right outside the dining room, sitting on a plush, cushioned loveseat next to a potted palm. When Emma saw her, she stood up and rushed toward her.

"That was a close call!" Emma said, her eyes glittering with excitement.

"I'll say. How did you ever manage to get the captain away?" Annie asked, still amazed she hadn't been caught out.

"I feigned disorientation—said I was lost. Men are always so eager to believe they can rescue a woman. He played right into my hands. Did you get what we needed?"

Annie tapped her pocket. "Right here."

"Let's have a look."

Annie pulled the note from her pocket and unfolded it. Emma took her elbow, and they went to the loveseat to examine the names.

"This woman," Annie said, pointing to the name. "Gail Tessen. Very odd."

"How so?"

"She was admiring Buck. She said she'd come from a well-to-do family, but her clothes were in tatters. And there is something strange about her demeanor, a deep unhappiness. I could see it in her eyes. She softened when she looked at Buck, but when she addressed me, her gaze was like ice."

"She might be someone to watch," Emma said.

Annie looked up to see Anna Parsons, Becky Brady, and John O'Brien as they took the stairs to the upper deck. "And those three. I spoke with them earlier. The older woman seems sweet as pie, but her companion is either very spoiled or very ill at ease with people. I got the sense she might be a bit touched in the head. The man said nothing."

"Who'd she say she was? The older woman?" Emma asked.

"Said her name was Anna Parsons."

"Hmm. She looks familiar to me. Have I told you I have an eidetic memory?"

"What is that?" Annie asked, always amazed at Emma's use of big words.

"I remember things with startling accuracy. That's why I am so good at my job. The boys at the *Herald* hated that about me at first—they were jealous, of course. But now, they quite rely on me."

"I know what you mean." Annie agreed. She knew all too well what it was like rising through the ranks of a male-dominated industry. "So you've seen that woman before?" Annie asked.

"Yes. In print, I think. Recently. I have scads of newspapers with me. I'll have a look through, tonight, after my engagement with the handsome chief."

Annie lowered the paper to her lap. "Your engagement? What do you mean?"

"What do you mean, what do I mean? He's coming to call, silly."

"Emma. Please do not toy with the chief like you did with Sitting Bull. I know Red Shirt seems tough and stoic, but he has a gentle heart. You are too much for him."

"Too much?" Emma raised her brows. "Oh, please, dear. The man has led men into war, fought bloody battles, and probably scalped more than his share of enemies—yet, I am too much for him?" Emma set her fists on her hips.

"Yes," Annie said with finality.

"Oh, darling. Relax." Emma looped her arm through Annie's. "'Indian Chief' is really not my type. I'm more of a 'Wealthy Land Baron' fan. I promise not to lead your chief on. We're only meeting for a sip of champagne. Besides, he might have some information on our murder. He seems very wise."

"He is." Annie said, not sure if she could really trust Emma with the chief's feelings. Emma had a magnetism about her that attracted men like deer to a flowering meadow. She flirted without intending to flirt. Annie hoped the chief would not get the wrong idea.

"Well, before you meet with him, there's something else I want to do." Annie clutched harder at Emma's arm. "Let's go."

Emma hesitated. "Where are we going?"

"I want to see Mr. Bhakta again."

"Really? But why?"

Annie stood up, pulling Emma along with her. "I don't know. I just need to see him again. Maybe the doctor missed something."

"Right-o, Sherlock. My sentiments exactly. Do you know where the body is?"

"The captain mentioned the refrigeration hold. I assume it's below decks."

"You assume correctly," Emma said. "Probably in steerage. When Mother, Daddy, and I traveled to the Orient on the RMS *Oceanic*, the captain gave us a tour of the ship. That was before they disinherited me for entering the disgraceful profession of journalism instead of marrying."

They walked across the foyer and down the staircase where they encountered a family of Indians cowering at the foot of the stairs. The mother held her two children close, her eyes wide with fear, and her face the color of day-old oatmeal. The father, slumped against the wall, held a bottle of whiskey in his hand. He looked as if he would fall asleep at any moment, but kept jerking himself awake.

Several of the Indian players gathered around a large pot hanging over a flame. Two women doled out bowls of stew to the others. Some ate heartily, but others simply stared at their bowls, their faces wan and their eyes downcast. Two children were vomiting in the corner of the room.

"Good Lord," Emma muttered.

"They're scared," Annie said, feeling as if she needed to defend them. "And there are no windows or fresh air down here."

"The chief said they don't like looking at the water," Emma said.

They walked down the length of the hallway and came upon a large wooden door.

"Do you think this is it?" Annie asked.

"Looks like."

"What if someone sees us? Asks what we are doing?" Annie turned to Emma.

"We tell them we are taking a tour of the ship. Simple."

"That's good." Annie pulled the heavy door open, the rusted hinges creaking.

They stepped through the doorway, their breath immediately turning to mist. Annie shuddered with the sudden drop of temperature. She blinked her eyes to adjust to the dimness. Shafts of foggy light sifted through three small portholes in the curve of the hold's wall. In front of them, stacked in neat rows, lay pig, chicken, and steer carcasses. A layer of ice gave them a shiny, pale glow. The metallic smell of blood and death filled the space.

Annie felt a sudden wave of nausea and took a deep breath of the cold air in hopes it would quell her urge to be sick. She didn't understand why she felt so horrible. She'd seen dead animals before—she'd butchered animals before, not to mention all the birds and game she used to shoot at home.

Emma covered her nose and mouth with her lace-gloved hand, and Annie gripped Emma's arm even harder.

"Where do you think they've stashed him?" Emma asked, her voice muffled behind her hand.

"Over there," Annie pointed to a sheet-covered object on the ground, in the corner, next to some crates labeled Milk and Butter. "Looks like a body, all right."

Annie pulled Emma with her as they approached the white sheet. Kneeling down, Annie pulled the sheet away from Mr. Bhakta's head. The face had turned an ugly shade of lavender-gray and the mouth hung open. A shiver of icy sweat trickled between Annie's shoulder blades. She felt Emma tremble next to her.

"Poor chap," Emma said, her voice barely a whisper.

Annie pulled the sheet further down the man's body. His shirt and suit had been neatly re-buttoned and smoothed, and other than the ghastly appearance of his face and the hoary icicles clinging to his black hair, he looked as if he'd just dressed and decided to take a nap. As the sheet passed over his stomach, Annie's breath caught in her throat. "Look!"

A crisply folded note lay neatly tucked in the waistcoat pocket.

Before Annie could say anything more, Emma yanked the note out of the pocket and opened it, holding it close to her face.

"What does it say?" Annie asked.

Emma lowered the note and turned her bright emerald eyes on Annie. "It says 'The queen is next.' This is proof Bhakta was murdered!"

Annie took the note from Emma and read it.

"Someone must have come down after the doctor placed him here and placed this note in his pocket. How strange. But why?"

"A plot to kill the queen," Emma said, her voice almost a whisper, her expression a million miles away. "We could be onto the story of a lifetime, Annie. A woman breaking a story like this could change the face of journalism—could change the world."

"Yes, but the note, Emma?"

"Right." Emma took the note back. "The killer placed it there thinking no one would find it until we disembarked in England. It could mean one of two things: either the killer somehow feels guilty and wants to be caught, or they are playing a game of cat and mouse. We must find out who did this before we get to London."

"I agree. It wouldn't do to arrive at the Queen's jubilee with an assassin." Annie tucked the note in her dress pocket and carefully replaced the sheet over Mr. Bhakta's body.

"I wonder why someone wants to assassinate the queen," Annie said.

"Well, she can't please everyone. There are people in her council who despise her."

"Like who?"

"Well, at the moment, Mr. Gladstone."

Annie nodded. "The Irish problem."

"Yes."

"But the victim was Indian," Annie said, a pang of sadness settling in her already unsettled stomach. She remembered Mr. Bhakta's smiling face. Such a pity.

"Indeed he was, and the queen's loyal servant," Emma said. "The queen has a great love of India, although Britain's relationship with that country has not been without its problems—many believe caused by the East India Company. After the Indian Mutiny in 1857, the Crown nationalized the company to soothe relations."

"Perhaps the murderer is just a deranged person," Annie said. "Have there been attempts on the queen's life before?"

"Yes, in fact." Emma held her gloved hands to her mouth and blew into them to warm them. "One of my mentors knew the English journalist who covered one story. The first attempt occurred in 1840, when Victoria was younger. A man by the name of Edward Oxford tried to shoot the queen as she and Albert were out driving on Constitution Hill. Some said he belonged to a secret society, but it was later determined that he acted on his own. He was, as you say, deranged. There have been a few more attempts throughout the years, but none in quite some time."

Annie moved away from Mr. Bhakta, crossed her arms, and grabbed her elbows to fend off the cold. She looked over the frozen carcasses and peered through the slats of the crates to see fruits and vegetables piled inside. She stepped over to a butcher's block and looked over the top, the sides, and on the floor for anything else that might be a clue.

Her gaze landed on something shiny under some crates, partially hidden under a piece of canvas. She marched over to the crates and pulled back the stained tarp.

"Emma, look." Annie pointed to a corked vial, about three inches long with a beautiful gold pattern etched into glass.

"Don't touch it!" Emma said, rushing toward her and nearly knocking over a burlap bag of potatoes.

They both stared down at the small bottle.

"Why can't I pick it up? It might be evidence," Annie said.

"It might be dangerous. I'm wearing gloves. I'll get it." Emma leaned down and picked up the vial. She held it up in front of her face. "Can't really see anything."

"The porthole." Annie dashed to the faint light and urged Emma to follow. Emma's heels clicked on the wooden floor as she hurried over and held the vial up to the light.

"It's beautiful," Annie said. "Is that a note in there?"

"Looks to be. I've seen this kind of decorative vial before. They're called 'tear catchers.' People use them to catch their tears after the death of a loved one."

"Fascinating! Let's read the note." A surge of excitement took away the sour feeling in Annie's stomach.

Emma shook the bottle. "It's partially wet from whatever substance was in here. I'm not sure we should touch it."

"You're right, Emma. Those lace gloves won't provide much protection."

Emma lowered the tear catcher and looked Annie in the eye, scorn on her face. "No, but they are fashionable."

"Right, Emma. But we need to read that note. It could be a clue." Annie scanned the refrigeration hold for any kind of tool they could use to pull out the note. Not finding anything small enough, she turned her attention back to Emma and saw the single hatpin holding the headpiece in her hair glimmering in the dim light.

"Your remaining hatpin. May I see it?"

"Yes, but whatever for?" Emma asked reaching up with her free hand to take it out of her hair.

"Open the tear catcher," Annie said.

Emma grasped the cork with her fingers and gently pulled it out.

"Hold it up to the light," Annie instructed. Emma complied, and Annie slid the hatpin into the opening of the tear catcher and, with it, pressed the note to the edge of the glass.

"You clever girl," Emma said.

Annie held it secure and then pressed the hatpin down, hoping to spear the note with the fine point. After several unsuccessful tries, she changed her tactic and tried dragging the note out of the top of the tear catcher with the hatpin. The note moved upward ever so slightly.

"You've got it," Emma said. "Steady now. Keep pulling."

Annie angled the hatpin to get a more secure hold on the note and pulled the pin upward. The top corner of the note peeked through the opening.

"Can you pinch that with your fingers, Emma?"

With her free hand, Emma pinched at the vial's opening. "It would be so much easier without gloves, but I think . . ."

"You've got it." Annie tried to steady her hand so the hatpin would not lose its purchase. With a smile on her face, Emma carefully pulled the curled paper from the tear catcher.

"Voila."

Chapter Nine

"Well done," Annie said as Emma held up the note. "Take it to the butcher's block so we can spread it out without coming into contact with it."

Annie's gaze fell on a small meat hook with a wooden handle next to the pigs. She tried not to look at the frozen swine with their sunken eye sockets and frosty snouts.

Emma dropped the note onto the butcher's block and held a tiny piece of the corner with the tip of her gloved thumbnail. Annie smoothed the note with the meat hook, catching the other corner and opening up the curled piece of paper to display the words printed on it in a neat hand. Emma read out loud:

Till the villain left the paths of ease,
To walk in perilous paths, and drive
The just man into barren climes.

Now the sneaking serpent walks
In mild humility.

And the just man rages in the wilds
Where lions roam.

"What does it mean?" Annie asked.

"I've no idea." Emma straightened. "It's from Blake's *Marriage of Heaven and Hell.*"

"Who is Blake?"

"William Blake, English poet, painter, and printmaker. A romantic."

Annie frowned. "A romantic. What do you mean?"

"He was an adherent of Romanticism, an intellectual movement that started in the early part of the century. The central characteristic of the movement is revolt, stressing self-expression and individual uniqueness, as well as the glorification of all the past and nature. It's medieval, Gothic."

Annie shook her head at the gibberish coming from Emma's mouth. She'd never heard of such a thing. She stared at Emma, her mind blank and her mouth open.

"Didn't you learn any of this in school?" Emma asked.

"School? I never went to school regularly. I was too busy trying to keep food on the table. I want to continue my education, but there's no time for that right now." Annie's declaration highlighted just how differently she and Emma had been raised.

"Oh, Annie. Forgive me." Emma's face crumpled. "I didn't mean to insult you. You are so well spoken and naturally intelligent, I forget that you haven't had much time for schooling."

Annie shrugged it off. "Forgiven. You on the other hand, seem to have an extraordinary education."

"Not really. It's the memory." Emma tapped her index finger against her temple. "I remember everything I see. It's like my mind takes a photograph. I read voraciously as a child, and much above my level. My father had an extensive library. William Blake was a favorite of his." Emma paused, staring at the tear catcher. "Do you think the thing contained some kind of medicine or poison?"

"What about tears?" Annie asked. "It's called a tear catcher, right? Or poison. Dr. Adams did mention poison. What if whoever decided to kill Mr. Bhakta was a fan of this William Blake you've just told me about? If so, they are probably well educated, like you, which means they might have come from a family with money. That rules out all the players and crew in the Wild West Show, except Frank—his family had some money, and he was fairly well educated, but not really the philosophical type."

"And he, too, may be in danger," Emma said, eyebrows pinched.

"Don't remind me." Annie's stomach clenched at the idea. "I don't know what I'd do without Frank. Emma, we *must* find the killer, and soon. We arrive in London in less than two weeks."

"We have to consider that these clues might have been laid out to send us on a wild goose chase. Throw us off the scent."

"A game of cat and mouse." Annie bit the inside of her lip. "But my gut tells me we're onto something here. We should at least explore it. Follow the clues to see where they lead."

"And if we're wrong?"

"Then we're wrong."

A conspiratorial expression crossed Emma's features. "But it's worth a try." The determination in her voice made Annie grin.

Emma took the tear catcher over to the porthole. Annie followed and watched as Emma slowly turned it in the light.

"Ah ha!" Emma said.

"What is it?"

"Just what I was hoping for. Look."

Annie squinted and focused on the tear catcher, partially lit in the dim light. Toward the top, a perfect oval appeared on the outside of the glass, with milky ridges and scrolls swirling within.

"That looks like a—" Annie's eyes met Emma's.

"Yes. A fingerprint." Emma said.

"A fingerprint?"

"Look at your thumb or index finger."

Annie held her hand up to the light, examining her nails.

"No, turn your hand over."

Annie obeyed.

"Now, can you see the lines on the tips of your fingers?

Annie squinted as hard as she could. She folded her fingers up and looked at her thumb. Lines, ridges and whorls appeared in the dim light. "A thumbprint," she whispered. "A thumbprint. I've read about a thumbprint somewhere. A man used red paint and a white piece of paper . . ."

"You continue to astound me, Annie." Emma lowered the tear catcher, turning to Annie. "I thought you said you didn't have much of an education. What you describe comes from Mark Twain's *Life on the Mississippi*."

"I didn't have time for an education, but I love to read. Mr. Shaw, my stepfather, gave me *The Adventures of Tom Sawyer* for my birthday one year—that was before he and my mother started courting. He's always been such a dear family friend. I told him how much I loved it, and he then gifted me with *Life on the Mississippi*. But what do we do with this fingerprint?" Annie asked.

Emma's eyes widened with excitement. "We analyze it and compare it with the fingerprints of the other passengers."

"How do we analyze it? Wouldn't we have to wait till we get to London?"

"Maybe not. At any rate, we might give it a try."

"Where would we get the necessary materials?" Annie asked.

"Who do you know who has access to talcum powder, paper, and perhaps a little paint?" Emma raised her brows, a Cheshire-cat grin on her face.

Annie returned the smile. "Hulda."

Annie made her way back to her stateroom and found Frank had returned. She was bursting to tell him of their discovery. Maybe he'd be more convinced he was in danger.

When Annie entered their room, Frank was lying on the bed, his eyes closed and his complexion an ashen shade of gray.

"Frank?" Annie rushed to the bed.

Frank opened his eyes and raised his head. When he saw her, his head flopped back down on the pillow.

"Frank, are you still feeling poorly?"

"I've been better," he said, raising his hand to pinch the bridge of his nose.

"What is it?" Annie sat next to him.

"Nothing to worry about, dear. Just a headache and a bit of nausea. I'm sure it's seasickness. It will pass as soon as I find my sea legs. Are you feeling all right?"

"Fine." Annie shrugged her shoulders. She couldn't let on that she felt less than fine. She didn't want to concern Frank. He clearly felt much worse than she did at the moment. "But I'm worried about you. Shall I bring you something? Tea perhaps? Some bread? Mother used to fix us tea and toast when our stomachs ailed us."

Frank patted her hand. "I'm fine for now, dear. Just a bit of rest is all I need."

"Frank, Emma and I have had the most interesting day. We found something incredible. Well, quite troubling, actually."

Frank grabbed her hand and held it in his, pressing her knuckles to his lips.

"Climb in beside me and tell me a story." His voiced sounded weak, but his blue-gray eyes crinkled in the corners, causing her stomach to flutter as it usually did when he became sentimental with her.

He released her hand, and she placed it on his brow, brushing his sandy blond hair off his forehead. She didn't linger with her caress as she was too excited about what she and Emma had found. She climbed onto the other side of the bed and, sitting cross-legged, arranged her skirt to circle her, covering her legs and lace-up, pointy-toed boots.

"Look at this." Annie pulled the handkerchief from her pocket. "But don't touch it. We don't know what was inside, and we don't want to smudge the fingerprint on the glass." She unwrapped the handkerchief to reveal the tear catcher and the note.

"What is it?"

"Emma thinks it's what is called a tear catcher. It could also be some kind of medicine vial. The note was inside." Annie told Frank about the excerpt from William Blake's poem and showed him the note she'd found on Mr. Bhakta's body.

Frank's eyebrows turned down, making a V on his forehead. "You found this in the refrigeration hold? What were you doing there?"

"We're trying to find out who murdered Mr. Bhakta."

Frank sat up. "You're what?"

"You heard me. We aim to find out what happened to Mr. Bhakta."

"Annie, the captain put the doctor in charge of any kind of investigation. You really shouldn't get involved. If there's a killer on board, I want you out of harm's way."

"I'll be fine, Frank. I wasn't the one pushed overboard—you and Mr. Bhakta were. This note about the queen is proof that Mr. Bhakta was indeed murdered."

Frank gave her a faint smile. "It also proves I was not the intended victim. Mr. Bhakta has a relationship with the queen. I do not."

"Probably, but we shouldn't take any chances," Annie said.

"My sentiments exactly. You will stay out of this."

"Are you absolutely sure there is no reason anyone would want to cause you harm?"

"I'm positive. You needn't worry, Annie. There is no reason for you to play detective."

Annie bristled at his words. "I'm not *playing* at anything, Frank."

"I'm sorry," he said. "It's just that we need you in fighting form for the performances in London. As your husband and manager, I insist you let the authorities handle the situation."

"We need you in fighting form, too, Frank. And you are ill."

"It's just a little seasickness." Frank's voice boomed. Annie leaned away from him and glared at him full in the face. She knew Frank meant no harm by his words or his tone, and he only intended to protect her, but she wouldn't abide his raising his voice to her.

"I didn't mean to shout," Frank said more softly.

Annie nodded, accepting his apology. "I just want to go through these names with you, to see if any of them seem familiar," she said gently, holding up the paper. She didn't want to quarrel with him.

"Where did you get this list?"

"The ship's manifest."

"And how did you come by the manifest?"

Annie bit the inside of her lip. "Emma." It wasn't really a lie. If it hadn't been for Emma, she wouldn't have gotten the list.

Frank let out a puff of air in an attempted laugh and shook his head.

"Just humor me. Please?" Annie said.

"Fine. I'll listen, but only if it will make you cease this inquiry."

Annie blinked at him.

"Go ahead," he said, resignation in his voice.

Annie straightened her legs out in front of her, the tips of her boots kissing. She rearranged her skirt and pulled the paper out of her dress pocket.

"Let's see. We know about Miss Parsons, Becky Brady, and Mr. O'Brien. Then there is Mr. Patel, Miss Tessen and . . . Haley, Mr. Richard H.? I believe it said in the manifest he is a general scenic artist of Wallack's Theater."

Frank shook his head.

"Lilford, Mr. Arthur Lilford and Mrs. Arthur. I'm not sure why they didn't give his wife a name." Annie smirked, irritated the woman had been written down like an extension of her husband, a possession.

Frank raised himself onto his elbow, wincing with the effort. "How were we listed?"

"Butler, Mr. Frank and Oakley, Miss Annie. Well, I suppose that is better than Butler, Mrs. Frank."

"Perhaps they don't know we're married and think we're living in sin." Frank grinned at her, his eyes twinkling.

"As I live and breathe, Frank Butler. Can we please concentrate on the matter at hand? What about Satterlee, Mr. Herbert L.?" she asked, not waiting for a reply. "MacKenzie, Mr. Alston? Crabtree, Mr. G.W.? Madame Mattei. Why Madame?"

"She must be of French origin," Frank reasoned.

"Oh. Name ring any bells?"

"No."

Annie pulled the list closer to her face, trying to read her hasty scrawl. "Ah. Mr. Reginald Cleary, his wife, and two children. That's all of them." Annie glanced at Frank, who was staring at her with glassy eyes and disheveled hair. The fringe at his forehead stood straight up as it often did after he'd raked his fingers through his hair. She reached out and smoothed it, running her hand down his temple.

"You feel warm. I hate to see you feeling so poorly."

"I'll feel better soon, I promise."

"Shall I fetch Dr. Adams?"

Frank shook his head. "No. Not necessary."

"If you're not feeling better by tomorrow, will you see him?" She wished he would agree to let the doctor come now, but maybe Frank just needed some rest.

"Yes, I promise. Will you stop nosing around the ship?"

"Have you seen Hulda? Is she in her stateroom?" She wouldn't be pulled into giving him a definitive answer.

"Annie?"

“I’m helping Emma,” she said, trying to deflect. “Breaking a story like this could change the world for women.”

“You are already doing that, my dear.”

“Yes, but I am helping her to make *her* mark in the world. Is Hulda in her room?”

“I haven’t a clue.”

Annie kissed Frank on the forehead and scooted off the bed. “I’ll check in on you later, dear heart. Try to sleep.”

Chapter Ten

Annie knocked on Hulda's door. "Hulda? It's me, Annie."

Loud, feminine laughter came from behind the door. Annie scowled. Lillie was in there with Hulda. For once, Annie wished Lillie would keep company with the cowboys as she usually did, instead of putting unseemly ideas into her sister's mind.

The door opened with a *whoosh*, sending Lillie's dark curls fluttering around her pudgy face.

"Oh, it's the famous Miss Annie Oakley. Do come in." Lillie gestured with a flourish of her arm for Annie to enter.

"What are you doing here, Lillie?" Annie tried to keep the irritation out of her voice.

"Visiting with your darling sister. She's making me a new costume for Her Royal Highness's jubilee performance."

Annie stepped into the room, casting a glance at Hulda, who sat at the desk surrounded by fabrics, and a pincushion fastened to her wrist. Her cheeks were flushed. At least she'd changed out of the crimson frock and got back into her more modest cotton dress. Lillie flounced back to Hulda's bed, plopped down on it, and pulled out her tobacco pouch to roll a cigarette.

"Lillie, what are you doing?" Annie asked. The woman really had no sense of propriety.

"Having a smoke, doll. Want one?"

"No, I don't want a cigarette, and I don't want you putting ideas into my sister's head. She's only thirteen."

"I'm sure she's seen someone smoke before." Lillie directed her gaze at Hulda and then pulled a matchbox out of her pocket. Annie glared daggers at her.

Lillie rolled her eyes and looked over at Hulda. "Don't smoke, kid. It's unseemly for Annie Oakley's younger sister to partake of the tobacco leaf." She then addressed Annie. "There. Feel better?"

Hulda stood up, the beaded suede fabric falling from her lap onto the table.

"I'm almost fourteen and you are not my mother," Hulda said, pointing at Annie. "It's my room, and I want Lillie to stay."

Annie took in a deep breath, biting her lip to keep from shouting at her sister in front of Lillie. She could deal with this situation later, when Lillie wasn't around. She had more important things to tend to at present, like trying to track down a murderer. She didn't need any more senseless arguments with her sister—or Lillie—at the moment.

"Fine, she can stay." Annie said in a low voice. Hulda sat back down, took the piece of suede back in her lap, and began poking at the dish of red beads in front of her with a long, thin needle. Annie swallowed her impatience as Lillie lit her cigarette. The smell of the smoke assaulted Annie's stomach, and she could feel the blood drain from her face and her knees weaken. As fast as the sensation took her, it went away.

"Do you have any paint, Hulda?" Annie asked, determined to focus on her task.

"Yes, some. Why?"

"Uh. Emma needs it. She's conducting an experiment. Where do you keep your costuming and make-up supplies?"

"Check in there." Hulda nodded to a basket sitting on the floor.

Annie walked over to the basket. Kneeling down, she opened the lid and started to search inside. She pulled out a jar labeled "beeswax."

"What is this for?" Annie asked.

Hulda looked up from her sewing. "To adhere wigs to the scalp."

"Adhesive. That might be helpful." Annie muttered under her breath. "May I take the whole basket? Do you need any of the items in here?"

"Not right now." Hulda went back to her sewing. "What does she plan to do with them?"

"I'm not sure." Annie didn't want Hulda knowing that she, not Emma, would be conducting the experiment. She didn't want any questions.

"Emma doesn't wear a wig, does she?" Lillie asked from the bed. She blew smoke rings into the air.

"No, Emma does not wear a wig. Like I said, I'm not sure what she wants with these things. She just asked for my help." It was all Annie could do to keep the exasperation out of her voice.

"Speaking of hair, did you see the bird's nest on that woman with the red coat? She could use a wig. And a new coat," Lillie said.

Annie, squatting on the ground, spun on her toes to face Lillie, her hand on the floor for balance. "Are you referring to Gail Tessen? You shouldn't make fun of people like that, Lillie. You don't know people's circumstances. You were taken in by people when you had nothing."

Lillie's eyes hardened and she blew smoke out of her nostrils in two determined streams, like a dragon in a fairytale picture book. "I wasn't making fun of her, just commenting on her hair. Could use a brushing."

"I like Becky Brady's hair," Hulda said with a dreamy voice. "It's so rich in color, and I like the way it curls."

"Becky Brady? Have you spoken to her, Hulda?" Annie stood, picking the basket up from the floor.

"Yes, when I was strolling the deck with Mr. Everett." Hulda sighed. "He's so handsome, don't you think, Lillie?"

Lillie let out a lascivious chortle. "And how. I wouldn't mind a roll in the hay with him."

"Lillie," Annie approached the bed. "I'm not going to tell you again. Stop your brazen talk right now or I'll—" Annie's limbs trembled with anger. She stepped over to Lillie, chest out, shoulders back, ready to slap Lillie's face if she needed to. She'd gone too far this time. Her sister was just a child and didn't need to hear this kind of talk. It was challenging enough to keep Hulda away from the cowboys with their loose tongues—and loose morals.

Lillie leaned back against the pillows with a smirk on her face. "All right, all right." She raised her hand in surrender, and blew smoke into Annie's face, Annie could practically feel the smoke burning her nostrils. She closed her eyes and swallowed down the nausea. "No need to get upset, Annie."

"I've asked you before to temper your words, Lillie. I mean it."

"Message received." Lillie took another long drag on her cigarette, her eyes narrowing at Annie. Annie ignored Lillie's surliness and turned back to her sister.

"What did you and Miss Brady talk about?"

"Oh, you know, the weather, the ocean. Nothing really."

"Did she say anything about her employer? Miss Parsons?"

"Her employer?" Lillie snorted. "She ain't no employer."

"But Miss Brady is her companion, isn't she?" Annie asked.

"Not the way they were arguing in the hallway outside my stateroom," said Lillie. "I heard the girl call her 'Mother.' I don't think they get on too well."

Annie remembered the terseness between the two earlier, when they all had left the dining room together. Why was Miss Brady noted as Miss Parsons's companion in the manifest? Why did Miss Parsons introduce the girl as her companion?

"Thank you, Lillie. I can scarcely believe I'm saying this, but you've been extremely helpful," Annie said, her voice wafting on the air, her mind preoccupied with this new information. Lillie's face contorted in confusion, her brows pressed downward toward the cigarette balancing in her mouth.

"Hulda, may I borrow this?" Annie said, holding the basket in the air. Hulda shrugged her shoulders, and bent her head low over her beadwork. Annie needed to talk to Emma right away.

"Thanks, dear. I'll return it quickly. I'm off then." Annie spun around to face Lillie again. "No more brazen talk. I mean it, Lillie."

"I said all right." Lillie took a small silver ashtray from her pocket. She pulled the butt of the cigarette out of her mouth and smashed the smoldering tip into the center of the small tray.

Annie stood her ground, her gaze fixed on Lillie's face. She needed Lillie to know she meant what she said.

Lillie raised her eyes to Annie's, her eyebrows arching in annoyance. "I got it."

Satisfied, Annie turned to leave the room.

"Your sister is a battle axe," Lillie said, loud enough for Annie to hear.

"She means well," said Hulda.

Annie bit her lip again but did not turn around, determined not to let Lillie get under her skin.

~

Annie headed up on deck to check on her horse. She climbed the stairs from the dark, over-paneled large foyer into the bright sunshine and squinted against the brilliance of the sun's rays as they touched the water, highlighting the small whitecaps dancing on the surface.

The sea was calm despite the brisk breeze. The air smelled of brine, and Annie couldn't help but tilt her head back and breathe deeply. She put her worries about Hulda and Lillie out of her mind and cleared her thoughts in preparation to see Buck. She liked to be completely present in his company, without any unpleasant thoughts or emotions playing their tune of anxious melodies in her head.

When she arrived at Buck's stall, she could see some of the other passengers milling about the deck. A couple stood in front of Isham's stall. The woman, clad in a day dress of sky blue with white lace trim, and matching blue, kid leather gloves, was stroking the white Arabian's forehead. Her ensemble, though beautiful, had a cheapness that Annie couldn't make sense of. Perhaps it was the bright white lace. The woman also wore too much rouge, and her lips were smeared with cherry-red lipstick. She was obviously many years her husband's junior.

Isham, his eyes closed, was basking in the attention. The man next to her, a corpulent fellow with a protruding belly, made even larger by the enormous fur-lined coat he wore, stood with his hands behind his back, smiling at his wife's attentions to the horse. Annie didn't know as much about clothing and fashion as her sister or Emma, but she knew garishness when she saw it.

"Hello," Annie said, leaning against Buck's stall door, her elbow propped on the top of the wooden railing.

"Good day," the gentleman said. "How are you, Miss Oakley? It's a pleasure to make your acquaintance. I am Lilford Arthur, and this is my wife."

Ah. The nameless wife.

"Mr. Arthur. Mrs. Arthur. It's nice to meet you."

"Fine piece of horseflesh here," he said, indicating Isham. Annie cringed at his demeaning use of the term "horseflesh." Isham, like Buck, was so much more than just a horse. He was the colonel's favorite companion.

"Yours is pretty nice, too," said Mr. Arthur.

Pretty nice? Annie attempted to smile through closed lips.

"Although he clearly doesn't have the breeding of Isham here," Mr. Arthur concluded, adding insult to injury.

Annie again forced a smile at the backward compliment. His taste in clothing matched his skill in social discourse.

"I love all horses," Wife said.

"How could anyone not," Annie agreed. "I'm sorry, I didn't hear your name?"

The woman's eyes shifted from Annie to her husband.

"Mrs. Arthur," he answered for her.

"Of course. Well, *Mrs. Arthur.* What takes you to England?" Annie couldn't help herself.

"Horses," said Mr. Arthur.

"My husband breeds racehorses," Mrs. Arthur finally spoke up. Annie could hear the distinct drawl of Brooklyn in the woman's accent. She leaned into her husband's bulk. "We have dozens of them. I can't seem to get enough of them, and my husband indulges me." She looked sweetly into her husband's face and he gazed back into her eyes with what could have passed for affection. He then turned to Annie.

"Good sport. Good business. Fine horseflesh is hard to come by, but when you find it, there's lots of money to be made." Mr. Arthur rolled back onto his heels in a matter-of-fact way. He did not share the same drawl as his wife. His voice resonated as one of the aristocracy. Annie hadn't met many people of nobility, but a few of America's rich and famous had attended her performances in New York.

"We have an appointment with the Duke of Portland, the queen's master of horse, once we get to England. We hope to make some purchases there." Mrs. Arthur's hazel eyes lit up and her nasal twang became exaggerated in her excitement. "I want to see some of the queen's ponies. They must be so adorable."

"Have you traveled to visit the queen's stables before? Did you know Her Majesty's servant, the late Mr. Bhakta?"

Mr. and Mrs. Arthur exchanged a glance.

"No, we never met him, not until we boarded the ship," said Mr. Arthur. "He was very gracious in greeting us and wanted to make us feel welcome."

"I think he thought we might be uncomfortable traveling with all the animals and cowboys and—well, you know, the red men and women." Mrs. Arthur scrunched up her face.

"You mean the Sioux and the members of other American tribes?" Annie felt her ire come up. She felt the term "red" was insulting when referring to her American Indian friends. "I'm sure you will find them to be very kind and abiding. They are essential to our show, and we treat them with the greatest respect." She hoped they picked up on her not-so-subtle hint.

"Oh. Well—I meant no disrespect." Mrs. Arthur's cheeks flushed pink again, but not out of excitement this time, Annie guessed. She may have gone too far in chastising the woman.

She heard the tapping of heels behind her and turned to see Emma marching toward them, newspapers folded in her gloved hand.

"Annie, there you are."

Annie made the introductions and explained Mr. and Mrs. Arthur's visit to England.

"Oh, so you are the man who purchased War Hero," Emma said. "Nicely done. I bet the queen hated to see him go."

The jovial, self-satisfied expression on Mr. Arthur's face melted into a frown.

"Ah, well, yes. I did, too," he said. "The horse died right after he won the race. Turns out he had an undisclosed injury. Cost me thousands of dollars in future revenues. I had plans to use the horse for stud fees."

An uncomfortable silence sliced the air. Emma glanced sideways at Annie.

"That must have made you very angry," Emma said to Mr. Arthur.

Mr. Arthur shrugged. "All is fair in love and horse racing. Of course, the press hid the story. Didn't want to taint the queen's name. They never get anything right."

Emma let out an uncomfortable bellow. "Oh, indeed. It does happen, doesn't it, Annie? Miss Oakley here knows all about that."

"It was a pleasure to make your acquaintance." Mr. Arthur bowed, placing Mrs. Arthur's arm in the crook of his elbow. "But we must go. Mrs. Arthur needs to take her beauty rest, don't you darling?" The last few words came out under Mr. Arthur's breath in such a way that Mrs. Arthur could not protest.

~

"Strange couple." Annie watched the Arthurs go and then opened the door to Buck's stall to step inside and greet him.

She stuck her hand out for him to sniff, and he responded by moving into her space and wrapping his neck around her body. She breathed deeply the earthy smell of horse and pine shavings.

"Do you think Mr. Arthur would be angry enough about War Hero to threaten the queen?" she asked Emma. "Kill Mr. Bhakta to send a message?" Annie ran her fingers through Buck's mane.

"Could be. Money and revenge are definitely motives for murder." Emma stepped into the stall and closed the door.

"They are an odd match," Annie said. "He seems much more refined than she. In speech, anyway."

"Huh. That fur-lined coat of his is an abomination," Emma said, reaching out to touch Buck's nose. "Hello there, gorgeous. Feeling better?"

"Emma, I have some interesting news. It's about Miss Parsons and her 'companion' Miss Brady."

"I have news, too. Miss Parsons is not Miss Parsons."

"What?"

Emma held the paper out for Annie to see. "I knew I'd seen her somewhere before. Look."

Annie let go of Buck and took the paper. Her eyes scanned a photo of Miss Parsons standing with her arms resting on an elaborately carved bureau, her voluminous skirts standing out stiffly behind her. The face was younger, the hair pulled up in braids rolled elegantly at the sides of her head. A hat rested on the bureau. The inscription below read, "Anna Parnell, sister of Fanny and Charles Parnell, leader of the Ladies Irish Land League."

"Who is she, and what is the Ladies Irish Land League?" Annie asked.

"Anna—Miss Parnell—is the sister of Charles. Charles was formerly the president of the Irish National Land League, started by a Michael Davitt, a known Fenian. In 1880, Anna and her sister, Fanny, started the New York Ladies League in New York, with the help of Davitt, to seek Irish American Funds to help support the men's league—Charles's Irish National Land League. Later that year, Anna returned to Ireland, and at Davitt's encouragement, they established the Ladies Irish National Land League, with Anna as president."

"What do these organizations do?" Annie perused the photograph more closely.

"The men's organization fought in parliament for Irish Home Rule to release Ireland from England's grasp, to fight for the rights of the Irish tenant farmers to own the land they worked on, and to abolish unfair landlordism practices in Ireland. They had Gladstone's support, and the passing of his Land Act seemed to pacify the Irish for a while, but not permanently."

Annie gasped. "Frank mentioned something about this."

"Did he? Well, anyone who is interested in international politics would have heard about it," Emma said. "Anyway, Parnell's association with the Fenian Brotherhood, and his speeches—filled with violent language—were said to have incited bloodshed between the Irish and the English. Parnell and others were imprisoned, and Anna's Ladies Land League continued the men's work, supplying food and goods to the evicted tenant farmers as well as their counterparts in jail."

"Sounds like a noble endeavor on Miss Parnell's part," Annie said. She knew what impoverishment and oppression felt like due to the state of her family after her father died, and her indenture with the McCrimmons. A helping hand in a time of crisis served to remind those suffering that there is still good will in the world. "Why do you think she is traveling under an assumed name?"

"Maybe wanting to avoid publicity?" Emma patted Buck on the neck. He nosed the papers in her other hand.

"Why would Anna want to travel incognito, lie about her identity?" Annie leaned into Buck's warm shoulder. "What about Becky Brady? Is she traveling incognito as well?"

Emma shrugged. "And the gentleman traveling with them, Mr. O'Brien?"

"Seems harmless," Annie said. "Miss Brady is an odd one, though. There is something about her. Something . . . frantic. Not right. I don't feel comfortable when I am around her. Do you know what I mean?"

"Yes. Quite the eccentric. Not the typical, obedient ladies companion," Emma said, shaking her head.

"Lillie said something about her. Said she saw Miss Parsons—Parnell and Miss Brady in an argument. Said Miss Brady referred to the older woman as 'Mother.'

Emma's eyebrows shot up. "Pet name?"

"Who knows?" Annie handed Emma the paper, walked over to the stall door, and picked up the basket of goods Hulda had let her take. "I've got paint, beeswax, powder, and paper, among other things."

"The great fingerprint experiment," Emma said, giving Buck a final pat and letting herself out of the stall.

"Indeed, Watson. Care to accompany me?" Annie followed behind her, careful to shut the stall door. Buck raised his nose from the pile of hay at his feet, acknowledging the two women's departure.

"No," Emma said. "I'll leave you to it, Sherlock. I'm going to see if I can find anything else in my trunk of newspapers about the Ladies Irish Land League. How do you think we should acquire fingerprints?"

"I've been thinking about that." Annie settled the handle of the basket in the crook of her elbow. "I have an idea if you're up to the task."

"You know me, dear. I'm up for anything." Emma tapped Annie on the shoulder with the newspapers.

"After the meal, I wonder if you could stash some used flatware in your reticule. You'll have to be discreet."

Emma grinned, leaning against the stall door. "I'm a journalist, remember. Discretion is my middle name. How will we know whose fingerprints are whose?"

"You'll have to figure out a system," Annie said.

"You are devious, Mr. Holmes. Not interested in pilfering yourself?" Emma asked, her pretty pink lips turning up in a smile.

"It's against my Quaker sensibilities, but—you. . . ."

"Really, Annie. I don't know if I am flattered or insulted."

Chapter Eleven

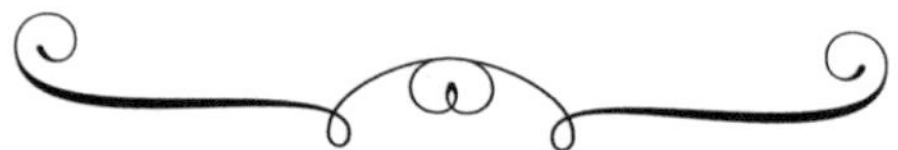

Annie returned to her stateroom and found Frank sitting in the rocking chair, fully dressed and reading a newspaper.

"Feeling better?" Annie rushed to him, planting a kiss on his forehead. His skin still felt like bread fresh out of the oven—warm and moist.

"Honestly, no. I just couldn't bear to lie around like an ailing old man anymore."

"I'm going to get Dr. Adams." Annie said, turning to leave the room again.

Frank lowered his paper. "You'll do no such thing. I'm fine. It's just a little seasickness. It will pass, I'm sure."

Annie sighed. "Your stubbornness defies logic."

"That is what makes me so loveable. I could say the same about you." Frank opened the paper again and continued reading.

Annie took the basket over to the desk and pulled out scissors, parchment paper, several small jars, powder pots, powder puffs, and brushes, and set them neatly on the corner of the desk.

She took the roll of parchment paper and cut out two neat squares approximately the size of her hand. She then pulled out a glass jar labeled "grease paint," the hue a burnished orange.

She bit her lip, considering her materials, and searched her memory for the passage in Twain's story. She then took a small, wooden-handled brush, thick with stiff bristle—almost like cat's whiskers—dipped it in the grease paint, and smeared a blob of the stuff on the paper. She worked the brush over the paper to get the thinnest layer of paint possible.

When she was satisfied, she took her index finger and lightly pressed it to the paint. She then flattened the tip of her paint-covered finger right in the middle of the clean square of paper. When she pulled her finger away, there it was—a perfect imprint of her finger. She examined the delicate swirls, lines, and fine ridges of her own signature print.

"Hah! Look, Frank."

Frank peered over his newspaper, his eyes glazed over in disinterest. "Right," he murmured.

"Now, to compare it with something else I've touched. Ah!" Annie walked over to the vanity where the silver hair brush, comb, and mirror set Frank had given her as a wedding present lay. She picked up the brush and examined the back of it where he'd had her initials engraved.

Annie smiled at the memory of his giving her such a thoughtful, personal gift. She peered closer, looking for fingerprints. She couldn't find any, so pressed her index finger to the silver. A faint image of the print appeared.

"Excellent." She took the brush over to the desk. Taking up one of the fluffy powder puffs, Annie dipped it into a dark brown powder that the Indians used for their tawny skin, and sprinkled it over the print on the back of the brush. Tiny curls, twists, and coils sprang to life. Annie compared the two. "I think this will work," she whispered.

"What will work?" Frank folded his paper and slowly stood up, rubbing his stomach.

"Did you use that glass?" Annie pointed to a water glass on the nightstand next to the bed.

"Yes."

"Where did you get that? Did you bring in from the dining room?"

"Actually, yes." Frank walked over to the glass, picked it up and brought it over to Annie. "When you were on deck, I ran into Miss Parsons and her ward, or her companion, Miss—?"

"Miss Brady," Annie finished for him.

"Yes. They commented that I didn't look well. I told them about my stomach ailment, and they gave me a packet of sodium bicarbonate. Miss Brady fetched the glass. I brought it to the room, drank it down, and lay down for a rest. That was right before you came in earlier."

"Oh." Annie couldn't help feel a bit wounded that Frank wouldn't allow her to help him in his time of discomfort. Or had she been too occupied with the murder investigation? Or her own stomach? "How kind of them. May I see it?"

Annie pulled Frank's handkerchief out of his waistcoat pocket and took the glass. She held it up to the light. The sunlight in the room had shifted with the passing of time, making it difficult to see through the glass.

"What in the world are you doing?" Frank asked.

"I'll tell you, but first, light that lantern, would you please?" Annie nodded to the lantern on the desk. Frank did as she asked. "Hold it up, here, so I can look through the glass," Annie said.

A faint smattering of fingerprints covered the glass. Annie lowered it, thinking. She bent over the desk and delicately sprinkled the dark powder over the sides of the glass. Then, using the handkerchief, she set it down on the desktop. She cut out two more pieces of parchment, spreading grease paint on one of them.

"Frank, put your thumb or index finger in this splotch of grease paint, would you?"

"I don't understand, but, for you, anything." He bent over to kiss her.

"Frank, not now. Put your thumb in the grease paint." He obeyed.

After he pulled his thumb away, she had him press it onto a square of paper. She held the paper and the glass close to the lantern. Some of the prints matched Frank's, but there were others, much smaller than his.

"Frank, was Miss Brady wearing gloves when she and Miss Parsons gave you the sodium bicarbonate?"

"For the life of me, Annie—what are you trying to get at?"

Annie set the paper and glass down on the desktop. "Do you remember the tear catcher I showed you? The one with the note in it?"

"Yes. I thought we had put this to rest. You aren't continuing with your 'investigation' are you?"

"Frank, please hear me out. That tear catcher had some fingerprints on it. What if it contained some kind of medicine—or poison? What if Mr. Bhakta was poisoned? I think it would be safe to surmise that if he was, whoever poisoned Mr. Bhakta handled that tear catcher, leaving their fingerprints on it."

"And you think Miss Brady's fingerprints are on the tear catcher?" Frank asked. "You think she could have possibly killed Mr. Bhakta? I think that is a stretch, don't you? Why would she want Mr. Bhakta dead? You don't seriously think Miss Brady is suspicious?"

Annie pressed her hands down on the rail of the chair-back at the desk, forcing her shoulders up to her ears. She rolled her neck in a circle to work out the kinks.

"Perhaps not, but I don't believe she is who she says she is. Miss Parsons isn't who she says she is, either. She's really Anna Parnell."

Frank's brows shot up. "Parnell? Of the Ladies Land League?"

"You know of them?"

"What honest Irishman doesn't?"

"So do you remember if Miss Brady was wearing gloves?"

"I think so." Frank rubbed his chin in thought. "Yes, I remember the hideous color. Puce, is it?" Frank crossed his arms over his stomach, and the color drained from his face. He clung to the back of the chair for support.

"Frank, sit down." Annie pulled the chair out for him and guided him toward it. "That's it. I'm fetching Dr. Adams. Don't move." Annie shook her finger in his face.

Frank eased himself into the chair, rested his arms on the desk, and held his head in his hands.

"I guess you probably should. I seem to be getting worse."

"I'll be right back."

Frank nodded, his forehead resting against his palms. Annie rushed to the door, but before she walked through it, she turned and looked back at her ailing husband. She didn't know anything about doctoring, but she did have a strong intuition, one that rarely failed her. She feared Frank's illness might be more than mere seasickness.

Annie sat on the bed next to Frank while Dr. Adams took Frank's pulse. Frank's face had gone white. Perspiration dotted his forehead and his sallow cheeks. He moaned, rolling his head back and forth on the pillow.

"What's wrong with him?" Annie laid her hand on Frank's chest.

"I'm not sure." Dr. Adams lowered Frank's wrist.

"More than seasickness?"

Dr. Adams placed his gold pocket watch back into the pocket of his tweed waistcoat. His eyes, nestled under bushy tawny brows sprinkled with gray, met Annie's.

"Could be food spoilage. When did he last eat?"

"With me, at luncheon—we had the same thing, and I feel fine." She wondered if she should mention her nausea, but that had started before they got on the ship.

"Has he had anything else?"

"No—well, actually, he mentioned that Miss Brady and Miss Parsons gave him some sodium bicarbonate."

Dr. Adams placed the first two fingers of each hand into the small pockets of his waistcoat. His mouth made a clucking sound.

"I don't see how that would have hurt. It should have made him better."

"Unless it was something else," Annie said.

The doctor raised his brows at her, as if waiting for her to explain.

"Someone pushed Frank overboard, along with Mr. Bhakta," she explained. "They chose their moment carefully, when everyone on deck was preoccupied with my horse. You said Mr. Bhakta's symptoms could have been caused by poison of some kind. What if someone was—is poisoning Frank?"

"I said Bhakta's symptoms could have been caused by a number of things. And we haven't been able to establish a motive—for why either man would be killed," said Dr. Adams, fingering his waxed mustache.

"Yes, but I think Mr. Patel was on to something when he stated that someone could be after Frank because of his supposed affiliation with the Fenians."

The doctor cocked his head. "But he himself denied that allegation."

Annie shrugged. "People believe what they believe. I myself have been defamed in the past with false allegations."

"I'm sorry, Miss Oakley, but it just doesn't hold water."

"Dr. Adams, look at this." Annie went to her desk and pulled out the note she'd found on Bhakta's suit. She held it up for him to see. "I found this pinned to Mr. Bhakta's suit."

"But I dressed him after I examined him. I didn't see any note." Dr. Adams took the paper, confusion written in his eyes.

"I went to the refrigeration hold. I wanted to look at him again, in case—"

"In case I missed something?" The doctor raised his brows.

Annie swallowed, embarrassed she'd admitted to second-guessing him. "Well, sometimes another pair of eyes . . . anyway, don't you see? This is proof Mr. Bhakta was murdered."

Dr. Adams' face clouded over. Annie couldn't tell if he was concerned or angry.

"Possibly," he said. "But what does it have to do with your husband? Based on your theory, it's obvious that Bhakta was the intended target, not your husband. Bhakta is much closer to the queen. One of her trusted servants."

Annie nodded. "Yes, I suppose. I've just never known Frank to be so ill."

Frank coughed and his eyes fluttered open. He tried to sit up.

"Oh, no you don't." Annie pushed down on his chest.

Frank lay back down, confusion in his eyes.

"How do you feel?" Dr. Adams held Frank's wrist again and took out his pocket watch.

"Better, I think. I'd like to sit up."

Annie looked up at the doctor for his opinion. He helped Frank to sit up, and Annie fluffed the pillows behind him.

"I want you to take it easy, Mr. Butler. Bland foods, no alcohol. This ailment just needs to run its course."

Annie took hold of Frank's hand, her chest aching with worry for him. His color had improved, if only slightly, but his usually heart-stopping smile looked forced.

"I'll be fine, Annie. Just a slight case of the grippe."

"Pulse rate is still elevated, Mr. Butler. You need to rest," Dr. Adams said, lowering Frank's wrist to the bed.

Annie knew Frank was putting on a good front to alleviate her worries, and she still had her doubts.

"What's all this?" Dr. Adams pointed to the mess on the desk.

"It's an experiment I'm conducting. I'm looking at fingerprints. You see, Dr. Adams, I also found this." Annie pulled the tear catcher from her dress pocket. She had wrapped it in cloth, so it wouldn't gather anymore fingerprints. "Miss Wilson and I are conducting an experiment to see if we can conclusively compare the fingerprints on this tear catcher to the possible murderer."

"Uh-huh." Dr. Adams rubbed his index finger over his lower lip. His voice betrayed his doubt. "Why are you doing this, Miss Oakley?"

"Because I want to find out who murdered Mr. Bhakta—and who might be out to harm my husband." She blinked up at him.

"Mr. Bhakta's symptoms—the bleeding in the eyes and gums—are nothing like your husband's. Mr. Butler is suffering from some kind of intestinal ailment, not poisoning."

"Perhaps, but don't you want to know if this tear catcher has anything to do with Mr. Bhakta's murder?"

"It is compelling," the doctor said, smoothing his mustache. "You do realize that neither finding proves anything. The substance in that vial could be perfectly harmless. As to the note you found in Mr. Bhakta's waistcoat—well, I'll admit, it does give rise to speculation. If you are finished with the vial, I will see if I can determine what was in it."

"Well, I haven't taken the fingerprints from it yet." Annie said. "But absolutely—you take it, just don't handle it without gloves or a handkerchief. You can keep this piece of fabric."

The doctor took the tear catcher wrapped in the fabric with a nod, amusement playing about his lips. Annie realized she probably did not have to tell the doctor how to handle the thing; she just wanted to make sure she could lift the fingerprints from it.

"As for your husband," he said, looking over at Frank who had fallen asleep sitting up. "I will give him some more sodium bicarbonate. You make sure he drinks it every few hours." He looked through his medical bag. "Oh, dear. I need to go to my office and retrieve it."

"I'll go with you to save you a trip," Annie volunteered. "Besides, I hate to wake Frank," she whispered.

The doctor took up his bag and led her out of the room. Once they were in the hallway, he turned to her.

"I'll check back in with him in the morning. I should also be able to evaluate the contents of the vial before then."

"Excellent, Dr. Adams. The sooner we find out who murdered Mr. Bhakta, the better we will all feel—I'm sure of it."

Chapter Twelve

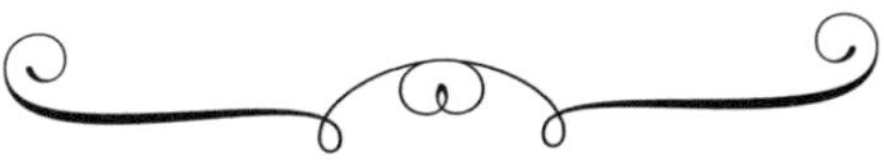

The doctor's infirmary, situated on the middeck at the aft end of the ship, resembled a tiny apothecary shop with glass bottles of all shapes and sizes, and round vials set in neat shelves. An examining table took up most of the compact room, and in the far corner sat a small writing desk with a lamp and stacks of papers.

A portrait of a woman hung on the wall. Annie admired the strong, yet feminine face with rounded cheekbones, square chin, and light eyes that shone with determination.

"Your wife?" Annie asked.

Dr. Adams stopped to admire the portrait. "No. My late mother. She died in a fire when I was young."

"How tragic. I'm so sorry."

"Yes. Thank you." Dr. Adams went to the desk and set down the fabric-wrapped tear catcher. He then took down one of the brown bottles from the top shelf. From a drawer in his desk, he pulled out a small, cloth bag and poured some of the contents of the bottle into it.

"Here you are," he said, pulling the strings of the bag tight. "Sodium bicarbonate powder. Put a teaspoon of this in some water, stir it up, and make sure he drinks it down. I think he should be feeling better by tomorrow."

"Oh, thank you, Doctor. I certainly hope so. I hate Frank feeling so awful. If I don't start feeling better soon, I may have to take some myself." Annie swallowed down the bile that threatened to rise in her throat.

"You feel ill?" Dr. Adams asked.

"Yes. Off and on. I've been able to keep my mind off of it—most of the time. I've also been so worried about Frank, and my sister Hulda. Well, I'm sure you don't need to know all about my troubles. My stomach hasn't been bad enough for me to want to take anything for it, aside from some ginger tea."

"Well, it wouldn't hurt you to take some medicine, either. Here," he said, opening the bottle again. "I will give you a bit more, just in case, eh?"

"Thank you, Doctor. Have you had any luck in your sleuthing?"

Dr. Adams shook his head. "I'm afraid not. I've spoken with a Mr. Richard Haley, Mr. Herbert Satterlee, Reginald Cleary and his wife, and Mr. Alston MacKenzie. I cannot link them to any motive for killing Mr. Bhakta." He poured more powder into the bag, pulled the strings tight again, and handed it to Annie.

"Thank you, Doctor. Hopefully you will be able to find the guilty party soon," she said. "We've only a week and a few days left on our voyage. I'm sure the Indians will be glad of that. What are your plans when we arrive in England, Dr. Adams? Will you attend the jubilee?"

"No, the queen's fiftieth year on the throne holds no magic for me. Her leniency toward the papists' agenda is an abomination, so I will not be celebrating." Dr. Adams's mustache twitched under stiff lips.

"Oh, I see." Annie didn't know how to respond to such a declaration. She hadn't expected such an unsolicited opinion from the doctor on anything but medical issues and realized she was embarrassed for not recognizing the doctor as a person with more dimensions. She herself had suffered from people's opinion of her as simply a performer and nothing else—having no other passion than shooting.

It did, however, surprise her to hear that the doctor had such a strong—and negative—opinion about the queen.

The next morning, Annie took her time rising from bed. Frank was sleeping peacefully, and she didn't want to disturb him. She also hadn't slept well during the night, and she woke feeling more tired than when she'd gone to bed. She'd gotten up a couple of times to make Frank his sodium bicarbonate. Although exhausted, she did feel less queasy, which pleased her.

She heard a gentle knock at the door.

Annie got up from the bed and wrapped herself in a dressing gown. She opened the door and found Dr. Adams and the captain standing there.

"Excuse me, Miss Oakley. We didn't mean to wake you," Dr. Adams said.

Annie ran a hand through her unruly hair. "Please, please come in."

Frank, who had begun to rouse when Annie got up, sat up in bed and rubbed his hands over his eyes. Annie left the door open for the captain and Dr. Adams to enter, and the captain closed it behind them.

"Mr. Butler, how are you feeling this morning?" Dr. Adams asked.

Frank blinked a couple of times. “Better—I think.”

“Excellent. Same rules apply as before; no alcohol, plenty of rest.”

“Of course, of course,” Frank said, pulling the covers over his lap. Annie sat down on the bed next to him.

“What was it you needed to discuss with us? Could you identify the substance in the tear catcher, Doctor?” Annie asked.

“Actually, I could, but I didn’t want to alarm you, since you feared that Mr. Butler was being poisoned—which, I must state again, I do not believe.”

“What is the substance?” Annie asked, her eyes darting to the captain who stood stoic as ever, his dark mustache making his frown seem all the more pronounced.

The doctor’s bushy eyebrows came together forming an ochre-and-silver caterpillar above his eyes. “I can scarcely believe it, but it looks to be viper venom.”

“Good God!” Frank said, his face going ashen again. “Where would anyone get that?”

The doctor handed Annie the tear catcher ensconced in the piece of fabric she’d given him. “The type of venom I found in the vial comes from snakes in the eastern regions—the tip of Africa, India, but most likely Sri Lanka.

“Oh my,” Annie said. “Captain, has this ship been to the tip of Africa? India? Sri Lanka?”

“Not to my knowledge.” The captain lowered his brow. “I’ve been captain of this ship for three years. The former skipper handed over all his logs and I examined them carefully. No voyages to that part of the world.”

“But are you sure there are no snakes aboard?” she asked.

The captain’s stern face grew sterner. “Miss Oakley, I don’t know what you are driving at, but Dr. Adams had the ship scoured from stem to stern. With these animals on board, we could not take any chances. That would be an enormous liability. Dr. Adams said he saw no evidence of bite marks or puncture wounds on Mr. Bhakta's person."

"Yes, yes, I know. But, as it is, Captain, our safety has been compromised." Surely, he could not argue the fact.

"Excuse me, Miss Oakley," the captain said, sounding a little too much like a strict father, unlike her own. "I assure you, there are no snakes aboard. But if you are concerned, perhaps you should remain in your stateroom. We can have your meals sent here."

Annie gripped at the bedsheets. How dare he speak to her this way? She'd done nothing but try to help, concerned for Frank and Hulda's safety, the safety of the passengers and herself.

"No snakes, you say." Annie bristled. "At least not of the reptilian sort." Clearly, someone wanted Mr. Bhakta dead, and clearly, the captain did not think her worthy of this discussion.

"A snake does not have to be on board for this to have happened," Dr. Adams said. "Viper venom can be medicinal. It can be used to treat apoplexy in emergency situations."

"And do you carry this sort of medicine?" the captain asked.

"Yes, a small amount. Not enough to kill."

"But who else would have access to this kind of snake venom? Where is Sri Lanka?" Annie asked.

The doctor looked from Annie to Frank, then back to Annie.

"Southeast Asia. Near India."

Annie stood up, her exhaustion suddenly gone. "Well, we need to find out from the passengers if they've visited that country in recent months."

"Annie," Frank admonished.

"I'm more determined than ever to help, Frank. You can't change my mind."

"We already know of one passenger who has visited Sri Lanka," said the doctor.

"Who?" asked Annie.

"Mr. Patel."

Annie gasped. "How do you know this, Dr. Adams?"

"He came to me complaining of seasickness, and we had a conversation. He told me he'd gone back to his homeland of Sri Lanka a few months back to attend his father's funeral."

"But why would Mr. Patel want to kill Mr. Bhakta?" Annie asked.

Frank reached for her hand. "It doesn't mean he did, Annie. It's just another piece of information. But he was on deck with Mr. Bhakta when we went overboard."

Annie held the tear catcher up to the light. Then she held the glass up to the light. Too hard to tell if the fingerprints smearing each object matched. Perhaps her test wouldn't work after all. She plopped down onto the desk chair.

"How frustrating. I need a way to get the fingerprints off the tear catcher and the glass and then compare them side to side," she said out loud to herself.

Half asleep, Frank mumbled something from the bed.

Annie looked through all of the items she had previously spread out on the desk. She found a glass pot with a honeycomb design on the label. Beeswax. Hulda told her it had been used to attach wigs to linen skull caps. Annie now remembered she'd seen Kimimela, her late costume designer, use beeswax to affix a fake strip of hair to one of the Indian player's heads. In the enactment of the scalping of Yellow Hair, the great Buffalo Bill "scalps" the fake hair off the Indian's head. Annie had been pretty impressed at how real it looked, especially at a distance.

Annie opened up the jar and pushed her finger into the waxy substance. It felt hard but malleable. She scooped a blob out with her finger, and realized she just left her own fingerprint in the stuff. She retrieved her oldest pair of gloves from her trunk, put them on, and returned to the desk. Taking out another blob with the tip of her gloved finger, she laid it on a piece of parchment and flattened it as best she could. She then took the tear catcher and held it under the light, to see which part of it had the most fingerprints and then pushed that side of the tear catcher into the beeswax. The print was impossible to see in the yellow waxy substance. She took the ochre powder she'd used before and sprinkled some on the wax. She lifted the flattened beeswax and shook off the excess powder. To her delight, the faint image of the fingerprints showed themselves on the wax.

"Success!"

"What's that?" Frank said, sitting up in bed.

"Just a minute." Annie completed the same process with the glass and then compared the two sets of fingerprints. The larger prints, obviously Frank's, had come from the glass, so she focused on the other sets of prints, the smaller ones. She looked from the blob with the glass's prints to the blob from the tear catcher. She blinked, trying to focus. She blinked again.

"Frank," she said, turning in the chair to face him. He'd put on his spectacles and was reading the paper.

"Yes, dear." He lowered the paper.

"The prints match." A surge of excitement sent her fingers tingling.

"What?"

"Whoever handled this glass also handled the tear catcher."

Frank's eyebrows pinched together. "Are you certain?"

"Yes. They look to be the same."

"But you and the doctor have also handled the tear catcher—and you've handled the glass."

"But not with bare hands. Don't you see, Frank? I'm on to something, here. I'll have to take your fingerprints to make sure they are the larger ones on the glass, and to be sure, I'll use my own to compare the tear catcher—but I can almost guarantee, the smaller set of prints won't be mine."

"If you are going to continue with this—and I wish you wouldn't—you need to be sure, Annie. Murder is a serious accusation."

Annie gritted her teeth at Frank's doubting her methods and his continual urging for her to stop her investigation. She would not be swayed. As much as she loved him, sometimes his authoritarian methods got under her skin.

"I'm doing this because I'm concerned about you, Frank. I'm concerned about all of us."

"I don't doubt you are brilliant, my dear. But you need to proceed cautiously. You are not a law enforcement official, nor are you a detective. I just don't want you to damage your reputation by doing something foolish like wrongly accusing someone."

Now he sounded like her manager, which he was, but still—it felt like a criticism, like he didn't believe in her at all. How could he be so dismissive of her theory? Her eyes welled up with tears.

"Annie? Are you all right? Are you crying?"

"No," she said, swallowing her emotions. Why did she feel so hurt? She knew her feelings were irrational, but she couldn't fight them off.

Frank got out of bed and came to her. She turned her back on him and sniffed her tears away. He put his hands on her shoulders.

"Darling, I'm sorry if I've upset you. I didn't think you would take offense to what I said. I'm just looking out for your best interest, your future."

"I know. I just—I'm, well. . . ." Annie didn't know what to say or how she felt. She couldn't believe this was happening to her. She wasn't the emotional sort.

"Talk to me, Annie. What has you so upset?"

"Nothing, Frank. It's nothing. I'm fine," she said, knowing full well she was not.

Chapter Thirteen

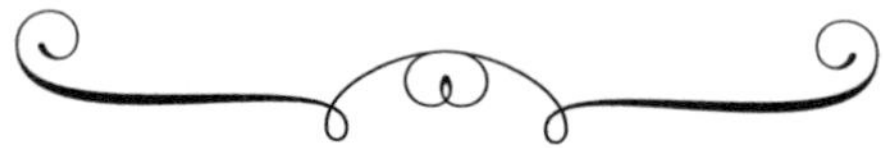

Unable to reconcile her hurt feelings with Frank, Annie left their room saying she wanted to check on Buck. Frank didn't protest—another thing that hurt her. Why didn't he insist she stay so they could work out their tiff? Why didn't he come after her?

She stood in the hallway a few doors down from their room, her back resting against the wall, unsure if she should go back to talk it out with him or go to see her horse. Why couldn't she make a decision? She slid down the wall, sat on the floor, and started to cry.

What was wrong with her? Typically not a weeper, there she sat, crying her eyes out—and over what?

A door opening startled her. She quickly wiped her tears and looked up and to her left, where she saw an older woman sticking her head out into the hallway.

"What is this?" the woman said. She stepped out of her room and stood over Annie. She had a kind face with large, dark eyes. A halo of gray wisps had come loose from the massive bun piled high on her head. She wore a high-necked, black lace gown with sleeves that culminated in a point at the back of her hand. "You are crying?"

"I'm sorry," Annie said, getting up. "I didn't mean to disturb you." She stood and faced the woman who stood about as tall as Annie—a mere five feet—but so much smaller. She had a child's body, but with a grandmother's face.

"You do not disturb me," the woman said, her voice thick with a lilting accent. "But you cannot sit out here crying. Please come in. I have tea. You will have a cup, and all will be better, no?"

"I don't want to trouble you—I'm fine, really." Annie said, sniffling.

"You are not fine, as you say. Do, come." She ushered Annie into her room with a wave of her hand. The smell of ginger tea filled the room. It was dark, as the woman had pulled the curtains over the window, but a few candles flickered on the bureau.

"Excuse the darkness," she said, motioning for Annie to sit in the armchair next to the reading table. "My eyes are sensitive to the light." She poured the tea into two cups. "Miss Oakley, I've been expecting you."

"You have?" Annie said. "But I—"

"I am Madame Mattei," the woman said with a nod of her head. She handed Annie a teacup. "Drink this. It will settle your stomach."

"But my stomach is fine. I—"

The woman raised an eyebrow at Annie.

"How did you know my stomach has been bothering me?"

The woman shrugged a shoulder. "Now, what did you want to speak with me about?" She asked, sitting in the chair next to Annie's.

Annie shook her head. Had she fallen asleep in the hallway? Was this some sort of strange dream?

"You have some questions for me?" Miss Mattei said.

"I do? Oh, well, maybe. Did you speak with Miss Wilson?" Annie figured Emma had spoken to the woman, asked her some questions.

"Who is this Miss Wilson? I have met no one. I stay in my room. My eyes cannot handle the light." Madame Mattei took a sip of her tea, set the cup in the saucer, and looked expectantly at Annie. Annie thought she could feel the hair on her arms rise.

"Then, you must have spoken with the captain? Dr. Adams?"

"No. I have spoken with neither. Sometimes I have a . . . connection with people. Certain people. I have one with you. You have a curiousness about you. Sometimes it gets you into trouble, am I correct?"

Annie set her teacup down and looked toward the door, wondering if she should bolt. This had to be one of the strangest conversations she'd ever had. She looked back at the woman who regarded her with such kindness in her face, Annie's skepticism about her started to abate. She did have questions for Madame Mattei. She had questions for all of the passengers.

Annie took another sip of tea and then cleared her throat. The tea had the pleasant effect of calming her and keeping her low-level nausea at bay.

"What takes you to England, Madame Mattei?"

The woman's face crinkled up in a smile. "I am going home, to Belgium. I have lived in America for many years, but it is now time for me to go home. From Dover, I will sail to Calais. *Comprenez-vous*?"

"Oh. I see. What did you do in America? Do you have a family? Children?" Annie finished her tea and set the cup and saucer on the table.

"No family. I am alone."

"I'm sorry."

"*Non, non*, do not be sorry. This is my choice. My parents are long dead, and I had no siblings. I am used to being alone."

"I hope you don't mind my asking, but how do you support yourself?"

"I have done many things in my life."

Annie waited to hear of the many things Madame Mattei had done to make a living, but she offered nothing more. It didn't matter. Given the woman's sensitivity to light, her advanced age, and the fact that she probably weighed eighty pounds at the most, Annie doubted she could be the killer. She probably had not left her stateroom since she'd boarded the ship.

"Well, I've troubled you long enough," Annie said. "I should be going. I need to see to my horse. He had some difficulty when we first boarded."

"You have been no trouble, *chérie*. I have enjoyed your company."

Annie smiled, realizing she felt much better after having spent time with this strange yet sweet woman. "And I yours." Annie stood up and walked toward the door to let herself out.

"Miss Oakley," Madame Mattei called after her.

"Yes?" Annie turned around to face her again.

"You will find your answers—in time. Your husband means you no harm. He loves you very much."

Annie stared at her, uncertain what to say. The woman couldn't have heard her tiff with Frank—their staterooms were separated by two others—and they hadn't raised their voices. At a loss for words, Annie simply smiled at her, turned, and left the room.

Annie stood in the hallway, thinking about what Madame Mattei had just said. It defied explanation how she could have known she had been upset at Frank, but Annie knew the woman was correct. Frank did love her. Beyond what she ever could have expected. She shouldn't have been so cross with him.

She went down the hallway to her stateroom and opened the door.

Frank had gone back to bed and was sleeping. She walked over to him and lightly kissed his cheek. His skin still felt warm, but he looked much improved. Tiptoeing out of the room, she quietly closed the door, and went in search of Emma.

Annie found Emma on deck, seated in a deck chair next to Red Shirt and Bobby. They looked as if they had just shared a joke. Emma tilted her head back, letting out a cheerful burst of laughter.

"Hey, Annie." Bobby tipped his hat to her, his freckled face beaming into a smile.

"Hello, Bobby, Chief. Emma, I need a word."

"Little Miss Sure Shot. Come sit." Red Shirt indicated a deck chair next to them.

Annie held up a hand in protest. "I really can't at this moment, Chief. Please accept my apologies."

"You need not apologize. It seems you have important business with this lovely lady." His eyes lingered on Emma and her cheeks flushed pink. Annie pulled in her breath and took hold of Emma's elbow. Emma rose from her chair, and the two of them walked to the railing, out of Bobby and the chief's hearing.

"I hope you are treading lightly with the chief, Emma." Annie gave her a pointed stare.

"Yes, dear. I've told him I'm engaged."

"You're engaged? Why didn't you tell me?"

"I'm not really engaged. Just a little white lie to thwart the chief's attentions. Doesn't seem to be working though. The man positively adores me." Emma reached a hand to the back of her perfectly coifed blond hair and patted it.

Unwilling to encourage Emma's vanity, and still a bit stunned from her conversation with Madame Mattei, Annie wanted to focus on her discovery of the fingerprints.

"I've done it Emma. I've found fingerprints that match the fingerprints on the tear catcher."

Emma's mouth dropped open. "Bloody brilliant!" she said.

Annie twitched at Emma's words. "Bloody?"

"Oh, don't look so shocked, Annie," Emma said, reading her thoughts. "It's just an expression. The Brits use it all the time."

"It sounds like a swear word to me."

"It is, but that's beside the point." Emma swatted the air. "Tell me, tell me. Whose prints are they?"

"I can't say for sure. I compared some fingerprints off the tear catcher with those off of a glass Frank brought into our room. Miss Brady and Miss Pars—Parnell gave it to him with a mixture of sodium bicarbonate and water in it."

"Really?" Emma's eyes flared, large and green as an owl's.

Annie nodded. "We also need to look into Mr. Patel. The doctor said the tear catcher contained viper venom—from a snake that hails from Sri Lanka—Patel's home country. He himself told the doctor he'd just been there to visit."

"Good work, Sherlock," Emma said. "I've done some more digging myself into Miss Parnell. According to some of the newspaper accounts, she may have had a dalliance with Mr. Davitt."

"Who is he?" Annie asked.

"He started the Fenian movement in the States."

"Really! What about Miss Brady? Anything on her?"

"Nothing."

Just as Annie was about to ask Emma another question, the captain strolled up to them, stiff in his uniform, with his hands clasped behind his back.

"Good afternoon, Captain." Emma batted her long, brown eyelashes at him.

"Hello, ladies. Are you enjoying the weather?"

"Yes. Thank you for commanding such a lovely, fine day." Emma touched the captain on the shoulder, transforming his stoic expression into the slightest of smiles.

Lillie came up from behind the captain and leaned against the rail, her body swaying, her complexion ruddy, and her eyes heavy and droopy. She'd been drinking. Annie's heart leapt to her throat.

"Where is Hulda, Lillie?"

"Her? She went strolling with Mr. Everett. He came by the cabin and invited her out. I know when I'm not wanted, so I've been *belooow* decks with the cowboys, if you know what I mean." She winked at the captain, whose lip curled up on one side. Annie blushed for all of them.

The captain cleared his throat. "Miss Oakley, I would like to extend an invitation for you and your husband to dine at my table tonight."

Annie tilted her head. Could this be an apology of sorts? "Oh, dear, Captain. Frank is still not well. I'm afraid dinner is out of the question for him. Bread and milk, more like."

"I'm sorry to hear that. Well, the invitation is still open."

Annie didn't really feel like dining with the stuffed shirt, but thought it might be rude to refuse. Besides, she needed to keep an eye out for any suspicious behavior from the other passengers.

"Thank you, Captain." She smiled at him.

"Perhaps Miss Wilson could be your dinner companion?" he asked, turning to Emma.

"That sounds—" Emma began, but Lillie interrupted her.

"I'm available, too, Captain. What time do we *diiiine*?"

The captain shot Annie a glance, the expression on his face pained, as if he'd just had a tooth extracted.

"Eight o'clock, Miss Wilson?"

"I'd be delighted." Emma beamed up at him.

"Captain, if I might be so bold—" Annie figured this might be the perfect opportunity for her and Emma to obtain the needed fingerprints. "I had planned to invite Miss Parsons, her companion, and Mr. O'Brien to dine with me tonight. Would there be room for them at your table? If not, I completely understand and I will ask them another time. . . ."

The captain forced a tense smile. Annie knew she may have crossed the line of politeness, but it would be so convenient to her plan. She'd have to come up with something else for Mr. Patel.

"Of course. I'll make the arrangements." The captain bowed to them, turned on his heel, and left them at the railing.

"I do love a man in uniform," Lillie said, her eyes lingering on the captain's backside as he walked away. "Even if he doesn't pick up on a lady's subtle hint for a dinner invitation."

"Subtle?" Annie said. Really, did Lillie have no boundaries?

Lillie smirked at her and walked off.

"She's right about one thing," Emma said. "The uniform does lend a certain panache."

"Oh dear," Annie said. She spotted Hulda and Mr. Everett near the horses' stalls. Mr. Everett let himself into Buck's stall while Hulda waited outside the stall door. Annie's heart skipped a beat. She hoped nothing was ailing her horse. She'd just checked on him a few hours ago.

To her annoyance, Hulda had changed her dress again. This time she wore a powder-blue gingham trimmed in white eyelet lace. Her sister had never produced so many garments so fast. She must be trying to impress the veterinarian with a new frock every day. While bemused with her sister's industriousness, she didn't fancy the reason for it.

"Emma, I'll see you at dinner," Annie said.

"Right-o." Emma walked back to Bobby and the chief, still sitting in the deck chairs.

"Is Buck all right?" Annie asked, approaching her horse's stall. Mr. Everett was running his hand along Buck's legs.

"Yes." Mr. Everett removed his hat when he saw Annie. "Just checking his legs for inflammation. He is a little swollen. He could do with a walk on deck."

Hulda suddenly squealed, and Annie turned to see what had caused the outburst. Bobby had come over and tossed Hulda a bean bag. The two started a game of catch, Hulda's ladylike decorum vanishing.

Annie cast a glance at Mr. Everett, who watched Hulda playing the game with complete enthusiasm, showing the inner child that still lurked in her woman's body. He pressed his lips together as if considering the same thing Annie knew to be true about her sister.

He caught Annie's gaze before refocusing on Buck. Annie hoped that Mr. Everett now saw Hulda's true self: a girl of thirteen who liked to play dress-up and still enjoyed a game of catch with the boys.

"That's a good idea, Mr. Everett. I'll take Buck for a walk." Annie said, distracting him from Hulda and Bobby. The two came over to the stall, sunny-faced and laughing from their game.

"Taking Buck out?" Bobby grinned. "I'd be happy to take him for a walk for you, Annie."

"I'll come too." Hulda said, her cheeks pink from exertion.

"I'll just check on the rest of the animals," Mr. Everett said, a hint of disappointment in his eyes. He replaced his hat and made his way out of the stall, nodding at Hulda, who smiled, bouncing on the balls of her feet.

Bobby took Buck's halter from the hook on the stall door, and Annie stepped aside, letting him attach the halter. She stroked Buck's forelock, and he nuzzled the waist of her dress. She let Buck and Bobby pass through, and she and Mr. Everett watched Bobby, Buck, and Hulda walk down the deck, talking like old friends.

"She's quite young, although she doesn't always seem it," Annie said as she closed the stall door.

"She is, Miss Oakley. Quite young. A lovely girl." As he walked away from her, there was resignation in his voice. Annie sighed with relief.

Chapter Fourteen

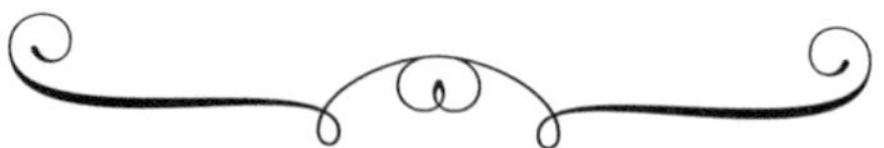

After dinner at the captain's table, Emma accompanied Annie to her stateroom. To Annie's concern, Frank was not in the room, although he'd left a note on the bed.

"He says he's gone for a walk on deck. I should go up and find him." Annie imagined him struggling with every step or, worse yet, being ambushed by someone who wanted to push him overboard again.

"Frank is a big boy. Poor man has been cooped up in here the entire voyage. The fresh air will do him good." Emma, still wearing her gloves, pulled silverware and a demitasse cup from her handbag. "Let's look at the evidence."

"Perhaps you're right. But if he isn't back soon, I'm going to go look for him."

"Give him some space, Annie. He's a grown man."

"You're right. I'm being a mother hen. Let's set to work."

"The demitasse cup is from Miss Parnell's place setting," Emma said. "The spoon from Miss Brady's, the fork from Mr. O'Brien's, and the knife from Mr. Patel's—I had to work my way over to his table. Made up some excuse to ask him about the queen and how he enjoyed her employ."

"And how does Mr. Patel enjoy her employ?" Annie asked.

"Greatly. He seems to believe that he will replace Mr. Bhakta, as he was his assistant."

"Interesting." Annie tried to remember how Mr. Bhakta and Mr. Patel got on, but she really hadn't gotten to know either one of them very well. "You've covered the lot, all in one meal, Emma."

"I like being Watson to your Sherlock. It's quite fun."

Annie frowned at her friend. "We're dealing with murder here, Emma."

"Oh, right. Sorry."

Annie bent her head over the objects and started the process of lifting the fingerprints to compare. Emma hung over her shoulder, so close Annie could feel her breath on the nape of her neck.

Annie compared the fingerprints from the glass and tear catcher with the fingerprints of Miss Parnell's demitasse cup. Not a match. Then the knife from Mr. Patel and fork from O'Brien.

"What are you doing now?" Emma whispered.

"Same thing I did with the other three objects." Annie tried to keep the impatience out of her voice. She loved being around Emma, but the woman's intensity wore on her nerves.

Annie then compared the fingerprints from the glass with the fingerprints from Miss Brady's spoon and the tear catcher. She turned to look into Emma's face, still as close as if she were a bird perched on Annie's shoulder.

"We have a match." Annie said.

Emma's mouth fell open. "Who?" Emma spoke with such force that Annie could feel the champagne vapor from the woman's breath on her face. Annie reached up and pushed Emma's shoulder.

"Please, Emma. Some room."

"I'm sorry. This is just so exciting. Whose fingerprints match?"

Just as Annie was about to tell her, Frank walked into the room.

"How was your stroll?" Annie asked. "You look better."

He took his hat and coat off, seated himself in the rocking chair next to the porthole, and took up a book.

"The pain and nausea comes and goes. Right now, I'm feeling better." Frank said. "The sea air is a restorative."

"Would you like for us to arrange to have dinner brought down?" Annie asked.

Frank winced.

"Perhaps soup?" said Emma.

"Maybe later. What gives us the pleasure of your company, Miss Wilson?"

"Fingerprints," she said.

Frank shot a look at Annie. "Ah, the big story. I thought we agreed you wouldn't pursue this."

"I never agreed or disagreed," Annie said. "Please don't be upset, Frank. I think we're on to something here."

"Your wife has good instincts. She's actually quite skilled at investigating." Emma smiled at Annie with pride.

"My wife is skilled at a number of things, sharpshooting primarily, which is her job, Miss Wilson. As her husband and manager, it is my job to see she comes to no harm and arrives in England safely and ready to perform."

"Exactly," beamed Emma. "She can outshoot anyone. I'm counting on her to protect me."

"I haven't been carrying my pistol with me, but I will if it will make you more comfortable," Annie said to Frank.

"It's so touching to see your concern for one another." Emma clasped her hands together, her face glowing with admiration. Annie stifled a grin. Emma was trying to work her magic on Frank. It was almost like watching a game between two cardsharps, knowing what cards each player had in their hand, but not knowing how they would play them.

"I'm getting the sense that I am outnumbered here. Neither one of you is going to give up on this quest to solve the crime."

"Then join us," said Emma.

"Yes, Frank, help us," Annie entreated.

"That way, you two can keep an eye on one another—and me." Emma looked very pleased with herself.

"Then it's settled," Annie said. "What do you say, Frank?"

Frank held a hand up in acquiescence.

"Excellent. So back to this glass and this spoon. What I see doesn't make sense," she said, engrossed in studying the two objects on the desk. "The prints match those of Miss Brady, but Frank said she wore gloves when she handed Miss Parnell the glass for the sodium bicarbonate, didn't you Frank? You remembered the shade of puce."

"Right. Miss Parsons was wearing gloves when she handed me the glass." Frank said.

"But I asked you about Miss Brady, and you said *she* was wearing gloves. You remembered the color."

Frank rubbed his hand across his forehead. "Honestly, my dear. I felt so horrible at the time, I doubt I could have remembered my own name."

"Come to think of it—" Emma interjected. "I've not seen Miss Parsons—I mean Miss Parnell—without her gloves unless she is at table. And I've never seen Miss Brady wear gloves at all."

"Well, my goodness." Annie let out her breath, not realizing she'd been holding it for most of the conversation. "I think we've found the murderer, but why on earth would Miss Brady want to kill the queen?"

Emma squared her hands on her hips. "More to the point, who exactly *is* Miss Brady?"

~

The next morning when Annie woke, she turned over and found Frank sweating profusely and moaning with delirium. He clutched at his stomach, and Annie could smell vomit coming from the chamber pot on his side of the bed. He'd taken a turn for the worse.

Annie and Emma had planned to visit Miss Parnell and Miss Brady for further questioning first thing before breakfast, but it would have to wait.

Annie jumped out of bed, took up the chamber pot, and put it outside the door for the staff to retrieve. She placed her unused one next to the bed. Then she dashed to the pitcher on the bureau and soaked a rag in the cool water. She leaned over Frank, placing the rag on his burning, damp forehead.

"Darling, I'm going to fetch Dr. Adams. Please don't try to get up."

Frank mumbled something incoherent in response, and Annie pulled on her blue velvet dressing gown, another gift from Frank. His love and generosity knew no bounds, and she hoped she would someday be worthy them. It still surprised her that, of all the women in the world, the handsome, dashing, talented Frank Butler had chosen her. She prayed his illness would not be life threatening.

When she ushered Dr. Adams back into their stateroom, she saw that Frank had vomited again, and this time missed the chamber pot. She set to work cleaning up the mess while the doctor examined Frank.

"I'm perplexed by this illness." Dr. Adams walked over to the ewer, soaked the rag again and placed it back on Frank's forehead. "You say he seemed improved earlier?"

"Yes. After you gave him the sodium bicarbonate."

"Did he have anything else before that? Did you give him some other stomach powder?"

"No. But Miss Parsons did. Remember? Frank saw her and Miss Brady on deck, and they gave him sodium bicarbonate. He seemed to have gotten worse after that. Oh, no!" Annie put her hands to her mouth.

"What is it?"

"What if I'm right, and someone is trying to poison Frank? It might be them."

"Who?"

"Miss Parsons or Miss Brady."

"I don't follow." The doctor shook his head, took a seat on the chair next to the bed.

Annie told him about the two women traveling under assumed names.

"Anna Parnell?" The doctor stroked his mustache with his thumb and forefinger, as if trying to register the name. "But why Frank?"

"I don't know. But I believe one of them killed Mr. Bhakta." Annie proceeded to tell the doctor about the fingerprint findings.

"That's astonishing. Don't you think you are jumping to conclusions? I fear your imagination is getting away with you, my dear. I can't think why they would want to harm your husband. He says he has no association with the Fenians, and even if he did, they support the Fenian movement."

"I'm just as perplexed as you are. But why would Becky Brady's fingerprints be on a tear catcher filled with viper venom? And she showed up at the captain's stateroom after Mr. Bhakta was retrieved from the water. She might have been checking to make sure she'd finished the job."

"Or the girl could have been lost as she'd explained."

"But the fingerprints on the tear catcher?"

"Can you be absolutely sure they belong to Miss Brady?" the doctor asked, his expression dubious.

Annie knew the fingerprints were a match. She was certain. But the doctor was unconvinced. She'd have to find more.

"Fine then. Before I notify the captain and accuse these two women of this horrible crime, I will speak with them one more time. Just to be sure," Annie said.

The doctor nodded. "Very well. I suppose there is no harm in that. But what about your protection? Your husband is ill."

Annie got up and walked to the bureau. She opened the drawer and pulled out her pistol.

"You seem to forget, Dr. Adams. Annie Oakley is a perfect shot."

Doctor Adams gave Frank some willow bark to bring down his fever, and more sodium bicarbonate for his aching stomach. He fell asleep immediately.

By the time Annie had dressed and braided her hair, twisting it into a neat knot, Frank was awake again.

"How do you feel, dear?" Annie rushed to the bed, sat down next to him, and took the damp rag from his forehead.

"What happened?" He asked, looking into her eyes with confusion.

"You woke in delirium. Dr. Adams came and gave you more medicine. You don't remember?"

"I thought it was a dream."

"I hope you are better for good." Annie pushed the sweat-caked hair away from his temples. "Would you like me to have a bath brought in for you?"

"That might be just the ticket." Frank took hold of her hand, and Annie kissed the back of his.

"I'll have it brought down right away. Will you be able to bathe yourself or do you need my help?"

"Well, if you insist." Frank's lip curled up into a half-smile.

"Frank, don't embarrass me."

Under the sheets, Annie was powerless against Frank's ministrations, but outside the love nest, she always tried to behave with complete decorum as a proper Quaker should. She had been raised to believe that lovemaking was purely for the purpose of bearing children. But, despite their frequent activity in bed, she had not yet conceived. She knew she should want children, but secretly, she wasn't sure if she did, at least not now. She loved the freedom of being on the road—traveling with the show. Her younger years had been full of responsibility, and she never dreamed she would have the freedom she was experiencing now.

"Annie?" Frank cupped her chin with his fingers. "You drifted away. I was only teasing you, dear."

"I'm sorry." Annie refocused on him. "Do you need my help?"

"Tempting as that sounds, darling, I don't need a nursemaid quite yet. There will be plenty of time for that when I am an old man."

Annie knew he had sensed her embarrassment and tried to make light of the subject, putting her feelings first.

She debated whether or not to tell him of her suspicions of Miss Parnell and Miss Brady, but she decided not to. She didn't want him upset. She would explain later.

"I'm off to see Emma." Annie stood, walked over to the basin, and retrieved the rag. "Put this on your forehead until the bath arrives, just for good measure. And it won't be a hot bath, I'm warning you. Mother always took us to the river after a fever. Said the cold water chased away the devil."

"I can hardly wait," Frank said, plopping the rag on his forehead.

Down the hallway, Annie knocked on Emma's door. When there was no answer, she headed out to the foyer to search for her in the dining room. To her surprise she found Emma in conversation with Miss Parnell, Miss Brady, and Mr. O'Brien.

"Annie, your timing is impeccable," Emma said, pulling her by the elbow into the conversation. "I was just telling Miss Parsons that we would like a word with her and her two companions." Emma's brows lifted, waiting for Annie's response.

"Oh yes," Annie said, turning to Miss Parnell. "It is of the utmost importance that we speak with you. Could we retire to your stateroom? I'm afraid the matter is a bit delicate."

"Of course, this way, please," Miss Parnell said with trembling lips. Miss Brady wrung her hands.

The three started ahead of Annie and Emma, but Annie caught Mr. O'Brien's sleeve.

"Please, Mr. O'Brien. I'm afraid the conversation is not for mixed company." If things went awry, Annie didn't want to have to defend herself against such a large man—although she didn't doubt that she could. She felt the weight of the pistol she'd put in her dress pocket and hoped the situation wouldn't bear her using it.

Mr. O'Brien's cheeks flushed even redder than his ruddy Irish complexion, his orange hair clashing with his pigmented skin. He cast a glance at Miss Parnell, who nodded her assurance and proceeded to lead Annie and Emma to her stateroom.

They entered to find the room tidy, the twin beds made, covered with lovely quilts. Not the standard ship's issue. They must have brought their own. Annie's eyes scanned the room, for what she didn't know, but it seemed a reasonable thing to do.

Miss Brady shut the door behind them and walked over to one of the beds. Annie noticed a book on the nightstand and her blood froze.

"I see you enjoy the works of Mr. Blake?" she said to Miss Brady, but her eyes traveled to Emma.

"Well, yes, I suppose. I've just started reading his book." She pointed to it on the nightstand. "It was in the room when we arrived. He's quite brilliant. I'm an admirer of his philosophies—and his belief that each of us reflects the contrary nature of God. We are all inherently good—and evil."

Annie wasn't sure she could agree, but that was beside the point. "You didn't bring the book on board with you?" Annie asked.

"No. Like I said, it was here when we arrived."

"Which brings us to the matter at hand." Emma pulled her notebook and pencil out of her skirt pocket. “Miss Parsons—or should I say, Miss Parnell—why are you *really* traveling to England? And what is your real name, Miss Brady?”

Miss Parnell’s face drained of color, and she sank to the floor in a faint.

Chapter Fifteen

Annie knelt down next to Miss Parnell, whose eyes fluttered open. Annie helped her to sit, and then she and Emma both took her elbows and helped her to stand. Miss Brady brought the chair from the desk over to them, but when they sat her down, the woman's head lolled back as if she'd lost consciousness again.

"How dare you upset Miss Parsons like that?" Becky glared at Emma. "You say you need to speak with us, get us down here in our room, and then verbally assault her."

Annie ignored Miss Brady's accusation and patted Miss Parnell's cheeks, trying to revive her.

"Please, Emma, fetch some water." Annie held Miss Parnell erect in the chair. The woman came to again, blinking her eyes, taking in deep gulps of air.

"I'm sorry we upset you, Miss Parnell," Annie said, "but we simply must know why you are traveling under an assumed name, and if Miss Brady is doing the same."

Emma handed Annie a glass of water.

"I'll give it to her." Miss Brady snatched the water glass out of Annie's hand and held it to Miss Parnell's lips. "Here you go. Drink it down," she ordered.

"I can keep up this charade no longer," Miss Parnell said to Becky through her tears. "We must tell them the truth. I'm so very tired of living a lie."

"We don't have to tell them anything." Becky's cheeks flushed a blotchy, angry red. Her eyes stabbed daggers at Annie and Emma. "Get out of our room."

"We just have a few questions for you, Miss Brady." Annie straightened, looking her directly in the eye.

"In regards to what?"

"Is Becky Brady your real name?"

"Yes, it's my real name. Why are you asking these questions?" She looked from Annie to Emma, and then back to Annie.

"It concerns the death of Mr. Bhakta," Annie said, gauging her reaction.

Miss Brady's jaw snapped shut, the muscles flexing with tension.

"Miss Oakley, what do you want to know?" Miss Parnell lifted her head, her voice weary.

"What is your current affiliation with the Fenians, Miss Parnell? We know you've worked on their behalf in the past. We also know that you have issues with the Crown."

Miss Parnell raised her gloved hands to her temples. "Yes, I've been involved with the Fenian movement. It is for the sake of the tenant farmers in Ireland. England has been a cruel landlady, Miss Oakley. The Irish are starving. They have no ownership of their own land—they have been evicted from the farms they've tended their whole lives. I was passionate about the movement, but no more. I gave everything

I had to it, and now I am seeking quiet solitude in England under an assumed name. I want no more affiliation with any political movement. I just want to live out my years in peace."

"The Fenians nearly killed this woman with work," Becky broke in. "She deserves some peace and quiet. You leave her alone." Becky's hand shook as she pointed her finger at Annie.

"Miss Brady, you and Miss Parnell can speak with us, or you can speak with the captain. We have information that could be damaging to both of you," Annie said.

"It's fine, Becky," Miss Parnell said. "The truth needs to be told."

Miss Brady took hold of the woman's hand. "They all but abandoned us—my—her brother and his *mistress,* that whore, Katherine O'Shea."

"It sounds as if *you* aren't fond of the Fenians at all, Miss Brady." Emma gave Becky a pointed stare.

"Becky is my daughter." Miss Parnell said.

The younger woman started to say something, but Miss Parnell held up her hand, signaling to Becky to let her finish.

"Before the movement started, I fell in love with a man in America. From our love, came Becky. And yes, Brady is her real name. When I told Mr. Brady of the pregnancy, he left me. I didn't know that my beloved Martin was already married, with a large family of his own. What was I to do? My family was in Ireland, and I was alone. After I gave birth to Becky in secret, I told people I had adopted her. I was free to pursue the cause of the Irish, unencumbered by the duties of a wife." Miss Parnell pulled a handkerchief from her sleeve and wiped her eyes.

"He abandoned us." Becky's voice trembled. "He was the first. Then my uncle, Charles Parnell, when he took up with that whore!"

Miss Parnell snapped out of her tearful reverie. "Becky! Stop this, now. You'll excite yourself."

"No. No!" Becky shrieked. "They've all abandoned us. The hateful lot of them." Becky's breath came hard and fast, and her eyes took on a wild and vacant stare. She picked at the buttons on her sleeves, her fingers moving rapidly.

Miss Parsons stood up from the chair, grabbing Becky by the wrists.

"Stop this, Becky. You'll have one of your fits. You must calm down. Where are your powders?"

"They hate us. They want nothing to do with us. We are alone. Alone!" Becky began pulling at her hair.

Miss Parnell moved Becky to the bed and sat her down. She waved the glass at Annie.

"Water, please."

Annie refilled the water and gave it to Miss Parnell, who took a packet of powder from Becky's reticule and stirred it into the water. She held the back of Becky's head and raised the glass to her lips. Becky was shaking from head to toe, her eyes mad, her lips clamped shut.

"Please, help me," Miss Parnell said to Annie and Emma. "Someone hold her for me. I must get her to swallow the medicine."

Annie and Emma went to the bed and took Becky by the arms. Becky twisted and turned, fighting against the three women trying to hold her still, shrieking as if she were being attacked.

Miss Parnell let go of Becky's head, stood back, and then slapped Becky hard across the face. The girl stopped shrieking, but her chest still heaved with shallow, short breaths. She stared at her mother with wide eyes, but when Miss Parnell shoved the glass at Becky's lips, she drank.

Annie could feel the muscles of the girl's arms relax, and within a few seconds, her whole body deflated. She closed her eyes and collapsed, falling on the bed on her side. Miss Parnell lifted Becky's legs onto the bed and straightened her inert body, tucking a pillow beneath her head.

"As you can see, my daughter has emotional difficulties." Miss Parnell stroked Becky's russet curls. "That is why we are going to England. My brother felt I should put her in an institution in America, but I will not. I can take care of my daughter. Mr. O'Brien is a family friend, along as a protector for us."

"Miss Parnell." Annie touched the woman's sleeve. "If you think Becky will rest quietly now, I'd like for you to sit down. Emma and I have something very important to discuss with you. It concerns Becky."

Annie and Emma let Miss Parnell make her way over to the chair and settle herself before delivering her suspicions.

Miss Parnell sighed, looking up into Annie's eyes. She bit her lip, as if preparing herself for terrible news. Annie's heart ached for her.

"Miss Parnell, it seems, well, we have found evidence—" Annie struggled to make herself say the words.

"We believe Becky may have killed the queen's servant, Mr. Bhakta." Emma finished for her.

"What? What are you saying?" The color drained from Miss Parnell's face, and her lips turned pale.

"We have evidence she may have poisoned him," Annie said.

Anna Parnell shook her head back and forth, her eyes wide with fear. "This cannot be. Becky would do no such thing. Why would she?"

Annie told her of the fingerprints and the note with the excerpt from Blake's poem.

"It all adds up, Miss Parnell. You yourself said that Becky is not emotionally fit. I don't know why she would wish to kill the queen, but the evidence is there. I also feel that for some reason, she might be trying to harm my husband."

"Your husband, why on earth—?"

"When Mr. Bhakta was pushed overboard, there is evidence that he might already have been poisoned. My husband was pushed overboard as well. Then later, you and Miss Brady gave him some sodium bicarbonate that made him very ill. We believe that Becky used a poison we discovered in a vial called a tear catcher. Her fingerprints were on it. Have you ever seen her with anything like that?"

"No. But why would she want to kill your husband?" Miss Parnell, obviously still reeling from the shock of the accusation, looked from Annie then to Emma, and back to Annie again.

"I believe she heard Mr. Patel say my husband is associated with the Fenian movement. When we were in the captain's quarters with the body, discussing what should be done with the body, I saw Becky lurking in the doorway right after Mr. Patel made the allegation. And she has just made it clear she has a grudge against the Fenians."

A loud knock on the door startled them all. Emma went to the door and pulled it open.

"We heard yelling over here." The colonel took off his hat and stepped into the room, followed by Nate Salisbury.

"Is everything quite all right?" Mr. Salisbury asked.

Annie placed a comforting hand on Anna Parnell's shoulder. "Yes, Colonel. I believe we have found the murderer of Mr. Bhakta. Would you please fetch the captain?"

The colonel replaced his hat and left without another word. Nate Salisbury stayed behind.

"Is there anything I can do to assist you, Miss Oakley?" He pointed to the unconscious Becky. "Is she ill?"

"She isn't physically ill, but I am afraid she isn't well mentally," Annie told him. Mr. Salisbury, impeccably dressed as usual, tugged at the bottom of his vest to straighten it. His handsome, usually stoic face registered concern.

"Are you certain?" he asked.

"I don't believe she killed anyone," said Anna Parnell, her voice almost a whisper. "She did despise the Fenians, but mostly because of one man, Michael Davitt. He and I had a relationship. He promised he would marry me and take care of me and Becky forever, but his love of the cause eclipsed his love for us, and he, too, left us. He abandoned us after one of Becky's fits. Said he wouldn't marry me unless I put Becky away in an institution. He and my brother agreed it was for the best."

Annie, her hand still on Miss Parnell's shoulder, knelt down in front of the woman.

"I can understand why she would have issue with the Fenians, Miss Parnell. Their cause directly affected her happiness. But can you think of any reason she would want to kill the queen?"

Miss Parnell held her handkerchief to her nose, shook her head. "No. She often blamed the queen for the troubles in Ireland. Said if it weren't for her, the movement would never have started and our lives would have been different. But that is no reason to want to *kill* her."

"But how do you explain the evidence, the fingerprints?" Emma stepped closer. She'd been quiet, scribbling on her notepad. Annie had almost forgotten she was in the room.

"I can't," said Miss Parnell. "Only that they weren't her fingerprints."

Emma sighed.

"We can show you how they match, if you'd like," Annie said. "I know this is a horrible shock, Miss Parnell."

The door burst open, and the colonel came in followed by the captain.

Annie explained the entire situation.

"We'll have to take her to the brig." The captain put his hands behind his back. "When she comes to."

"No!" Miss Parnell stood up, facing the captain. "Please. I can keep her here with me. She can't be alone. She needs to be monitored. Please, Captain, I beg of you. Let me take care of my daughter."

The captain pressed his lips together, considering. Annie put an arm around Miss Parnell's shoulders.

"You could place a guard at the door, Captain."

"I suppose we could," the captain said. "We only have four more days till we arrive at port in England. The authorities there can handle the rest."

Miss Parnell broke into tears, her knees weakening again. Annie helped her to the chair.

"They will take her away from me now," Miss Parnell said, her voice trembling with emotion. "I know they will. Even if she is innocent, our secret has been revealed. She will be taken away, and I will be ruined and alone."

Annie looked up at Emma, her heart crumbling in her chest. Sometimes, she wished she didn't have a gift for finding the truth.

PART TWO

Chapter Sixteen

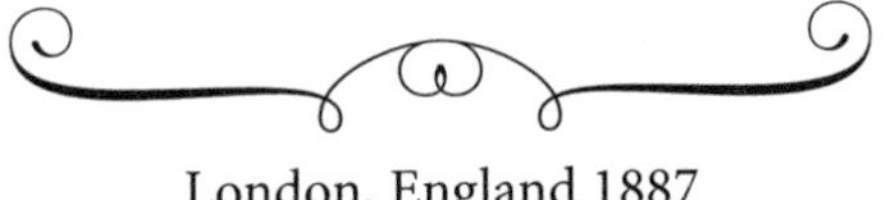

London, England 1887

Annie sat at her vanity in the tent she and Frank shared, pulling tight the strip of leather onto the bottom of the braid running down her back. The previous day's disembarkation from the S.S. *Nebraska* and their move to Earl's Court in Kensington, smack dab in the middle of London, had exhausted her. Frank, still not feeling well, lay in bed watching her at her toilette.

"I'm impressed with the grounds." Annie said, trying to cheer both herself and Frank. She pinched her cheeks and turned away from the mirror to face him. "The colonel said that seven acres of the American Exhibition here at Earl's Court have been reserved for the Wild West Show. Everything is so green and manicured. Perhaps if you are feeling better later, we can take a ride through the exhibition."

"Yes, perhaps." Frank's voice sounded weak and defeated. She had never seen him so listless. She thought getting off the ship might help with his condition, but so far, it hadn't. At least he would be safe from the deranged Miss Brady. Frank's body just needed time to heal, she tried to convince herself.

"Did you ask? Is Dr. Adams staying on with us throughout the tour?" Annie asked him.

"Yes, he said he was."

"I may go seek him out if you don't rally by this afternoon."

Frank didn't answer, but turned over in bed and fell back asleep.

Annie got up from the vanity and walked over to him, watching him breathe. His face had grayed again, and for the first time, she saw him as a much older man. Her heart sank. Her hero, her love, her cherished Frank had, in two weeks, become a shell of his former self.

Her theory that Miss Brady and Miss Parnell had attempted to poison him seemed silly now. They hadn't had contact with him for the last week while they were confined to their stateroom. If they had poisoned Frank, he should be healing by now. As much as she wanted to convince herself he was improving, he seemed to be no better, perhaps even worse.

Of course, Frank had been exhausted by the activities of the previous day. Annie tried to tell him he needed to rest, but he wouldn't listen. He had to help.

Their day had been full of activity—greeting the tremendous crowd at the Royal Albert Dock and taking the train to West Brompton. Buck had again become agitated, but the train trip seemed such a short time compared with the sea voyage.

When they arrived at Earl's Court, Frank had seen to securing their belongings while Annie got Buck settled in his pen. It hadn't taken him long to relax and start eating.

Frank and Annie then helped with the erection of their tent, as well as Hulda's and Emma's. Annie hadn't done nearly the work Frank had, but still felt exhausted, despite being in perfect health. He probably just needed another day to rest. She'd let him sleep.

"I'll check on Hulda," she whispered to Frank, knowing he wouldn't hear her, but it made her feel better to say it.

Annie stepped out into the sunshine to see a woman standing outside Hulda's tent. She recognized her immediately.

"Miss Tessen, how are you? I'm surprised to see you here."

"Hello, Miss Oakley." Miss Tessen's hands shook and her face was drained of color, all but the dark circles under her eyes. "I'd like to have a word with you, if you have a minute." The woman looked on the verge of collapse. She placed her hand against the tent wall for support.

"Are you well, Miss Tessen?"

"Yes. Just a bit hungry. Haven't had a meal since we disembarked. Couldn't keep much down when I was below decks on the ship."

"Come. I'll see if Cook has anything to eat." Annie reached out and took Miss Tessen by the elbow, afraid the woman would crumple. "I'm not sure they've got the dining tent completely set up, but I'm sure there is some food available."

Annie guided her through the rows of tents, some completely erect, some still in the process of being put together. Cowboys and crewmen from the show, as well as an English crew, were milling about. The loud clink of sledgehammers hitting spikes, rolling cart wheels, wagon wheels, and orders being shouted back and forth rang through the air as the Wild West Show took form.

The large, white-and-red-striped tent they used as an eating hall lay on the ground, the poles erected but nothing else. Annie noticed Hal, their chief cook, working at his coal-burning stove. A steaming pot hung over a stone-ringed fire pit, and the aroma of fresh meat-and-vegetable stew made Annie's stomach rumble with hunger—for the first time since she'd left America, she realized.

"Hi, Hal." Annie said, her arm linked through Miss Tessen's as she approached the cook. "I'm famished. Could my friend Miss Tessen and I have a bowl of that delicious smelling stew?"

Hal, a short, round fellow with a ginger colored bushy mustache, beard, and eyebrows that had a life all their own, frowned at Annie's request. The caterpillar across his brow rippled downwards in consternation.

"'S not quite finished stewing."

"We don't mind, do we Miss Tessen?"

The woman shook her head. She leaned heavily on Annie's arm, her face ashen.

"Please, Hal." Annie feared Miss Tessen would buckle if she didn't get food into her fast. "And some bread if you have it."

Hal bent over a large crate and pulled out two wooden bowls. He set them down on the stove with an irritated clunk. He reached into the camp oven and pulled out a large round of freshly baked bread.

"'S'not eatin' time. Don't let them cowboys see you with this food, or they'll come over here like bees to honey. Can't keep their bellies full no matter what I do."

"We'll just take it back to my tent," Annie said.

Hal took the bowls to the pot and scooped out two servings. He handed the bowls to them, plunked a spoon in each one, and cut each of them a slice of bread. He never made eye contact with Annie, and she knew she'd angered him, but she couldn't watch Miss Tessen suffer another moment. She thanked Hal and he gave a grunt in response.

They walked back to Annie's tent.

"Frank, my husband, is still not feeling well," Annie said, setting her bowl on a table that stood outside the tent with a chair next to it. "You sit here and start, and I'll be back in a moment with another chair."

Annie slipped inside the tent with her bowl of stew, hoping Frank would want to eat it. He lay sleeping peacefully, so she decided not to disturb him. She lifted a chair by one of the back rungs and, holding her bowl, made her way back outside. Miss Tessen had finished her bread and was tucking into the stew like a starving animal. Annie set the chair down opposite her and began eating.

When Miss Tessen was finished, she lifted her head and wiped her mouth with the back of her tattered jacket sleeve.

"Thank you for your kindness." She gave Annie a curt nod.

"You're welcome."

"I told you a bit of a fib." Miss Tessen's eyes did not meet Annie's. Annie continued to spoon the stew into her mouth. "I'm not visiting family. I have no family. I didn't have any luck finding work in America—well, not the kind of work a woman likes to do, if you know what I mean."

Annie pressed her lips together, completely understanding. She knew what a hungry belly and desperation felt like. Luckily, she'd never had to resort to the kind of work Miss Tessen spoke of.

"So you hope to find work here, in England," Annie finished for her.

"Yes. Well, actually, I want to find work here, at the Wild West Show."

Annie tried not to show her shock and surprise. Why hadn't she said anything on the ship? She'd had complete access to the colonel and Mr. Salisbury for the entire voyage.

"Why didn't you mention this before, Miss Tessen, on the ship?"

"I wanted to see what kind of people you all were." Miss Tessen stared into her empty bowl. "I haven't had much luck with people. But then I saw you and your husband and how you are with your horse. I saw how the colonel treats his people, the American Indians, and his horses. You are good folk."

"I'd love to help," Annie said, warmed by the woman noticing their kindness and respect for one another. That feeling of kinship made Annie proud. She also knew what it was like to feel the ache of hunger and despair. "What kind of skills do you have?"

"I can take care of horses. I loved doing it as a girl. My mother didn't like me in the stables all of the time—thought I should be sewing or singing or dancing."

"That sounds familiar." Annie couldn't help smiling. She knew all too well the pressures of trying to live up to feminine expectations, but oh, so much wanting to do almost anything else.

"I'd like to take care of your horse, Miss—Annie."

"Buck? Well—" Annie hesitated. She didn't want anyone but Mr. Post, Bobby, or herself taking care of Buck. How could she explain that three years ago, he'd been poisoned and stolen from her? She'd never let him be out of her care ever again. Not for a moment.

"Please don't take offense, but I don't think that would be a good idea. Buck is rather particular about who takes care of him. He only eats for me, Mr. Post, or Bobby. I hope you understand." *That I have embellished the truth.*

Miss Tessen waved her tattered gloved hand in front of her face.

"I do understand. Just thought I would ask. What about the other horses? You have about two hundred head here, don't you?"

"Yes, we do."

"I know how to shoe horses. I used to help our blacksmith all the time. Who does blacksmithing for the show?"

Annie tried to hide her surprise. Blacksmithing had been the last occupation Annie expected from the petite, almost frail woman. The art took hard, lean muscles, the strength of an ox, and a tolerance for extreme heat. Gail Tessen hardly fit the bill. But she supposed many people said the same thing about her. In fact, she knew they did.

"Most of the Indian ponies are barefoot," Annie said. "The cowboys trim their own horses' feet, make their own shoes—usually at a campfire."

"What about you? What about the colonel?"

The questions hung in the air. Before Annie knew Bobby, she or Mr. Shaw, owner of the North Star Mercantile, had always taken care of Buck's feet. Since she'd joined the show, it had been Bobby. He also took care of Isham and Charlie's feet, and Fancy's when Frank had her before she passed of old age.

Annie put a spoonful of stew in her mouth to stall. Now that Bobby was a featured performer of the show, his duties had grown, and he would love to have some help. But something made her hesitate.

"I can't speak for the colonel, but I can ask him, or Mr. Salisbury, if there are any available positions. I will also mention your skills at the forge."

"I thank you for your kindness." Miss Tessen stood up.

"Come back tomorrow and hopefully I will have an answer for you."

The woman nodded and trudged off toward the tree-lined road, leading out of Earl's Court. Annie had almost asked if she had a place to stay, but then decided against it. She couldn't figure out why the woman made her so uncomfortable.

Hulda popped out from behind the flap of her tent, the apples of her cheeks ripe with enthusiasm.

"Did you hear, Annie? We're invited to a society gala!"

A society gala. Annie felt a sudden itching and dampening of her palms.

"We'll have to find you a suitable dress since you ruined the last one I made for you," Hulda prattled on. "You must have one in that old trunk of yours, but I'm sure it's not in the latest fashion. I'll have to spruce it up a bit. I suppose I could alter the neckline and sleeves. . . ." Hulda swept past her, talking a blue streak as she started to enter Annie's tent.

Annie grabbed her by the sleeve. "You'll wake Frank. He needs to sleep. I'm sure whatever I pick will be suitable enough. Mind what you wear, little sister. Don't forget who you are and where you come from."

Hulda scowled and marched back to her own tent.

Annie sighed, stood up, and stepped from the shadow of the tent. She turned and gazed out toward the road, wondering where Gail Tessen would sleep tonight.

Later that evening, after Annie and Frank had shared a piece of apple pie—the only thing Frank felt like eating, much to Annie's concern—Bobby appeared at their tent with a note from Mr. Salisbury stating, "The former Prime Minister of England, Mr. William Gladstone will be visiting the encampment at 2:00 in the afternoon. Please be in costume and ready to receive him at that time."

"Oh, dear," Annie said aloud, crushing the note in her palm. She looked over to tell Frank the news, but he'd climbed onto the bed, still clothed, and was already asleep. She hoped he'd be up to meeting Mr.

Gladstone tomorrow. With Frank by her side, Annie always felt less awkward when meeting important people, like when she'd met the Governor of Ohio or the Mayor of Greenville. While others fawned over people of "authority," Frank always treated them like they were old friends. His buoyant personality and natural charm smoothed the way for her to do the same.

She felt they'd hardly had time to catch her breath since disembarking from the ship and setting up camp. Already, they had to make appearances and greet people. Annie set the note on the nightstand, dressed for bed, and after blowing out the lantern, molded her body to his, reciting prayers in her head that he would be back to himself soon. She missed the old Frank.

In the morning, Annie woke to find Frank tossing and turning in his sleep. She nudged his shoulder.

"Frank, wake up. I think you are having a nightmare."

He rolled over to face her and opened his eyes. "Yes, I was," he said, his voice thick and groggy. "I was in the water with Buck again. The ship was sailing away with you on it."

Annie laid her hand on his cheek. "I'm right here, Frank. Always."

He smiled and closed his eyes again.

"Mr. Gladstone is coming today to visit the exhibition. Will you be up to meeting him?"

Frank opened his eyes wide. "Yes, of course. I'll be fine."

"You look like you didn't sleep at all," Annie said, concerned by the pallor of his skin. He still did not look well.

"I'll be fine. I just need a little sleep. Wake me in a couple of hours."

After she'd dressed, Annie went to Hulda's tent in search of one of her new costumes, relieved that the colonel had insisted they wear them to meet Mr. Gladstone. She always felt more comfortable in costume as opposed to the fancy dresses Hulda liked her to wear.

Hulda had not yet completed the new costumes, so Annie had to make do with one of the older costumes that Kimimela had made for her. Putting it on made Annie's heart ache for her dear friend who had died at such an early age. She wondered how Kimi's little daughter, Winona, was faring with her new family. The child must be four years old by now.

The former prime minister and his wife entered the grounds of Earl's Court in a shiny black coach pulled by four chestnut geldings with gleaming white blazes and four white socks each. They rounded the 1200-square-foot exhibition building and came across the dirt road to the encampment, where they were greeted by visiting Americans and English nobility.

The colonel had instructed his cowboy band—all dressed in gray shirts, slouch hats, and moccasins—to strike up "Yankee Doodle" as Mr. Gladstone and his wife made their way out of the carriage to meet the troupe.

Mr. Gladstone had a grandfatherly face, snow-white hair, and downturned lips that gave him a perpetual frown. His eyes too, turned down at the corners, but quickly brightened, pulling up his mouth when he smiled as he stepped out of the carriage. Holding out his hand, he assisted his wife, a tiny woman with silvery hair topped with a velvet hat trimmed with a bright scarf that cascaded down her back. Her bright blue eyes popped open in wonder as she saw all the Indian players lined up to greet them.

Chief Red Shirt and Black Elk, who had both dressed for the occasion in full war paint and feathers, with brightly colored blankets wrapped around their shoulders, stood stoically next to Annie and Frank.

Frank had slept till noon, and when Annie returned to their tent with a plate of Hal's pork chops and potatoes for him, he was up, dressed, and sitting in his rocker. He still looked like a ghost of his former self, and Annie could tell his strength had not returned. She hoped the food would restore him but was disappointed when he ate only the potatoes and a small portion of the meat.

She turned to look at him as they waited to meet Mr. Gladstone. His eyes looked glassy and out of focus, and perspiration shone on his forehead. At least he was up and eager to meet England's former prime minister.

Red Shirt's handsome face, with its broad forehead, long straight nose, and square jaw wore a mask of proud stoicism and was framed by his thick wavy hair. The long tails of a bright red scarf he had wrapped around his head hung in unison with the thick braid that trailed down to his slender hips. Next to Frank, Annie thought Red Shirt the most handsome man in the outfit, and she was not alone.

After greeting the American officials and English noblemen, the colonel, Mr. Salisbury, and Mr. Gladstone—his wife's delicate hand nestled in the crook of his elbow—strode directly over to Red Shirt.

"Chief, this is the former prime minister, the great white chief of England," the colonel said. Gladstone held out his hand.

Red Shirt drew his blanket closer around his chest, his gaze settling somewhere on the distant horizon. The colonel repeated the introduction to Red Shirt in Sioux. He added, "You must take his hand, Chief."

Finally, the chief took the former prime minister's hand, but remained silent.

"What think you of the English climate, Chief?" Gladstone asked.

The chief did not answer.

"Do you see those similarities in Englishmen and Americans which might be expected to exist between kinsmen and brothers?" Gladstone tried again.

Annie held her breath, hoping the chief would answer the question.

"I don't know so much about being kinsmen and brothers," the chief said, his voice monosyllabic.

All the gentlemen let out uproarious laughter, but the chief's face never changed. Annie was a little taken aback by the laughter. She knew that Chief Sitting Bull and Chief Red Shirt had some resentment toward the American government, and rightly so—how could he feel a kinship with the people who had taken everything from him?

She supposed Mr. Gladstone would never understand. Even though the colonel had formed a genuine friendship and partnership with his former enemies, others had more trouble bringing themselves to understand the Indians.

"Ah. Well. It's a pleasure to meet you, Chief Red Shirt. I look forward to seeing you perform," Mr. Gladstone said.

The chief gave a curt nod and left the group. Mr. Gladstone turned to the colonel.

"I understand Miss Parnell traveled with you—under an assumed name."

"That is true, Mr. Gladstone."

"Yes. Unfortunate business with her brother," Gladstone continued. "We tried to work together on some of this Home Rule business for the Irish, but he's just been recently accused of taking some kind of role in the Phoenix Park murders five years ago—one of the victims was brother to one of my ministers."

Annie listened with rapt attention. If Miss Parnell's brother had in some way been involved with the murder of one of Mr. Gladstone's ministers, what would stop him from employing his sister or his niece to do the same to one of the queen's private staff? Annie couldn't imagine Miss Parnell doing anything so horrible, but this squabble between the Irish and the Crown was much more malicious than she'd ever considered.

Lost in her thoughts, Annie almost didn't hear the colonel address her.

"This is Miss Annie Oakley, Mr. Gladstone. Pride of the Wild West Show."

Annie snapped back to attention. "Oh, Colonel. Don't embarrass me."

"I've heard about you," Mr. Gladstone said, his face beaming. Annie took his hand and then greeted his wife.

"I'm so looking forward to seeing you perform," the tiny woman said.

"We're giving the former prime minister and the Prince and Princess of Wales a private showing," said Mr. Salisbury. Annie wished she had known sooner. She had hoped Buck would have more time to get acquainted with his surroundings.

"I hope you enjoy the show," Annie said, releasing her hand.

The colonel introduced Frank, and the two men exchanged a few words about English politics, the weather, and Annie's success. Frank, always proud of her, boasted about her talents, but with less than his usual enthusiasm. The weakness of his voice conveyed the weakness in his body, and Annie's heart broke a little.

The colonel and Mr. Salisbury stepped forward. "Nate, should we give them the tour?" the colonel asked his manager, tucking his fingers into the pockets of his waistcoat.

"Splendid idea." Mr. Salisbury held his hand aloft for the group to pass by. After they had filed past him, he turned to Annie.

"There is a party tonight and we need you to be there. We are to be presented to the Prince and Princess of Wales."

"Wonderful," Annie said, giving him her brightest smile. "I look forward to it."

She hoped he could not hear the dread in her voice.

Chapter Seventeen

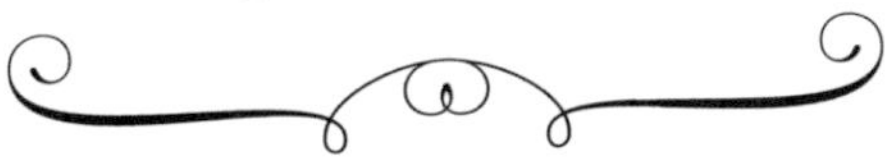

After their names had been loudly announced by a man wearing a stiff, tailed tuxedo and an equally stiff expression, Annie and Emma entered the grand parlor of the estate and settled into a corner of the ballroom to view the crowd. Frank, still weak, had opted to stay in their tent, at Annie's insistence. She needed him to be well when she started performing.

The room's expanse seemed never-ending, with large crystal chandeliers casting a rainbow of colors on the white carpet decorated with silk-threaded roses intertwined in the weave. Elegant silk sofas and chairs, all in white, sat clustered throughout the room, with handsome potted palms strategically placed to encourage private conversations. Other areas of the room had been left wide open to accommodate group discussions.

The walls of the ballroom, which soared high to the ceiling, were covered in silk damask and trimmed with dark wood wainscoting. The silk walls were hung with elegant tapestries and portraits of stoic looking men in tailored suits and puffy white ascots accompanied by beautiful ladies in silk, jewel-toned gowns.

"Who is hosting this extravagant party, Emma?" Annie laid her hands against the bones at the front of her corset, fighting for breath. She'd chosen one of the dresses she'd been given by the show's former manager, Derence LeFleur, three years ago, as opposed to a new one Hulda had made. The new dress, bright green with a daring décolleté, made Annie feel like a doll on display. She knew the older dress wasn't the latest fashion, as her sister pointed out in disgust, but she felt it complimented her soft brown hair and her famously tiny waist, which was all she cared to show off.

Trimmed in fine ecru lace at the throat and the cuffs, the dress fit Annie's torso like a second skin—after Hulda had sewn her into it for the evening—and the skirt billowed out modestly with the help of petticoats and a bustle. Hulda had also expertly arranged all of Annie's shooting medals above her left breast. Annie cringed at "showing them off" but the colonel had insisted. She hoped she wouldn't faint dead away from embarrassment at the crude display of her accomplishments, or the lack of air in her lungs.

"I believe it is a Mr. George Glyn—or should I say, Baron Wolverton?—who owns the manse," Emma replied. "I assume he is the host. Rumor has it we are to be presented to the Prince of Wales and Princess Alexandria tonight. I'm all aflutter."

"You don't easily impress, Emma. I'm surprised."

"I know. But, Annie, they are *royalty*—the fairy prince and princess of my old schoolgirl storybook days. It's thrilling. I'm on air!"

"I wish I *had* some air." Annie pulled at the neckline of her dress. Already, she could feel a trickle of sweat slip down her spine. "I also wish Frank could have come. I hope he gets better soon. He handles these types of events so expertly. I usually let him do all the talking."

"You'll have to make do with me, tonight." Emma patted her blond coif adorned with pearls and crystals. The pale blue of her gown brought out the intense green of her eyes and the pink luster in her cheeks. Emma had an elegance that Annie would never possess, but her rock solid loyalty to Annie eclipsed her porcelain beauty.

"I'm sorry, Emma. You know I love your company," Annie said, grimacing as she tried to adjust her corset.

Boisterous laughing pulled their attention across the room toward Lillie, who was unabashedly flirting with a group of well-dressed gentlemen. Her short, plump figure, all the more bulky in a white lace gown with a wide black ribbon at her ample waist, drew the eye. She wore heavy paste jewels that somehow overpowered the pomp and circumstance of her dress. Annie knew nothing about fashion, but knew that what Lillie was attempting did not suit her at all.

"Poor girl. She really does herself no favors," Emma said with a sigh. "I might have to make a new project of her. What do you think?"

Annie swallowed down her distaste of the idea. Lillie was already threatening to steal Annie's thunder in the show arena with her improving marksmanship and her naturally social nature.

"I don't think she would listen. Stubborn as a donkey, that one," Annie said.

"You might be right," Emma agreed. "Actually, her garishness lends her a sort of charm, don't you think?"

"Charm? Yes." As Annie choked out the words, she noticed a couple staring at Emma and her, talking behind their gloved hands. The man, striking in appearance with a puffy white bejeweled ascot, wool suit, and fur-lined crimson cape, oozed a mischievous sort of charm. His light, narrow-set eyes sparkled beneath his broad forehead and his mane of thick, sandy-brown hair. The woman had a regal, commanding presence, as if she herself had been born of royalty, with her plunging neckline, silks, and sparkling jewels. But something in her eyes told a different story. A hit of the survivalist—an existence Annie knew all too well—brewed in the woman's gaze.

"Do you know who they are, Emma?" Annie tilted her head in the couple's direction.

"I would say from everything I've heard about the peacock, that he might be the poet Oscar Wilde. Who else would wear such a cape?"

As if the couple could hear the conversation, or read their minds, they turned toward Annie and Emma.

"Well, I suppose we will find out," Emma said, plastering on a glittering smile.

The man approached Annie with an outstretched hand. "You must be the charming Annie Oakley. I would have known you anywhere. My name is Oscar Wilde."

Annie took his hand. When she looked up into his eyes, she saw in them a passionate soul. "Pleased to meet you. This is my friend Emma Wilson," Annie nodded toward Emma.

Mr. Wilde took Emma's hand and then turned to his companion. "This is my friend, Mrs. Lily Langtry, or as I call her, J. L., which stands for the Jersey Lily that she is."

The woman's bright eyes settled on Annie's, and she offered a hand ensconced in an ivory silk glove. The fabric felt warm and soft against Annie's palm.

"Excuse Mr. Wilde's eccentricities," Mrs. Langtry said. "You will grow to love him as I have. I'm from one of the Channel Islands, south of England, called Jersey."

"And she is beautiful as a lily, don't you think?" Mr. Wilde leaned into Mrs. Langtry's hair and breathed deeply, as if he'd been transported to heaven. "And she smells divine."

"You two make a lovely pair," Annie said. She didn't know what to make of this odd play of affection.

"Oh, we aren't together." Oscar's eyes grew wide. "The prince would have my head. Only he can enjoy the purest beauty of the J. L. She is his mistress, after all."

"Oscar, you've had too much wine," Mrs. Langtry said with a charming smile, grabbing him by the arm. "We must get you some air. Please excuse us, ladies. It was such a pleasure to meet both of you. I hope to see you again, soon."

"Bang, bang! Right, Miss Oakley?" Mr. Wilde said, putting his thumb and finger into the air like a gun. "We've tickets to your performance. I'm simply on pins and needles to see you shoot a cigarette out of someone's mouth," Mr. Wilde said as he let himself be led away by Mrs. Langtry.

"What an peculiar man." Annie turned to Emma. "Do you think it is true? Is Mrs. Langtry really mistress of the prince?"

"So the scandal goes," Emma said, eyebrows raised. "She's married, too."

"I don't care for that." Annie couldn't imagine such a thing. "Why would someone want to interfere in another's marriage, or cause harm to their own?"

"Look, there's the colonel, the chief, and Mr. Salisbury," Emma said, changing the subject. "Let's go talk to them." Emma strode off before Annie could protest. She'd just noticed Hulda speaking with a group of gentlemen. They all looked completely enchanted with her, and Hulda was basking in the attention. Annie could tell by the high color of her cheeks and the way she twisted her body to make her skirt swing.

Hulda had chosen a modest yellow gown, but the cut and fabric made her appear much older than her thirteen years. Although she looked like a grownup, her mannerisms and speech remained childlike, and Annie hoped her sister wasn't getting herself into trouble.

She marched over to the group, took Hulda by the elbow, made her apologies to the gentlemen, and walked her sister over to a corner near one of the potted palms.

Hulda wrenched her arm out of Annie's grasp. "I was having a conversation."

"You were making a fool of yourself, Hulda. This is a fast crowd. I don't want you getting in over your head. Where's Bobby?" Annie asked scanning the room. Right now, she'd even take the dashing Mr. Everett as her sister's escort. Hulda milling around alone looked unseemly, improper.

"He didn't want to come. Said he felt like an imposter in such fancy company," Hulda said.

Annie knew exactly the feeling. "You stay with me this evening. I don't want you leaving my side."

"Oh, Annie. You are such a bore."

Annie turned to Hulda. "I am your sister and I love you, Hulda. I'm responsible for you. Please don't make this more difficult than it already is."

"So I'm a responsibility. A burden. Difficult. As usual." Hulda's lower lip protruded in a pout. "You act like you take care of us, Annie, but you're too busy trying to find fame and fortune to care about me, or John Henry, or Mother. I don't know why you even brought me along."

Annie wanted to slap Hulda for her insolence and disrespect, but refrained when a tall, elegant gentleman and a woman bejeweled in pearls down to her waist walked past them, their expression questioning why she and her sister were hiding behind a plant. Annie forced a smile and nodded as the couple glided past.

"Hulda, we're making money to support our family. Don't you see the importance in that?"

"Why is it our responsibility, Annie? What if I want to be on my own?"

"You are thirteen."

"You were fifteen when you joined the Wild West Show, left home, and traveled the United States. Why can't I do that? You are mother's strength and John Henry is the favorite. No one understands me." Hulda's face had turned an unpleasant shade of crimson and she looked as if she were about to have an outburst.

"Hulda, you aren't making any sense—"

But before Annie could finish her sentence, Hulda ran to the white-paned, glass doors and out into the night.

Annie had started after Hulda when Lillie caught her by the elbow. Lillie's cheeks, bright pink from the whiskey, puffed up as she stifled a belch. She smelled of alcohol and tobacco, and her smile tilted across her face as if someone had smeared her lip pomade.

"Hey, doll. You're needed at the party. We're going to be presented to the Prince and Princess of Wales. Can you imagine?" Lillie let out a bull horn of a laugh, her hands on her hips, her body swaying in an imaginary breeze.

"I can't right now, Lillie. I have to find Hulda. She just ran off." Annie started for the doors but Lillie pulled her back.

"She'll be fine. Just needed some air, I'm sure. You have no idea how hard it is to measure up to 'Sure Shot Annie.' Believe me, I know."

Annie's breath caught in her throat. She hadn't seen things from that perspective. She never thought Hulda would think she needed to live up to her big sister's fame, or that somehow, she *couldn't* live up to it. She'd never meant to make her sister feel inferior.

It all made sense. The extravagant, sometimes bold clothing Hulda wore, her rebellious attitude, her friendship with Lillie—whose recklessness unnerved Annie—and Hulda's sometimes sullen mood were all indicative of a young girl with a famous sister, desperately seeking to find herself. Find a way to make her mark on the world.

"You coming?" Lillie blew her nose in a lace hanky she'd pulled from her sleeve.

"But, what about Hulda?"

"I'll go find her after we meet the royal anuses—I mean highnesses." Lillie doubled over laughing at her own crude joke. "You are the last cowgirl Hulda wants to see right now."

"I'm not a cowgirl." Annie felt her temper flare. She shouldn't let Lillie know she got under her skin, but the woman brought out something in her that made her act unlike anything she was or wanted to be.

"Well, aren't you full of yourself? Let's go. We need to get in line." Lillie grabbed Annie by the wrist and dragged her toward a crowd of people lining up to greet the prince and princess.

Mr. Patel approached them wearing a dark suit and a tall, beaver-skin fez.

"Hello, Mr. Patel," Annie said, nodding to him. She still wasn't certain how she felt about him, considering he was one of her prime suspects in the murder investigation of Mr. Bhakta. But both she and Emma felt certain they'd found the killer. The evidence against Miss Brady was too overwhelming to deny.

Mr. Patel graciously bowed and took Annie's hand. His hand felt small as a sparrow and just as fragile.

"I'm here to instruct you on how to greet their royal highnesses."

Lillie snorted, obviously in reference to her previous joke. The guests again turned a disapproving eye on the two of them. Annie cringed inwardly, but focused her attention on Mr. Patel.

"Do we shake their hands?" she asked.

"You must first address His Royal Majesty. Curtsy with your eyes cast downward. Once you rise, then you may make eye contact and whatever you say, be sure to address him as 'Your Royal Majesty.' Then you may move on to the princess."

"Aye, aye, Captain." Lillie gave Mr. Patel a stiff salute. Annie stifled a groan.

"Have a good evening." Mr. Patel bowed again and then moved on down the line where more of the performers, including Buffalo Bill, the chief, and Mr. Salisbury, waited their turn to meet the royals.

"Please show some taste, Lillie. We don't want to reflect badly on the colonel. I don't think the people of Europe have seen anything quite like us." Annie scanned the room, noting the appraising eyes of the gentry.

It had taken her so long to be comfortable in front of a crowd performing. Now, that seemed easy compared with standing in a fancy parlor of an estate, unable to move—or breathe. Her corset dug into her waist, and Annie envisioned the angry red lines she would see on her skin when she undressed. To rid herself of these binds and sink into a warm, soft bed with Frank seemed like a fantasy, and one that wouldn't manifest for hours yet to come.

"We *are* special," Lillie said tugging at the teardrop pearls hanging from her earlobes. "My ears feel afire! Are they red?"

"Be quiet, and stop grabbing at your ear." Annie said through a clenched and forced smile. "You're getting too much notice."

The line quickly moved forward, and Annie and Lillie were only one other couple away from meeting royalty for the first time.

The woman behind them cleared her throat, and Annie stole at glance at her; her nose rose straight in the air. Annie took in a steady breath, praying that Lillie wouldn't do anything even more embarrassing.

As the prince addressed the man in front of them, his eyes traveled to the back of the room. Annie turned to see Mrs. Langtry blow the prince a kiss. She turned back and saw a mortified expression on the face of Princess Alexandra. Her mouth twitched at the corners, and her eyes narrowed slightly, but she still held her bearing and smiled graciously at the couple in front of Annie and Lillie, exchanging a few words with them. Annie's heart went out to the princess. She must be so humiliated at Mrs. Langtry openly flirting with her husband. The couple ahead of Annie and Lillie moved away from the royal couple, leaving the two of them left to face the prince and princess.

Lillie stepped forward first and bowed low to the ground, her head almost between her knees. She lost her balance and had to put her hand to the floor for support. Giggling, she stood up, red-faced, her bosom nearly falling out of her dress. She held her hand out toward the prince. He looked over to his wife, as if for an explanation. The princess blinked several times in rapid succession, her smile close-lipped and tense. The prince took Lillie's hand, his crooked smile belaying his astonishment at the young woman's clumsiness.

"Charmed, I'm sure," Lillie said, batting her eyelashes.

Annie wanted to sink into the floor. Instead, she turned her full attention to the princess, dipped to a small curtsy and then rose, holding her hands together at her waist.

"It is a pleasure to meet you, Your Royal Highness," she said.

A collective gasp filled the room. Mr. Patel had instructed her to greet the prince first, but she couldn't bring herself to do it because of his behavior with Mrs. Langtry.

The princess smiled wide at Annie and held out her hands. Annie placed one of hers in the princess's warm grasp.

"I'm delighted to meet you, Miss Oakley. I hope you have found everything to your satisfaction in our fair kingdom so far."

"It's lovely." Annie then turned to the prince and curtsied. "Your Royal Highness."

"Miss Oakley." His eyes met hers for a brief moment and then he focused on the couple behind them. Annie grasped Lillie's plump arm and guided her away from the royals. Lillie shook her off and walked away.

In seconds, Emma was at Annie's side. "Oh, dear, darling. I'm afraid you've slighted the prince. Annie, what were you thinking? You know this will be the talk of the town."

Annie led Emma over to a small alcove off the main parlor that led into a great hallway lined with paned glass windows that soared to the ceiling. When she felt they could not be heard, she whispered to Emma, "He is unabashedly unfaithful to his wife and flirts with his mistress in front of everyone. My heart went out to the princess."

"Annie, the royals do things differently."

"I don't care." Annie planted her fists on her hips. "It's cruel. I don't suppose the princess can go off and have affairs with anyone she pleases. A man and woman are equal partners in a relationship."

"Not here, and not in most cases, Annie. You have something very special with Frank, but believe me—not everyone is so fortunate." Emma's gaze penetrated Annie's heart, and she felt a sudden pity for Emma. She always seemed so strong and fiercely independent. Annie never considered she might be lonely.

Annie sighed. "I understand. But I still don't regret my actions. In that moment, Princess Alexandra needed to know she is valued."

"You have a true heart." Emma patted her shoulder, the earlier sadness in her eyes gone.

Annie heard voices echoing down the long hallway and turned to see Dr. Adams speaking with another party guest. From the tone of their voices and the rigid body language of the two men, the conversation seemed to be heated.

"Is that Dr. Adams?" Emma asked. "And why is he wearing that appalling orange ribbon on his lapel? The color does not suit him."

"He seems very upset. I'd like to speak with him about Frank." Annie tilted her head to see if she could hear the conversation. They listened to the voices. "Do you hear that, Emma?"

"No, I can't hear what they are saying. You have good hearing, my dear."

"It's not what they are saying it's *how* he is saying it."

"I don't get your meaning."

"He is speaking with an Irish accent." Annie turned to look at Emma. "Don't you hear it?"

Emma shook her head. "Are you sure?"

"Absolutely. On the ship, he had an English accent, didn't he?"

"Yes."

"But how—?"

A white-gloved servant holding a small silver tray appeared in the alcove.

"Miss Oakley. A letter for you."

"What? Here?" It seemed strange to get a letter delivered at a party. Everyone who knew her was in attendance. Why would she receive a letter at Baron Wolverton's estate? She hoped it wasn't about Frank.

The servant stood silently, his back straight and the tray held out to her. She removed the letter and held it to her chest. "Thank you."

The servant bowed his head and left.

"How very strange," Emma said, leaning in to get a look at the letter. "Well, open it."

Annie turned the letter over and saw a red seal was holding the folded paper closed. She couldn't make out the mark, which was blurred as if the sender had been in a rush. She opened the paper and unfolded it. All of the life melted out of her body. She raised her hand to her mouth.

"You look wretched, Annie. What is it?"

Annie stared at the paper. "It's not a letter. It's a message."

Emma grabbed the paper from Annie's hands and read.

"Without contraries is no progression. Attraction and repulsion, reason and energy, love and hate are necessary to human existence. From these contraries spring what the religious call good and evil. Good is the passive that obeys reason. Evil is the active springing from energy. Good is Heaven. Evil is Hell. The queen betrays these laws. She should not be allowed existence."

"Another section from Blake's poem. And another threat about the queen," Emma said, raising her eyes to meet Annie's.

"But what does it mean?" Annie shook her head in confusion. How could this be? Another letter? And why sent to her? Was this person aiming to torture her, to play with her, to prove how wrong she had been? She swallowed hard, her mouth turning dry as a dust.

"I'm not sure. I think this part of the previous poem. Here Blake speaks of contraries: good and evil, Heaven and Hell. His theory explains that both are necessary and part of human nature. I think the person who sent this note feels that the queen has put herself above good and evil, and so she should not exist, but I'm not certain. I'm not sure what it means," said Emma.

"I do." Annie took back the letter and crushed it to her chest. "It means the murderer is still at large, and I've accused the wrong person."

Chapter Eighteen

Annie suddenly felt lightheaded, and her knees wobbled. She had to sit down. Pushing past Emma, she headed toward one of the plush sofas and sank into it, grasping onto the arm and digging her fingers into the fabric.

"That poor girl!" Annie exclaimed as Emma sat down beside her. "What have I done? What did they do with her? Where is Miss Brady?"

"Annie, calm down." Emma grasped her by the shoulders.

Annie's mind reeled. "Do you know where they've sent her? We have to get her out. I was wrong. How could I have been so stupid?"

"Are you sure, Annie? We compared the fingerprints."

"Yes, I know, but who else would be quoting Blake? The fingerprints were not substantial evidence—that is obvious, now. We have to find out where she was sent." Annie's heart raced. How could she have been so quick to judge Miss Brady? But the evidence had seemed so solid.

"All right, we will find her," Emma said, in an obvious attempt to soothe her. "Dr. Adams is here, remember? He examined Miss Brady on the ship before we disembarked."

Annie closed her eyes, remembering. The girl had sunk into a deep depression. She wouldn't talk, wouldn't eat, and couldn't sleep. She had walked down the ramp of the ship like a ghost, her eyes vacant, her skin sallow, and her cheeks bony and sunken.

"We have to find Dr. Adams." Annie stood up too fast. Suddenly dizzy, she grasped the arm of the sofa again for support. "I hope he hasn't left the party yet. Was he to meet the royal couple?" Annie swayed, her head feeling airy and light, her breath shallow.

Emma stood up and grabbed hold of her elbow. "No. Only those of you in the Wild West Show. Are you all right, Annie?"

Annie waved her free hand in the air. "I'm fine. A little lightheaded. I can't breathe in this damned corset. Oh, I'm sorry, excuse my language. I'm just—I suppose it's also from the shock of knowing I've accused an innocent woman of a crime so heinous—" Annie pressed her fingers to her lips, squeezing her eyes shut, fending off a wave of nausea. She took a deep breath and gazed into the eyes of her friend. "I have to make this right, Emma."

"And we will, Annie. How were we to know? All the evidence pointed to Miss Brady. You did nothing wrong."

Annie felt a little steadier on her feet. She took in another breath and squared her shoulders. "Let's find Dr. Adams."

"You stay here. I'll find the doctor." Emma indicated for Annie to sit again.

"No. I have to find him. I have to do this, Emma."

Emma sighed. "All right. Let's go together, then."

Annie shook her head. "No. It would be better if we split up. We can cover more of the party if we aren't together." Annie felt the blood rush back into her limbs, along with her determination.

"Fine. I'll go this way—" Emma took off before Annie could say anything more.

Annie headed in the opposite direction. She weaved in and out of little groups, trying to smile as she slid past people. Many made eye contact with her, as if they wished to speak to her. She hated to appear rude, but she had to set things right for Miss Brady. God only knew what she had been going through. All because of her.

To her relief, she spotted the doctor talking to Mrs. Langtry and Oscar Wilde, of all people. She tried not to appear rushed as she glided over to them. Her eyes went immediately to the orange ribbon he had pinned to his lapel. She thought it a very unorthodox accessory.

"Miss Oakley!" Oscar Wilde beamed. "Your greeting the princess was highly entertaining. I'm sure you made her feel the belle of the ball."

"Bertie was none too pleased, but I admire your spunk," said Mrs. Langtry. "He's a man who needs to be kept on his toes."

"Which you manage to do quite well, my lovely, I must say." Mr. Wilde held his champagne glass up to Mrs. Langtry in a toast. She burst into a hearty laugh.

Annie bit her lip. She would love to tell Mrs. Langtry how she felt about the situation between her and "Bertie" but she had other pressing matters to attend to.

"Dr. Adams, may I speak with you, please?" Annie directed her gaze at the doctor.

Dr. Adams bowed to Mr. Wilde and Mrs. Langtry. The two raised their brows at Annie's request and walked away, but she refused to let their flippancy bother her.

She swallowed hard, not knowing how to begin with the doctor.

"That is a lovely ribbon, Dr. Adams."

He glanced down at his lapel. "Yes. Thank you. In remembrance of my late mother. It is the anniversary of her death today."

"Oh, I'm terribly sorry for your loss."

"Wonderful woman, my mother."

"Yes, you've told me. May she rest in peace. Dr. Adams, I have to know, who alerted the queen about the death of Mr. Bhakta? I'm sure she was quite distressed."

"I don't know. The captain sent word before we arrived in London."

"What became of Miss Brady?"

"The police came aboard when we docked. After all the passengers disembarked, they took Miss Brady away. It is my understanding she was sent to the Middlesex County Asylum at Hanwell."

"Asylum?"

"Yes. For the mentally disturbed. I am sure she is being adequately taken care of. Why do you ask?" Dr. Adams focused on Annie with rapt interest.

Annie could barely make the words come out of her mouth.

"She didn't kill Mr. Bhakta."

"How do you mean?"

Annie told him about the note she'd just received, with the continuation of Blake's poem, "The Marriage of Heaven and Hell."

"So, you see," Annie continued, "not only have I accused the wrong person of the crime, but the murderer is still at large, and the queen's life is still in danger. We must get word to the queen's security people. And we must get Miss Brady out of that asylum."

"Excuse me." Mr. Wilde appeared again. He peered around the doctor's shoulder, smiling. "I couldn't help but overhear. You say our beloved queen's life is in danger?"

Annie took in a shaky breath. She hadn't meant for anyone else to hear.

"It appears so, from what Miss Oakley just told me," said the doctor.

"What makes you believe this is true, Miss Oakley?" Mr. Wilde asked. Mrs. Langtry rejoined them, and leaned into Mr. Wilde's arm.

"What's this? Old Vic in danger?" she asked.

Annie wasn't sure what to say. It could be a disaster if too many people knew what had occurred on the ship. She didn't know how to reply. Before she could think of anything, the doctor began recounting the story. When he finished, Mr. Wilde addressed Mrs. Langtry.

"J. L., did you know this Indian servant, Mr. Bhakta?" Mr. Wilde asked.

"I've seen several Indian servants at the queen's beck and call. She's grown quite fond of their people. I usually do not move in the same circles as the royal family, well, for obvious reasons, so I don't know the gentleman you are referring to." She smiled prettily at the doctor, who seemed enchanted with her.

From the corner of her eye, Annie saw Lillie on one of the sofas speaking to a man in uniform, leaning in so close to him that she was nearly resting in his lap. Lillie had said she would look for Hulda, but Hulda was nowhere to be seen. Panic gripped Annie's heart. Where was her little sister? If someone had taken the time to send the threatening note to Annie, it could mean Hulda was in danger too. At this point, Annie couldn't be too careful.

"Dr. Adams, Mrs. Langtry, Mr. Wilde, I must go. I have to find my sister. She was upset with me and ran off. She is very young and new to all of this—this—"

"Miss Oakley, you are distressed." Dr. Adams placed his hand on

Annie's shoulder. "I think you should find your sister, go back to Earl's Court, and get some rest. I'm sure you haven't recovered from your journey yet. I hope your husband is doing better."

The lightheaded feeling returned. She wanted to scream that no, Frank was not better; in fact, he was worse; her sister had left the party upset and unchaperoned; and she, herself, had committed a grievous error resulting in the false institutionalization of an innocent woman—*and* she could be responsible for an assassination attempt on the queen.

"He's not well. I—I must go. Please see if you can alert someone about the queen." Annie's head pounded, and her insides churned. Dear God, what had she eaten? When was the last time she ate? The room grew hot and her corset tighter by the moment. Perspiration dampened her palms and armpits. It suddenly occurred to her that Dr. Adams's English accent had returned. The Irish brogue she had heard bellowing in anger down the hallway before had vanished.

"Miss Oakley, you look quite pale; please sit down." Dr. Adams grabbed hold of her arm and led her to a salon chaise.

"I really must go," Annie protested. "I need to find my sister—to see that she is all right."

"You need to sit right here until you are recovered." The doctor helped her to sit and then took her wrist and placed his fingers on her pulse.

She studied his face, deciding if she wanted him to see Frank again. Given what she'd heard earlier—his Irish brogue—she didn't know whether to trust him.

"Are you feeling warm?" he asked.

"Yes. It's just the corset. I'm not used to it."

Oscar Wilde came forward with a glass of water and handed it to

Annie. She thanked him and gulped it down. Mrs. Langtry knelt down next to her and patted her brow with a monogrammed lace handkerchief. She was so close that Annie could see the tiny pores in her powdered, perfectly alabaster skin and the brown flecks in her violet eyes. No wonder the prince had fallen for her. Annie thought her the most beautiful woman in the world.

But it still didn't excuse adultery.

"All this fuss," Annie said, suddenly embarrassed at her racing thoughts and all the attention. "Really, I'm fine. Just a bit overwrought." The crush of everyone made the room seem warmer and the air thicker. All she wanted to do was to go outside and get some fresh air. How she wished she ridden Buck here. A night ride in the cool breeze always cured whatever ailed her.

"There you are, you found him." Emma's voice pierced through the crowd, and, like the words of Ali Baba summoning the cave to open, Mr. Wilde and Mrs. Langtry stepped away, allowing Emma into their circle. At the sight of Annie, the brightness of her eyes dimmed with concern.

"Oh, my dear. What's happened?" Emma knelt down next to her.

"Nothing, Emma. I'm fine. I just want to find Hulda and go home."

"Of course, of course." Emma sat next to her and took her hand.

"Pulse normal." Dr. Adams let go of her wrist. "A good night's rest will help, although I'd like to examine you in the morning. I'd also like to check in on your husband."

As much as she wanted to protest, she probably shouldn't, given Frank's condition. She hadn't had time to solicit the services of another doctor.

"Fine. Tomorrow. But now, we must find Hulda." Annie stood, the wobbly feeling in her legs gone. "Come on, Emma. Goodnight and thank you for your kindness." Annie took Emma's hand and then linked arms with her. They made a circuit of the grand room twice, looked down hallways and out three sets of French doors that led to terraces.

"Where could she be?" Annie fought the dizziness that threatened to consume her again. "I never should have scolded her. I never should have argued with her."

Emma stopped, forcing Annie to stop.

"Annie, she's probably found a way back to camp. She certainly isn't here anymore. We need to get back, and you need to get into bed. I've never seen you look so fatigued."

Annie shut out Emma's words. She couldn't be sick. Not now.

They would go back to the camp and find Hulda asleep in her tent and Frank resting comfortably, she told herself. Tomorrow, she would set everything straight. She would write to Mrs. Langtry and implore her to get word to the queen through the prince of the impending assassination threat. She only hoped it wouldn't be too late.

With the help of Oscar Wilde and Dr. Adams, Annie and Emma retrieved a coach and made it back to Earl's Court without issue.

They pulled up to the entrance to the Wild West Show camp and found Bobby standing there, as if waiting for them. Annie didn't wait for the driver of the coach to open the door for her, but instead pulled the handle herself and climbed down the stairs.

"Bobby, have you seen Hulda?"

"Yes, Annie. She's all right. Lillie put her in a coach and sent her back here. I was gathering wood for a fire when the coach pulled up. She's had a little too much to drink. She was awful sick, but I cleaned her up and put her to bed. She's going to feel mighty bad in the morning."

"Oh, thank God! Wait—drinking? Alcohol?"

Emma came up behind her. "It's not then end of the world, Annie. If she was that sick, she probably won't do it again, at least not in the near future."

"Emma, we believe in temperance." Annie couldn't hide her annoyance at the situation. "Our bodies are temples of the holy spirit."

Emma put her hands up in surrender.

"Don't come down on her too hard, Annie," Bobby said. "I think she's terribly homesick." His eyes implored hers. Annie hadn't thought of that. Annie loved being on the road, traveling the world, meeting new people. That didn't mean Hulda felt the same way.

"I won't be harsh with her, Bobby," Annie said, trying to calm herself. "Thank you for taking care of her. You are a gem of a friend."

"Aw, Annie, you know I'd do anything for you," Bobby said, a smile splitting his face.

"Yes. I do. You remind me all the time."

"Well, I'm calling it a night," said Emma. "Are you feeling better, Annie?"

"Yes. Go to bed. I'm going to check on Hulda and then go to bed myself." She kissed Emma's cheek and then Bobby's, all the while reciting a quiet prayer of gratitude for such honorable friends.

Chapter Nineteen

Early the next morning, nausea woke Annie. She looked over at Frank, who lay quietly, beads of perspiration dotting his forehead. He still had a fever. Could she have contracted whatever ailed Frank? She had assumed her nausea on the ship had been due to a mild case of seasickness.

She pressed her palms to her cheeks. They felt flushed and warm, but she passed it off as overheating from the piles of blankets they had on the bed. She reasoned with herself that she didn't feel feverish, but the churning of her stomach drove her to get up. She could no longer lie there and feel that way.

She went to her vanity, dipped her hands into the ewer of cold water, and splashed it on her face. Looking into the mirror, she curled her lip at her wild hair and the pink flush of her cheeks.

Dressing as quietly as she could, Annie tiptoed out of the tent and made her way over to Hulda's tent. Her sister lay sleeping under the blankets. She hadn't seemed to move since Annie had checked on her the night before. Her boots, wrap, and handbag lay on the floor.

"Hulda." Annie shook her sister's shoulder. "Wake up."

Hulda squinted, opening her eyes to small slits. "Oh, my head. Go away, Annie."

"Get up, Hulda. I'll not let you lie in bed all day. You need to get moving. You'll feel better."

Hulda rolled over on her side, her back to Annie. Annie could see she still wore her clothes from the previous night.

"How would you know?" Hulda asked.

"I've taken care of Lillie after a drunken night out, many times. You need to get up."

"I feel terrible, Annie. I'm sick. I can't."

"The exhibition opens in two days, and we have our first performance." Annie grabbed Hulda's blankets and dragged them onto the floor. "Do you have Lillie's and my costumes finished? No, I didn't think so," she said before Hulda could answer. "Drinking alcohol is a sin, Hulda. Your body is a temple, a gift from God. You will not sit here all day nursing a headache that you yourself caused. Now, get up and get moving. I'll be back in a few minutes. I need to send for Dr. Adams." He'd been so helpful and kind to her last night, and since Frank still hadn't improved, she felt a visit from Dr. Adams would be a good thing.

Hulda flopped over onto her back, her face stricken with panic.

"I don't need to see the doctor, I'm fine."

"Good, then get up. The doctor is for Frank, and—"

"And?"

"I have a few questions for him. Nothing you need to concern yourself with. Now, out of bed and get dressed. I'll be back in a few minutes, and we can go to the dining tent together. What you need is a good, solid breakfast."

Hulda groaned and turned back onto her side, curling her knees up to her chest.

Although furious at her sister, Annie didn't want to concern Hulda with any of her own health issues. The girl had enough to deal with.

She looked at her sister's small body in the bed, her dress twisted around her waist, and suddenly, Annie felt the weight of responsibility and regret. Hulda had the talent for her job, but Annie now recognized her little sister did not have the maturity to handle life on the road with the Wild West Show. Hulda had always been protected from the world, unlike Annie, who had been forced to be an adult way before her time. Adjusting to life on the road had been difficult for Annie at first, but having been farmed out as a young child to help support the family and having lived under the abuse and neglect of the McCrimmons had made her tough, although she knew in her heart she'd been given the gift of resilience by God.

Hulda, although bestowed with many other gifts, didn't have the mental and emotional capacity to deal with a life full of change and upheaval. Or with people who had different cultural beliefs, lifestyles, and extravagances. People who might take advantage of a young, innocent girl.

Annie would have to be much more vigilant and attentive to Hulda. With the killer still on the loose, and with Annie as his prime conduit of communication, they were all in danger. She had to protect her sister.

"I mean it, Hulda. I'll be back in a few minutes."

Without turning over, Hulda flapped her arm at Annie, who pinched her sister's little toes. "Up!"

Annie went back to her tent and found Frank awake and sitting up in bed. The collar of his night shirt was stained with sweat. She rushed over to him.

"Why are you sitting up? Lie back down, Frank. You don't look well."

Frank lifted the covers and swung his legs out of bed. "I can't lie here anymore. I want to get dressed. I'll sit in a chair. I just don't want to be in bed anymore."

Annie knew incapacitation had been hard on Frank. As her manager, he made sure she had everything she needed to perform her best. As her husband, he made sure she had everything she wanted to be her best self.

"I'll help you dress, and then I'm going to call for Dr. Adams." Annie tried to sound chipper, but Frank's illness was wearing on her. Since she'd met him, he'd been her rock, her protector, her buffer against the harshness of life and the feeling of vulnerability that came with fame. She'd come to rely on his strength. It had been so wonderful to lean on someone after having to carry the burden of her family. Now, the tables had turned, and Frank needed her to be strong for him. Her one refuge, her safe place, and the sense of balance Frank brought her were teetering on the brink.

She took in a deep breath, prayed for continued strength, and helped Frank to dress. Afterwards, she led him to the rocker and placed an afghan over his knees.

"This is intolerable," Frank said. "You are running yourself ragged taking care of me and your sister and going to parties. Have you even had time to practice?"

"Mr. Salisbury hasn't called for practice yet. But don't you worry—Buck and I run like a well-oiled machine. You know that."

"I do. I feel as if I'm fading away." Frank pinched the bridge of his nose, closing his eyes. It was the first time he showed any kind of emotional weakness since he'd become ill.

"Don't talk so, Frank. I need you. I need you to be well. We'll find the answer to this illness. I know it." She had to believe her own words. Life without Frank would be unbearable.

With renewed vigor in her voice, Annie told him she would bring him some breakfast and then went to fetch Hulda, who, to Annie's surprise, was out of bed, dressed, and working on her hair at the vanity.

"I'm not hungry. I still feel awful," Hulda said.

Annie had to admit Hulda's complexion had taken on an ashen green hue.

"I know, but some good, strong tea and toast, at least, will fill your stomach." Annie hoped that some sustenance would make her feel better as well. She fought to keep her own stomach from spasming. "And Hulda, please don't ever leave like that without telling me first. We are in a strange country, unfamiliar to us both. I worry about you and don't want anything bad to happen to you."

Again, to Annie's surprise, Hulda didn't argue, but got up from the vanity, put her arms around Annie's waist, and hugged her tight.

"I don't ever want to feel like this again, Annie. I'm sorry for having worried you. I promise I'll behave from now on."

Annie wrapped her arms around her sister's bony shoulders and pulled her close.

"We have to stick together, Hulda—you, me, and Frank." Annie couldn't keep the waver out of her voice. "Not everyone shares our Christian values, and there are people in this world who wish us and others harm. Don't forget what happened to Mr. Bhakta." Annie's stomach sank, remembering she'd accused poor Miss Brady of the terrible crime. She had so much to set right, and on top of everything else, she bore the responsibility of knowing someone was out to kill the queen. Someone who wished to directly involve her, which meant she wasn't safe, nor Hulda, nor Frank. All this, and their tour hadn't even begun yet.

The two of them walked over to the dining tent. Despite her protests, Hulda ate a hearty serving of eggs, bacon, and toast. Annie could see the usual rosiness of her cheeks reappear.

Annie silently choked down a couple of dry toast points and a cup of Earl Grey tea, which settled her stomach, but she didn't dare eat more for fear it would only come up again.

She sent Hulda back to her tent to work on the costumes and then went in search of Mr. Salisbury, the show manager. She found him in his tent, seated behind his desk, with the colonel sitting in a chair across from him, his thigh-high beaded and embroidered boots resting on the corner of the desk.

"Annie, good morning." Mr. Salisbury stood up from his chair, but the colonel didn't move.

"Good morning, Mr. Salisbury, Colonel."

"What can we do for you, this morning?" The colonel took his hat off his head and swiped a hand over his long, wavy hair.

"I'm afraid I have some bad news."

"What's this?"

"Last night at the party, I received an anonymous note with a continuation of Blake's poem written on it. I'm afraid Mr. Bhakta's killer is still at large. Miss Brady was not at fault."

"Are you certain? Could this have been a joke, albeit in poor taste?" asked the colonel.

"The only people who knew of the note were me, Emma, Frank, Dr. Adams, Mr. Patel, and the two of you. I'm sure none of us would think that was funny."

"But why send the note to you?"

"I don't know. But it makes me ill at ease."

"We should call the police," said Mr. Salisbury.

"Yes, I think we should," Annie agreed. "And we need to see about getting Miss Brady out of the asylum she's been sent to. It's my fault. I take full responsibility." Annie swallowed the bile that rose in her throat. She wished her stomachache would go away.

"The girl was hardly stable, Annie." The colonel said, in an obvious attempt to make her feel better.

"Maybe not. But she isn't our killer, and that is why she's in the asylum. I need to make this right, Colonel."

"Well, then, let's get the police out here." The colonel stood, towering over Annie. "I'd like to get this situation rectified before we start our performances. I don't want any of this mess getting in the way of entertaining these fine ladies and gentlemen. It's an honor for us to be here, and I don't want the taint of any murder scandal following us around."

"Do you know if the queen plans to attend?" Annie asked.

"Word has it Her Majesty rarely makes public appearances anymore," Nate Salisbury said.

Annie let out her breath. "Good. I am worried about her safety."

"We will tell the police everything," the colonel said.

"There is one more thing." Annie placed a hand on her stomach, trying to hold down the sickness that threatened to overwhelm her. "I'd like to have Dr.—" Annie hesitated. "Colonel, is Dr. Adams English or Irish?" Annie asked.

The colonel and Mr. Salisbury exchanged glances.

"English as far as I know. Looks like an Englishman, walks like an

Englishman, talks like an Englishmen. Why do you ask?" said the colonel.

"That's just it," Annie said, stepping closer to the two men. "Last night, I heard him in an altercation of sorts with another man, and he was speaking with an Irish accent."

Mr. Salisbury let out a chuckle. "Why would he do that?"

"I don't know. I thought it very strange."

The colonel sat down and leaned his elbow against his knee.

"You've not traveled abroad before, my dear. With all due respect, how would you know an English accent from an Irish one? I think you might be confused."

"Colonel," Annie said, keeping her irritation at his condescending tone at bay, "have you forgotten? Frank is Irish. His accent is all but gone, but he still has a certain lilt to his speech that I heard in Dr. Adams's voice. I know an Irish accent when I hear one."

"What are you getting at, Annie?" Mr. Salisbury asked.

"Can we trust him?"

"I don't see why not. He's been caring for Frank for three weeks now," said the colonel.

"Yes, but Frank seems to be getting worse."

"And you think the doctor might be responsible?" the colonel asked.

"I'm not saying that. All I'm saying is, I think the doctor is not who he says he is."

"I don't think we can make judgments about people based upon how they talk," said the colonel. "I've dealt with the man and think he is a fine doctor. I think you might be a little distressed about Frank, and perhaps it's clouding your thinking."

"Perhaps you are right." Annie's stomach lurched again, and she remembered why she had come in the first place, to ask to see a doctor. Keeping Dr. Adams close would give her an opportunity to explore the nagging feeling she had about him. Especially now, since Miss Brady was clearly innocent. She'd been wrong about her, and was probably wrong about the doctor. She didn't want to make the same mistake twice.

"Could you please see that he comes to examine Frank, again? He said he would check in, but I want to make sure he comes," she said.

"I'll get right on it, Annie." Mr. Salisbury said. "I'll have a message sent to him right away."

"Thank you." Annie turned to leave. "And please send the police to my tent as well, the moment they arrive."

~

Annie handed Frank one of the bowls of broth she'd retrieved from the dining tent after leaving Mr. Salisbury. She set her own on the nightstand and sat down on the bed next to Frank. His clothes were spread across the covers, and he had put his nightshirt back on.

"Sitting in the chair didn't last long," she said, smoothing his sandy blond hair away from his eyes.

Frank shook his head. "Nothing I do makes me feel better."

"Here." She lifted the spoon from his bowl and held it to his mouth. "Take some soup."

Frank was able to drain the bowl, and then he settled under the covers and fell asleep. Annie forced herself to drink her broth, and when she'd finished half of it, Dr. Adams announced himself at the entrance of their tent. Annie stood and walked to the opening, pulling the tent flap back for him to enter. She was surprised to see Mr. Everett standing there. Dr. Adams stood behind him.

"Mr. Everett! How are you?"

"Miss Oakley. It's good to see you. How is your sister?" Mr. Everett removed his hat and looked at Annie expectantly.

"She is well, thank you. Quite busy with the show starting in a few days." She hoped she would dissuade him from seeking out Hulda.

"I ran into him while he was checking the horses." Dr. Adams slapped Mr. Everett on the shoulder. "I decided to bring him along to see Frank. I don't know if he told you, but before becoming a veterinarian, he was a physician. I wanted his assessment of Mr. Butler's situation." His gaze travelled to Frank, who lay sleeping. "So tell me, how is Mr. Butler feeling?"

"The same, I'm afraid, if not worse," said Annie. "He was able to drink some soup and keep it down, though." She felt encouraged about Dr. Adams by the fact that he brought Mr. Everett along for his opinion. If he had nefarious motives, why would he do such a thing?

"How long has he felt this way?" Mr. Everett asked.

"Since before we got off the ship. The vomiting has gotten worse. He seems very weak," Annie said, looking over at Frank, her heart heavy with worry.

Frank opened his eyes and blinked, surprised to see them standing over the bed. The doctors greeted him and repeated the question.

"She's right, since the voyage," said Frank.

"Did you feel this way before going overboard?" Mr. Everett asked.

"I felt a little seasick, but didn't have this bone-crushing malaise. I feel I hardly have the energy to move."

"Why do you ask, Mr. Everett?" Dr. Adams asked.

"I can't be certain, but this reminds me of an incident that took place in my family years ago. One of my ancestors, a sailor, on an expedition of the central Pacific coast in 1793, suffered similar symptoms after eating mussels. I've done some research into this, and we still don't know what caused the illness, but when Buck and Mr. Butler were in the water, Miss Oakley mentioned the water looked red. I later remembered the story. The captain recorded in his log that the water surrounding them had a curious red hue. Several of the crew came down with the same symptoms exhibited by Mr. Butler. Others' limbs became paralyzed.

"Could the mussels have been tainted?" Annie asked.

"I can't be certain, but I believe a bloom of algae created a poison, infecting the mussels. I've observed that when plankton grows rapidly, its massive numbers turn the water a reddish color."

Annie inhaled sharply. "I thought Buck had cut himself while jumping overboard."

"But I haven't eaten mussels, ever." Frank pulled his body up to rest his back on the headboard. Annie rushed over and fluffed the pillows behind him.

"But you were submerged in the water," Mr. Everett said. "You could have ingested some."

Annie suddenly had a sinking feeling in her stomach, which did nothing to make it feel better. "Mr. Everett, I, too, plunged into the water. Buck was there as well, and he hasn't been ill either."

"Horses may not be affected like humans. And, perhaps you did not ingest as much water, or any at all."

"You haven't felt well of late, dear," Frank said. "You try to hide it from me, but I can see it in your face."

"If Miss Oakley had this malady, I think she would be much more ill, exhibiting the same symptoms as you."

"I have felt like vomiting, but haven't so far," Annie admitted.

"I've been watching you, Miss Oakley. I have a feeling your symptoms might be indicative of something else entirely," Dr. Adams said with a smile. "And I think Mr. Everett might be of help."

Confused, Annie looked up at both of them with a frown on her face.

"How can Mr. Everett help?" she asked. She hoped she didn't sound rude, but what could he possibly do to help with her nausea.

"He has access to rabbits," said Dr. Adams, laughing.

"I don't get your meaning, Doctor." Annie had already tired of this game, and of the expression on Dr. Adams face.

"I'm joking Miss Oakley. What I'm saying is you might be with child."

The room blurred, and a deep, deafening hum filled Annie's ears. She stared at the two doctors, their faces beaming. Her chest caved in on her, pressing all the air out of her lungs. Time slowed, and the steady beat of Annie's own heartbeat filled her ears. She felt as if she were swimming through a cascade of water, pelting her with its weight. She could barely move, and slowly she turned to Frank, who stared at her with fevered but dancing eyes.

With child. Pregnant. Responsible for the life of another human being. It can't be true. It mustn't be true.

"Miss Oakley?" She heard Dr. Adams's voice, thick and drawn out, as if he were under water. Her heart beat faster, and her limbs began to shake. She had to get out of here, away from these men, away from her own dread. She stood and fled from the tent.

Chapter Twenty

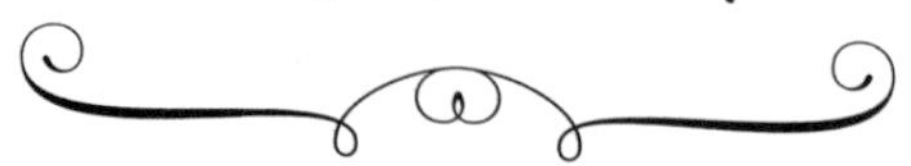

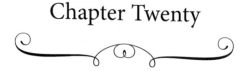

Annie ran as fast as she could past the tents, past the large exhibition building, and toward the stables. She ran through the barn and out to the open pens where Buck stood, his nose buried in a pile of fresh, green hay. She climbed the fence and landed on the ground with a thud, making Buck look up from his meal.

Annie approached him softly and wrapped her arms around his neck. She leaned her chest into his muscled shoulder and buried her face in his mane. Buck turned his head to look back at her and wrapped his neck around her body, his nose nuzzling her lower back.

It couldn't be true. She couldn't be pregnant. She didn't want to be pregnant.

And that was a sin.

What a hypocrite she had been. Preaching to her sister about living by their beliefs. A child is God's greatest gift to a couple. But Annie didn't want that gift. She didn't want the burden. She wanted to be free.

Buck nickered, the sound coming low from his throat.

"I can't think about this right now, Buck. I have to make up for the horrible mistake I made in accusing Becky Brady of murder. I have to find a way to protect the queen from an assassination attempt. I have to help my husband become whole again. I have to provide guidance for my sister. I have a career." She dug her fingers into Buck's thick black mane and made a fist around the course hair. "I don't have time for a baby." Annie swallowed down her anger, released Buck's mane and stroked his long golden neck.

She had barely been able to keep an eye on Hulda who, at thirteen, was relatively self-sufficient. How was she supposed to raise a child who would be dependent on her for everything?

Dr. Adams said pregnancy was a possibility, not assured. He didn't know anything for sure. He didn't even know what was wrong with her husband. Mr. Everett knew more about what could be causing Frank's illness than Dr. Adams, and he was a veterinarian, for God's sake!

And then there was the business of the fake English accent. She thought she could definitely hear the lilt of Irish in his voice. He obviously didn't want people to know he was Irish, and why was that? Maybe he had been or was still involved in the Fenian movement that was so violently opposed to the position of the Crown.

His appointment as the ship's doctor gave him access to the Wild West Show, which would give him access to the queen. He said he didn't have enough snake venom on board the ship to kill, but could he have lied?

Annie inhaled a deep breath and let it out, trying to center herself, trying to figure out what to do next. First, she needed to go back to her husband. She shouldn't have run away like a spoiled child. Right now, he needed her.

She let go of Buck and he lowered his head to continue eating while Annie gathered her thoughts.

"Miss Oakley?" A sturdy man with a hawkish nose approached Buck's stall. His tweed suit and wool overcoat seemed a size too small as the buttons of the waistcoat strained against the width of his belly. The hem of his pants hung well above his ankles. A diminutive, uniformed police officer stood next to him, small notebook in hand. "I'm Inspector Grange, and this is Constable Markus. I've just spoken with Colonel Buffalo Bill Cody concerning the murder on board the S.S. *Nebraska*. We met your husband when we went to your tent, and he gave us the vial that contained the viper poison, and the notes you received on the ship and at the recent party. We have been and will continue to question all those who were on board. Do you have any other information for us?"

"I don't think so, Inspector, but I believe Miss Brady to be innocent."

"Is there anything other information you can give us? Anything at all?" he asked, ignoring her assertion.

Annie thought about mentioning her suspicions about the doctor, but she had no reason to do so. Faking an English accent seemed hardly criminal. She needed to have more to go on before accusing yet another person of a crime.

"No."

The Inspector handed Annie a calling card. "Please let Colonel Cody know you'd like to see me if you can think of anything else. Rest assured, we will take all precautions—alert the queen's guards."

Annie took the proffered card. "Thank you, Inspector."

The man tipped his hat and turned to go, but he hesitated and then turned back to face her again.

"And Miss Oakley?"

"Yes, Inspector?"

"We are thrilled that the Wild West Show has come to England. Everyone is so fascinated by the Wild West of America. I've heard that you are very good at what you do—and so am I. Why don't you do your job of riding your fine horse, shooting clay pigeons and glass balls, and leave the detective work to the professionals, would you? We don't need any more mistakes."

Although embarrassed and remorseful about accusing Miss Brady, Annie felt some sense of relief knowing the police had more information. With any luck, they would find the murderer of Mr. Bhakta soon and prevent an attack on the queen. Then she, Frank, and Hulda would be safe.

Still stinging from the Inspector's reproach, Annie took her time heading back to her tent. She didn't want to burden Frank with her emotional ups and downs, her self-doubt and self-loathing. She had behaved like a child, running away at the news of a possible pregnancy. She should be overjoyed, but as much as she tried to look at the situation in a positive light, all she could see was darkness. She had never considered that she would marry, much less have children.

As she neared her tent, Bobby approached at a fast clip.

"The colonel and Mr. Salisbury are calling a practice in thirty minutes. Can you be ready?"

"It's rather short notice, but yes, I can be there." She had never missed a practice, and as much as she wanted to make a visit to the asylum to see Miss Brady and Miss Parnell, her job took precedence.

"I'll tell Mr. Post to get Buck ready." Bobby jogged away from her toward the stables.

Standing at the entrance to her tent, Annie took in a deep breath and then let it out, forcing all of the negative thoughts from her mind. She had to be strong for Frank.

After a few minutes of deep breathing, she stuck her head back into the tent. Both Dr. Adams and Mr. Everett had gone.

"Annie. Are you all right?" Frank was still sitting upright in bed.

"Yes, I am, darling. I'm sorry I ran out like that." Annie walked over to the bed and kissed his forehead. It didn't feel as hot as it had before, to her relief. She sat down on the bed next to him.

"Dr. Adams says it's normal for a woman to be overwhelmed by the idea of pregnancy. Especially the first one." Frank took her hand. She noticed a spark in his eyes that she had not seen in weeks. Annie shook her head.

"I'm not pregnant, Frank. Don't you think I would know if I was?"

"But—"

"Dr. Adams said there was a *possibility* of pregnancy."

"Yes. That is why he wants to examine you." Frank's grip tightened on her hand.

How could she tell him she didn't want this? She couldn't bear the conflicting emotions surging through her. She wanted Frank to be better, but she didn't want to be pregnant. At least, not now.

She stood up. "Well, I have other matters to tend to first. Like taking care of you, and I have practice in thirty minutes. What did the doctors suggest?"

Frank's face fell a little. "He gave me this." He held up a dark brown vial. "Said it was a tisane. It's making me pretty sleepy. But before I nod off, we should talk about the possibility of your being pregnant. You'll have to slow down. We should inform the colonel and Nate."

"No, Frank." Annie dropped his hand and immediately regretted the bite in her voice. "We must wait and see before telling anyone anything. Promise me you'll keep quiet about this until we know for sure."

"But you must be examined."

"Not now. I have too much to do." She wished he would stop pressing. Her head felt like it would explode.

"Annie, please." Frank's eyes implored her with such sincerity and concern that she could feel her resolve melting.

"I will, Frank. Just not today, besides, Dr. Adams has left already."

"He said he would be back later today. And Annie, the police came by, too."

"They found me. Frank, please rest. I'll be back in a few hours. Do you need anything?"

"No." She knew he was disappointed in her attitude toward the possible pregnancy. She could tell from his expression the moment Dr. Adams mentioned it that Frank was delighted with the idea. Of course he would be. It would have no effect on his daily life, his aspirations, or his dreams. Only hers.

She kissed him on the forehead and pulled the covers up around his neck. He closed his eyes as if shutting her out. A fissure of regret cracked the edge of Annie's heart, but she ignored it and walked away from him, determined not to let his disappointment fracture her determination.

~

The minute Annie got into the saddle, all her thoughts and worries vanished. It felt so good to be riding again. She trotted Buck around the arena to warm up his joints and muscles. When he began to canter, Annie knew he had loosened up. She melted into the saddle, feeling Buck's energy, and let him run.

Once Lillie and Bobby arrived—Bobby on a new sorrel horse the colonel had given him—the crew set up the mounted course. Annie pulled Buck to a stop next to Lillie, who sat on the fence railing smoking, her rifle in her lap. They watched Bobby and his horse start the course.

"Buck looks good," Lillie said. Compliments from Lillie were few and far between, and they always made Annie suspicious.

"He feels good. Much better than I thought, given the situation on the ship." Annie adjusted the pistols more squarely on her hips and checked her rifle in the scabbard that lay flat against Buck's side, beneath her leg.

"You on the other hand, don't look so good. You look tired." There it was—Lillie's one- two-punch.

"I have a lot on my mind."

A whistle pierced the air, and Annie turned to see Mr. Salisbury waving her onto the mounted course. She steered Buck to the fence railing on the other side of Lillie and urged him into a canter. She shifted her torso to the right, pulled one of her pistols, and turned Buck onto the course. Their bodies moved in perfect unison they weaved through the first stage of the course while she successfully shot each of the tripod-mounted colored glass balls into sparkling confetti.

Buck knew the routine of the course, making Annie's job a lot easier. Still at a canter, Annie holstered her pistol and laid the reins on Buck's neck while he veered toward the second stage of the course. She pulled her rifle from its scabbard and continued steering Buck with her hips, shooting all her targets with ease.

For the final stage, Annie took Buck wide, while securing her rifle and taking out both pistols. Buck turned and gathered speed as they thundered between the straight line of tripods. Annie shot the targets on either side of her with both pistols at the same time. While she secured her pistols back into her holsters, Buck came to a stop and reared into the air—their grand finale.

"Good boy!" Annie said as he came down. She leaned over his mane and wrapped her arms around his neck.

Mr. Post was at her side in seconds to take Buck. Annie strode over to Lillie and Bobby and they took turns shooting metal targets with rifles and pistols. To Annie's dismay, Lillie outshot her, ten targets to seven—something that rarely ever happened.

"Wonder what the people of England will think of that, Miss Oakley." Lillie rested her rifle on her shoulder, a smug smile on her face.

"It's only practice, Lillie," Annie said, trying to sound as if her defeat didn't sink into her pride with the sharpness of a knife.

"Nice work, everyone," said Mr. Salisbury. "Annie, better luck next time."

Annie forced a smile and strode away from the arena. She remembered Emma's words when they had first boarded the ship about Lillie's skills improving. As much as it rankled her, she knew it would be good for the show to have the performers exhibiting healthy competition. She just wished Lillie didn't act so self-righteous about it.

She heard her mother's voice echo in her head. "We are all equals in God's eyes." She repeated the mantra, letting it soothe her wounded pride.

"It was only practice," she repeated to herself. "Pride is a sin . . . the truly humble people are not affected by praise or criticism because they know who they are."

Annie knew who she was, and she knew when she needed to make things right. And she needed to make things right with Becky Brady.

Annie stepped out of her tent, intending to make her way toward Emma's in hopes her friend could accompany her to the asylum. She imagined it would be a horrible place to visit, and she didn't want to go there alone. Asking Hulda or Lillie was completely out of the question. Emma would give her the strength she needed to face the asylum, and the reporter also knew how to pull strings to get in. Annie hoped together they could convince the doctors that Miss Brady might need special care, but that her mother was entirely capable of providing that care.

As she set her buttoned boot outside her tent and ducked through the tent flap, she almost ran headlong into Gail Tessen. The woman still wore the same tattered red coat, but her unruly hair was fixed neatly into a bun under a fetching maroon hat. She wore what looked like men's trousers.

"I am ready to be put to work at the stables," she said, smiling at Annie for the first time.

Annie's heart plummeted to her still aching stomach. "Oh, Miss Tessen, I am so sorry. I haven't been able to talk to the colonel or Nate Salisbury about your employment yet."

Miss Tessen's face fell. "Oh. I see."

Her expression tugged at Annie's compassion, but she really didn't have time to deal with this at the moment. She hadn't wanted anyone else to care for Buck, but the woman seemed quite harmless—and Annie had a million other things to do before the performance.

"I'll tell you what. I need someone to clean and oil my tack. I will also talk to Mr. Post about you assisting him as Buck's groom. I can pay you for today, and then I'll speak to the colonel. I promise."

Miss Tessen's face brightened. "Thank you, Miss Oakley. I'll be able to afford my dinner tonight, and maybe find a room to let."

"You still have nowhere to stay?" Annie asked.

Miss Tessen shook her head. "Found some shelter on the street."

Annie made up her mind. "You will eat here at the camp tonight and I will see that you have proper lodgings. You can stay with my sister. I'm sure she won't mind." Annie smiled, pleased with herself at helping Miss Tessen, and perhaps thwarting Lillie's tendency to avail herself of Hulda's tent after a night of drinking. Lillie often complained about the discomfort of her own bed, and more than once, Annie had walked into Hulda's tent to see her poor sister in a nest of blankets on the floor, and Lillie in her bed snoring loudly. Lillie clearly took advantage of Hulda's sweet nature, and it irritated Annie—but then, most things about Lillie irritated Annie.

"Come." Annie reached for Miss Tessen's elbow. "I'll take you to meet Mr. Post and show you where everything is laid out."

Annie led Miss Tessen to the stable and showed her Buck's stall. While Miss Tessen fed Buck one of the apples from a bucket nearby, Annie called out to Mr. Post. She met him several feet from Buck's stall.

"What can I do for you, Annie?" Mr. Post took off his hat and wiped his balding head with a handkerchief.

"That woman over there was on the ship with us. I think she is in a bad way financially. I told her I'd help her find a job at the show while we're here. Could she help you with Buck?"

"We usually don't let strangers around Buck. You sure?"

"Only if you supervise her. I don't want to add to your burden, and if you don't want her, I'll send her away."

"A girl groom? Well, any hand is always welcome. I hope she doesn't have a problem with cleanup," said Mr. Post. "I'll have to clear it with the colonel, but I'm sure he'll give it the go-ahead."

"Thank you, Mr. Post." Annie gave him a peck on the cheek which always made him chuckle.

Annie continued familiarizing Miss Tessen with the stables. She showed her where Mr. Post stowed the rakes and pitchforks, the vast collection of brushes, hoof picks, and rags used for grooming, and the tent where the tack was kept. She also showed Miss Tessen her array of saddles, bridles, and saddle blankets and directed her to the waxy soaps for leather and the polish for the silver accoutrements.

"Mr. Post feeds Buck at around two o'clock in the afternoon, and Buck loves to be brushed while he's eating. Perhaps Mr. Post will let you groom Buck. You won't need the halter or lead line. He basks under the attention. As long as you're grooming him and he's eating, it would take an earthquake to move him." For the first time all morning, Annie's stomach felt calm. She loved talking about Buck as much as he loved food and a good round of brushing.

"This is fine tack." Miss Tessen ran her hands over the leather of the saddles and bridles. "Of the highest quality. I have so missed the smell of good leather. Your saddles and bridles will be gleaming by the time you return, and so will your horse. You have my word. Thank you so much for your kindness, Miss Oakley."

Annie felt her spirits lift at being able to help someone after all that had transpired in the last few days. Perhaps she would be able to make up for her horrible mistakes. The image of a pudgy baby popped up in her mind, but she dismissed it, resigning herself to think about that possibility later.

"Before you do anything, you must always clear it with Mr. Post, understand?"

"Yes, ma'am. Completely."

"I'm off to run an errand. I'll be back in a few hours."

Annie left Miss Tessen happily seated at a stool, scrubbing her silver-trimmed leather reins, with Mr. Post standing over her, pointing out the spots she missed.

Annie headed for one of the coaches that Nate Salisbury had rented for the duration of their stay at Earl's Court. Before she got there, she saw Mr. Patel, his white suit and turban gleaming in the sun, striding toward her.

"Miss Oakley." He waved a piece of paper in front of him.

"Mr. Patel. What brings you here?"

"I have a message for you from the Prince of Wales. He would like you to come by the royal box tomorrow, on your horse, after your performance. He is a great admirer of horses, and his wife wishes to see you again. You made quite an impression at the party." He placed the sealed letter in her hand.

"So Emma told me. I did not mean to offend, Mr. Patel. Sometimes my opinions get me in trouble."

"I believe all is forgiven," Mr. Patel said with his customary bow. Annie smiled, wondering if Mr. Patel had been questioned by the police yet. And if he had, was he on their list of suspects?

Chapter Twenty-One

Annie clutched at her stomach as the coach lurched forward. She hoped Emma, sitting across from her, hadn't noticed. She probably hadn't, as she was busily admiring herself in a small hand mirror.

"I'm sorry the policeman was so condescending. They have mastered the art of that behavior. Trust me, I know. They also paid a visit of admonishment to me." Emma straightened her skirt, smoothed down the lace at her bodice, and pulled at the hem of her gloves.

"He's right, though, Emma. We have no business getting involved in police work."

"Well, a conversation with the police isn't going to stop me. I hope it won't stop you." Emma's eyes were wide with indignation.

"Of course not. I won't be able to rest until we find Mr. Bhakta's killer. I feel responsible for my mistake, and I must make it right."

"Oh, Annie, I do admire your spunk," Emma said, beaming, her eyes shining bright under the pink brim of her enormous hat, trimmed in red and pink roses. Her lips bore a consistent smile that Annie always found endearing, but today, there was no solace in Emma's rosy smile.

Annie stared out the coach window as they passed the perfectly straight row of trees lining the drive of Earl's Court. She found it hard to breathe with the weight of the burden on her chest, and she tried in vain to press down the nausea that made her whole body ache. She hadn't told Emma about her possible pregnancy, and she wouldn't. Not until she knew for sure. The less said about it, the better.

Emma must have sensed Annie's moodiness and busied herself with notebook and pencil. The sound of the lead scratching across the paper soothed Annie, and she was grateful for the silence. Annie closed her eyes, shutting out the thoughts in her head, and focused on breathing through the nausea.

The sound of shouting startled her. She opened her eyes.

"What is going on out there?" Emma said. She had removed her hat and leaned her head out the window.

Annie looked out her window and saw a hoard of people camped around a large statue, tents, pallets, and blankets spread upon the bricks. Men, women, and children sat in groups around crudely build fires and cook stoves, sweaters and coats wrapped around their bodies. A group of men surrounded two others who were engaged in a fist fight, egging them on.

"Where are we?" Annie asked.

"Trafalgar Square." Emma said. "Driver! Stop!"

The coach came to a stop and bounced as the driver jumped down from his seat. He came around to the window, his lanky arms and legs swinging as he walked. He perched his long fingers along the edge of the open window. His whiskered cheeks were sunken below protruding cheekbones. Bushy eyebrows framed his large, round eyes.

"Miss?"

"What's going on here?" Emma asked.

The driver rubbed a finger across his nose. "Bit of civil unrest. Irish, and the poor of London."

"What are they doing here?"

"The English are protesting that they have no work and no money, and the Irish are protesting for the release of one of their blokes who's in jail."

"Who is the man in jail?" Emma jotted something on her pad.

"A representative in the Irish House of Commons, ma'am. Name of Charles Parnell."

Annie and Emma exchanged a glance.

"Guess he caused a ruckus over a coercion act. Was also accused of being involved in a murder. These folks are demanding his release. Been camped here for weeks. The English don't like it none, sharing the space and all, so things get a bit fractious at times. There is at least one riot a week. Keeping the police in business, I'd say."

"Let me out, please, sir. I need to cover this story." Emma stashed her pad of paper and pencil in her reticule.

The driver held up a hand. "I wouldn't advise it, Miss. They're a pretty rambunctious bunch."

"Emma, you can't go out there. It's chaos." Annie grabbed hold of Emma's wrist.

"Annie, these people are protesting Gladstone and the queen. By talking to them, it may shed some light on this proposed attack against Her Majesty." All traces of Emma's persistent smile had faded.

"But this protest could be entirely unrelated."

"True. But we won't know until I find out. Give my best to Miss Brady and Miss Parnell." Emma pushed through Annie's hold on her wrist and nearly knocked the driver down as she forced open the door.

Annie beseeched the driver with wide and indignant eyes to stop Emma, but he simply shrugged his shoulders and walked back toward his perch on the driver's seat of the coach.

Annie slammed her back against the velvet seat of the coach in frustration and immediately regretted it as her stomach lurched again. She should know better than to try to convince Emma of anything. The woman was as headstrong and stubborn as—well—as she was!

Still, Annie worried Emma could get hurt if she asked the wrong person the wrong question. The people in Trafalgar Square obviously weren't there for a Sunday picnic. They wanted justice, and many of them were hungry and angry. Not a good combination.

The coach surged forward with a jerk. Looking out the window, Annie winced at the screaming faces, the fistfights, the women clutching their children to their skirts, and the children crying.

She scanned the crowd and stopped when her gaze rested on a woman dressed in black, wearing a large, black hat, and standing with her hands resting on her cane, watching the mayhem go on around her. There was something vaguely familiar about her. The coach sped past, and the woman vanished behind the crowd of anguished people.

Annie steadied herself against the rocking of the carriage, her stomach uneasy with the motion. She'd have to visit Miss Brady in the asylum alone. The thought did nothing to ease the ache in her stomach or the oppressive weight of regret that settled deep in her heart.

By the time they finally reached the massive gates of the Hanwell Pauper and Lunatic Asylum, Annie had convinced herself she could handle whatever might come up in conversation with Miss Brady and Miss Parnell. Still, it hadn't escaped her thoughts they might refuse to see her. Or that Miss Brady's condition might be so advanced or so serious there was nothing to be done. Either way, Annie needed to face the situation and make her apologies. She would do whatever she could to help the two women.

They coach pulled up to the imposing, massive gates below a tall arch, flanked on either side with security buildings as large as a country manse. A stately wall, lined with silver maples, surrounded the immense property, much like a fortress stronghold. The grounds were comprised of several acres of land, complete with several outbuildings surrounding an enormous elegant spired building that Annie took for the main hospital.

The driver pulled the carriage up to the guard at the entrance under the arch.

"State your business." A stout man with a demeanor like an overly protective father approached the window. His bushy mustache covered his mouth and bounced with each word he spoke.

Annie had been rehearsing what she would say to enter the asylum ever since Emma had jumped out of the coach.

"I am Annie Oakley—performer for the Wild West Show."

"Ah, yes. So you are! You look just like the drawings on the posters." The guard's eyes softened and his mustache broadened into a smile. "My wife has been pestering me to buy tickets to your show."

"Well, you tell the ticket master you are my personal guest." Annie pulled a calling card from her reticule. "Just give him this."

"Why, thank you, ma'am. The missus will be pleased as punch." He placed the card in his pocket.

"I am here to bring some cheer to the patients," Annie said, giving him her brightest show smile.

"Yes, ma'am. I will alert the office you are on your way." He pointed to another guard sitting atop a well-muscled chestnut horse, and the latter nodded and rode toward the hospital building at a brisk trot.

Annie waved at him and leaned back into the cushion of the seat, pleased to have gained entrance. The driver of the coach guided the horses through the gates and down the long, tree-lined drive to the stairs of the main building. He hopped down from the bench seat and helped Annie out.

A woman clad in a lavender cotton dress with puffy sleeves and a full-sized white pinafore cinched tightly at her waist waited for Annie at the top of the stairs. A large lace doily-like cap sat atop the woman's fire-red, neatly upswept hair, and a strip of lace-edged fabric, denoting her status, trailed down her back past her waist.

Annie straightened her skirt and climbed the dozen steps to the door of the main building.

"Miss Oakley. Welcome. So kind of you to visit. I am Matron Dixon." The woman had a pleasing face with soft wrinkles at the corners of her bright, Kelly-green eyes, and around the lines of her smile.

"I am happy to do it. I have a friend here. Miss Becky Brady."

"Ah yes. I believe she is in the garden."

"Is her mother here as well?"

"Yes," the matron said. "She has hardly left the girl's side. I worry Miss Parnell hasn't gotten enough rest. Miss Brady's illness has been a trial for both of them."

"Has her condition improved?"

Matron Dixon opened the door to the building and gestured for Annie to enter. Annie obeyed and ducked through the doorway into an expansive hallway with gleaming tile floors and windows that soared up to the high arched ceiling, filling the hallway with light.

"I'm afraid not," said the matron. "Her condition has worsened."

Annie faltered, her stomach again reminding her of its distress.

"Miss Oakley, are you all right?" Matron Dixon took Annie's elbow.

"I'm fine, Matron Dixon. Really." Annie straightened her spine and again put on her best show smile.

The matron led her down the spartan, gleaming hallway and out the back doors to a beautiful garden sanctuary filled with trees and dozens of defined allotments separated by neat dirt pathways.

"It's like a fairy land here," Annie said in wonder. Based on some of the stories Emma had told her about asylums, this was not what she had expected. She had steeled herself for people wailing in the hallways or pounding on locked doors. Instead, the patients here were engaged in trimming bushes and picking fruit from the trees or tomatoes from the vines. Several were digging tidy rows for planting.

The matron's face shined with pride. "Yes. The doctors here feel it is beneficial for the patients to be industrious on a daily basis. We have a rigorous schedule with morning meals, exercise, and bathing. Then we send the patients outdoors. The air is very healing, you know. The food grown here is used in our kitchens, and we give of our abundance to the poor. We believe nothing must go to waste. This type of activity makes the patients feel like they are contributing to society, instead of wasting away in a hospital."

As they neared one of the small plots, Annie recognized Miss Parnell seated in a white wicker rocker, watching Becky work the soil with a three-pronged hand cultivator. Miss Parnell looked up at their approach, but Miss Brady continued with her digging.

Annie was struck with alarm at the dark half-moons under Miss Parnell's eyes. The woman looked as if she hadn't slept in weeks.

"Miss Parnell, it's so good to see you." Annie knelt down next to the rocker.

Miss Parnell glanced at her and then turned away. "What are you doing here?"

"I've come to see you and Miss Brady. To apologize for my mistake. I am so terribly sorry." Annie pivoted on her heel to face Becky, but the girl continued to work the soil.

"She's been like this for a week now," Miss Parnell said, an edge to her voice. "She doesn't respond to anyone, except me, on occasion. If she were at home with me, she'd improve. I know it."

Annie stood and walked over to Becky. She knelt next to her in the dirt.

"Becky—Miss Brady. It's Annie. I am so sorry if I caused you any distress. I hope you will be feeling better soon."

To her surprise, Becky turned and looked directly into Annie's eyes.

"He did it. He sent me here," she said, her voice hoarse from lack of use.

"Did she speak?" Miss Parnell leaned forward, the fringe of her shawl sweeping the ground as she stood up. She knelt down next to her daughter, who continued working. "Oh, my dear girl, you've come back to me."

"Who, Becky? Who are you talking about?" Annie asked.

"Miss Oakley, must you persist? This is a breakthrough. Don't set her back again with memories of the—"

"I'm sorry, Miss Parnell, but the killer is still at large. People are in danger." Annie tried to reason with her.

"He did it, I tell you. He wanted me to be quiet. So I am quiet. I don't tell." Becky looked up at Annie.

"Who told you to be quiet?" Annie asked.

Becky stood up and her mother held her by the shoulders. "The doctor. He hates the Fenians. I am born of a Fenian. My mother is of the Fenians. We must fight for our land. Our rights. He did this," Becky said.

"Are you speaking of Dr. Adams?"

"The doctor."

"Becky, I must know. Do you speak of Dr. Adams?"

"Miss Oakley, I implore you."

Becky shook free of her mother's grasp and knelt down, turning her attention again to her gardening.

Annie stood up and stepped away from the girl. "Do you think she is talking about Dr. Adams?"

"I don't know." Miss Parnell wrapped her shawl tighter around her shoulders. "After we left the ship, she saw many doctors. Many before we came here. I was in such a state when they took her away, I—I have left my life of public service and only wish to be left alone." Miss Parnell's gaze fell away from Annie's.

"I understand your brother has been imprisoned for his alleged participation in the Phoenix Park murders. Do you know anything about this?"

"Why do you persist?" Miss Parnell looked into Annie's eyes with exasperation.

"Because I made a mistake, and I'm trying to make things right, Miss Parnell. Surely, you want to see justice done."

"How will that justice make my daughter better?"

"I don't know, but you seem to be a woman of character. If you have any information that could help me or the police—"

"I've told the police everything I know. They don't believe me because of my former association with the Fenians." Miss Parnell looked away from Annie, her gaze settling on her daughter.

"I would like to understand," Annie said.

The silence grew between them. Finally, Miss Parnell sighed, shaking her head. "I have nothing to do with my brother anymore, Miss Oakley—it is no longer my concern."

"I would like to know more about the Irish who are so unhappy with the queen. You are obviously well versed in the subject. We saw many people at Trafalgar square protesting Mr. Gladstone and the queen. Do these protesters support your brother and his efforts?"

Miss Parnell made her way over to her chair and sat. "Many do. But there are so many other factions of unhappy people. It is not only the Irish who are unhappy with the queen, but many of her own countrymen."

"Do you think your brother is guilty of this Phoenix Park crime? Do you think he might have something to do with the threat to the queen?"

Miss Parnell looked pointedly into Annie's eyes. "My brother is very passionate about the cause, but he would never murder."

Annie held her gaze. "But would you?"

Chapter Twenty-Two

Miss Parnell appraised Annie without flinching, her eyes cold. "Miss Oakley, I do not believe getting rid of the queen will help the plight of the Irish. She is just a figurehead in matters of politics. Her prime minister, Mr. Gascoyne-Cecil, and her cabinet are the real forces behind the Crown, just as Mr. Gladstone was. My focus now is my daughter. I hope to bring her back to health so we may live our lives in peace."

"I understand. I apologize for the question, but I had to ask." Annie placed her hand on Miss Parnell's shoulder. She understood the need to protect family over one's own welfare. Hadn't she done the same time and time again? She knew she had to leave Miss Brady and Miss Parnell in peace, but there were still some things she had to know.

"Miss Parnell, as I mentioned when Miss Wilson and I spoke with you and Miss Brady on the ship, I'd found a vial, a tear catcher. It's very beautiful, with gold etching. Your daughter's fingerprints were on it. Had you ever seen anything like that?" Annie wondered if the smaller fingerprints she had found on the tear catcher could belong to Miss Parnell.

"I'm finished answering questions, Miss Oakley. If you don't mind, I'd like my daughter to garden in peace."

"If you could just answer the question."

Miss Parnell remained silent.

"Perhaps I can help you with her case," Annie said.

"How can you help me?"

"I can speak to the police again. I can assure them that your association with the Fenians is over. I can advocate on your behalf."

Miss Parnell put her hands to her temples and sat down again. After a moment she turned her face up to Annie. "What do you want to know?"

"About the vial, the tear catcher."

Miss Parnell's brow rose. "Yes. Before she stopped talking, Becky mentioned something about it. She said she found it on the gangway as we boarded the ship—we figured it had fallen out of someone's trunk, or perhaps a pocket. Becky picked it up. The police didn't believe her."

"What did Becky do with the tear catcher?"

"She placed it in a box labeled 'lost and found' on the ship."

Then how did it end up in the refrigeration hold?

"Why do you ask, Miss Oakley? And what has this to do with the doctor?"

Annie blinked away her musings and focused on Miss Parnell's question.

"Someone has threatened to kill the queen. If it is Dr. Adams Becky is talking of, she obviously feels he has something to hide. Is there any reason Dr. Adams would want your daughter put away? Any reason at all?"

Miss Parnell turned away from Annie and stared off into the

distance. The silence grew. Just as Annie was about to repeat the question, Miss Parnell turned back to face her.

"Dr. Adams is Irish—and he despises the queen."

Annie's heart flipped. "How do you know this?"

"I didn't, until we were brought here. One of my brother's associates, a Mr. Shaunessey, is also receiving care here. He immediately recognized Dr. Adams on one of his visits. Apparently, Dr. Adams and Mr. Shaunessey had been on opposite ends of an argument during a Protestant protest in Ireland."

"But what does that have to do with the queen?"

"Dr. Adams opposes Catholic freedoms in Ireland. You know, he is of the Order of the Orange."

"The ribbon. Yes. I saw the ribbon he wears pinned to his lapel."

"The order is fiercely Protestant. They formed when William of Orange defeated the Catholic King James in the Battle of the Boyne in 1690. The Orangemen feel that the queen has let the Catholics in Ireland run riot. Apparently, Dr. Adams's mother was killed in a house fire caused by the Catholic faction for independence. He blames the queen."

"Oh, dear." Annie's mind whirled with this new information. So her suspicions about Dr. Adams had not been unfounded. The man had a bias against the queen because of the death of his mother. Annie remembered the portrait of his mother hanging in his office on the ship. Could he have lied about the amount of viper venom he had on board? Could he be Bhakta's killer? If so, wouldn't it be have been convenient for him to keep quiet when Annie accused Becky Brady?

Matron Dixon walked toward them. "It's time for Miss Brady to take some rest," she said, her eyes crinkling with her wide smile.

"Thank you for this information, Miss Parnell. Again, I am sorry for any distress I may have caused you and your daughter. I will do my best to convince the police of her innocence. I hope she becomes well again, soon."

"I do, too." Miss Parnell held a handkerchief to her mouth. "She is everything I have now. Everything to live for. I will stay with her until she is well, or until. . . ." Miss Parnell turned her face away.

Matron Dixon leaned over Becky. "Miss Brady, it's time to come in. We have some tea and cakes waiting for you inside."

Becky placed her gardening tools in a canvas bag at her feet, and then stood up, handing the bag to Matron Dixon. Miss Parnell took Becky's arm and led her away.

At the entrance to the hospital, Annie climbed into the carriage and told the driver to head back to the grounds at Earl's Court. She stared out the window, her mind whirling with this new information about Dr. Adams.

Overwhelmed by her thoughts, she set them aside and let her mind drift. She took in a deep breath and let it out slowly. Since they had arrived in London, Annie had not had the time or the ease of mind to enjoy this once in a lifetime opportunity. She decided to put all her efforts into releasing her worries, so she could at least enjoy the sights and sounds of the city during this carriage ride.

Were a few brief minutes of peace and happiness too much to ask for?

People from all walks of life teemed in the streets. The air, thick with smoke, left a haze in the sky, but the people seemed unaffected as they bustled to their destinations or strolled looking into shop windows.

As they passed one of the larger hotels, Annie's gaze settled on a woman walking a few feet ahead of her, wearing a red, tattered coat. Could it be Gail Tessen? The woman walked at a fast clip and then suddenly stopped. She turned her head toward the carriage, looking to cross the street, but Annie couldn't see her face clearly. Where was she going in such a hurry?

Annie pulled on the bell, signaling the driver to stop.

He leaned his head body back toward the window. "Ma'am?"

"Follow that woman in the red coat," Annie instructed him.

"Aye!" he said.

The carriage turned to go down the street the woman had taken, but then stopped again. "What is it?" Annie called out, leaning her head out the window. "Follow that woman!"

"Got an overturned cart in front of us."

Annie was about to open the door to get out and tell the driver to wait for her, when the carriage started to move again. Annie could see the red coat in the distance. They followed her for some time and then the woman turned, crossing the street again to take a different road.

In minutes, they ended up at Trafalgar Square. The woman hurried past the monument, folks camping there watching her walk past. She headed down a narrow street—too narrow for the carriage. The driver leaned toward the window again.

"That's as far as I can go," he said. "Do you want to get out?"

Annie watched as the woman stopped at a doorway, looked in both directions as if worried about being followed, and entered the dwelling.

"No," Annie said. "We can return to the grounds."

She settled back into the seat as the carriage turned and headed back the way they had come.

"If that's Miss Tessen, what is she up to?" Annie wondered aloud.

Miss Tessen had told her she'd no place to stay, so whose house had she entered? Perhaps she was visiting a friend—a friend who had no room for her. Maybe she was running an errand for someone, like Mr. Post, although Annie couldn't imagine what the errand could be.

In truth, there could be any number of reasons Miss Tessen had left the grounds to visit the dwelling. And in truth, it really wasn't any of Annie's business.

But when had that ever stopped her?

When Annie arrived back at her tent, she found Frank dressed and reading the paper.

"There you are," he said. "Nate was looking for you. He wants to do another practice before your performance tomorrow. I thought I would go with you. See how the course is set up. Where have you been?"

Annie told him she'd gone to see Miss Parnell and Miss Brady. She didn't tell him anything else. He looked wretched.

"Are you sure you're up to it?"

"I need to get out of bed."

Annie knew his inactivity was contributing to his disheartened spirits. Although she worried about him, it might be good for him to get out. She looked at the watch pinned to a ribbon on her chest and sighed. She would be late for practice.

After slipping into her tan buckskin skirt and white cotton blouse, she buttoned her knee-length leather gaiters over her boots, retrieved her guns, and dashed out of the tent, calling to Frank that she would see him at the practice arena.

When she arrived back at the barn, Buck was groomed and saddled, and Miss Tessen was securing the bridle over his ears. Annie saw no sign of the red coat. If it had been Miss Tessen she'd seen in the streets, how had she returned so quickly? Could she have made her way back shortly after Annie had seen her—and gotten Buck ready as Annie dressed?

Mr. Post stood some distance away, leaning against a fence railing, watching the young woman's every move. Annie knew he didn't like that she had hired Miss Tessen, and she also knew if Miss Tessen made even the slightest error, she would never hear the end of it. Annie had to give him credit, though, for his diligent concern about her and her horse.

"Mr. Post, how did she do?" Annie walked up to him, securing her gun belts around her waist.

"Did all right. Knows a horse, that's for sure." Mr. Post spit some chaw on the ground.

"Was she here the whole time I was gone?"

"She finished cleaning Buck's stall and your tack pretty quickly. I told her to go cool her heels for a while."

"Oh. Do you know where she went?"

"Nope." He picked up a bucket at his feet. "I gotta go see if the colonel's horse needs any water. Are you good here?"

"Yes, thank you, Mr. Post."

"Miss Tessen?" Annie asked as she approached Buck. "Did I see you in town earlier?"

"Me? No. I've been right here on the grounds."

Could she have been mistaken? She could swear she had seen Miss Tessen in town.

"He looks quite handsome," Annie said, still distracted with the image of the woman in the red coat walking past Trafalgar Square.

Buck nickered at her, and she slipped him a sugar cube she'd stashed in her pocket. She then checked the position of the saddle, the tightness of the girth, and the position of the bridle. All looked in order.

"Nice work."

"Thank you," said Miss Tessen. "I've missed working with horses. It's so soothing for the soul."

"Don't I know it!" Annie could already feel her muscles relax and the tightness in her chest subside as she stroked Buck's neck. He closed his eyes and exhaled loudly.

She loved that she brought him peace, as he did for her. She felt like she'd been holding her breath for days. Even the persistent, low grade nausea had subsided. Thoughts of pregnancy slipped into her awareness, but she pushed them aside. She didn't want anything to ruin her time with Buck. She had to be focused for practice.

As she was about to mount, she saw Lillie, Bobby, and Hulda walking toward her. Lillie's ensemble included buckskin trousers, a pistol belt, a man's shirt and suspenders, and a beat-up hat that looked like it had come from the garbage bin. It severely contrasted with the make-up she'd caked on her face. From the neck up, she looked like a parlor girl, and from the neck down, she resembled a cowboy.

Odd as Lillie looked, she was nothing compared to Hulda. Her sister looked like a parlor girl all the way around: eyelids coated with coal-dark shadow, rouge like two ripe apples, and lips the color of blood. Hulda all too much resembled a lady of the evening. The black, laced trim neckline of the dress she wore showed considerably more bosom than Annie wanted to see. The hem barely reached her knees, exposing her stockings and lace-up ankle boots. Much to Annie's annoyance, Bobby was grinning like a fool, never taking his eyes off her baby sister.

"Hulda, what are you wearing?" Annie tried to keep the anger out of her voice. She remembered her last skirmish with her sister and didn't want to go there again. She would have to tread lightly, but still get her point across.

Hulda placed her hands on her hips. "A dress, silly."

"Go change your clothes right now, and wash your face."

"Oh, lighten up, Sure Shot." Lillie puffed on a cigarette.

"Was this your doing?" Annie turned to face Lillie, unable to control her temper. "I thought we talked about this, Lillie. Hulda is still a child. I won't have her looking like a harlot—why, she is the spitting image of Twila Midnight!"

"I'm not a child!" Hulda stomped a foot. "Bobby said I look beautiful and sophisticated."

Annie shot Bobby a look. The silly grin faded, and his face turned the color of Buck's salt lick. Tipping his hat, he quickly retreated into the barn. Lillie stepped up to Annie, her nose inches from Annie's. Her eyes flared with anger.

"You take that back, Miss High and Mighty."

Annie stood her ground. She knew it was cruel to bring up Lillie's adopted sister and Annie's nemesis, who'd passed away a few years ago—it had just slipped out—but Lillie seemed hell-bent on ruining her sister.

"Lillie, I would appreciate it if you left my sister to me." Annie tried to keep her voice even.

Lillie's eyes softened, but not much. "Well, maybe if you were around more and left the detective work to the police, she wouldn't be so lonely. What kind of a big sister are you, anyway?" Lillie spit a flake of tobacco off her lip and sauntered away. Annie turned to Hulda whose eyes were brimming with tears.

"I hate you!" Hulda said.

"Hulda, I'm sorry—"

"I hate you!" She turned and ran toward the tents.

Annie sighed, shaking her head. She shouldn't have scolded Hulda—again. She just couldn't abide the girl wearing such outlandish clothes. It sent the wrong message.

"I had a little brother," Miss Tessen said, her voice quiet and even. "I know you mean right by her, but she just wants to be her own person. She's finding her way."

Annie bit her lip, afraid to speak for fear her voice would crack. She held her breath to keep tears from forming. She never thought bringing Hulda to England would be so challenging. She placed a hand on her belly. How could she be a mother when she was failing so miserably as a sister?

The sound of a loud whistle filled the silence. It was Mr. Salisbury, calling everyone to practice. Annie composed herself, and lifted her calf to get a leg up from Miss Tessen. Once she had mounted, Miss Tessen handed up her pistol belt, then her rifle. A little shooting practice would do her good.

The rehearsal went well, without a hitch, except for the fact that Annie couldn't seem to hit many of the targets. Frank, standing at the fence watching, called her over.

"What seems to be the problem?" he asked. "You never miss."

"I got after Hulda again. I shouldn't have. I guess it threw me off."

"Try it again."

Annie turned Buck and repeated the course, this time, hitting all of her marks.

Frank, standing at the fence clapped his hands together applauding her. She trotted Buck over to him.

"That's more like it," he said. "You're going to have to keep a cool head when it comes to your sister."

"I know. I'll go find her."

Frank headed back to their tent. Annie watched him go, his usual swagger diminished by the constant ache in his belly. She wished she could make everything right again, and Frank well, but nothing seemed to be working out as she had hoped.

Annie sought out Hulda and found her sulking in her tent, wearing her dressing gown, her makeup smeared, and the tawdry dress lying on top of her bed.

"Hulda, I'm sorry I was so harsh. I know things have been difficult for you, and I haven't been able to spend much time with you."

Hulda refused to look at her and picked up one of the Indian costumes. She took up her thin needle and began sewing colorful beads onto the suede. She had designed an intricate and beautiful pattern.

"You're not going to say anything?" Annie said, trying to keep her tone soft.

"I want to go home." Hulda still had not made eye contact with Annie. "I miss Mother."

Annie sighed. She missed their mother, too. She would be able to smooth things over between the two of them. She always had.

"Well, you can't right now. You have a job to do. And you do it so well, Hulda. You really are quite talented. I don't know what I'd do without you."

Hulda finally looked up at her. Annie smiled, hoping to ease Hulda's anger.

"Stop trying to act like my mother, Annie. I can't stand it. You are so bossy." Hulda set down her work, waiting for Annie to react.

Hulda still needed mothering. She hadn't made the best choices since they'd left New York. As much as Annie wanted to tell her so, she bit her tongue. Keeping the peace with Hulda was her most important job—even though it seemed the hardest.

Chapter Twenty-Three

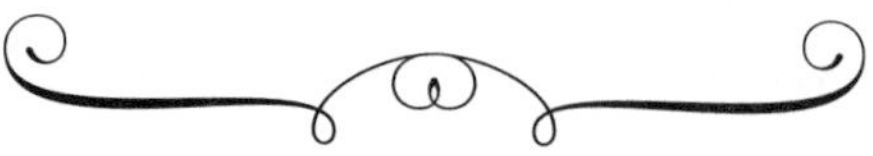

Sitting atop Buck, waiting for her first international performance, Annie breathed deeply, trying to settle the butterflies racing around in her stomach. She always got a little nervous before a performance, but today felt different. Hulda was still not speaking to her; Frank's health had not improved, so he wouldn't be ringside, cheering her on; and Lillie had beaten her again in practice the day before.

From where she and Buck stood, near the corrals at the outskirts of the grand stadium, Annie could see several people filing into the immense, all-white, American Exhibition building where the performances were held.

The idea of a private show for the prince and princess made Annie tense with anticipation. She looked out over the green expanse of Earl's Court gardens, watching as people strolled the flower-laden paths and lined the road to get a look at their future sovereign when he arrived in his carriage.

Annie closed her eyes, visualizing the course she had run with Buck yesterday. She envisioned the red, white, and blue swags, commemorating the relationship between England and America, decorating the royal box where the prince and princess would sit. Opulent displays of flowers, fragrant and colorful, surrounded the stadium. She remembered the placement of all of her targets and imagined herself hitting each and every one.

"How are you doing, Annie?" She opened her eyes and saw Bobby standing next to her, twirling his pistols in each hand—something he did to settle himself before performing.

"I'm all right, Bobby. A little nervous."

Bobby slipped his pistols into his holster, then took them out and twirled them again. "I've come to fetch you for the colonel and Mr. Salisbury."

Annie nodded and turned Buck to follow Bobby. The colonel and his manager always wanted a meeting with the players before their first performance in a new location. He'd never admit it, but the colonel got nervous, too. He felt personally responsible for everyone—the players and the spectators—and liked everything to run smooth as butter.

Once the meeting had adjourned, the players headed toward the exhibition hall where they would wait to enter the stadium. After the famed "Enactment of Yellow Hair," featuring the colonel, Chief Red Shirt, and Black Elk, Annie would run the mounted shooting course.

While she was waiting to go on, Annie took Buck for a few laps in the practice arena. When she brought him to a stop, she saw Oscar Wilde and Lily Langtry standing on the other side of the arena fence. She trotted Buck over to them.

"Miss Oakley!" shouted Mr. Wilde. "Fine day for a performance, is it not?"

Annie pulled Buck to a stop and greeted the two of them. "Will you be watching the performance?" Annie asked, surprised the prince's mistress would be present.

"Of course, dear. Your horse is lovely," said Mrs. Langtry. "He reminds me of my Copper, one of the horses Bertie purchased for me."

"Thank you," Annie said, not completely appreciative of the compliment, as it was a reminder of the prince's treatment of his wife. Annie struggled to reconcile the words Emma had told her about the relationships of royals.

Mrs. Langtry held her hand out for Buck to sniff. Annie couldn't deny she was impressed. Most people, especially those who claimed to know horses, walked right up to Buck and slapped him on the neck. Mrs. Langtry showed a respect for Buck that Annie had to admire.

"We may have some information for you, my dear," said Mr. Wilde. "J. L. heard some scuttlebutt around Buckingham about a disgruntled servant who was overlooked for the late Mr. Bhakta's coveted position."

"Oh?" Annie suddenly forgot about her nerves.

"We've also heard that Old Vic has received some threatening notes at Windsor," said Mrs. Langtry. "It's not entirely unusual—Vic has her enemies great and small, but we gathered from what we witnessed at Georgie's soirée, and also from your friend the reporter, that you are investigating what happened to Mr. Bhakta aboard the ship. You also believe it might point to danger for the queen."

Annie couldn't be sure of Mr. Wilde's and Mrs. Langtry's motives, but they certainly had her attention.

"I do believe there is a connection, yes."

Mrs. Langtry stroked Buck's forehead. Annie could feel him melt under her, and she, too began to relax.

"The queen certainly has her opinions about me, but she is my sovereign and I her subject. And I have the greatest respect for her son, who has been very good to me. I don't wish any harm to come to the old girl." When Mrs. Langtry smiled at her, Annie couldn't help being charmed.

"We are at your service," Mr. Wilde added, sweeping his hat off his head and bowing with a flourish. Annie didn't know what to think about their offer. She supposed it couldn't hurt to have some connection to the palace. Behind them, near the American Expo building, Annie spotted Bobby waving her over. She pointed to him.

"That's my cue. I must go now."

"Very well," said Mr. Wilde. "We will be cheering you on in the stands. J. L. has a box behind the prince's box."

"Yes, and the prince and I are throwing a party after the show," said Mrs. Langtry. "We do wish you would come."

"Yes," Mr. Wilde chimed in. "Everyone who's anyone will be there, you know."

"I thank you for your kind offer, but my husband is not well, and I wish to spend the evening with him. Maybe some other time?"

"We understand, don't we, J. L? Anyway, you must be off. Break a leg, my dear!"

Annie trotted away from them thinking they were the most eccentric people she had met to date.

~

As the colonel, Chief Red Shirt, Black Elk, and the other cowboys and Indians left the arena, Annie and Buck stood by waiting for the announcer to invite them in. Annie checked her pistols to make sure they were ready to fire. She then adjusted the Winchester in its scabbard, and checked to see that it fit securely under the saddle's fender.

Chief Red Shirt, riding bare-chested and bareback on his favorite pony, Dancing Feather, approached her. Sweat glistened off his muscular, war-painted chest, and his face bore his familiar proud expression, but it melted to a smile when he made eye contact with Annie.

"They are a most appreciative audience," he said as he steered Dancing Feather next to Buck. "I think this first performance bodes well for the show."

"That's excellent news, Chief." Annie said, scratching Buck's withers. She could feel his pre-performance anxiety surface, as usual. Buck made it clear he loved performing but, like her, he experienced some jitters right before going on. The mass of butterflies she'd experienced before felt as if they had organized themselves and were now flying in formation—still there, but less jumbled.

"Did the prince and princess seem to enjoy the show so far?" Annie asked.

"Yes. They said so. The colonel and I exchanged some words with them. They asked about you and Miss Smith and would like to greet you when you're finished."

"Yes, so I've been told. Thank you, Chief."

"May the Great Spirit bless you and your horse. May you give an astounding performance, Watanya Cecilia." Red Shirt reached over and laid his hand on Annie's shoulder.

Annie heard the announcer introduce her, so she bid the chief a quick goodbye. She turned Buck toward the stadium gates and trotted him around for a moment, collecting herself, and allowing him to burn some energy. When the gates open, she urged him into a canter and then an all-out run.

Buck's muscles flexed beneath her as he stretched his neck out and raced around the arena. Annie lifted one of her pistols from its holster and shot it into the air as the small crowd of fifty or so people whooped with excitement.

As they made their way around the arena, Annie set her gun back into its holster, and took note of her targets, mentally preparing for the course. Two dozen multicolored glass balls sitting atop as many tripods covered one half of the arena. The other half held props, including a makeshift shack, the Deadwood Stagecoach, and several buffalo and "wild" horses contained in a pen.

After two laps, Annie set her weight deep into the back of the saddle, encouraging Buck to lift his shoulders and bring his hind end under himself to come to a sliding stop in front of the prince and princess. It made Annie's heart glad to see them smiling and clapping.

Tapping Buck's shoulders with her toes, Annie cued Buck to raise his forefeet into a rear. When he came down, she urged him into a run again and they began the course.

Laying her reins on Buck's neck, she pulled her pistols from their holsters. She used her body to navigate Buck through the serpentine course, shooting twelve of the glass balls off their tripods. She put her pistols back in their holsters and pulled her rifle out of the scabbard. Turning her hips to the left and then to the right, cueing Buck to do the same as they raced through the course, Annie shot the rest of the glass balls.

Without picking up her reins, Annie held the rifle over her head, tucked her hips forward and Buck came to another resounding sliding stop. The crowed whooped and yelled with abandon.

Adrenaline pulsing through her body, Annie waved to the small crowd, giving them her best show smile. To her surprise and delight, Buck lifted himself into another rear, his front legs kicking wildly in front of him.

"You love this, don't you, boy," she said to him, patting his neck as he came down. Settling her rifle back into its scabbard, Annie approached the prince and princess, still out of breath from her performance.

The Wild West crew set about clearing the course in preparation for Annie and Lillie's shooting contest. At Annie's approach, both the prince and princess stood, clapping with great enthusiasm. To her surprise, Annie saw Mr. and Mrs. Arthur standing too, behind the prince and princess.

"What a wonderful little girl," said the princess. "I so enjoy watching you ride."

"Thank you, Your Highness," Annie said with a bow of her head, the compliment tingling all the way down to her toes.

"Hey, Miss Oakley," Mr. Arthur yelled. "Remember us? From the ship?"

The princess turned around, annoyed that Mr. Arthur had interrupted their conversation.

"Yes," said Annie. "How lovely to see you."

"We were anxious to see you perform," said Mrs. Arthur, dressed in a garish shade of pink with a white fox stole wrapped around her shoulders. "The queen and the prince have been so generous. They even gifted us with a new horse in reparation for War Hero. We are simply delighted!"

"How generous."

It seemed the Arthurs no longer posed any threat to the queen—if they had in the first place.

"You are quite skilled I must say," said the prince. "You are as good as they say you are."

Before Annie could thank him, Princess Alexandra said, "We've also heard much about your husband, Mr. Butler. You two used to perform together?"

"Yes—but he's retired from performing. He's my manager now."

"How novel!" said the prince, raising his brows.

"We must have you both to tea at Buckingham Palace." Princess Alexandra clapped her hands together.

Annie hated to turn down such a lovely invitation, but Frank's condition hadn't improved.

"I'm honored by the invitation, Your Highness, but I am afraid my husband is ill—he's been ill since the voyage over. He's scarcely been out of bed."

"Oh dear. I am sorry." Princess Alexandra glanced at her husband, who gave her a nod. "Then, there is nothing to it. You and your husband will come stay at the palace where he will be seen by the royal physician."

Annie smiled, wishing she could find a graceful way to refuse. She wasn't sure Frank would be up for a move, close as Buckingham Palace was to Earl's Court, and she didn't want to leave Buck—or Hulda, who would be left to Lillie's influence. She decided she'd do what her mother always did—tell the truth.

"I'm so honored by your invitation Your Highness, but I am responsible for my sister, and I don't like to be far from my horse."

"Your sister is most welcome, and your horse can stay in our stables. You may bring a groom if you wish; we will have lodgings for them. What do you say, Miss Oakley?"

It would be good to have Frank examined by another doctor as she wasn't sure about Dr. Adams's integrity anymore—and if Buck could be kept nearby, and Hulda out of Lillie's clutches. . . .

"I will have to check with Mr. Salisbury and the colonel, of course."

The announcer's voice rang through the air introducing Bobby and Lillie. As usual, Mr. Post entered the arena to retrieve Buck. Annie bid the prince and princess farewell and handed Buck off to Mr. Post.

Bobby and Lillie mugged for the crowd while Annie loaded her pistols.

They started with the card trick that had made Frank so famous. Neither Bobby nor Lillie could split the card in half. Bobby, cheerful as ever, shrugged and then wowed the audience by hitting all of his targets while standing on his head, Lillie and Annie holding his ankles.

As Bobby was about to fire off a second round, the crowd murmured with excitement, anticipating the spectacle. Annie, helping Bobby stand on his head again, suddenly felt the ground shift beneath her feet. She looked over at Lillie who was grinning for the crowd, waving her plump arms in the air.

"Lillie—a little help?" Annie said. The ground shifted again and Annie blinked, trying to fend off her dizziness. Lillie curled her lip at Annie but grabbed Bobby's other ankle.

Annie glanced over to the royal box where the prince and princess sat smiling, eager to see if Bobby would hit all of his marks again. Bobby didn't disappoint, and flipped back onto his feet. Far to the side of the royals, Annie could see Mrs. Langtry and Oscar Wilde as well, grinning with admiration.

Next up, a competition between Annie and Lillie with live pigeons. Bobby ran to the box that housed the birds, while Annie and Lillie walked to the weapons table to gather their rifles. When Annie lifted her rifle to make sure it was loaded, her head spun again and nausea gripped her stomach.

The announcer explained the contest. Lillie would go first.

Bobby released six pigeons and Lillie hit them all within ten seconds. The crowd cheered with enthusiasm. When Annie's name was announced the cheers turned to a static roar. Mr. Arthur stomped his feet on the wooden floor of the box.

Annie wished she could appreciate the enthusiasm, but was distracted by the cold sweat that overtook her body. The pigeons were released. Annie raised her rifle, took aim and hit the first two birds, but nearly fell backward with the impact of the rifle. She lowered it and pressed her hand to her head.

"Shoot, Annie!" Lillie yelled at her.

Annie raised the rifle again, but another wave of nausea seized her stomach. She tried to focus on the pigeons, but they flew out of the stadium. A collective groan echoed through the crowd. Annie closed her eyes, humiliation pounding at the edges of her heart. What was wrong with her?

Lillie, delighted with her win, jumped up and down. "Lillie Smith beats Annie Oakley!" she crowed at Annie. "Now, that's a cause for celebration!"

Bobby ran over to them to prepare for the cigarette trick. "Are you all right, Annie? You don't look too well. I've never seen you miss so much."

"I'm fine, Bobby," Annie said, frustrated and angry at her sudden weakness. She could not be sick. Not now. "But I'll be the target for the cigarette trick. I don't trust myself."

"Are you sure?" Bobby said, incredulous.

"Yes, Bobby, don't argue." Annie took her spot and lit the cigarette. Bobby shot it out of her mouth, and the crowd applauded. Bobby held the cigarette for Lillie and she hit her mark as well.

Finally, their time was up, and the three of them grasped hands, Bobby in the middle, and held them up to uproarious applause. They bowed collectively and ran out of the arena.

When the gates closed behind them, Annie leaned against the stadium wall, her head pounding and her stomach feeling like it was going to come up.

"Annie, are you all right?" Bobby asked again.

"Maybe you should practice a little more instead of running around with that reporter," Lillie said with a sneer. "Or maybe you're just losing your edge."

"Be quiet, Lillie," Annie said. "Take your win graciously." She motioned for Mr. Post to bring Buck over to her.

"What happened in there, missy?" Mr. Post asked, handing her the reins.

Annie bit back her annoyance at the situation. Settling the reins around Buck's neck, she held her leg up for a boost.

"I don't know, Mr. Post. It was horrible." Annie felt like her insides were collapsing. She had never performed so dismally before—her first international performance had been a disaster. How would she ever recover? She could already see the headlines in the next day's paper: "Annie Oakley, a has-been at 18, Lillie Smith's star on the rise!" She swallowed down the bile that rose from her throat. She hated the thought of explaining to Frank what had happened.

Mr. Post took hold of her shin and lifted her up. She swung her other leg over the saddle and reached for the stirrups.

"Wonder what the prince and princess think of you now, little Miss Sure Shot," Lillie said, her fists resting on her plump hips.

Chapter Twenty-Four

By some miracle, reports of Annie's poor shot with the live birds did not make the local papers as she had feared. Perhaps reporters were not among the fifty or so persons invited to the prince's private performance.

"It was terrible, Frank," Annie said as she draped a blanket across Frank's lap, despite the summer heat of May oozing into the tent. Her dizziness had subsided, but the nausea persisted. Annie didn't dare mention to Frank she was late in her cycle. It happened all the time. She never could keep track. In fact, she hadn't even tried.

"What do you think happened? It's so unusual for you to miss," Frank said, his voice gravelly from sleep. Annie handed him the bowl of oatmeal Bobby had brought to the tent for the two of them. Annie had swallowed down two bites, but the texture of the gruel sent her senses into overload. Frank took the bowl, looking down at it with apprehension.

"You must eat, darling. You're wasting away," Annie said.

"I know. Problem is, I don't feel like eating." He handed the bowl back to her and she placed it on the floor.

"Well, we are to move to Buckingham Palace for a few days, where the princess has arranged for the royal doctor to care for you." Annie took a pillow from the bed and stuffed it between Frank's head and the back of the chair.

"But we have Dr. Adams—here."

"Yes, I know. But it wouldn't hurt to get a second opinion." Annie didn't feel it prudent to discuss her reservations about Adams while Frank felt so poorly. She wanted to remain as positive as she could—or at least impart that positivity to Frank.

"I agree. No one can seem to find what is wrong with me, and I'm sick of lying in this damned bed. But what about the show? You need me here," Frank said.

"I need you well. We don't have a performance until next week, thank goodness. I think some rest will do both of us some good. And you could be well by then, God willing. I'm hoping to get a little more practice in before then, too."

"Rest? You?" Frank said, teasing her. "You're determined to find out who killed Mr. Bhakta, and who may be out to kill the queen."

"And you." Annie finished buttoning her dress and sat down at her vanity to tackle her unruly mane of hair. "I am obviously missing something, Frank. I can't let it go. I'm responsible for falsely accusing Miss Brady, and I'm determined to rectify my mistake."

Annie rose early the next morning and asked the colonel to summon the police again. She wanted to make good on her promise to Miss Parnell. Inspector Grange and Constable Markus arrived at Annie and

Frank's tent as she was finishing a late breakfast. Annie explained the situation between Miss Parnell and her brother, and that they were no longer associated.

"Miss Parnell cares nothing about the Fenian agenda anymore, Inspector, only the well-being of her daughter, and I believe her daughter is innocent."

"So we should just take your word for it?" the inspector said, grinning at the constable.

"Sir, I believe you asked Miss Parnell about the tear catcher. She told you the truth. Miss Brady found it on the gangway as she boarded the ship. That is why her fingerprints were on it. That was my mistake."

"Very well," the Inspector said with a dismissive sigh. "Is that all?"

"Yes. But you will take into account what I've said?"

"I will. Good day, Miss Oakley, Mr. Butler."

"But—" Annie called after them. "Oh, how condescending can one be?" She whirled around to look at Frank, hands on her hips.

"You've done what you could do, Annie. You told Miss Parnell you would speak the police again, and you have. You need to focus on the show."

"If only they would—"

"Annie. . . ."

Annie realized staying at the palace might give her access to more information about the threat to the queen. "Oh, you're right, Frank. Especially after that last performance. And we need to focus on you getting better."

"That's my girl."

A town carriage pulled by four black horses arrived for them the next morning. The footman, dressed in a smartly fitted deep-red coat, with gold trim and tails, loaded their trunks on the back of the handsome closed coach. Annie had heard of the elaborate coaches used by the royal family, and this seemed quite tame in comparison, but it certainly made more of an impression than the Deadwood Stagecoach.

Miss Tessen arrived with Buck, who was saddled, bridled, and ready to go. Annie wanted Mr. Post to come with them, but he was responsible for all the other horses. If Annie wanted Buck near her, she would have to make use of Miss Tessen. Buck seemed to have taken to the woman well, and she'd given Annie no reason to doubt she was a fine groom. Mr. Post had also given her the seal of approval. Hulda followed behind Buck and Miss Tessen, accompanied by Lillie.

"Oh, isn't this splendid!" said Hulda. "I feel like a princess."

Annie smiled at her sister, glad that her spirits were brightened.

"Got room for one more?" Lillie said, out of breath from the long walk from the tents. She glared at Annie. "Well, la-dee-dah, Miss Oakley. Getting special treatment as always, despite your performance yesterday." Sweat glistened on her upper lip and her eyes, droopy from drink, seemed out of focus.

"It is for Frank's benefit that we are going to the palace. Not mine, Lillie."

"I'll tell you all about it when we get back," Hulda said, giving Lillie a tight hug.

"I'm counting on it, princess," Lillie said back.

The coachman in his red coat, gleaming with gold trim and a top hat adorned with a gold band, got Frank and Hulda settled inside the coach, and then held his white-gloved hand out to help Annie up.

"Oh, thank you, sir, but I will be riding my horse. My groom can ride in the coach with Mr. Butler and my sister."

The coachman stared at her as if he didn't know what to say. Annie felt sure she had broken some sort of protocol, but she didn't care. She longed to ride Buck through the expansive beautiful park in peace—not be bounced around in the interior of a carriage, lovely as it was. She knew if Frank were able, he'd be riding, too.

"Very well, miss," said the coachman, gesturing for the footman to help Miss Tessen into the coach.

The two-and-a-half-mile ride to the palace was too brief for Annie's liking. She so wanted to gallop through Hyde Park on the enchanting bridle path lined with flowering hedges. A canopy of tree branches soared high above them. Buck seemed to enjoy the ride as well. He took long, relaxed strides, his head bobbing up and down and his ears pricked at all the new sights and sounds.

Annie's breath caught in her throat as they turned the corner to face the long, wide, perfectly straight, neatly groomed mall to the palace. Annie marveled at the impressive, stately architecture of the massive building. She rode to the front of the coach.

"It's so grand," she said to the coachman.

"It is indeed, miss, the pride of London."

"Is it very old?" Annie asked, mouth agape.

"Built in 1702 as a town house by the Duke of Buckingham. He sold it to King George the Third in 1761, who doubled the size of it. Her Royal Highness, Queen Victoria, was the first monarch to use it as a royal residence, with her Prince Albert, of course, may he rest in peace. She is here on occasion, but since the prince died, she feels more at home at Windsor."

The guards at the gates, with their tall, furry, imposing hats and resplendent red coats, opened the gates as they approached. The coach pulled up to the front of the palace, and Annie and Buck followed. She dismounted while the footman helped Frank and Miss Tessen out of the coach.

"Heavens, this is magnificent," said Frank, leaning for support on Hulda, who stood with her mouth hanging open and unusually quiet.

"I have him, thank you, Hulda," Annie said, coming to Frank's aid. He wrapped his arm around her shoulders. The footman motioned for Miss Tessen and Buck to follow him.

"Where are they going?" Annie asked the coachman.

"To the Royal Mews, ma'am. Where your horse will be staying. There are lodgings for your groom as well."

Annie turned her face up to Frank's. "Once I get you and Hulda settled, I will see that Buck is feeling comfortable."

"I want to come," said Hulda.

"Yes. I would like the company." Annie chucked her sister under the chin. She hoped this might be a way for her to rebuild the bond she once shared with Hulda. A stay at the palace might be good for all of them.

The coachman helped Annie get Frank up the stairs, where he handed them off to another royal servant—a tall, reedy man with a stern face and a monocle.

"I'm Henry Stanley from the office of the lord steward. Welcome to Buckingham Palace."

Mr. Stanley led Annie, Frank, and Hulda into the grand entry hall. White walls trimmed with gold rose up to a ceiling resplendent with

candle crystal chandeliers. Alcoves built into the walls housed marble busts and statuary. Annie had never even imagined a place of such splendor. She felt Hulda tug at the sleeve of her dress.

"Annie, look," Hulda whispered, "a naked boy!"

"Shh, Hulda. Don't be rude."

"It is a marble statue of a young David, by the artist Michelangelo," said Mr. Stanley.

Annie blushed at his overhearing Hulda's outburst. She grasped Frank's arm tighter as they headed up the long staircase, rising onto the palace's main floor. As they rose, the light became brighter, and the furnishings, ceilings, and wall coverings grew more illuminated.

Frank slowed, catching his breath.

"Are you all right?" Annie asked.

"Yes. A bit overwhelmed by all of this," he whispered.

"I know what you mean."

After a long walk through corridors laden with portraits of royals, noblemen and women, children, and pastoral landscapes, Mr. Stanley finally stopped.

"May I present the Belgian Suite," he said, motioning for the three of them to enter.

Annie gasped as they entered a large, yellow room with gold furniture covered in lively floral fabrics. A gold screen adorned with the same fabric stood in front of the white marble fireplace. The mantle was topped with elaborate candelabras flanking a beautiful gold clock. A crystal chandelier blinked rainbows across the white carved and paneled ceiling.

"This is named the Belgian Suite in honor of Prince Albert's cousin Leopold the First, King of the Belgians and a favorite of Her Majesty.

Mr. Butler and Miss Oakley, you will reside in the blue bedroom, while Miss . . . Miss?"

"Miss Mosey," Hulda said, her voice filled with pride. "Oh, Annie, what would Mother think? I must write to her as soon as possible."

Annie smiled at Hulda, reaching out to stroke the back of her head. "I'm sure she will scarcely believe you."

"Miss Mosey, you will retire in the Spanish room." Mr. Stanley led Hulda to her room where Annie heard her squeal with delight.

Mr. Stanley soon reemerged and led Annie and Frank to their room. Two large canopied beds occupied the room, along with two blue sofas and several chairs surrounding a low, marble table with gold legs. Three large portraits of the queen adorned the walls.

Frank made his way to one of the beds.

"I understand Mr. Butler is not well. I will send for the physician directly. Do you require any sustenance? I can have something brought to your rooms. Tea perhaps?"

"That sounds perfect," said Annie with a sigh.

"Very well. Mr. Ingle will serve as your personal butler, and he will see to your every need." With a nod of his head, Mr. Stanley left the two of them sitting on the bed.

Frank blew air through his lips, drawing Annie's attention. The previous flush of his cheeks had vanished, and his forehead glistened with perspiration.

"Let's get you into bed," Annie said, turning down the covers.

"Don't fuss, Annie. I can get myself to bed."

She ignored his ill temper and helped him take off his boots, his coat, and his trousers. She laid his clothes on the back of the chair next to the bed and then helped him to get in, fluffing the pillows behind his back and tucking the covers around his legs. When she straightened up, the room shifted. She closed her eyes to will away the dizziness. Tea might be just the thing she needed, she reasoned. She did feel a bit peckish.

She made her way to the chair and sat down, shifting Frank's trousers to the arm of the chair.

Hulda bounded into the room. "I've never been in a place so big, Annie. And we are in just a small part of the castle. Can I go exploring?"

"I don't think that would be wise, Hulda. This palace is so immense you might get lost. Besides, the butler is bringing us tea."

"What's a butler?" Hulda asked, scrunching her nose.

"A servant," Frank said.

"Our own servant! I can't wait to tell Lillie. But we will get to see the palace, won't we Annie?"

"We'll see." Annie put a hand to her temple, suddenly exhausted. They'd had a completely overwhelming day, and it was just nearing three o'clock. How would she make it through the evening?

A man appeared in the doorway of the bedroom, dressed in the vibrant red of the queen's staff and holding a tea tray. Another servant carried a three-tiered tray with sandwiches and pastries.

"Emma would be in heaven," she said, grinning at Frank.

"I *am* in heaven," said Hulda.

Once the servants had laid the table in the reception room and poured tea for the three of them, they left Annie and Hulda to enjoy their treats. Annie took Frank's tea and a plate of food to his bed. He didn't want the food, but welcomed the tea. Annie joined Hulda again in the reception room, where Hulda prattled on about the splendors of the palace. To her surprise and annoyance, the nourishment did nothing to ease Annie's exhaustion.

When they had finished their tea, Hulda retreated to her room to write a letter to their mother. Annie was about to check on Frank when she heard a knock at the door. She rose and went to open it when she felt the blood drain from her head. As she clutched the chair, her limbs weakened, and then she fell into utter darkness.

Chapter Twenty-Five

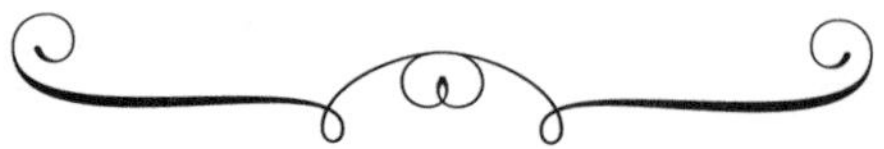

Annie felt something tapping at her cheeks. She opened her eyes to find herself on the second bed, and a man with a pointy nose and chin sitting next to her, staring into her face.

"There you are," he said. He took hold of her wrist, feeling for her pulse.

"Is she all right, Doctor?" she heard Frank ask. "She hasn't been feeling well, lately."

"Is this true?" the doctor asked her.

Reluctant to admit the truth, Annie nodded her head. The doctor asked about her symptoms and she told him. She also mentioned she hadn't experienced her time of the month in quite a while. She couldn't very well lie in front of Frank, who knew her so well.

"Do you think I am pregnant, Doctor?" Annie asked.

The doctor pried open her eye lids, felt around her neck and told her to open her mouth.

"I can't be certain, but your symptoms do reflect the possibility—especially since you've not had your menses in a couple of months. I suggest bed rest until you can be certain."

"Bed rest?" Annie bolted upright. "I have performances, responsibilities. I can't lie about in bed, especially if you're not certain. And if I am pregnant, it doesn't mean that I am ill—just with child." Annie never remembered her mother lying in bed during her pregnancies with John Henry and Hulda. She had functioned the same as before. The lying about in bed came later, with the stress of poverty.

"Annie, perhaps you should listen to the doctor," Frank said.

"You are the person who needs medical attention. Why don't you ask Frank about his symptoms?" Annie pointed over at Frank. She knew she was behaving irrationally, but she just couldn't be pregnant. Not now.

"Hysteria is another symptom of breeding," the doctor said with a patronizing smile. "Most women are elated to find out they are in the family way. I'm sure your husband welcomes the possibility."

Annie wanted to scream. Why was this man telling her how she and Frank should feel? She had no idea agreeing to come to the palace for Frank's benefit would be so taxing.

She swallowed down the vortex of emotions threatening to overwhelm her.

"I just want to be sure," she said, trying to keep the tone of her voice even. "But the major concern right now is Frank. Can you help him?"

The doctor stood and turned his attentions to Frank. Annie breathed a sigh of relief. They discussed what Frank had experienced since his time on the ship, Mr. Everett's algae poisoning theory, and the idea that someone could be poisoning him intentionally.

"Poisoning by algal bloom is an interesting theory, and that could have been the case, but it's been a few weeks since you've left the ship," the doctor said. "You should have returned to health by now.

As far as someone intentionally poisoning you, we have no way to be certain—I recommend blood-letting by leeches. They will draw out any toxins in the body. It's my prediction we'll have you feeling better in no time."

Although Annie didn't care for the doctor's opinion about what ailed her, she felt that perhaps, finally, Frank would get a treatment that made him better. Emma had told her stories of miraculous cures from the use of the slimy creatures.

Hulda reemerged from her bedroom, holding a letter.

"For Mother," she said. "Annie, can we go exploring now?"

"I think that sounds splendid, Hulda," she said, climbing off the bed.

"Annie, don't you think you should—" Frank started.

"I'm feeling so much better, darling. I think the doctor should expend his energies on you. That's why we are here, after all. Besides, I would like to visit the mews—to see where Buck will be staying, and also to find out how Miss Tessen is settling. There really is so much to be done." She grabbed Hulda by the hand and led her toward the door. "We will leave you to your privacy." They slipped out before Frank or the doctor could protest.

Annie closed the door behind them to find an older man wearing the same red-and-gold uniform standing next to it, his back to the wall, arms at his sides, as if at attention. He turned to face her.

"Miss Oakley, Miss Mosey," he said, "I am Mr. Ingle. May I be of service?" At first glance, Mr. Ingle reminded Annie of Mr. Shaw. Ingle had the same round face and bright blue eyes, but they differed in the area of the mouth. Mr. Shaw wore a perpetual smile, where Mr. Ingle's mouth turned down at the corners, lending him a dour expression.

"We'd like to see the royal mews, where my horse has been taken."

"And we'd like to see more of the palace," Hulda said, bouncing on the balls of her feet.

"Forgive my sister, Mr. Ingle, she is overexcited."

Mr. Ingle gave a slight nod. "I can give you a limited tour, as the prince and princess are in residence."

"Goodie!" said Hulda, clapping her hands.

Annie took Hulda's arm in hers, hoping to preventing further outbursts. She hated to dampen Hulda's enthusiasm, but feeling way out of her element, Annie also didn't want to draw undue attention.

Mr. Ingle took almost an hour guiding them through the gallery, the council room, the library, dining room, and plate room. Annie and Hulda strolled silently next to him, listening as he explained the important features of each room, including the furnishings and artwork.

As they stood in one of the corridors listening to the history of one of the paintings of Napoleon Bonaparte, a man in a white suit and turban approached them.

"Mr. Patel!" Annie could scarcely believe her eyes.

Mr. Patel bowed at the waist. Annie noticed a small gold medal hanging from a chain around his neck fall forward from his chest as he bowed. "It is I, memsahib. What brings you to the palace?"

Annie explained Frank's condition.

"We are getting a tour of the palace," Hulda said.

"So I see," said Mr. Patel. "You are in good hands with Mr. Ingle."

The downward angle of Mr. Ingle's mouth increased and he refused to make eye contact with Mr. Patel.

"Would you care to join me for tea?" Mr. Patel asked.

Anxious to get to the stables, Annie almost declined, but then thought joining Mr. Patel for tea might be a way to find out more about his former relationship with Mr. Bhakta and his present relationship with the queen.

"I'd love to."

"But the tour, Annie!" Hulda said.

"Mr. Ingle, can you finish without me? Mr. Patel will direct me to the stables."

"Very well," said Mr. Ingle. "I will see the young miss back to your rooms."

Pleased, Hulda put her arm through Mr. Ingle's, ready to continue. Mr. Ingle looked less than pleased, but Annie knew Hulda would be safe.

Mr. Patel led Annie through more rooms and down a flight of stairs.

"The servant's quarters," he said, holding out his arm in invitation. "I will fix some tea for us in my rooms." Annie instantly felt more at ease in the modest quarters.

Mr. Patel led her through a narrow hallway and into his rooms—a sitting room with a small stove and a doorway that led into what must be his bedroom. He directed her to one of the chairs at a small wooden table and set about preparing their tea. He pulled a tin from one of the shelves above the stove and took out several biscuits and placed them on a plate.

While he worked, Annie scanned the room. She got up to examine a small painting on the wall which depicted a quaint row of thatched buildings below a grove of palm trees. A charming well stood prominent in the forefront of the scene.

"This is lovely," Annie said. "I like its simplicity."

"Yes. That is where I grew up—my home, before the British East India Company took it."

"Sri Lanka?"

"No. Cawnpore—in India." He stopped working and grasped the medal at his neck, staring at the teapot.

"I thought you were from Sri Lanka," Annie said.

He took two teacups and saucers down from another shelf.

"I have family there, but I am from Cawnpore."

Annie studied the workmanship in the painting. "It's beautiful, like nothing I could ever imagine." Annie thought about the tear catcher with the remnants of viper venom, supposedly from Sri Lanka, found on the ship. Now that Becky had been cleared of the crime, she wondered again if Mr. Patel could have murdered Mr. Bhakta. Mr. Wilde and Mrs. Langtry had mentioned a disgruntled servant who failed to get Mr. Bhakta's post. Could it be Patel? It didn't seem likely, but she couldn't be sure. She hadn't thought she'd ever see Mr. Patel again. This was a stroke of luck.

"It was a beautiful place," he continued. "But terrible things happened there."

"What things?" Annie asked. She noticed he took hold of the medal again. He held it out from his neck to show her.

"I wear this to remember. It commemorates the great siege in 1857, during the Indian Rebellion. It is a long story. The East India Company had taken over Cawnpore for the queen, along with much more of India.

I was a soldier, a sepoy rebel, but I remained loyal to the British when India wanted her country back, for I was in love with a British girl. But my brothers in arms, they did terrible things during the rebellion—to the English women and children. I escaped during the siege and was later hunted by my fellow soldiers. I was shot in the leg, but crawled to safety. Somehow, I made it to Lucknow." The ghost of a smile played at Mr. Patel's lips, as if the memory stirred something in him. "I will be returning there, soon."

Annie noted a hint of sadness in his voice. "Oh?"

"I have no place here at the palace anymore. Not since Mr. Bhakta—"

"I'm sorry," Annie said.

"The English servants do not like us, even though we are far below them in rank. They tolerated me because Mr. Bhakta endeared himself to the queen, but now he is gone . . ." He brought over the two teacups on saucers, and then retrieved the plate of biscuits. "Sugar?" he asked, indicating the small bowl of sugar on the table.

"No, thank you." Annie sipped her tea. It was good and strong. "How long will you be here?"

"A few more weeks. I am in the process of securing passage home."

Annie thought she should take advantage of this time with Mr. Patel. Who knew when she would see him again—if ever.

"Mr. Patel, have you ever seen a tear catcher?"

He shook his head. "I do not know of this tear catcher. Why do you ask?"

Annie shrugged. "It was found on the ship. It might have something to do with Mr. Bhakta's death. It may have contained the poison that killed him. Poison that comes from Sri Lanka. Venom from a snake, a viper. Mr. Patel, do you know of anyone on the ship who would have access to that sort of substance?"

"No, memsahib. Truly."

A knock on the door interrupted their conversation.

"Come in," Mr. Patel said.

A young woman wearing a simple black dress entered the room. "Forgive the intrusion, but I have a letter for Miss Oakley. Mr. Ingle said I would find her here." Annie stood to retrieve the note and opened it.

It was from Dr. Adams.

"He wants to see Frank," Annie said out loud, and she wondered why. She had told the colonel if Dr. Adams showed up at the grounds to tell him Frank would be attended by the royal physician. Perhaps he still felt a responsibility to his patient—or was there something more? Now that she knew for certain he was Irish, she wondered if he had some kind of political agenda and wanted to include Frank.

"Is everything all right?" Mr. Patel asked, setting down his teacup with a clink.

"Yes, yes, but I must go. Miss, did Dr. Adams deliver this note? Is he still here?"

The woman shrugged. "I don't know, ma'am. It was given to me by Mr. Ingle."

"Well. . . ." Annie tucked the note into her dress pocket. "I will reply later. Mr. Patel, would you mind taking me to the mews?"

"It is quite a long walk, memsahib. I will secure a carriage for you."

"But are you not coming?"

"Oh no. It is not permitted for me. My duties require that I stay in the palace."

~

By carriage, the ride through Green Park to the royal mews took less than a quarter of an hour. When Annie alighted from the coach after passing through the grand archway, she was greeted by a royal groomsman, as Mr. Patel had promised. The young man was small in stature and had a broad, shining face and yellow-blond hair that he wore parted down the middle.

"You have come to see your horse," the young man said, handing her down from the coach. He stood only a few inches taller than she.

"Why, word travels fast around here. Yes, I have."

"May I show you around? The queen is very proud of her stables and the fine horses within."

The young man strode next to her, hands behind his back, as they toured the quadrangle. They stopped at the coach house which housed the queen's many beautiful conveyances, the most impressive being the queen's golden state coach.

"Is this real gold?" Annie asked.

"Yes. Gilded, but gold. The interior is fashioned with velvet and satin. The queen will use this coach for all of her jubilee celebrations."

Annie couldn't believe her eyes. This much gold could feed all the people of North Star, perhaps even all the people of Ohio.

"Annie! Isn't this magnificent?" Hulda, accompanied by another groomsman, ran up to her.

"Unbelievable," Annie said.

"Your horse is down this way," said the blond groomsman.

He led them down a row of stalls with horses grazing on hay, or with their heads over the stall doors to watch them pass. Finally, they reached Buck. When he saw Annie, he gave a low nicker and met her at the door.

"Hello, boy," she said, stroking his head. "Aren't you living in luxury?"

Buck nudged her with his nose. Hulda and her escort moved on to continue their tour.

"Meet you in our rooms directly after you view the stable?" Annie called after her.

"I want to see the park," Hulda said.

"I will make sure she is looked after," said the groomsman accompanying Hulda.

Annie sighed with resignation. "All right. Be sensible, Hulda."

"Oh, Annie, stop fussing." Hulda turned on her heel and put her arm through her groomsman's as they continued down the aisle.

Annie turned to the blond groomsman.

"Have you seen Miss Tessen? Has she gotten settled?"

"I saw her earlier. Yes, we have quarters for the grooms over there." He pointed to one of the wings of the quadrangle. "I believe someone helped her get moved in and showed her around. Do you have a message for her? If I see her, I can relay your message."

"Yes, actually. I will need to ride Buck to Earl's Court in the early mornings for practice and performances. She will know what to do to get him ready. I've brought my costumes with me, so I will be ready to go. Will she be able to come to me in the palace?"

"We are not permitted in the palace, I'm afraid."

"Oh." Annie remembered Mr. Patel told her he was not permitted in the stables. This palace sure had a lot of rules.

"I will see that Miss Tessen gets the message. Are you ready to go back to the palace?"

Annie nodded and gave Buck one last pet on the nose. "You behave, mister. No getting nervous and pacing in your stall. You need to be fresh for practice in the morning."

She left Buck munching on hay while she and the groomsman made their way back to the arch where Annie's carriage awaited. She asked him many questions about the queen's horses, and he was kind enough to oblige her with a history of many of them. He proudly told her the queen had started a breeding program for her carriage horses.

"She also loves to ride every day—well, not so much anymore. Not since Mr. Brown passed away."

"Who was Mr. Brown?"

"He was a personal favorite of Her Majesty's. They were quite close. He used to walk with her for hours through the park—she on her favorite horse, Fyvie, and Mr. Brown on foot."

"Does she still ride?" Annie couldn't imagine not riding every day if she was able.

"Occasionally, but she misses Mr. Brown sorely—I'm told, almost as much as she misses her late husband, Prince Albert. She grows very attached to people, if you are lucky enough to have her approval."

"Have you her approval?" Annie asked, teasing him.

"Yes. She is very kind to me when I have occasion to see her."

"I'm glad of it. I am anxious to meet her. I'd love to be in her good graces. Do you have any words of wisdom for me?"

"Only the usual. Do not speak to her unless she speaks to you first. You may make eye contact, but do not stare. Be honest and forthright—she likes that." He smiled, his blue eyes twinkling.

As they turned the corner to approach the arch, something caught Annie's eye by the grooms' quarters. She saw Miss Tessen talking with Dr. Adams. The conversation looked intense, with both of them standing close. Annie stopped.

"There is your Miss Tessen," said the groomsman. "Would you like me to retrieve her?"

"No, I've been away from my husband too long."

Annie continued to watch Miss Tessen and the doctor, and nearly gasped when she saw Dr. Adams leaned in to kiss her. She did nothing to stop him. They embraced for a few seconds. When they broke apart, she said something to him, and they went their separate ways. Miss Tessen walked toward Buck's stall.

Annie continued walking toward the arch, stunned by what she had just witnessed. Dr. Adams and Miss Tessen—lovers? She tried to reconcile exactly what that meant. Was this a new courtship? Had it started on the ship? Miss Tessen had claimed she had no friends, no support. She had to inform Emma and get her opinion immediately.

"Thank you for showing me around," she said to the groom. "I need to return to the palace and my husband. Tell Miss Tessen I will speak with her tomorrow."

The groomsman helped her into the carriage, closing the door behind her. The carriage jerked to a start and Annie sank back into the velvet cushion, the image of Miss Tessen and Dr. Adams embracing etched into her mind.

They were the last two people Annie ever imagined as a couple.

Chapter Twenty-Six

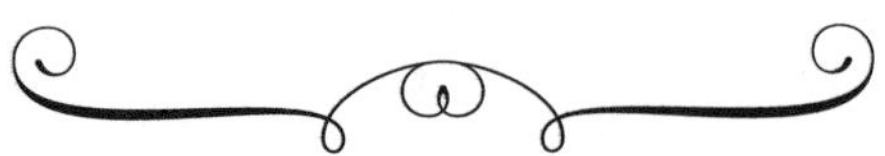

Annie walked into their suite and found Frank sitting at the table in the reception room, a blanket wrapped around his shoulders, playing cards with Hulda.

"My goodness, Frank, you look quite restored." She walked over and bent down to give him a kiss. "The treatment did you well."

"I feel better than I've felt in weeks. The royal physician is a miracle worker. No disrespect to Dr. Adams, but maybe he could learn a thing or two from the man," Frank said, smiling. Annie couldn't agree more. As pleased as she was to see Frank better, it raised her suspicions about Dr. Adams.

"Your sister is also a miracle worker with these cards. She's beaten me every time. We may have a cardsharp in the family."

Hulda beamed at him. "I don't want to play cards, Frank, I want to sew."

"You have many talents," said Annie. It was good to see Hulda happy again, and Frank feeling so much better. Any reservations she had about staying away from the show grounds evaporated.

She laid a hand over her belly and caressed it. She thought about her mother and how she had poured her love out to all of her children—and how she'd wept when she lost the three who had gone to be with God. She thought about Miss Parnell and her fierce devotion to Becky. A mother is a pillar of strength, a wonder to behold, the embodiment of love. Bringing a child into the world—even though the idea frightened her to her core—was noble and courageous and beautiful.

"Hulda, could I have a private word with Frank?"

Hulda looked up from her hand of cards. "But I'm winning."

"I forfeit," said Frank laying down his hand. "My ego can't take much more of this."

Hulda rolled her eyes and gathered up the cards from the table.

"Very well, I will *retire to my chambers*," she said in an affected voice. "I will play solitaire with a much more worthy opponent."

"I'm sure you will win," said Frank with a chuckle. Hulda stuck her tongue out at him and left the room.

"Mr. Ingle is having dinner sent up to the room shortly," Frank said. "I thought we could all use a little peace and quiet."

"That sounds wonderful." Annie took his hand in hers. "Frank, I'm sorry I have been dismissive of this possible pregnancy."

"It's a lot to consider." He squeezed her hand. "But if you are pregnant, there is nothing to be done about it except embrace the idea."

"I'm scared, Frank. What if the colonel fires me from the show?"

"We will manage, darling. If need be, I can work for my family—run the horse operation. I know a thing or two about farming, too." He kissed the back of her hand, and Annie melted into his words. He always knew how to comfort her.

"But what about Mother, Hulda, and John Henry?" She'd been taking care of them for so long, she couldn't imagine not doing so.

"Your mother has Mr. Shaw and the mercantile. He makes a fine living with the store and his farm. Hulda will always be able to find work as a seamstress, and John Henry is turning into a strapping young man. He's smart, and he can work hard. We can help if necessary."

He made good points, all of them, but something still poked at her resolve.

"But I enjoy working, performing, traveling. I love what I do, Frank. It's a part of who I am now." She looked into his eyes, waiting to see the disapproval, the disappointment, but they only softened with her gaze.

"Who says you have to stop performing? You will for a short time once we know for sure—and for a short time until you heal—but I have no objections to you working if it's what makes you happy. We will find a way, Annie. I promise."

Annie's eyes brimmed with tears. "You are so good to me, Frank. I've been such a fool." She reached across the table and wrapped her arms around his shoulders. She squeezed her eyes shut and said a silent prayer of thanks for Frank and his improved health.

Their embrace reminded her of what she had seen in the Royal Mews. She told Frank about Dr. Adams and Miss Tessen. She also told him that Dr. Adams had asked to see him.

"I don't think I want him treating you again, Frank. You're so improved since you have been out of his care," Annie said, wrapping the blanket tighter around his shoulders.

"No. We should let him come. I'd like to see what Dr. Adams has to say about my improved condition. His reaction might tell us something."

"You're right, Frank. As always."

~

Early the following morning, Annie and Frank received a note from Mr. Patel stating that Dr. Adams had been to visit him that evening, and now wanted to see them both. He would be by at half past eight, and Mr. Patel would escort him to their rooms.

Annie looked at the ornate, golden clock above the marble fireplace mantel. It read half past seven. She would need to dress soon.

"He sure seems anxious to see us," Annie said, handing Frank the note. Frank's color had returned, and he seemed more energetic than he had in weeks. He also managed to eat all of his breakfast and part of hers.

"I agree he is a peculiar man, and I'm concerned that I remained so sick under his care, but I also can't find a motive for him trying to harm me. What would be the point? And what would be the point of keeping me sick but alive, when he could easily have killed me before now and blamed my illness?"

"He is hiding something, Frank. I don't know what, but he is," Annie said, picking at a piece of toast. "And look how much better you are now."

"I don't disagree, love," he said, his eyes brighter than they had been since before the voyage. "We'll both stay vigilant."

Annie wrinkled her nose. "I'll need to go to Earl's Court for practice directly after Dr. Adams's visit. I also want to tell Emma what I've learned about Miss Tessen and the mysterious doctor."

"Will you take Hulda?" Frank asked.

"Must I go?" Hulda said, coming out of her room. "Mr. Ingle said he would arrange another carriage ride in the park for me today."

Hulda had been so happy since they'd arrived at the palace, and at least here, she would be away from Lillie's influence. Certainly the royal guards could keep her safer than Annie herself. Besides, Annie's costumes were up to date and fit perfectly, and she wasn't to have a performance until day after tomorrow.

"You may go to the park," Annie said. "But first, help me dress."

Hulda squealed and flounced back into her bedroom.

After they had dressed, Hulda went in search of Mr. Ingle, who was probably standing right outside their suite, as always. Annie wondered if the man ever slept or ate. Annie helped Frank back into bed.

"I really don't think I need to be in bed anymore. My backside is killing me," he said in protest. "And I'd love to get out into the air. I've been cooped up for so long."

"Why don't we see what the royal physician has to say? He said he would drop by this afternoon."

"I see the motherly instincts are starting to manifest," Frank said, grumbling.

A knock at the door prevented Annie from a retort. She opened it and found Mr. Ingle, Mr. Patel, and Dr. Adams there.

"You have visitors," said Mr. Ingle. "Is there anything you require?"

Annie told him no and invited the two men inside.

"Well, you have quite a setup here," Dr. Adams said looking around the reception room and smoothing his mustache. "The queen's excess shows no bounds. Mr. Patel has fine quarters as well, for a servant. He provided me with some strong coffee."

"It was my pleasure," said Mr. Patel. "Now, if you will excuse me, I have duties to attend to." He bowed and made his way out of the room. Annie couldn't blame him, having been subjected to Dr. Adams's rudeness. She wanted to comment on it, but decided it probably would do no good.

Instead, she led Dr. Adams to the bedroom.

"Mr. Butler, you look quite well," he said.

"Thank you, sir. I am feeling better."

The doctor opened his bag and took out some of his instruments. He examined Frank and then handed Annie a small, dark brown bottle.

"The blood-letting is a good treatment, but results vary. I recommend you take this tonic in addition to anything the palace physician might prescribe. Check with him, of course, first, but it is my recommendation."

"Is it more of the tisane?" Annie asked. "Frank did not respond to what you gave him earlier."

"No. This is something to restore the blood. I will be back tomorrow to check on you." Dr. Adams collected his instruments. Annie wanted to tell him it wasn't necessary to return, but how would she find out what he was hiding if she kept him away?

She thanked him and saw him out the door.

Frank would not be taking the tonic she held in her hand. Not until she knew what was in it.

Annie opted to walk to the stables, even though she ran the risk of showing up late to practice. She checked her pocket for the bottle of medicine and felt it secure deep inside. She adjusted her gun belt and buttoned her duster over it, fending off the chill of the morning.

As she approached Buck's stall, she saw her saddle and bridle placed neatly on a saddle rack next to the stall door, and Miss Tessen inside the stall, grooming Buck to a gleaming gold. He noisily ate his hay and grain as Miss Tessen worked.

Annie noticed that somewhere along the line, the woman had abandoned the red, tattered coat and replaced it with a better-fitting sweater, though drab in color. She'd also put some meat on her bones and lost the gaunt look of the malnourished.

Since Miss Tessen was working for Annie for room and board, she wondered where the woman had come up with the money for the sweater. Perhaps Dr. Adams had bought it for her.

"Fine morning, Miss Tessen. Is Buck almost ready to go?" Annie asked.

"Yes, Miss Oakley. I just have to clean his feet and tack him up," she said, avoiding eye contact with Annie.

"How are the accommodations here in the stables?"

"Right fine, they are. Small, but warm."

"I see you have a new sweater."

Miss Tessen looked down at her clothing. "Yes. One of the grooms was kind enough to give it to me. The morning can be downright brisk."

"Yes." Annie agreed as she pulled the lapels of her duster closer together. "Dr. Adams came to see Frank today." Annie's words hung in the air as Miss Tessen slowed with the brush.

"Did he? Dr. Adams from the ship?" Miss Tessen bent over to work on Buck's feet. "How is Mr. Butler feeling?"

"Oh, much better. Should be up and about in a day or so, according to the royal physician."

Miss Tessen stood, resting her arm across Buck's back. "That's excellent news."

"Did you happen to see Dr. Adams yesterday?" Annie asked, eager to see her reaction. Miss Tessen busied herself with another hoof.

"Can't see why I would, not being in the palace and all. Why do you ask?" Miss Tessen stood up again and this time made direct eye contact with Annie.

"No reason."

She opened the stall door and reached for Annie's saddle blanket. She hoisted it up onto Buck's back, then saddled him. Annie paid particular attention, making sure Miss Tessen pulled the cinch snug but not too snug. She picked up the bridle and inspected it, running her hand over the bit, checking for rough edges or dirt. She followed Miss Tessen as she led Buck out of the stall. She'd make a point to keep a closer eye on the woman when Buck was in her care.

Miss Tessen held the reins while Annie mounted.

"I should be back early this afternoon," Annie said, taking the reins and wondering why Miss Tessen had lied to her—again.

As she had feared, Annie showed up late to practice, despite trotting Buck through the park at a fast clip. She made her way to the arena where some of the cowboys were working the mounted shooting course. Several of the Indians stood talking in a circle on their ponies, and several of the crew herded the buffalo into their great pen.

Annie rode up to Bobby, who stood next to a table, cleaning his rifle.

"There's the fine lady," he said, looking up at her with a broad smile. "So what's it like living like a queen in a palace?"

"Lovely, but I'd much rather be here. Frank has improved." Annie scanned the area looking for the colonel or Mr. Salisbury.

"That's good news," said Bobby, checking the barrel of his rifle.

"Where is everyone?"

"By everyone, you mean Lillie? She hasn't been seen this morning. Neither have Mr. Everett and some of the cowboys. Probably gone to find a saloon. Old Charlie's got a belly ache, so the colonel is fit to be tied. He's worked up because we just got word that we are to perform for the queen in a week's time."

"What about practice this morning?" Annie asked.

"Been postponed till we can get things right. Nate said probably a couple of hours."

Annie sighed. She needed the practice, especially after her abysmal performance for the prince and princess. Lillie would not get the upper hand again.

"Care to set up the clay pigeons? I could use the extra practice," Annie said.

"Sure. I could use the practice, too."

Annie frowned at the idea of Mr. Everett cavorting with Lillie and the cowboys. He seemed more dignified than that. It wasn't the saloon that concerned her, but the company. Namely Lillie. And to think Mr. Everett had been sweet on Hulda. She still feared her sister would be hurt by his attentions. She tried to put it out of her mind, and concentrated on shooting.

While Annie and Bobby took turns pulling and shooting, Annie heard her name called from somewhere in the distance. She spotted Emma coming toward her, her dress pressed against her legs and her arms swinging at her sides. She looked in a hurry. Annie turned Buck and walked toward her, meeting her halfway.

"Hello, dear! How are things at the palace?" Emma asked, out of breath.

"Lovely. You are just the person I'd like to see. Bobby and I are just finishing here."

"You hit them all, Miss Oakley," Bobby said reloading his rifle. "Looks like I'm the one who really needs the practice."

"Still the best," said Emma, winking at Annie.

"I wish I had shot this well in front of the prince and princess."

"You may have another chance," said Emma.

"Let's go to my tent where we can chat," Annie said. "I think I have some tea."

Chapter Twenty-Seven

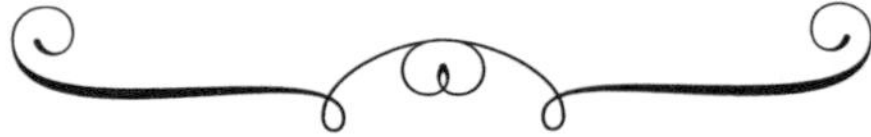

Annie took Buck to the stables, and Mr. Post shuffled over to them to receive the horse. His back had become more bent in the last couple of years, and his hair and whiskers were whiter than ever.

"I sure don't like not having eyes on this here yellow horse," he said with a frown. "Don't know why you couldn't a just left him here. I sure would feel better about things."

"I know, Mr. Post." Annie handed him the reins. "It won't be long. Frank is nearly well. Will you tend to Buck while I go to my tent with Miss Wilson? Just whistle when you see the colonel."

Once inside her tent, Annie got the water boiling and took off her duster and gun belt. While Emma set the teacups and saucers on the table, Annie told her about Miss Tessen and the doctor.

"Well, Annie, you must understand. Miss Tessen probably fears she will lose her position if she has a liaison with the doctor. There are a million reasons why she would keep a relationship with someone else in your employ a secret."

Annie agreed she had a point.

"The doctor left this with Frank." Annie pulled the bottle from her dress pocket. "I don't trust that it isn't something harmful. Is there any way you can work your magic with your connections in town to find out what this is?"

Emma took the bottle from her, holding it up to see the liquid inside. "Do you really think the doctor wants to harm Frank?"

"I don't know. I do feel like he has an agenda. Given how he feels about the queen, I don't trust him. Especially with the care of my husband—someone who is rumored to have connections with the Fenians. The unrest in this country astounds me."

Emma laughed. "And you don't think the unrest in our country is astounding? The way the government is rounding up all the native peoples and throwing them into internment camps?"

"I'm sorry, Emma. Yes, you know I am sympathetic to the Indians' plight. I guess I'm just at odds as to who is justified in their outrage in this country. It seems all are unhappy."

"It's true," said Emma, stirring sugar into her tea. "The *London Times* is allowing me to cover the situation at Trafalgar Square. The place is run riot." Her eyes sparkled with excitement.

"Wonderful, Emma. A big story! You're setting the standard for women in journalism—for the world in general." Annie's heart swelled with pride for her friend.

"Sisters in empowerment, you and I," Emma said with a giggle.

"Yes, Emma. It is thrilling, isn't it?"

"Quite." Emma lifted the cup to her lips and blew on it to cool the tea.

"Are the Irish at Trafalgar Square still up in arms about Mr. Parnell? Has he been released?" Annie asked.

"No, he hasn't. As you know, he is but one reason the Irish—and the English—are fighting mad."

"So the queen is still in danger." Annie nibbled on a biscuit.

"On many accounts."

"Well, we can't stop all the threats, but if we could understand why Mr. Bhakta died and why someone wants to hurt Frank, perhaps we can help with one threat," said Annie.

"But now that we have gotten off the ship, how can we track down who killed Mr. Bhakta and wrote the notes? It all seems to be unraveling," Emma said.

A memory flashed into Annie's mind. "There might be a connection after all, Emma. Do you remember when you got out of the coach at Trafalgar Square the day we went to visit Miss Parnell and Miss Brady at the asylum?"

"Yes, you were not pleased, I recall."

"I wasn't. But as we pulled away, I saw a woman standing among the crowd, dressed all in black. I thought she looked familiar, and now, I just remembered who she is."

"Well, spill it, darling. The suspense is killing me."

"Madame Mattei."

"The old woman? Who never left her stateroom, like a vampire?" Emma asked.

"Yes, I could swear it was her I saw at Trafalgar Square. She said she wouldn't be staying in London, but traveling on to Belgium. Why would she lie? Why would she be with the malcontents at Trafalgar Square?"

Mr. Post's familiar whistle echoed through Annie's tent.

"I have to go to practice, Emma. Perhaps Lillie and Mr. Everett have returned. I guess the colonel is hopping mad."

"That girl really has a lot of nerve, doesn't she?"

"You have no idea. She tests my patience on a daily basis." Annie swallowed down the last of her tea. She stood and secured her gun belt in place once more.

"But I guess the colonel and Mr. Salisbury would be fools to replace her. She's right on your heels as the sweetheart of the Wild West Show." Emma raised her teacup to her lips, a teasing light shining from her eyes.

"You realize I'm carrying a gun," Annie said.

"I'll have the medicine checked, dear." Emma raised her teacup in a toast.

"And I'll make a visit to Trafalgar Square after practice," said Annie, throwing her duster over her arm.

~

Annie went to the stables to retrieve Buck. He was tied to a hitching post, dozing, while Mr. Post, sitting on a barrel nearby, gnawed on an apple.

"The colonel cancelled practice. He's mad as a blue hornet at Miss Smith for not turning up," he said, spitting some seeds out of his mouth.

"How is Old Charlie feeling?"

Mr. Post pointed to one of the corrals where Charlie stood dozing in the sun.

"He's fine. Just getting old. I think he needs his teeth filed—doesn't seem to want to eat much these days. The colonel is right upset about it."

"I can understand that." Annie unfurled her reins from the hitching post. "Do you suppose Mr. Everett and Lillie are together?" Annie didn't know how she felt about the prospect. Although she didn't want

Hulda involved with the handsome veterinarian, she also didn't want Hulda's feelings hurt by her "friend" Lillie.

"That girl could corrupt just about anyone, I suppose. I hope for his sake they aren't. He's probably off just enjoying the exhibition—Lord knows there is a lot going on around here. Downright distracting. It's been a frustration for the colonel with you off at the palace, Lillie carousing around, the Indians scattered all over the place, and the cowboys at the whorehouses."

Annie stifled a smile. The poor colonel. "Well, you tell him I hope to be back in a few days—well before the queen's performance. It will all come together."

Annie shot some practice rounds with Bobby, and then sought out Red Shirt and Black Elk for a quick visit. She found the two chiefs seated by a fire they had made. She spent some time talking with them and afterwards, anxious to see if she could locate Madame Mattei, headed back toward the palace.

The streets of London were full of excitement as people traversed the parks, either on foot or in gleaming carriages. Street vendors sold peanuts and sweets. People stared at Annie in her American Western garb as she trotted in her Western saddle with its gleaming silver trim. Everyone else she saw riding in the park used English style saddles. Annie paid them no mind, trying to put together the pieces of the puzzle that had started with Mr. Bhakta, included Frank, and ended with the threat of an assassination attempt on the queen.

She passed by the palace and headed toward Trafalgar Square. The people encamped at the base of the monument sat on the steps or huddled in their makeshift tents. Some of the women had made fires under hanging kettles.

She and Buck walked the area for three quarters of an hour, looking for Madame Mattei, but saw no sign of her. Emma agreed to come to the square in the coming days for her story, and would also be on the lookout for the old lady in black.

Annie returned to the mews and deposited Buck with Miss Tessen, who greeted her at Buck's stall. Distracted by her thoughts, Annie did not make conversation with her but strode briskly back to the palace.

She nodded to Mr. Ingle, who stood stationed next to the Belgium Suite, and entered to find Frank dressed in his favorite black slacks, white shirt, and red-and-black waistcoat, reading the paper.

"Don't you look back to yourself," Annie said, her heart filled with happiness at seeing Frank completely restored.

"I even took a walk around the palace today," Frank said, sounding joyful.

"Did Hulda have a nice day?" Annie asked, heading toward her sister's room.

"I haven't seen her since she left for the park this morning. I thought perhaps she was with you," Frank said.

"No, she wasn't with me." Annie raced back to the door. "Mr. Ingle. Mr. Ingle. Have you seen my sister?"

Mr. Ingle came to the opened door, his posture erect, hands behind his back. "Not since this morning, madam. I arranged a carriage ride for her in the park. She has not returned."

"Oh, Frank, what is that girl up to? I can't leave her for a minute!"

"Calm down, darling," Frank said, gently taking her by the arms. "You should not get overwrought."

Annie shook off his hands. "Frank, this is no time to coddle me. I feel fine. But I have to find my sister."

"Let's go see if we can find her."

"Mr. Ingle, may we have permission to peruse the palace?" Annie asked.

"Certainly, but I must accompany you."

"I'd like to see if perhaps Mr. Patel has seen her. Would you take us to his quarters?"

Despite his stoic nature, Mr. Ingle's already stern expression visibly soured at the mention of Mr. Patel.

"If you insist," he said.

When they reached Mr. Patel's room, they found several people there, including Dr. Adams.

Mr. Patel was seated at his table, undergoing verbal interrogation by the other two men in the room, one of medium stature with a square head that somewhat resembled an icebox, and the other who was taller and reedy with pale hair and the light eyes of a ferret. Both looked to be palace officials by their uniforms.

"What is the meaning of this?" said Mr. Ingle, pushing past Dr. Adams.

"He is being questioned," said Dr. Adams in a whisper.

"What's happened?" asked Annie. Dr. Adams turned to face Annie and Frank.

"I came to see Mr. Patel, to inquire after Mr. Butler, who was not in his room," he said, still in a hushed tone. "Mr. Patel offered me tea, and when he reached onto the shelf to pull down the tea tin, this fell to the floor." Dr. Adams held up the remains of a tear catcher, almost identical to the one Annie had found on the ship. "And there was a note inside." He handed it to Annie.

"The road of excess leads to the palace of wisdom. The tigers of wrath are wiser than the horses of instruction." She lowered the note. "More contradiction."

"Blake, I presume," said the doctor. "I excused myself for a moment and alerted the palace officials. I believe Mr. Patel murdered Mr. Bhakta, and may have reason to harm the queen."

"But that can't be true, Dr. Adams," said Annie. "Mr. Bhakta saved Mr. Patel's life, during the Indian rebellion."

"It is *not* true," said Mr. Patel. "I would never harm Mr. Bhakta, or Her Majesty. Someone has been in my room. I have proof—my necklace, the medal I wear around my neck, is missing."

"Quiet," said the heftier guard. The taller one was writing furiously in a notebook.

"It's about time," said Mr. Ingle under his breath.

The taller official turned to him. "Do you know something, sir? Who are you?"

"I work for the queen's household. My name is Ingle. I have been assigned as personal butler to Mr. Butler and Miss Oakley."

"What did you mean, 'it's about time?'"

"It is the opinion of many of Her Majesty's servants that Mr. Patel expected to take the position of personal assistant to the queen when Mr. Bhakta died. He was overheard saying as much to one of his Indian cronies. The queen has replaced Mr. Bhakta with an English servant. I'm sure Mr. Patel resented being passed over."

"That's ridiculous," said Mr. Patel. "I said nothing of the kind."

"Does this tear catcher belong to you?" The tall guard asked Mr. Patel.

"I've never seen it in my life. I tell you, someone was in my room. They planted it here."

The guard turned to Dr. Adams. "You say this resembles the tear catcher found on the ship?"

Dr. Adams nodded. "It does. As does the note inside. Wouldn't you agree, Miss Oakley?"

They all turned to face Annie, who stood staring, mouth agape. She couldn't deny they looked the same. "Well, yes, but I am sure many people have similar tear catchers. What's important is what might be inside the thing. Dr. Adams was able to determine that the substance inside the tear catcher was poison. The same analysis should be done on this one."

"And the handwriting on the notes compared," added Frank.

"Do you still have this item that was found on the ship?" the guard asked the doctor.

"We turned it in when we reached London. To the police. They had another individual in custody for the crime," said Annie, the pain of accusing Miss Brady coming back to her.

The tall guard scribbled on his pad. "Who was this individual?"

Annie told him the story of what happened.

"Very well. You all might be further questioned by the police," he said, snapping shut his pad of paper and placing the pencil behind his ear. "Until more can be determined, Mr. Patel here will be in custody of the London police."

"But what if he is telling the truth?" said Annie. "What if someone did plant it here. He said his medal was stolen."

The bulky guard took Mr. Patel by the arm, forcing him to stand. "It will all get sorted out."

"I did not commit these crimes," Mr. Patel said, his eyes imploring Annie's. "I did not."

Annie and Frank bid Dr. Adams good night after he'd made some inquiry into their health. He seemed satisfied with their answers.

"I have the strong sense Mr. Patel is telling the truth, Frank," Annie said. "I can feel it in my gut."

"I agree. He looked truly surprised."

"Yes. And so sincere in his conviction that he'd been set up."

Mr. Ingle took them back to the main gallery in search of Hulda. Not finding her, they decided to go back to the Belgium Suite to see if she'd returned. They opened the door to find Hulda sitting at the table in the reception room playing cards with Lillie.

"Hulda! Where have you been?" asked Annie, marching over to her, "I've been beside myself with worry. And what is Lillie doing here?"

"Hey, doll," Lillie said, smirking at her.

Hulda stood up, taking hold of Annie's hand. "I'm fine, Annie. As you can see. Mr. Ingle arranged a carriage for me to see the park again. While I was there, I saw Lillie and—"

Lillie snorted. When Annie glared at her, she cast her eyes back down to her cards, a mischievous smile playing at her lips.

"And Mr. Everett?" Annie said, trying to maintain calm.

"Yes, but Lillie was with us the whole time. When the carriage driver returned us to the palace, I got special permission from Mr. Stanley for Lillie to come back with me. To keep me company. He cleared it with the guards and everything," Hulda said.

"Lillie is a far cry from an appropriate chaperone, Hulda." She turned to Lillie. "Why won't you leave her alone?"

Lillie shrugged. "I'm not that bad, Annie. I thought we were friends."

"Lillie, you missed practice today. The colonel is furious. We are performing for the queen in less than a week. He and Mr. Salisbury are beside themselves with anxiety over it. And you continue to set a bad example for Hulda. Mr. Everett is far too old for her. What were you thinking?" Annie realized her voice had raised a few octaves. Her hands shook, and she could feel her heartbeat pulsating up to her ears.

Frank came up behind Annie and put his hands on her shoulders. "It's been a long day, Annie."

"It *has*, Frank," Annie said.

"Don't raise your voice to me, Annie. Hulda, you have caused your sister a good deal of distress with your behavior. Go to your room." Frank said.

"You can't tell me what to do." Hulda's face pinched with indignation.

"Show some respect, Hulda!"

"Calm down, both of you," Frank commanded.

Annie couldn't abide her sister sassing her husband, nor her husband telling her to calm down. She wanted to scream. She placed both palms against the sides of her head and paced the floor, incensed that their stay at the palace had come to this humiliation.

Frank, Lillie, and Hulda remained silent, watching her as if she were a raving lunatic—which, at the moment, she was.

"Hulda, you had no right to invite a guest to the palace, nor do you have the right to disrespect my husband. Lillie, go back to Earl's Court—now. I don't care if you have to walk. Hulda, you go straight to bed, and Frank, help me pack. We are leaving in the morning."

Chapter Twenty-Eight

Annie awoke in Frank's arms. She lay staring at the swirling dust motes that danced in the shaft of sunlight peeking through the heavy brocaded curtains. She had not slept well and had only fallen asleep a few hours earlier when Frank had reached out to comfort her. The stillness of the morning and the steady rhythm of Frank's breathing gave her some solace as she tried to sort out all that had transpired since they'd departed from New York.

How could she have so failed with Hulda? Had she left her at home, would she be giving her mother fits? She thought getting away from the show for a few days would be good for Hulda—and would also allow them to spend some time together. But it had all gone wrong.

At least Frank's health had improved. She couldn't be sure if whatever ailed him had just run its course, as Mr. Everett had said it would if Frank had contracted the illness from the algae, or if Dr. Adams, or someone through him, had set out to harm Frank because of his alleged association with Irish unrest.

She felt him stir beside her.

"Have you been awake long?" he asked, kissing the top of her head.

"No."

"Penny for them."

Annie sighed. "I was just thinking about Hulda. What kind of a mother am I going to be if I can't seem to do right by my sister?"

Frank stroked her arm. "You will be an excellent mother. Hulda is going through what many young people do at her age. She's just testing the waters."

"Testing me, more like."

"That too." A chuckle reverberated through Frank's chest.

"And I can't help feeling sorry for Mr. Patel. He spoke so fondly of Mr. Bhakta. I have trouble believing he would have killed him." Annie propped herself up on an elbow. "What do you think?"

Frank rolled on his side to face her, adjusting the pillow more securely under his neck.

"I think we will know more when it is determined what was in the tear catcher. Viper venom is a very unusual type of poison. There are so many others that are much more readily available. And he does have the connection with Sri Lanka where the particular viper hails from. Or. . . ." Frank raised himself on an elbow. "Dr. Adams only claimed the poison was viper venom. It could have been something else. Maybe he wanted to make Mr. Patel look guilty."

Annie shook her head. "We're missing something. It all seems such a jumble—but one thing is sure."

"What is that?" Frank asked, smiling at her.

"You are returned to me, Frank Butler, and I am so grateful." She leaned into him and kissed him. She had missed their tender embraces, their lovemaking. Frank must have missed it too, because he kissed her back with the passion she so fondly remembered, crushed her body to his, and then pulled the covers over their heads.

They woke again a couple of hours later, dressed, and summoned Mr. Ingle to tell him they wished to return to Earl's Court. When he offered to have breakfast sent to their suite, they readily agreed.

While they dined on cheese, bread, boiled oatmeal, and bacon, Hulda came out of her room looking sheepishly chastened.

"I'm sorry for upsetting you yesterday, Annie. Must we really leave the palace?"

Annie cast a glance at Frank and he winked at her.

"I accept your apology," Annie said, using an authoritative but compassionate tone, "but, yes, we are leaving the palace. I think it would help the colonel to have us all in one place."

"So it's not just because of me?" Hulda asked, worry lining her brow.

"Not entirely," Annie assured her.

They heard a knock on the door, and Mr. Ingle and the royal physician entered the reception room.

"Mr. Butler, the royal physician would like to see you again before you go," said Mr. Ingle.

"By all means," said Frank rising from the table. "Please come in."

"No need to get up," said the doctor. "I can see you are much improved." He came over to the table and reached for Frank's wrist. He pulled a pocket watch from his waistcoat and studied it while he took Frank's pulse.

"I think you'll be fine," he said.

"I feel great. Better than I have in weeks."

Mr. Ingle came into the room, cleared his throat, and looked pointedly at the doctor.

"Yes, Ingle. What is it?"

"Your presence is required in the yellow drawing room."

"By whom?"

"The police, sir."

"Ah, yes. Well, it's been a pleasure serving you, Mr. Butler."

Frank shook the doctor's hand. "I can't tell you how much I appreciate your talent, Doc."

"Yes, thank you, Doctor," Annie said, also shaking his hand. She wondered what the police wanted with him. Or had he requested they come to the palace? Did this have something to do with Mr. Patel and the tear catcher? How she would love to be a fly on the wall when he spoke with the police.

The doctor took up his bag and left the room, Mr. Ingle behind him. Annie followed them to the door and let it click shut before she opened it again and peeked out to see if anyone was guarding the door in Mr. Ingle's place. The hallway looked clear.

"Where are you going, Annie?" Frank was right behind her.

"I'm going to follow them. I forgot to ask the doctor something about my pregnancy." She didn't like lying to Frank, but she knew he would try to dissuade her.

"What about it?"

"I'll tell you later, I don't want to miss him. Please stay here with Hulda. Don't let her out of your sight."

Before Frank could protest, Annie dashed down the hall in the direction Mr. Ingle had led the doctor. She came to a marble stairway to her left. She thought she could hear voices down below. Tiptoeing so her boots did not clack on the marble, she descended the stairs as fast as she could and stopped when she reached the bottom, straining to hear.

The staircase led to a great carpeted hall, with an arched glass ceiling and ornately carved wood-paneled walls. She heard muffled voices to the right, so she followed them. The voices grew louder, and she thought she recognized the voice of Inspector Granger.

When she reached what must have been the yellow drawing room, she stopped.

"Thank you for meeting me, Inspector. I have some news regarding the tear catcher that was found in Mr. Patel's room."

"Let's hear it," said the Inspector.

"The residue of the substance within the tube was indeed a toxin of some sort. I'm afraid the evidence against Mr. Patel is substantial. Unfortunate, but not surprising."

"What do you mean, not surprising?" the doctor asked.

"Given his past as a young sepoy rebel. The authorities believe he manipulated Mr. Bhakta, a known favorite of the queen, into his position here at the palace. The rebels are known for their hatred of the English—and our queen, damn them all, the darkies—but she is so desirous of peace between our two nations, she sometimes does not see ill intent. We also believe Mr. Patel was in league with someone outside the palace."

"What makes you think that?" asked the doctor.

"Because Dr. Adams was found dead this morning in Hyde Park."

Still reeling from the news about Dr. Adams, Annie opted to ride in the carriage with Hulda, Frank, and Miss Tessen back to Earl's Court, instead of riding Buck. She didn't want the distraction of the bustle on the street. The footman, standing on the back of the carriage, held Buck's line as he trotted behind.

Annie had shared the news of Dr. Adams's death after they'd gotten into the carriage. She paid particular attention to Miss Tessen when she divulged what she had heard. The woman seemed nonplussed, which perplexed her. Emma had mentioned the relationship might be a secret for any number of reasons. Perhaps, one of them was married? Miss Tessen seemed a strong woman, but for her to show so little emotion gave Annie pause. The woman grew more mysterious every day.

The four of them sat in silence as the carriage passed through the gates of Buckingham Palace and onto the street.

"It's a terrible thing," said Annie. "It's hard to believe Dr. Adams is gone."

Miss Tessen, sitting directly across from Annie and Frank, stared out the carriage window. Hulda, seated next to her, did the same. Annie worried about Hulda's state of mind. She'd been so quiet since their altercation the previous evening. Annie couldn't tell if her current mood was the result of leaving the palace or the shocking reality that another person had been murdered. Again, it gave rise to the thought that she should never have brought her sister to England.

"Well, it looks like Mr. Bhakta's killer has been found," said Frank. "Perhaps the threat to the queen we feared has been has been eradicated. Now, we can focus on the show and enjoy this wonderful country."

"I don't believe Mr. Patel guilty of either crime," said Annie. "He insists someone has set him up."

"Convenient excuse. Of course he won't admit to it." Miss Tessen finally spoke, venom in her voice.

At last, some kind of reaction, Annie thought.

Miss Tessen turned toward the window again, anger lingering in her eyes. Perhaps she did mourn the death of the doctor—she just didn't want to admit to the relationship, as Emma had suggested.

Annie wanted to see Buck settled again, and also wanted to question Miss Tessen further about the nature of her relationship with Dr. Adams, thinking she might open up without Frank and Hulda present.

She accompanied Miss Tessen to the stables. While Miss Tessen got Annie's tack organized and put away, Annie led Buck to his pen. She then took the pitchfork leaning against the haystack, and scooped some hay for him to eat.

Miss Tessen, finished with the tack, brought a bucketful of water to fill Buck's trough.

"I'm sorry, Miss Tessen," Annie said.

"Sorry? What for?" Miss Tessen swept a lock of errant hair behind her ear.

"Dr. Adams. I saw you, you know." Annie leaned against Buck's shoulder. "In the mews courtyard. I saw the two of you kissing. You needn't fear judgment from me."

Miss Tessen set down the bucket. "Oh, that."

"I'm sorry for your loss," Annie said. "He must have meant something to you."

"Well, he didn't. It wasn't like that."

"I don't follow."

"He—Dr. Adams—he made advances. I didn't return his affections, and it made him angry. He figured a girl like me—without friends, without family—would be happy for his attention. But I wasn't. So no, I'm not broken up about his death. Is that terrible?" She dropped her fists to her sides, but did not unclench them.

Annie shook her head. “No. No, it isn’t terrible. I didn’t understand, but now I do. Thank you for telling me.” Annie was disappointed in herself for never considering the doctor might be pressuring Miss Tessen in some way. A poor woman being taken advantage of by an older, wealthier man. It happened all the time. “I’m sorry.”

Miss Tessen waved a hand. “It’s over. I’ll go see if Hulda needs any help. Is there anything I can do for you, Miss Oakley?” she asked, her features and her hands relaxing.

“No, thank you. I’ll just stay out here with Buck for a while.”

Miss Tessen headed back toward the tents. Annie saw Emma coming toward her, crossing paths with Miss Tessen.

“The prodigal daughter returns,” said Emma. “I’m surprised to see you back.”

“It’s a long story. Make me a cup of tea?”

“Sounds good to me.” Emma opened the gate to the pen to let Annie out. “It’s no palace, but you are welcome in my tent.”

Annie stepped into Emma’s tent and took in a sharp breath, struck by the lavish furnishings. A large sleigh bed, angled in the corner and covered with a silk floral quilt, took up most of the space. A charming wooden tea table draped with a silk scarf and two floral cushioned chairs graced the opposite corner. Her desk, as large as the colonel’s and strewn with papers, took up another corner, while the last corner was reserved for a small, pot-bellied, wood-burning stove. All but the stove stood atop a finely woven, plush Persian rug.

“I don’t know how you do it, Emma. These furnishings are lovely.

Not that what the colonel has provided for us is not, but you have outdone yourself."

Emma set a teapot on the stove and then threw some wood into its belly. Annie took a seat in one of the cushioned chairs. "Did the *Chicago Herald* provide this?"

"Oh, heavens no, silly." Emma spooned some tea from a tin into two cups. "My taste is too high for them. The stipend they give me barely covers the cost of my hats. A little trip to Tottenham Court Road and voila! Furnishings. Oh, I almost forgot." She went to a small vanity next to the bed and picked up two letters.

"This came for you." Emma held out an envelope for Annie.

She took it and turned it over. The seal on the back read L. L. "Must be from Mrs. Langtry, Mr. Wilde's friend."

"And the prince's paramour," said Emma with a twist of her lips.

Annie tore open the envelope. The tea kettle rumbled as the water boiled. Emma poured the water into a teapot, and brought it and two teacups over to the table.

"It's an invitation to dinner at the Ruben's Hotel, Mrs. Langtry's private suite," said Annie, a sinking feeling in her stomach. The latent nausea returned. She felt she was about to be put on display—the quaint American little girl sensation. Even the princess had referred to her as "a clever little girl."

"I received one, too." Emma held up the other envelope. "Oh, don't look so mortified, Annie. It's an honor. I, myself, feel quite privileged. She knows all of the important people. Artists, musicians, actors—you name it. She knows all the scuttlebutt around town."

"Do you think she knows about Dr. Adams?"

"Everyone will know about Dr. Adams. I heard from some friends of mine at the *Times* that Mr. Frank Butler's personal physician was found murdered in the park. The story will hit the papers tomorrow."

"Oh, dear," Annie said. "The colonel won't like the negative publicity."

"He will love it, dear. It will bring people to the show—not that you all need any help. The Wild West Show is a sensation. I understand there will be a performance for the queen next week."

"Yes. And did you hear about Mr. Patel?"

"No. What about him?" Emma poured them each a cup of tea.

Annie told him what had transpired the night before Dr. Adams was killed.

"And they think Patel is responsible—for all of it?"

"Yes. I would like to believe that we have found the murderer, and at least one threat to the queen, but, Emma, I don't feel we have." Annie spun her teacup in its saucer.

"Annie, you have a strong intuition. It has served you well in the past," Emma said, sipping her tea.

"Not with Miss Brady, poor soul. I made a horrible mistake."

"You followed some evidence—not your intuition. Rely on your sensibilities, my dear. Did you track down Madame Mattei?"

"No. I saw no sign of her."

"I, too, asked about her around the square," Emma said. "I did speak with a man who might have seen her. He was quite drunk, though. Couldn't be sure."

"Are people still railing against the queen?" Annie couldn't discount the notion that whoever killed Mr. Bhakta could be associated with the angry mob.

"Oh yes. Until some of these prisoners like Mr. Parnell are released, and the Irish problem is solved—they will continue to protest."

"Hello?" A voice came from outside the tent. It sounded like Bobby.

"*Entrez*!" sang out Emma.

Bobby stuck his head through the opening. "Oh, Miss Tessen said I might find you in here, Annie. Telegram for you." Bobby came in, ripped off his hat, and handed Annie the piece of paper.

"Join us for tea, Bobby?" Emma asked, giving him her most flirtatious grin.

Bobby's face flushed bright red. He mercilessly crumpled his hat in his hands. "Oh, no thank you, ma'am. The colonel and Mr. Salisbury need me to shoe their horses. I just wanted to bring Miss Annie her telegram."

"Another time." Emma's dimples sank charmingly into her alabaster cheeks.

Completely flustered, Bobby nearly ran out of the tent.

"Emma, you are cruel," said Annie.

"I like to have a little fun. I'm not getting any younger—approaching the spinster age far too rapidly. So are you going to open your telegram? Could be from an adoring fan."

Annie unfolded the paper and scanned the type. Her stomach folded in on itself. She handed the message to Emma.

"Oh my goodness," Emma said, grabbing hold of Annie's hand. "You were absolutely right. Mr. Patel is not the murderer."

Chapter Twenty-Nine

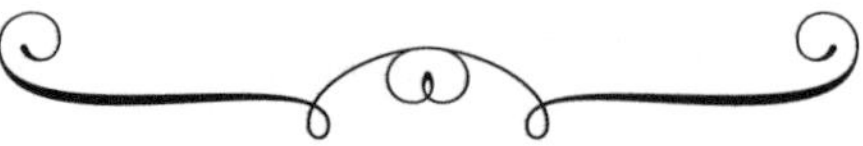

Annie, clutching the telegram in her hand, walked up to Lillie's tent.

"Are you in there?" she called.

Lillie came to the tent flap and folded it open. "Oh, it's you."

"Lillie, I need to speak with you. It's of the utmost importance." Annie didn't have time to bicker.

"Well, then I guess you'd better come in." Lillie sighed, holding the tent flap open for her.

Annie stepped through and was not surprised at what she saw. Clothes everywhere, guns strewn across the bureau next to a bottle of whiskey and two crystal glasses, powders and toiletries scattered across the vanity, and her bed an unmade, crumpled mess. Annie did not miss sharing living quarters with Lillie.

"Want a cigarette?" Lillie asked, running a match across a flint stone and then holding it up to the cigarette she had placed in her mouth.

"No. You know I don't smoke."

"Yes. The prim Miss Oakley—no smoking, no drinking, no fun." Lillie took a long drag.

"I'm not here for trouble, Lillie. I need a favor."

Lillie walked over to her bed and lounged across it, holding the cigarette aloft. She raised her eyebrows expectantly, waiting for Annie to continue.

"I've received a disturbing telegram. Whoever sent it has threatened Hulda."

"What?" Lillie sat up, suddenly interested. "Whatever for?"

"The sender said if I don't stop investigating Mr. Bhakta's murder, something will happen to Hulda. This proves that I'm on the right track, and also whoever this is—" she held up the note—"was on the ship, and is here in London, close to us. The note I found on Mr. Bhakta's waistcoat alluded to a threat to the queen. We also found a note in a tear catcher containing poison on the ship, quoting the poet Blake, and this telegram contains another quote from him."

Lillie held a hand in the air. "Slow down, sister. What does this have to do with me?"

Annie took a deep breath, hoping she would not regret what she was about to say.

"I know we've had our differences, Lillie, but am I correct that you genuinely care for my sister?"

"I do. She's a nice kid."

"Remember when Twila died, how upset you were?" Annie asked. When Lillie's adopted sister Twila took poison to end her sorrowful life, Lillie had been clipped at the knees. Annie had helped her through the stressful time, and the two had come to a temporary mutual understanding, although they never really liked each other. Annie hoped she could rely on Lillie's memory of Annie supporting her through that difficult time. Lillie never really had a family, aside from Twila.

"I can't believe I am asking this, but, I'd like you to keep an eye on Hulda tonight. Don't let her out of your sight. I have to attend a dinner party, and Frank will be with me, as well as Emma."

"I thought I am a bad influence on the girl." Lillie smirked.

"You don't have to be," said Annie. "Since you say you care for her—even though I don't necessarily trust your influence on her—I am going to trust you with her safety. If not for me, then do it for Hulda. Keep your gun handy and loaded."

Lillie pulled the stub of the cigarette from her mouth and tamped it in a crystal ashtray lying on the bed. She leaned back against the pillows again, never taking her eyes off Annie. Annie remained silent, waiting for her reply.

"I don't want anything to happen to her, you're right. I'll do it, Annie. Thanks for your trust in me."

"No drinking, no smoking, no cowboys, no Mr. Everett" Annie warned. "Just for tonight. Promise?"

Lillie rolled her eyes. "Promise."

"I don't want her to know she is in danger. I don't want to scare her."

"All right, all right. I got it. Geez, Annie, you're so bossy."

Mrs. Langtry's suite at the Rueben Hotel was nothing less than Annie had anticipated.

They entered into a brightly lit parlor with blue walls and a white, elaborately patterned ceiling, with a large crystal chandelier hanging in the center. A marble fireplace with a carved wooden mantelpiece dominated the room. Two powder-blue-cushioned sofas and several matching chairs surrounded the fireplace, creating a cozy place to relax and talk.

The dining room, off to the back of the parlor, housed a large, round dining table laden with a white silk table cloth, silver place settings, a profuse floral centerpiece exploding with pink roses, and fine crystal stemware. Judging from the ten place settings, Annie gathered the party would be small. She, Frank, and Emma were the first to arrive. A smiling butler with coal-black hair and bright blue eyes showed them into the parlor and encouraged them to settle into the plush sofas.

Emma, dressed in a dusty rose, pearl-beaded gown and a gigantic hat wrapped in chiffon with roses pinned to one side of the crown, made herself comfortable in one of the chairs. Annie and Frank sank into one of the sofas, making breathing for Annie even more of a challenge. She glanced over at her husband, who looked so handsome in his dark dinner jacket and burgundy waistcoat.

"I do love society parties," Emma said. The handsome butler, holding a tray of filled champagne glasses, offered one to her. "Don't mind if I do. What is your name?" Emma asked, her dimples deepening as she gave the man a coy smile.

The butler, clearly uncomfortable with the personal question, cleared his throat. "I'm Mr. Chaucer, ma'am."

"Oh, like the esteemed writer—charmed. Don't stray too far, Mr. Chaucer. I have a feeling I'm going to be thirsty."

The butler nodded to her and offered Annie and Frank champagne. Frank obliged, but Annie held up her hand, declining. She wanted to apologize for Emma's boldness, but knew it really wasn't her place.

Mrs. Langtry entered from one of the rooms at the same time Oscar

Wilde was let in the door. He handed the butler his knee-length, fur-collared cape to reveal a burgundy coat trimmed with ivory piping. He wore matching velvet pants that gathered at the knee and were tucked into knee-length brown leather gaiters. His tie, of white silk, was knotted into a large bow that draped down his chest.

He and Mrs. Langtry exchanged air kisses and then greeted Annie, Frank, and Emma.

"Oh, I am delighted that we are all here," said Mrs. Langtry as she and Mr. Wilde seated themselves on the other sofa. "I've been so eager to visit with you all again. I have a few more guests arriving, but I invited you early so we could chat. So tell me, how was the stay at the palace? We heard about Mr. Patel and that fine doctor."

"The stay was excellent," said Frank. "Cured what ailed me. The royal physician worked wonders."

"So pleased you are feeling better, old chap," said Mr. Wilde, reaching over and slapping Frank on the shoulder. He then rested his hand against Frank's collar, a bit too long in Annie's estimation, before he reached for a champagne glass.

Somewhere in the room a bell chimed, and the butler went to the door as the five of them chatted. He soon returned, and standing with his hands behind his back and his chest jutting forward, announced, "His Royal Highness, the Prince of Wales."

Taking Mrs. Langtry and Mr. Wilde's lead, they all stood when the prince entered. Annie was surprised at his casual dress. He wore a simple, dark wool suit, white shirt, and waistcoat. He carried a hat in his hand, and gave it to the butler.

"Darling," said Mrs. Langtry as she went to greet him. She threw her arms around him and gave him a lingering kiss on the lips. Annie turned away, annoyed at the display. She wanted to ask after the whereabouts of the princess but refrained.

Mrs. Langtry and the prince squeezed in on the sofa next to Mr. Wilde, the prince's hand resting on Mrs. Langtry's knee.

"We were just discussing Mr. Butler and Miss Oakley's stay at the palace—and all the mischief that happened while they were there."

"Terrible business," said the prince. "You are all well, I suppose? Kept out of danger?"

"Yes, Your Majesty, for the moment. But I fear the queen is not, nor is my sister."

Annie, Frank, and Emma explained what had transpired since they embarked on their journey.

"So the killer is still at large," said the prince.

"Yes, but I have an idea how to draw him out," said Annie. "I will need cooperation from the palace—and the colonel and Mr. Salisbury of course. And what I tell you may not leave this room. No one must know, not even our closest companions."

"Goodness, how cryptic," said Mr. Wilde.

Annie turned to Emma. "I will also need you to enlist some of your friends at the *London Times.*"

"Anything for you, dear." Emma said, raising her glass.

"Well, do tell, Miss Oakley," said the prince leaning forward. "The suspense is killing me."

Chapter Thirty

Annie and Buck sat at the gate, waiting to go on for the three-o'clock performance. For two days, she and the rest of the players and crew had rehearsed their acts to perfection and were ready to perform for the queen. Even Lillie put in her best effort and hadn't had a drop of whiskey since Annie had confided in her about Hulda.

The colonel, Chief Red Shirt, and Chief Black Elk got the crowd of ten thousand roused up for a good time.

Frank, waiting with her at the gate, told her the queen had arrived in a covered carriage, to great fanfare in the streets, and was brought into the American Exhibition arena through a back entrance and seated in her box. A small party accompanied her, including the prince and princess, Mrs. Langtry, Mr. Wilde, and Emma, as well as attendant servants to the royal party.

"And where is Hulda?" Annie asked.

"She's with Miss Tessen and Mr. Post in the paddock area, waiting for you to finish."

As the colonel and his crew finished with their act and thundered out the gates, Annie heard the announcer call her name.

"And now, America's little darling, the best sharpshooter and all-around cowgirl, the petite, the daring, and the wildly famous Miss Annie Oakley and Buck the Wonder Horse!"

"Go get 'em." Frank slapped Annie on the thigh.

"Let's hope this works," she said.

She cued Buck and they raced into the arena. As she always started her act, she shot her pistol into the air a couple of times as Buck raced around the outskirts of the mounted tripod course. As she passed by the queen's box, she waved to the party, including the queen in her customary black dress and the veil that routinely covered her face when she was in public.

Annie managed the first ten obstacles with ease, her body in sync with Buck's as they sped through the turns and serpentines. When she'd shot her last bullet, she holstered her pistols and pulled her rifle out of the scabbard. She finished the course, and raced to the queen's box where she brought Buck to a sliding stop, and he raised himself up in a rear.

Mr. Post ran into the arena to get Buck. Lillie and Bobby accompanied him, rifle and pistols blazing.

As they set up for the card trick, a commotion at the other end of the arena got their attention. The gates had burst open, and a large group of men were running into the arena, shouting and shooting into the crowd. Some of them carried signs stating, "Shame on the Crown," "Death to Gladstone," and "Death to the Queen." As two of them ran toward the queen's box, Frank and Mr. Salisbury jumped into action and hurried the party out of the box.

Annie, her heart pounding with adrenaline, signaled Lillie and Bobby, and together, rifles drawn, faced down the men. The colonel, Red, Shirt, Black Elk, and several of the other cowboys and Indians entered the arena, trapping the group of men. Realizing they were outnumbered, they threw down their weapons. Within moments, the police had infiltrated the arena and, with the help of the cowboys, escorted the recalcitrant group out of the arena to uproarious applause from the crowd.

"What just happened?" Lillie asked, a look of confusion on her face. "Those men tried to kill the queen!"

The announcer's voice rang through the air. "Ladies and gentlemen, please remain calm. The situation is in hand, but because of the circumstances, the rest of today's performance will be cancelled."

A collective groan rippled through the crowd, accompanied by some shouting and the waving of arms.

The announcer continued. "Tickets will be honored for the next several performances."

With that, the people quieted and started filing out of the stadium.

"Annie figured out what was happening, and we put a stop to it." Bobby's voice rose an octave from the excitement. "I bet the queen will give us some kind of medal or something for saving her life."

Annie, coming down from the rush of adrenaline, let her rifle drop.

"Don't count on it Bobby," she said. "That wasn't the queen. She was a plant."

"What are you talking about, Annie?" Lillie asked, perspiration dripping down the sides of her face. Her cheeks were pink from exertion.

"Emma, Mrs. Langtry, Mr. Wilde, and I came up with a plan to draw out Mr. Bhakta's killer. Hopefully, one of the people in that group was associated with someone on our ship. The someone who wants the queen dead. They will be interrogated by the police. Hopefully, this time, it's over."

"But aren't we going to perform for the queen?" asked Bobby. "I thought she invited us special."

Annie took hold of Bobby's shoulder. "We sure are, Bobby. We are giving her a private performance tomorrow. Mr. Salisbury has it all worked out with the queen's people."

"I would have been real disappointed to not have performed for Her Majesty," said Lillie. "Seasick for days for nothin'."

"Me too. Now, let's go get some rest so we are at our best for the queen tomorrow," said Annie.

"One more day of no whiskey," said Lillie, her expression downcast.

"It will be worth it," said Bobby. "I won't have any either."

Annie laughed, feeling lighter than she had for days.

After Annie had said her goodbyes to the impersonator queen and her party, and seen Buck comfortably bedded down in his stall for the evening, she, Frank, and Emma walked back to the tents together.

"How long do you think it will take to question the men?" Annie asked Emma. She wanted to make sure her plan had truly worked.

"It could be some days," said Emma. "In these situations, people are reluctant to snitch on their friends or admit their guilt. They are trying to make a statement."

"Let's hope your plan worked, darling. I'm anxious to start enjoying this tour," said Frank. Annie laughed, but stopped when she felt a twinge of pain in her belly.

"Annie, are you all right?" asked Emma.

The twinge gone, Annie waved her hand. "I'm fine. Just worn out from the excitement."

"We can have a quiet night and get some rest," said Frank. "I'm still a bit weary."

"I told you, you needed to slow down," said Annie.

"You did," Frank said, giving Emma a sideways glance. Emma laughed, kissed them both good evening, and strolled toward her tent. When they reached theirs, Annie decided to check on Hulda in her tent. Frank said Bobby had walked her back.

"Hulda?" Annie called. "Lillie?"

She stepped inside and found the tent empty.

"She's not here," Annie said, stepping outside.

Frank had lit a cigar and pulled the smoke into his mouth. He let it out with a rush.

"She's probably with Lillie in the mess tent. It's about suppertime. Are you hungry?"

Annie put a hand to her stomach. She wasn't sure if it was from all of the excitement, but she wasn't hungry at all.

"I think I'll lie down."

"I can bring you something," Frank said.

"Yes, that would be good. How about some bread?"

"That it?"

"Yes. I'll make some tea. When you see Hulda, will you tell her to come see me? And make sure Lillie isn't drinking."

Frank lowered his cigar. "I'm not telling that girl what to do. She's mean as a hellcat."

Suddenly exhausted, Annie kissed Frank's cheek and went inside. She took off her gun belt and gently draped it over the bedpost. She then made her way to the bed and flopped down onto it. Her head barely hit the pillow before she was fast asleep.

She didn't know how long she'd slept when she felt Frank shaking her awake.

"Did Hulda come see you?" he asked.

"No. I guess I fell asleep. Have you not seen her?" Annie sat up, her head still groggy from sleep.

"I didn't see her in the mess tent. I've looked everywhere." Frank raised his hands in exasperation.

"How long have you been gone? How long was I asleep?" Annie stood up, rubbing the sleep from her eyes. She ran her hands through her hair, her mind starting to come back into focus. *Hulda was missing.*

"About an hour. I thought I could find her by now. Bobby and some of the cowboys are searching for her."

"Frank, we have to find her. She could be in danger. That telegram!"

Frank took Annie by the shoulders. "Now, don't get yourself worked up. We've likely lured out the killer, so just relax. You know how Hulda can be. She's been giving you fits of late."

Annie remembered all too well.

"Where's Mr. Everett? She might be with him."

"I've asked around. No one has seen him," Frank said, reluctantly.

"Oh, God. What if they've run off together?" Annie's heart started to pound. "I'll kill him." Another cramp seized her belly, but she ignored it.

"You are jumping to conclusions, Annie. You need to calm down."

"Don't tell me to calm down, Frank. I'm getting Buck. I'm going out looking for her." She grabbed her gun belt off the bedpost and secured it around her waist.

"Not alone, you aren't." Frank went to one of their trunks and pulled out his gun belt.

When they went to the corrals to saddle up, they alerted Mr. Post and Miss Tessen to keep an eye out for Hulda. They also asked Mr. Post to tell the colonel and Mr. Salisbury she was missing. Frank instructed the cowboys to go out again, and to meet back at Earl's Court at eight o'clock.

Annie and Frank searched the streets of London until half past eight. They rode through Green Park and Hyde Park, and past Trafalgar square, which was ominously quiet. When they came down Buckingham Street in front of the Mews, Frank halted his mount.

"We need to head back," he said.

"I want to keep looking." Annie urged Buck forward. Frank trotted his horse up to them and took hold of Annie's rein, bringing Buck to a stop.

"Someone may have found her, Annie. We need to go back to find out."

"What if they haven't?" Exhausted and still feeling a little crampy, Annie couldn't keep the sob out of her voice.

"If she isn't there, we'll have the colonel alert the police. They know the city much better than we do."

Annie raised a shaking hand to her eyes and pinched the bridge of her nose. She didn't want to go back. She wanted to keep looking, but Frank's argument made sense. He always made sense.

"We'll alert the police if she isn't back?" she said, her voice coming out in a whine.

"Immediately," said Frank. He laid a hand against her cheek. "We'll find her, darling. I promise."

When Annie and Frank arrived back to Earl's Court, it was as Annie had feared. No sign of Hulda. Mr. Everett had joined the campaign to find her and said he would search the streets all night with a couple of the crewmembers so Annie and Frank could rest.

Annie lay in bed, staring at the nearly burned out candle, listening to Frank's soft, consistent snore. The intermittent cramping she had felt the previous afternoon and throughout the evening had calmed. She figured her menses might be on its way, as she often felt like this before it happened.

Her mind reeled with questions of why Hulda was gone, and what would happen to her. She couldn't get the words of the telegram out of her mind. *Stop your investigations, or your sister will meet the same fate as the doctor.*

Frank tried to soothe her by telling her Hulda may have just gone off exploring and gotten lost. Could he be right? Had she decided to go walking in the city and gotten turned around in the maze of narrow streets? Could she have tried to find the port to get on a steamer and go home? Was she hurt, or hungry? Had someone harmed her?

Frank reasoned that Hulda had gone off on her own before, during their stay at the palace. The police would find her, he said. She would be fine.

The candle, burned down to the nub, sputtered and went out. From the faint, gray light glowing on the tent wall, Annie guessed it to be early morning. She flopped over onto her other side, facing Frank. He slept with his mouth open, his chest rising and falling in a steady rhythm.

Annie closed her eyes, willing herself to rest before she had to rise. The queen's private performance would take place at half past ten in the morning, before the crowds became a crush at Earl's Court with all of the visitors coming to see the Expo.

She had tried to persuade the colonel to postpone the engagement, but he'd received word that the queen's hectic agenda would not allow for a change of schedule. Nor would Her Majesty be swayed by an alleged assassination attempt. She was counting on seeing the "two clever female marksmen."

According to Mr. Salisbury, the palace official quoted the queen as saying, "I've been shot at before, and I'll be shot at again. I'll not let fear rule my life."

The colonel assured Annie he would send out the performers after their act to search for Hulda.

As much as she wanted to get up and start combing the streets of London again, she would comply with the colonel's wishes to go on.

Annie flipped over onto her other side again and stared at the pool of wax the candle had left in the lantern. The words of the telegram, as if imprinted on the back of her eyelids, came into her mind again. *Good is the passive that obeys Reason. Evil is the active springing from Energy.* Another quote from Blake's *Marriage of Heaven and Hell.* Someday, she would read the bloody thing, as Emma had referred to it, to try to understand the reasoning behind the madness it prompted in the killer. Right now, in her current state of mind—none of it made sense at all.

At ten o'clock that morning, Miss Tessen helped Annie to mount. Buck had been brushed to gleaming, and his mane and tail shone like dark pools of water in the moonlight. Annie checked her gun belt, securing it low on her hips, and pulled one of the pistols out to make sure it had been loaded.

"Miss Tessen, there are some bullets missing here. Would you hand me the other set of pistols?"

Miss Tessen took the two pistols from Annie and went to Annie's tack trunk and pulled out two more—the first pistols she'd ever owned—a gift from Frank before her very first show. It seemed fitting to use these pistols for a performance for the queen. Annie took them from her and secured them in the holsters.

Miss Tessen checked the rifle and then loaded it into the scabbard while Annie swung her leg over the saddle horn to make the process easier.

"You all set, Annie?" Mr. Post ambled over to them, followed by Frank.

"I think so," Annie said. "Miss Tessen has done a fine job of cleaning my tack and making Buck look his best."

She wished she could sound more appreciative, but her mind was heavy with worry about Hulda. Mr. Post, perfectionist that he was, looked everything over. He checked the saddle's girth for snugness, ran his hands over the leather and silver, looking for dust, and picked up each of Buck's feet, to make sure no pebbles or grit had lodged in the tender frogs of his hooves.

"How are you holding up?" Frank asked, laying a hand on her thigh.

"All right. I just want this performance over with so we can find Hulda." Annie found it difficult to keep the emotion out of her voice.

"The police are still looking for her. All is in hand, my dear. Just concentrate on your act. I'll be watching from the box—for moral support."

"I know, Frank. Thank you." Annie bent down and kissed him.

"We'll find her, Annie," Miss Tessen said. "I have something for you, but I wasn't sure if you wanted to see it before the performance." Miss Tessen pulled a note from her pocket. "I found it early this morning—near Buck's pen."

Annie took the note and read.

The queen is expecting you. Perform your best and your sister will be returned. The apple tree never asks the beech how he shall grow; nor the lion, the horse, how he shall take his prey.

Annie handed the note to Frank, tears starting to surface in her eyes. The niggling of a cramp fluttered across her belly.

Frank looked up at her and gently took her arm.

"Let's take this person at face value. Perform for the queen, do your best. We *will* get her back, Annie."

Chapter Thirty-One

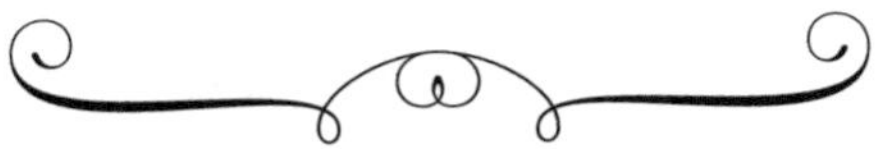

Before the gates to the arena opened, Annie said a silent prayer that Hulda be returned to her in good health, both physically and mentally. She then prayed for a good performance.

She took in a deep breath and let it out slowly. At the bottom of the breath, another cramp tightened in her belly. Annie breathed in again, willing away the pain until it subsided. She wished she would start menstruating soon, to be rid of these cramps. Frank would be disappointed, but they had plenty of time.

The gates opened.

"Okay, boy. Here we go." Annie urged Buck forward.

He picked up a canter on her cue, and they started their laps around the arena. When they passed by the queen's box, Annie smiled at the queen, noting the four guards surrounding her, as well as several other people she assumed to be her servants. The colonel and Mr. Salisbury, and Emma and Frank were seated behind everyone else.

Annie made eye contact with Frank, and he winked at her, giving her a silent nod of support.

She pulled out her pistols and started through the course. Buck performed to perfection as they weaved in and out of the tripods, Annie smashing all the glass balls into a rainbow of brilliantly colored shards.

She set her pistols back in their holsters as Buck careened around the corner. She pulled her rifle from the scabbard and peered through the site at her next target. She pulled the trigger, but nothing happened. She tried again at the next target, and nothing.

Grabbing her reins, she pulled Buck to a stop.

"Of all the times to have an equipment malfunction," she said under her breath. She opened the bolt and found there were no cartridges in the rifle. "Damn it!" Quickly, she pulled some bullets from her gun belt and started to load them, embarrassment and humiliation slowing her movements. She couldn't make her fingers work fast enough.

Suddenly, a shot rang out in the air. Annie looked up to the queen's box and saw one of the servants had fallen. The guards threw themselves on top of the queen. Annie looked around the arena but saw no sign of a shooter.

"Annie, get down!" shouted Frank.

Ignoring him, Annie finished loading her rifle and urged Buck to a canter, circling the arena, looking for the shooter. She hollered at the person working the gates to open them up and let her out.

Speeding out of the arena, Annie stopped when she cleared the gates, trying to decide which way to go, but all was quiet outside of the Exhibition Hall. Bobby and Lillie stood waiting for their cue to go on. People strolled through the park casually, enjoying their morning.

"What are you doing out here, Annie?" Bobby asked.

"Someone shot at the queen," she said, looking around. "Have you seen anyone with a gun?"

Bobby and Lillie exchanged glances. "No. Nothing suspicious."

"Any sign of them?" The colonel, Mr. Salisbury, Frank, and Emma joined them.

"Nothing. Damn it!" Annie couldn't believe she'd failed again. She suddenly lost all hope that whoever had taken Hulda would return her as they had stated in the note.

A cramp seized at her belly, and she crumpled over in the saddle.

"Annie!" Frank came over to her.

"I'm all right," she said, holding up a hand. The pain faded away. "How is the queen? I saw someone go down."

"It was one of her servants," said Emma. "He's going to be fine. He was hit in the shoulder. She's been taken back to the palace, and the police have been alerted."

"This person, whoever he is, has Hulda," Annie said. "We have to find them."

"The police are working on that," said Frank.

Annie, annoyed at his consistently trying to calm her, opened her mouth to yell at him.

"But we can go look as well," he said, stopping her. "You get Buck back to the corrals and get him settled. I'll get a carriage. We can meet at the entrance to the Expo in thirty minutes."

Annie breathed out her anger. "Thank you, Frank."

Taking up her reins, she trotted Buck back to the corrals. Miss Tessen, filling up Buck's water trough, put the bucket down and came to meet her. Annie noted Miss Tessen's cheeks were flushed, and she seemed out of breath.

"That was fast," Miss Tessen said.

"We didn't finish. Someone shot at the queen."

"Oh. Is she all right?"

"Yes. Can you see to Buck?"

"Of course." Miss Tessen took the reins from Annie and led Buck toward his pen.

Annie took off her gun belt to reload the pistols. She walked over to the tent where the tack and weapons trunks were stored to look for more ammunition.

Opening one trunk, she rummaged around. All she could find were pieces of scrap leather and tools for saddle making. She opened the trunk next to it, and saw what she needed. Boxes of bullets. She put one of her pistols down on the lid of one of the closed trunks and picked up one of the small boxes, about the size of her palm, by its lid. Not realizing it was slightly opened, it tipped it over, spilling the ammunition.

"Drat," she said, scrabbling around to gather the bullets with her fingers. She grabbed a few and loaded the chamber of the pistol she held in her hand. Putting the pistol in her dress pocket to free her hands, she moved another ammunition box out of the way to get to the bullets that had fallen between the cracks. Impatient to search for Hulda, she decided she didn't have time to clean up the mess.

She reached for another box of the same size and opened it. She sucked in a breath when she saw what lay within. A gold medal, strung through with a thin gold chain. She'd seen this before.

"Mr. Patel," she said, aloud.

"Put it back," she heard someone behind her say. She turned around to see Miss Tessen, pointing a pistol at her.

"You stole this," Annie said, holding up the necklace. "It belonged to Mr. Patel."

"Put it down, Annie." Miss Tessen shifted from one foot to the other. Her eyes glowed with the madness Annie had witnessed when she first saw her on the ship.

"I was due," Miss Tessen said, her voice shaking. "He was there, at Cawnpore—they destroyed the village, burned it. They raped some of the women there. *They threw us into a well*! To starve, to die. My mother and brother were killed by those who tried to claw their way to the top, desperate to get out. I was knocked unconscious. Somehow, I survived. *I was the only one*! Now, I know I was spared to make them pay. Make them all pay. The queen most of all. Patel wore that damn medal as a trophy—like a badge of honor. Well, he paid. He will suffer in prison like my family and I suffered in that well, and then he will die a traitor's death."

Knifelike pain shot through Annie's abdomen. She doubled over.

"Don't you move! What's wrong with you?" Miss Tessen said, her eyes wide and wild.

"My stomach is cramping. Just let me sit down." Annie clutched her middle. Panic rose up inside. Something was terribly wrong. She broke out into a cold sweat, the pain almost unbearable.

"And Dr. Adams?" Annie said, between breaths.

"He served a purpose."

"You two were romantically linked?"

Miss Tessen laughed, the sound like a high-pitched cackle. "So he thought."

"You used him."

"We met in New York. We bonded over our hatred of the queen. He told me he was boarding passage to England with the Wild West Show—would I like to come? Imagine my delight when I saw Mr. Bhakta and Mr. Patel—the dirty Indians—and the medal Patel so proudly wore."

"You intended to kill Mr. Patel, not Mr. Bhakta." Annie felt the weight of her gun in her skirt pocket. Another zing of pain shot through her belly. She thought she felt a trickle down the inside of her thigh. She bit her lip, breathing low and slow to endure the pain.

"They both needed to die. I wanted to send a message to Victoria."

"Where did you get the viper venom?" Annie's head was swimming, and she blinked, trying to regain her equilibrium. The pain in her gut intensified.

"Dr. Adams, of course. He had some in his medical stores. When it went missing, he claimed he'd never had it, or said it wasn't enough to kill—at least that's what he told you. He was worried he'd be accused of killing Mr. Bhakta—that it would come out that he himself had intended to kill the queen—but she was *mine*! I thought the tear catcher appropriate, given what I'd gone through."

"But Dr. Adams took the tear catcher from me. When he realized the liquid remnant was viper poison, he implicated Mr. Patel."

"Worked out well for me." Miss Tessen smiled.

"But that wasn't proof. We didn't have any kind of proof, until the fingerprints. And Mr. Patel's fingerprints weren't on that tear catcher. You let me accuse an innocent woman. A woman of delicate sensibilities," Annie said, her fear turning to anger.

"Delicate sensibilities? Crazy as a bed bug, more like."

"And the references to Blake?"

Miss Tessen laughed again. "It was so much fun watching you and that prissy blue blood trying to figure it out. Mr. Blake knows all, Miss Oakley. Heaven and hell, good and evil. According to him, it's all the same. One is necessary for the other to exist."

Annie took in gulps of air, trying to deal with the pain coursing through her stomach like a rusty dagger, and the trickle down her thigh turning into a gush of hot liquid. Her legs began to tremble and her vision blurred.

"You made Frank sick," she groaned. "You nearly killed him."

"I had to keep you distracted. You are determined, I must say. Downright bull-headed." Miss Tessen shouted the last three words.

"Where is Hulda?" Annie practically growled through gritted teeth, her stomach feeling as if it was being eaten from the inside out.

"Oh, you'll never find her," said Miss Tessen, the gun shaking in her hand.

"If you've harmed her, I'll—"

"You'll what? Kill me? You see, I can't let that happen. The queen is still alive. She hasn't paid."

In a moment of clarity, Annie saw Miss Tessen's finger pulling back on the trigger. Annie reached into her dress pocket, drew her gun and fired, hitting Miss Tessen in the shoulder. The woman fell backwards, the gun going off as she went down.

Pain seared through Annie's middle and she crumpled to the floor. Miss Tessen yowled in pain, rolling around on the ground. She tried to sit up, but couldn't. She leveled the gun at Annie again.

Light penetrated the tent as Frank came through the flap. He quickly assessed the situation and kicked the gun out of Miss Tessen's hand. She yelped again in pain, writhing on the ground.

"What happened here, Annie? Are you all right? I heard gunshots." Frank knelt down next to her.

"Don't let her get away, Frank. She has Hulda somewhere. She's the murderer, Frank. She did it all!"

Frank pulled Miss Tessen to her feet and she hollered, trying to get out of his grasp. He pulled her arms behind her, and she howled, screaming like a lunatic.

"What the hell?" Annie heard the colonel's voice. Frank explained what had happened and handed Miss Tessen over to the colonel.

"We have to find Hulda!" Annie yelled, no longer able to bear the pain in her stomach. She rolled up in a ball on the floor.

"Annie, what's the matter with you—?" said Frank, stroking her hair. "Oh, dear God. You're bleeding."

"Where is Hulda?" the colonel shouted, shaking Miss Tessen by the arm.

"Somewhere safe," said Miss Tessen. "She doesn't need to pay."

Annie suddenly remembered when she saw Miss Tessen head down the street and into a dwelling near Trafalgar square.

"I know where she is, Frank. You have to take me there," she said, the words coming out in gasps. Her vision was clouded, her head was on fire, and she fought to remain conscious.

"You need a doctor, Annie."

"Hulda!" she screamed.

"Where? Where is she? I will alert the police and we will find her," Frank said, desperation reverberating in his words.

"A street off Trafalgar Square, kitty-corner from the monument. About . . . halfway . . . down. . . ."

The sound of something tinkling against metal woke her. She could sense movement around her, but struggled to open her eyes. Bright light flooded her senses, and she felt someone take hold of her wrist.

She thought she heard a bird singing, but it didn't make sense to her. Her wrist was released.

"Her pulse is normal. She's doing well," the voice was soft and melodious—comforting.

She felt warmth cover her hand, and then it lifted and pressed against something prickly. She opened her eyes to see Frank, holding her hand against his lips, his whiskers tickling her fingers. His eyes widened when she blinked.

"Hello, my lovely," he whispered, lowering her hand.

Annie blinked again and took in her surroundings. The light was so bright it was hard for her to keep her eyes open, but she did anyway. An open window behind Frank let in a cool breeze, and Annie could see a small bird in the tree, singing to her.

"Where am I?"

"The London Hospital." Frank smoothed her hair from her face. "You are going to be fine."

Annie's abdomen felt swollen and sore. She remembered the searing pain she'd endured.

"I was pregnant. I lost the baby."

Frank nodded, his eyes welling with tears. Her heart caved in on itself. She'd so hoped he'd tell her she was mistaken, that the baby would be all right.

"I'm so sorry, Frank. It was my fault. I didn't want it. That's why I lost it." How could she have been so selfish? What kind of a person was she?

"That makes no sense, Annie."

She remembered thinking herself incapable of raising a child, because of how she handled Hulda. Bits of memory resurfaced, and she remembered facing down Miss Tessen and shooting her in the shoulder.

"Hulda!" she said, trying to sit up, but feeling a spike of pain in her belly.

"Don't, Annie. Hulda is fine. She was exactly where you said she'd be. We had some help locating the building."

"What do you mean?"

"Madame Mattei, from the ship. Turns out she is an Irish sympathizer and wanted to lend her support to the cause. She recognized Miss Tessen from the ship, and saw her turn down the street."

"But Hulda is all right? Is she here?"

"She's right outside the door. With Emma. Would you like to see her?"

"Please, Frank. Yes."

"The doctor said you can have visitors for only a few minutes. He's coming back around to speak with us." Frank went to the door and motioned for them to come in. Hulda rushed to the bed and leaned down to kiss Annie.

"I'm so sorry I've caused so much trouble, Annie. I've been terrible and I apologize. You can send me home if you'd like—but I really want to be here, with you."

"Come here, you silly monkey." Annie wrapped her arms around Hulda, not minding that lifting her arms caused her some pain. "You are staying with me—but only if you want to."

"I do, Annie. Really, I do." Hulda stepped away to let Emma approach the bed.

"You're so brave and so clever, Annie. I admire your strength so much." Emma's eyes glistened with moisture. She took hold of Annie's hand. "And I'm very sorry about—your loss," she whispered.

Annie, unable to hold back her tears anymore, let them flow down her cheeks. She rested her cheek against the back of Emma's hand.

"I think that's all for now," said Frank. "Annie needs to rest." He ushered the two of them out of the room, and took up his seat next to Annie once again. He reached into his pocket, pulled out a handkerchief and handed it to her, letting her cry until she had no more tears left.

Chapter Thirty-Two

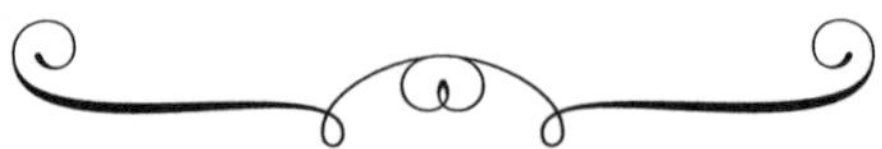

Annie sat with her eyes closed, luxuriating in the feeling of the sun bathing her face with warmth. A blanket draped across her knees staved off the chill of the morning. She breathed in the fragrance of the blooming trees, the aroma intensifying with the ebb and flow of the sea air.

The sun drenched her in light, and her thoughts, like leaves, drifted by on the river of consciousness. She wanted to stay in this place of momentary peace—free from the sorrow that had pressed in on her heart for the last month. Could this moment of unencumbered bliss be a sign that she had passed through her darkest heartbreak—the child that would never be?

While she recovered at the London Hospital, the doctor had broken the news she would never bear children. A weak cervix and the massive hemorrhaging she'd endured had rendered her barren. How could she have taken for granted the gift of bringing life into the world?

Mrs. Langtry had offered her seaside home in Bournemouth for the inconsolable Annie's recovery.

"It is a place of love and healing," Mrs. Langtry said. "The sea air and sunshine will wash away your troubles."

Called the Red House, from the red shakes on the peaked roof, the Tudor style dwelling had been purchased by the prince as a love nest for his beloved mistress during the time of their intimate affair. What Annie had learned in the past month was that the affair between the prince and Mrs. Langtry had ended long ago, but the two remained the best of friends.

Somehow discovering this had eased Annie's prejudice against the woman. For, if she really thought about it, love was really all that mattered. Who was she to judge who loved whom and how they loved them?

Annie recalled the words Madame Mattei had spoken to her when she came to see Annie in the hospital.

"You are destined to bring love to the world through your talent. Any woman can be a mother. You can set the example for women to embrace their talents and make something of themselves in this world, whether they are mothers or not. Motherhood does not define a woman."

At the time, Annie could not reconcile herself to Madame Mattie's words, but now she began to see their wisdom through the fog of her pain.

"Annie."

She opened her eyes and saw Frank standing before her.

"Something came for you today." He presented her with a small, filigreed metal box, adorned with jewels and a thick purple ribbon wrapped around its middle, knotted into a bow.

"How lovely. Who is it from?" She sat up and lifted the blanket off her knees. The chill of the morning had melted away with the warmth of the sun.

"Open it to find out."

"It's almost too pretty to open." She delicately pulled at the ribbon. It cascaded from the box and fell to her lap. She lifted the hinged lid to find a miniature portrait, about the size of an egg, inside.

The image of a young Queen Victoria stared back at her, with eyes as tiny as a mouse's. She stood tall and proud, wearing a flowing white, jewel-encrusted gown with a thick purple sash draped across one shoulder and anchored to her hip with a diamond brooch. Atop her head was a stunning diamond tiara with a dark blue jewel set in the middle.

"Look, Frank." Annie handed the portrait to him. "Isn't it stunning?"

She reached back into the box to pull out a note with the queen's monogram embossed on top. She read it aloud to Frank.

Dearest Miss Oakley,

I hope this gift finds you well and recovering. I am terribly sorry for your loss. Although the good Lord bestowed upon me nine children, the loss of my beloved Albert has deeply affected me. Cherish your husband. You will have a fulfilling life in his love.

Please accept this token of my appreciation for your valiant efforts to save my life. I am not naïve to the fact that others may attempt assassination in future, but you have spared me for the time being. Your cleverness and bravery are to be commended.

You have a gift to offer the world, and I so admire your courage. May God bless you on your journey.

Fondly,

Victoria R.

She set the note down in her lap, and wiped a tear from her cheek. Frank knelt down next to her, and took hold of her hand.

"You touch the hearts of others, my dear. Even the Queen of England."

Annie smiled, the chains of sorrow burdening her for the last few weeks starting to break loose.

Emma had always told her she had much to offer the world with her talent, and so had Frank. This letter and this gift were a sign to her that they were right. She had a calling—and it wasn't motherhood. She would take her newfound resolution and give back to the world in the way she was meant to do.

"I have more news," said Frank. "I've received a letter from Mr. Salisbury. The Wild West Show is continuing the tour of England, and he and the colonel are asking if you will be returning. They don't want to pressure you, but you know the show won't be the same without you."

Annie leaned over and wrapped her arms around Frank's neck.

"No, it won't. The show needs me, and I am ready."

About the Author

Empowered women in history, horses, unconventional characters, and real-life historical events fill the pages of Kari Bovée's articles and historical mystery musings and manuscripts. Bovée is an award-winning writer: She was a finalist in the Romantic Suspense category of the 2012 LERA Rebecca contest, the 2014 NTRWA Great Expectations contest, and the RWA 2016 Daphne du Maurier contest for her unpublished manuscript *Grace in the Wings*. She was also honored as a finalist in the NHRWA Lone Star Writer's contest in 2012 with the unpublished manuscript of *Girl with a Gun*. Bovée and her husband, Kevin, live in New Mexico with their cat, four dogs, and four horses. Their children, who live happy lives as productive entrepreneurs and professionals, are their greatest achievements.

About SparkPress

SparkPress is an independent, hybrid imprint focused on merging the best of the traditional publishing model with new and innovative strategies. We deliver high-quality, entertaining, and engaging content that enhances readers' lives. We are proud to bring to market a list of *New York Times* best-selling, award-winning, and debut authors who represent a wide array of genres, as well as our established, industry-wide reputation for creative, results-driven success in working with authors. SparkPress, a BookSparks imprint, is a division of SparkPoint Studio LLC.

Learn more at GoSparkPress.com